BADGE OF HONOR

W.E.B. Griffin's electrifying epic series
of a big-city police force...

P9-DHJ-979

THE CORPS

*W.E.B. Griffin's bestselling saga of
the heroes we call Marines...*

The Captains

BROTHERHOOD OF WAR

OF

WAR

BOOK

II

BY W.E.B. GRIFFIN

JOVE BOOKS, NEW YORK

*For Uncle Charley and The Bull
RIP October 1979*

*And for Donn.
Who would have ever believed* **four** *stars?*

Brotherhood of War was written on a Lanier
"No Problem" word processor.

THE CAPTAINS

A Jove Book / published by arrangement with
the author

PRINTING HISTORY
Jove edition / October 1982

The Putnam Berkley World Wide Web site address is
http://www.berkley.com/berkley

ISBN: 0-515-09138-3

A JOVE BOOK®
Jove Books are published by The Berkley Publishing Group,
200 Madison Avenue, New York, New York 10016.
JOVE and the "J" design
are trademarks belonging to Jove Publications, Inc.

PRINTED IN THE UNITED STATES OF AMERICA

40   39   38   37

I

At approximately 0500 Sunday, 25 June 1950, Koreans awakened Major George D. Kessler, USA, Korean Military Advisory Group advisor to the 10th Regiment at Samch'ok and told him a heavy North Korean attack was in progress at the 38th parallel.

U.S. Army in the Korean War, Vol. I, p. 27
Office of the Chief of Military History, U.S. Army, Washington, D.C., 1961

(One)
Seoul, Korea
25 June 1950

The 38th parallel bisects the Korean peninsula. From a point near Ongjin, on the Yellow Sea, to another near Yangyang on the Sea of Japan, the parallel stretches just over 200 miles.

If the forces of the Immun Gun, the Army of the People's Democratic Republic of Korea, had been spread out equally across the 38th parallel, there would have been one Immun Gun soldier every twelve feet. There were 90,000 of them.

And one in three of these was a veteran of the Chinese Communist Army, which had just sent Chiang Kai-shek fleeing to the island of Formosa.

They were not, of course, spread out across the line. They were formed in Russian-style military organizations. There were seven infantry divisions, one armored brigade, equipped with the Russian T34 tank which had stopped Germany's best, a separate infantry regiment, a motorcycle regiment, and a brigade of the Border Constabulary, the Bo An Dae, North Korea's version of the Waffen SS.

They had 150 tanks in all, and 200 airplanes, large quantities of 76 mm self-propelled howitzers, and even more 122 mm truck-drawn howitzers. They were "advised" by a large contingent of Russian officers and technicians, and they were equipped with Russian small arms.

They also had boats, and they made two amphibious landings behind the South Korean lines between Samch'ok and the 38th parallel on the Sea of Japan in coordination with an attack by the 5th Infantry Division on the 10th Regiment of the Republic of Korea's (ROK) 8th Infantry Division.

The 2nd and 7th North Korean Infantry Divisions attacked the understrength ROK 6th Division at Ch'unch'on. The 3rd and 4th North Korean Infantry Divisions, reinforced by the 14th Tank Regiment, attacked the ROK 7th Division at Uijongbu. The North Korean 1st and 6th Infantry Divisions, reinforced by the 203rd Tank Regiment, attacked the ROK 1st "Capitol" Division (less the 17th Infantry Regiment) at Kaesong on the route to Seoul and Inchon. And on the extreme left of the front, that peaceful Sunday morning, the North Korean Border Constabulary Brigade and the 14th Infantry Regiment attacked the ROK 17th Infantry Regiment, which held the Ongjin peninsula on the Yellow Sea.

(Two)
The Ongjin Peninsula, Korea
0400 Hours
25 June 1950

When, without warning, the positions and the headquarters

of the 17th Infantry Regiment of the Capitol Division were brought under artillery, mortar, and heavy automatic weapons fire by the Border Constabulary of the People's Democratic Republic of Korea, the three American officers—a captain and two lieutenants—of the U.S. Army Korean Military Advisory Group were asleep in their quarters on a knoll overlooking the regimental headquarters, a sandbag bunker erected on the near side of one of the hills.

Their quarters, now fixed up to be as comfortable as possible, had once been a farmhouse. The floor was baked mud, through which vents carried heat in the winter, a device alleged to be the world's first central heating system. The walls were mortared stone, eighteen inches thick, and the roof was of foot-thick thatch.

Because they recognized the need to do so, the three made a valiant effort to live as much like their Korean counterparts as they could, yet there were things in the ex-farmhouse to be found nowhere else in the 17th Infantry. There was a General Electric refrigerator and a Zenith combination radio-phonograph and a Sears, Roebuck three-burner electric hotplate, all powered via a heavy rubber-covered cable by a skid-mounted GM diesel generator. And there was a Collins BC-610 radio transmitter and an RCA AR-88 communications receiver, used for communication with KMAG in Seoul, forty-five or fifty miles, as the crow flies, to the east.

For all practical purposes, the 17th Infantry (Colonel Paik In Yup commanding) was on an island, although the Ongjin peninsula was of course connected with the peninsula of Korea. When the Great Powers had partitioned Korea after War II, they had made the 38th parallel the dividing line. The Russian and Red Chinese-backed People's Democratic Republic lay north of it, while the American-backed Republic of Korea lay south.

The 38th parallel crossed the Ongjin peninsula very near the point where it joined the Korean peninsula; the line was fortified on both sides, and there was no land passage between the Ongjin peninsula and the rest of South Korea. All commerce (what there was of it) and all supply of the 17th Infantry had to be accomplished by sea.

It was generally agreed among the three American officers assigned to the 17th that if the gooks north of the parallel started something, they were really going to be up the creek without a paddle.

Seconds after the first artillery shell whistled in from North Korea, it was followed by another and another. Simultaneously, there came the different whistle of incoming heavy mortars, and off in the distance, the dull rumble of heavy machine guns. It was apparent that the shit had indeed hit the fan.

The three officers dressed hurriedly, in crisply starched fatigues and highly shined combat boots (laundry and boot polishing were available for three dollars per month, or the equivalent in PX merchandise) and picked up their personal weapons. Technically, as instructors of the 17th Infantry, they were supposed to be unarmed. But the North Koreans were capable of infiltration, and the South Koreans were capable of stealing anything not firmly embedded in concrete; personal weapons to defend themselves against either happenstance were as necessary to their survival as the water purification pills and toilet tissue (1,000 sheets per roll) that reached them at irregular intervals via the South Korean Navy's LSTs.

The senior instructor, clutching a U.S. .30 caliber carbine in his hand, announced that he was going over to the CP to see what the fuck was going on. His two subordinates, one armed with a carbine, the other with a privately owned Smith & Wesson .357 Magnum revolver, turned to firing up the diesel generator (shut down at bedtime because of the horrific roar it made) and to warming up the BC-610 and the AR-88 radios.

By the time the generator had been running long enough to warm up the radio tubes, the senior instructor was back from the 17th Infantry's command post.

"Any luck?" he asked the lieutenant at the microphone. The lieutenant shook his head, "no." The captain took the microphone from him.

"Victor, Victor, this is Tahiti, Tahiti," he said into the mike. And he said it again and again without response for fifteen minutes as artillery whistled in to explode deafeningly, sending white-hot fragments of steel ricocheting off the foot-thick stone walls of the hootch, until the voice radio operator on duty at

KMAG returned from taking a liesurely crap secure in the knowledge that absolutely nothing was going to happen at 0400 on a Sunday morning in the Land of the Morning Calm.

"Tahiti," a bored voice finally came over the AR-88's speaker. "This is Victor. Read you five by five. Go ahead."

"Where the fuck have you been?" the captain demanded, furiously. And then without waiting for a reply, he went on. "Victor, stand by to copy Operational Immediate, I say again, Operational Immediate."

The radio op's voice was no longer bored: "Victor ready to copy Operational Immediate. Go ahead."

"From Tahiti Six to KMAG Six, 17th ROK under heavy artillery mortar and heavy automatic weapons fire since 0400. Believe ground assault will follow shortly. All KMAG personnel at CP. Advise. Signature is Delahanty, Captain. You got that?"

"I got it, Tahiti," Victor said. "Stand by."

(Three)
Headquarters
Korean Military Advisory Group (KMAG)
Seoul, Korea
25 June 1950

The commanding general of KMAG had boarded a ship the day before in Pusan to go home; his replacement had not officially assumed command. The slot called for a brigadier general, and there had been no rush among the army's one-star generals to ask for the command. Korea, "Frozen Chosen," was generally recognized to be the asshole of the globe, and serving as senior advisor to its raggedy-assed army was not considered to be a desirable assignment.

Pending the assignment of a new general, command had been temporarily vested in the KMAG chief of staff, a colonel of artillery. When the word of the North Korean invasion reached him, when it became apparent that it was not an "incident" but a bona fide invasion of South Korea by a four-pronged land assault across the parallel and by two amphibious invasions on the east coast, the colonel had serious doubts that anything could be done to stop it. The only American troops in South Korea were his, and they were not organized in any kind of military formation that could be committed to combat. And while the colonel believed that the South Korean Army would fight, he knew better than just about anyone else that they didn't have much to fight with.

That made evacuation, or withdrawal, or whatever word one wanted to use for getting the hell out of Seoul, the only reasonable action to take. Doing that was not going to be easy. There were a thousand problems to be solved almost immediately, and among these was what to do about those three poor bastards stuck on the Ongjin peninsula with the ROK 17th Infantry.

The only sure way to get them out was by air, by Stinson L-5, a single-engine aircraft used by the army to direct artillery fire from the air, to supervise movement of armored or logistic columns, and as sort of an aerial jeep. But it would take either three L-5s, or three flights by one L-5, because the tiny aircraft were capable of carrying only one passenger at a time. Furthermore, the colonel realized that he had better things to do with his L-5s. They were not only the best eyes he had, but they were absolutely essential to carry messages. Communications, never very reliable, had already started to go out, probably because of sabotage. He was very much afraid that he was going to have to leave the three KMAG instructors to fend for themselves.

And then the colonel remembered that there was a Supreme Commander, Allied Powers (SCAP) L-17 Navion sitting at Kimpo Airfield. One of MacArthur's palace guard, a colonel in military government, was enamored of a State Department civilian lady at the Embassy, and had arranged to fly over from Tokyo to see her. It was a four-passenger airplane, big enough to pick up the three officers at the 17th ROK Infantry CP. The colonel considered begging the use of it from the SCAP colonel, but decided not to do that. The SCAP colonel, probably still asleep in the arms of love, might very well decide that the Big Picture required his immediate return to the Dai Ichi Building. There was time, the colonel decided, for the L-17 to rescue those poor bastards on Ongjin, and then fly the SCAP colonel out.

He motioned a master sergeant to him.

"Take a jeep and go out to Kimpo, and find the pilot of a SCAP L-17, and ask him to go get the officers with the 17th ROK," he said. "If he won't do it, you get him on the horn to me. At pistol point, if you have to."

(Four)
Kimpo Airfield
Seoul, Korea
25 September 1950

Captain Rudolph G. "Mac" MacMillan, Army Aviation Section, Headquarters, Supreme Commander, Allied Powers (SCAP), had flown one of SCAP's L-17 Navions to Seoul from Tokyo the day before, landing just before noon after a two-day, 1,000-mile flight.

MacMillan was Scotch-Irish, out of Mauch Chuck, Pennsylvania. He had enlisted in the army ten years before, at seventeen, after two years in the anthracite coal mines where everybody else he knew worked out their lives. He had no idea what the army was going to be like, but it couldn't be worse than the mines. The possibility of becoming a commissioned officer and a gentleman had never entered his mind. His vaguely formed dream then was to get up to corporal in four years, so he could marry his sweetheart, Roxy, and maybe up to staff sergeant before he had thirty years in. With a staff sergeant's pension, he had dreamed, he could save enough money to buy a saloon, and then he and Roxy would be on Easy Street.

World War II had changed all that.

There were three L-17s in the fleet of army aircraft assigned to the U.S. Army of Occupation in Japan. The Navions (from North American Aviation) had been bought "off-the-shelf" with funds reluctantly provided by Congress, less to provide the army with airplanes than to assist North American Aviation in making the transition from a manufacturer of warplanes (North American had built thousands of P-51s during World War II) to a manufacturer of light aircraft for the civilian market.

The L-17 Navion bore a faint resemblance to the P-51. There was a certain sleekness in the Navion that no other light aircraft, except perhaps Beech's "Bonanza," had; and the vertical stabilizer of the small aircraft looked very much like the vertical stabilizer of the P-51. But it was a civilian airplane, despite the star-and-bar identification painted on the fuselage and the legend us army painted on the sides of the vertical stabilizer.

The seats were upholstered in leather, and the instrument panel, probably on purpose, looked like the dashboard of a car. There were four seats under a slide-back plexiglass canopy. There had been a notion among certain North American executives that all it was going to take to fill America's postwar skies with Navions flown by business executives and salesmen, and even by Daddies taking the family out for a Sunday afternoon drive through the skies, would be to convince the public that the Navion was nothing more than a Buick or a Chrysler with wings. They had designed the Navion to fit that image.

An airplane, of course, is not a car, and the idea never caught on as people hoped it would, but a number of Navions were built, and about forty of them were sold to the U.S. Army. They were used as transport aircraft for senior officers who wanted to fly, for example, from Third Army Headquarters in Atlanta to Fort Benning when there was no convenient (or available) means to do so by commercial airlines.

Some of the Navions were sent to the army overseas, to Germany and the Panama Canal Zone, to Alaska and Japan. Unofficially, they were assigned on the basis of one per lieutenant general and higher. By that criterion—which worked in the States and in Europe—Supreme Headquarters, Far East Command, U.S. Army, Japan, should have received but two L-17 Navions, for there were only two officers in the Far East in the grade of lieutenant general or above.

Lieutenant General Walton H. Walker commanded the Eighth United States Army, the Army of Occupation of Japan. Above him was General of the Army Douglas MacArthur. Custom, not regulation, dictates the rank of senior officers immediately subordinate to a five-star general. When General of the Army Dwight D. Eisenhower commanded the Army of Occupation of Germany from the Farben Building in Frankfurt, his chief of staff had been a full, four-star general, who himself had a three-star lieutenant general for a deputy. Five other lieutenant generals were scattered through the command structure.

When five-star General of the Army Douglas MacArthur had requested a suitable officer to serve him as chief of staff in the Dai Ichi Building in Tokyo, the Pentagon could find no officer suitable to serve the Supreme Commander except a lowly major general, Edward M. Almond, whose most distinguished previous service had been as the commanding general of a division in the Italian campaign whose troops were almost entirely black.

MacArthur rose above that studied insult, as he rose above others, including the somewhat unequal distribution of L-17 Navion aircraft. Headquarters, European Theater got thirteen of the winged Buicks, and Headquarters, Far East Theater got three. MacArthur simply made the L-17s availble to whoever needed aerial transportation around Japan and to Korea.

At the lower echelons, however, among the brigadier generals and the colonels in the Dai Ichi Building, and especially among the small corps of army aviators, use of the L-17 became a matter of prestige, of privilege, of honor.

The SAC (for Supreme Allied Commander) army aviation officer, a full colonel, and his deputy, a lieutenant colonel, flew most of the missions in the L-17s. With the exception of Captain Rudolph G. "Mac" MacMillan, the other pilots permitted to fly the tiny fleet of L-17s were the other lieutenant colonel aviators, and a few, especially well-regarded majors.

MacMillan, who frequently got to fly one of the L-17s, was a special case. He had several things going for him, even though, having learned to fly only four years before, he was a newcomer to army aviation. For one thing, in 1940, Rudy MacMillan had brought prestige to the Department of the Philippines by winning the All-Army Light-Heavyweight Boxing Crown. The contests had been held that year at Fort McKinley, near Manila; and MacArthur, then Marshal of the Philippine Army, and a boxing fan, had watched MacMillan train, and had personally awarded him the golden belt.

MacMillan had not been with MacArthur in the Philippines during the war—which always granted a special cachet—but he had done the next best thing. He'd won the Medal of Honor. If there was one little clique around General MacArthur for whom he did not try to conceal his affection, it was those few men entitled to wear, as Douglas MacArthur himself wore, the inch-long, quarter-inch-wide piece of blue silk, dotted with white stars.

MacMillan's award had been for his "intrepid gallantry and valor in the face of overwhelming enemy forces." MacMillan had been trapped on the wrong side of the river during Operation Market-Garden, his fifth jump into combat with the 82nd Airborne Division. He didn't learn that he had been awarded the Medal, or the battlefield promotion to second lieutenant and officer and gentleman, until some months after the action. He spent some of that time in a German POW camp in Poland, and some of it escaping from the camp and leading twenty-two others on an odyssey to freedom that earned him the Distinguished Service Cross to go with his new gold bars and the Medal.

So no one had really been surprised, when the orders were cut for Colonel Jasper B. Downs, General Staff Corps, Hq, SCAP, to proceed by army aircraft to Seoul to confer with KMAG, that Captain MacMillan had been assigned as his pilot. A flight to Seoul was a good deal.

Mac MacMillan had come to Seoul with instructions from Mrs. Roxanne "Roxy" MacMillan, the twenty-eight-year-old redheaded woman to whom he had been married for a decade, to get her eight yards of a really nice green silk brocade. Roxy wanted some to make herself a dress, and some to send home to her sister in Mauch Chunk, Pennsylvania.

There were a number of things available in the enormous Tokyo PX that were unavailable in Korea. If you knew what you were doing, you could make the Seoul trip with one extra, nonsuspicious Valv-Pak full of the right things, and come home with an empty Valv-Pak and a nice stack of either Army of Occupation script or real green dollars; or if you liked that kind of stuff, with the Valv-Pak full of silk brocade, maybe wrapped around some three-hundred-year-old vase.

When the master sergeant from Headquarters, Korean Military Advisory Group (KMAG), burst into MacMillan's room at the bachelor officer's hotel at Kimpo Airfield, the silk brocade was in his Valv-Pak, wrapped around a nearly transparent china tea set MacMillan had been solemnly informed was at least three hundred years old.

In his bed was a large-breasted blond he had not planned on, but who had been at the Naija Hotel roof garden when he'd gone there for a drink, and who had soon made her desires known. Mac MacMillan's philosophy was that while he didn't go running after it, he didn't kick it out of bed either. He always wore his wedding ring. If he was going to get a little on the side, it was better to screw a commercial attaché, or something like that, an American broad from the Embassy who had as much to lose as he did, than fuck around with either the nips in Tokyo, or the slopes here.

But he was embarrassed when the master sergeant came barging into his room at the BOQ and caught him in bed with her like that.

"What the hell?" he said, sitting up in bed. "Goddamnit, Sergeant, didn't anybody ever teach you to knock?"

"Captain, the North Koreans are attacking all over the god-damned parallel."

The blond looked at him in disbelief for just a minute, saw that he was serious, and covered her mouth with her hand.

"Oh, my God!" she said.

"Jesus Christ!" MacMillan said, and got out of bed and picked up his shorts where he'd dropped them on the floor.

"Are they coming here?" the blond asked, holding the sheet in front of her, more frightened now than embarrassed or out-raged.

"It's no raid," the sergeant said. "It's a war, that's what it is."

"Jesus Christ," MacMillan said again. He pulled his tropical worsted Class "A" trousers on, and then dipped into the nearest of his two Valv-Paks and came up with a small Colt .32 caliber automatic pistol. He ejected the clip, confirmed that it contained cartridges, replaced it, and put the pistol in his hip pocket.

"The colonel sent me to ask you to pick up three officers on the Ongjin peninsula," the master sergeant said.

"Why?" MacMillan asked, as he put on his shirt.

"Because they're cut off, is why," the sergeant said.

"I got my own colonel to worry about," MacMillan replied.

"Unless you go get them," the sergeant said, "they're gonna get run over."

"I didn't say I wouldn't go get them," MacMillan replied. "What I said was that I got my own colonel to worry about."

"What happens to me, Mac?" the blond asked. She was now out of bed, her back to the men, picking up her underpants from where she had dropped them the night before.

"The sergeant will take you into Seoul to the Embassy, or wherever you want to go," Mac said. "If I were you, I'd go to the Embassy first."

"All right," she said, as if making a decision.

"The guys at Ongjin know I'm coming after them?" MacMillan asked.

"We told them we'd try to get somebody up there," the sergeant said.

"That's not what I asked," MacMillan said angrily.

"Their radio's out," the sergeant said.

"Which means they could already be rolled over, doesn't it?" MacMillan said.

"We have to try," the sergeant said.

"*We* have to try?" MacMillan said. "Shit!"

There was a peculiar whistling sound outside. MacMillan's face screwed up as he tried to identify it. Then there came the scream of propellers on aircraft flying low.

"Goddamnit, they're strafing the airfield," MacMillan said and went to the window, pushing the curtain aside. He saw a Russian-built YAK fighter pulling up after a run on the terminal building across the field. "Shit, if they get the Navion, we'll all be walking," he said.

The blond, oblivious to the amount of thigh she was displaying, hooked her stockings to her garters, pulled her dress down, and slipped into her shoes. MacMillan sat down and put on his shoes and socks.

"Let's go see if I still have an airplane," he said. He put his leather-billed cap on, picked up his two Valv-Paks, and walked out of the BOQ.

The Navion, parked across the field from the air force and civilian terminals of the airfield, was intact. MacMillan put his Valv-Paks in the plane, one in the luggage compartment, one in the back seat, and then turned to face the blond and the sergeant.

"I want you to find my colonel," he said. "Colonel Downs, he's in the Naija Hotel. Tell him what I've done and that I should be back here, if I can still get in here, in an hour. If I can't get in here, I'll go down to Suwon."

"Yes, sir," the master sergeant said. He had just noticed the fruit salad on MacMillan's tunic. He didn't think much of army aviators, and wondered if this one was really entitled to wear the blue ribbon with the white stars on it.

"You'll be all right," MacMillan said to the blond. "They've got an evacuation plan, in case something like this happens."

She raised her face to be kissed. It turned into a passionate embrace. MacMillan was grossly embarrassed. She was hanging on to him like that not because she was horny, but because she was scared.

He freed himself, stepped up on the wing, and crawled into the cabin. He busied himself with the preflight checklist, not looking up until he heard the sounds of the jeep starting up and driving away.

Then he got out of the cabin again and walked around the plane, making the preflight. After that, he got in again and cranked it up. When the propeller was turning and the engine smoothing out, he closed the canopy, released the brakes, and moved onto the taxiway.

There was no response when he tried to call the tower, so he simply turned onto the active and pushed the throttle to the firewall. Even if he was taking off downwind, he had enough runway to get it into the air.

He took off toward the city, made a steep, climbing turn to the right, passing over the KMAG Skeet and Trap Club on the banks of the Han River, and then changed his mind about the altitude. The YAK fighters might come back. He lowered the nose and flew at treetop level through the low mountains until he reached Inchon and the sea. Then he pointed the Navion's nose toward the Ongjin peninsula.

(Five)

MacMillan made a power-on approach to the command post of the 17th ROK Infantry Regiment. With his flaps down and the engine of the Navion running at cruise power, he had two options. If he saw the Americans he had come to fetch, he could chop the throttle and put the Navion on the ground. If he didn't see the Americans, or, as he thought was entirely likely, he saw North Koreans, he could dump the flaps and get his ass the hell out of there.

There was nobody in sight as he flew over the command post, and he had just about decided the unit had been rolled over when he spotted three people furiously waving their arms and what looked like field jackets at the far end of the short, dirt runway. He was too far down the runway by then to get the Navion on the ground, so he went around again, came in even lower, dropped his landing gear, and when he was halfway down the dirt strip, touched down. He hit the brakes as soon as he dared.

Now that he was on the ground, rolling toward the three men, he could see they were Americans. As he taxied toward them, he wondered where the hell everybody else was. And then there was an explosion which both shook the Navion and sprayed it with dirt and rocks. He had landed at the 17th ROK Regiment thirty seconds before they blew up the CP.

The first of the three Americans scrambled onto the Navion's wing before MacMillan had finished turning around and before he had the canopy open. He lurched to a stop, unlatched the canopy, and slid it back on its tracks. One by one, almost frenziedly, the three American officers climbed into the cockpit.

MacMillan was pleased to see that the last man to climb in was the senior of the three officers. The senior officer would most likely be the last. But it wouldn't hurt to ask.

"Is that all?" MacMillan shouted, over the roar of the engine.

The officer beside him vigorously shook his head, "yes."

MacMillan turned to slide the canopy closed. There was a pinging noise on the side of the fuselage. He turned around and rammed the throttle to the firewall. The Navion began to move. The officer beside him slid the canopy home and latched it in place. The Navion lifted off the ground. MacMillan pulled the wheels up and then immediately pushed the nose down to put a rise off the end of the dirt strip between him and the machine gun.

Sixty seconds later he was over the water and safe.

He thought that if Roxy's silk brocade and the nearly transparent, 300-year-old tea set got shot up, she'd really be pissed.

With the canopy closed and the engine throttled back to cruise, conversation was possible.

"Captain," the major said, "thank you very much."

"My pleasure," MacMillan said.

MacMillan realized there was going to be a confrontation between him and Colonel Jasper B. Downs, Deputy Chief, Office of Military Government, Headquarters, Supreme Commander, Allied Powers, the minute he touched down at Kimpo Airfield in Seoul.

Colonel Downs was sure to be waiting for "his" L-17 to land, more than a little pissed that "his pilot" had taken the aircraft assigned for his use on a flight without his permission. Colonel Downs was very much aware of his status as a senior member of the SCAP staff. In the present emergency, the chair-warming sonofabitch would see his duty clearly: He would be obliged to return to his headquarters immediately.

Fuck him.

It was not that Captain MacMillan was in the habit of frustrating the desires of his seniors, or for that matter, even privately questioning any orders he received. It was simply that he thought of himself as a warrior, and of Colonel Downs as a rear-echelon desk trooper. For the first time since he had arrived in the Far East—for that matter, for the first time since he had been in a drainage ditch in Belgium in the closing days of War II—MacMillan was sure of what he was doing.

As far as he was concerned, there were only two kinds of soldiers. There were those who lost their heads at the sound of hostile fire, and those who didn't. The warriors and the chair-borne. MacMillan believed himself to be a warrior, despite his present status as an army aviator. He had won the Medal as a paratrooper. And perhaps more important, General of the Army Douglas MacArthur, SCAP himself, was a warrior. He'd gotten the Medal in War I, and he liked to have people with the Medal around him.

All of these things combined to convince Captain Mac MacMillan that there was nothing really to worry about with Colonel Jasper B. Downs, even if the chair-warming sonofabitch would be waiting at Kimpo with his balls in an uproar.

MacMillan's prediction that Colonel Downs would be impatiently, even furiously, waiting for the Navion to return was quite accurate. Moreover, Colonel Downs was accompanied by Miss Genevieve Horne, a Foreign Service officer attached to the U.S. Embassy, Seoul, to whom (with, of course, the permission of the ambassador) he had offered transportation out of Korea. Obviously, there were going to be few cultural exchanges in the near future (Miss Horne was deputy cultural attaché), so her presence was not only not essential to the conduct of the Embassy's affairs, but actually an impediment to it. Flying her to Tokyo in the L-17 would not only insure her safety, and take advantage of passenger space that otherwise would be wasted, but would also give the colonel and Miss Horne the opportunity to spend some time together in Tokyo before she had to go back to Seoul after this incident with the North Koreans blew over.

Colonal Downs was therefore more than a little annoyed when he and Miss Horne and her luggage arrived at Kimpo Airfield and found his L-17 was gone. While it would be an exaggeration to say that Colonel Downs panicked when he couldn't find either the L-17 or anyone who knew what had happened to it, it would not be an exaggeration to say that he was enraged when he finally learned where the L-17 was. And when the plane touched down, he was quite prepared to give Captain MacMillan the benefit of his thinking.

Also waiting at Kimpo Field were two officers from KMAG, bearing with them a note scrawled on a message form by the acting commander, KMAG, authorizing them to commandeer any KMAG aircraft for the purpose of conducting an aerial reconnaissance of the land approaches to Seoul. While they knew full well that the L-17 was not assigned to KMAG, they approached it nevertheless the moment it taxied up before the army hangar. If the pilot was not impressed with their authority to commandeer, perhaps he would listen to reason.

MacMillan did just that, over the violent protests of Colonel Downs, which included both a recitation of the urgent need of his services at the earliest possible moment in Tokyo and a direct order to Captain MacMillan that he make immediate preparations to board himself and Miss Horne and fly them there.

"I'll split it down the middle," MacMillan said to the KMAG captain. "I'll take one of you guys with me for a recon. One hour. No more. The other one stays here and sits on that fuel truck. I don't want anybody blowing it up while I'm gone."

"Goddamnit, MacMillan," Colonel Downs said, with mingled disbelief and rage, "I've given you a direct order, and I expect to be obeyed."

"While I'm gone, Colonel," MacMillan replied, "you ask the lady to get what she really has to have into one of those suitcases. We can't take all of them."

Colonel Downs resisted the temptation to tell MacMillan what he intended to do with him when they got back to Tokyo. If he went too far, MacMillan conceivably would not return to pick him up at all. He could settle his hash in Tokyo. Congressional Medal or not, captains do not go around refusing to obey direct orders from colonels.

MacMillan actually gave the KMAG officer a two-hour recon flight. It took that long, and that's all there was to it. He landed at Kimpo again at a quarter past one, and it was another forty-five minutes before he could refuel the Navion and take off for Pusan.

MacMillan took on thirty gallons of gasoline in Pusan, more than enough for the Pusan-Kokura leg of the flight over the Straits of Korea, but not enough to fill the tanks. He was over Maximum Gross Weight as it was. If he had topped off the tanks, he'd never have gotten the Navion into the air.

When he landed at Itazuke Air Force Base near Kokura, he noticed unusual activity and had some trouble getting somebody to fuel the Navion. The ground personnel were too busy with fighter aircraft to bother with a little army liaison airplane.

It was nearly 0300 hours when MacMillan landed the Navion at Tachikawa Airfield at Tokyo. The long ride had done nothing to calm Colonel Downs's rage, and possibly it had been fueled by the last, long, Itazuke-Tachikawa leg, during which he had ridden in the somewhat cramped back seat. Miss Horne had requested that she be allowed to ride up front, and of course there was no way he could refuse her. Neither had he been able to participate in the long conversations she had had with MacMillan, because they were conducted via earphones and microphones, and the back seat was not equipped with them.

He would have been even more disturbed had he been able to eavesdrop on the conversation.

"Can I ask a personal question?" Miss Horne had asked MacMillan, over the intercom.

"Sure."

"Isn't that the Congressional Medal of Honor?"

"Yeah," MacMillan replied and actually flushed.

"I really don't know what to say," she said. "I've never met anybody before who had the Congressional Medal."

"There's a bunch of them around," MacMillan said.

"Oh, no, there's not!" Miss Horne insisted, touching Captain MacMillan's arm for emphasis.

"Yeah, there is," MacMillan insisted.

"I feel a whole lot better, I don't mind telling you," she said, "with someone like you around. I was really getting worried back there at Kimpo."

"There was no reason to be worried," MacMillan said. "I wouldn't have taken those KMAG guys on that recon flight if I didn't think there was time to do that and pick you up, too."

"Jasper, I mean, Colonel Downs was very worried."

MacMillan said nothing.

"I suppose," Genevieve Horne said, "that someone like yourself thinks clearly under stress. I mean, I wish I had known who you were before you left us standing on the field."

"I have this rule," MacMillan said. "I never leave pretty women stranded."

She chuckled with pleasure.

"I'll bet your wife has to watch you closely around women," Genevieve Horne said.

"She tries hard," MacMillan said.

"And does she always succeed?"

"Not always," MacMillan said. "I took a course in evasive action one time."

"If it wasn't for the circumstances, I'd say that meeting you has been quite an experience, Captain MacMillan."

"Does the colonel watch you pretty closely?" MacMillan asked.

"I don't think he's going to have much time to do that," she said.

"You'll be staying at the State Department's transient hotel?"

"And probably bored out of my mind," she said.

"Maybe I could do something about that."

"I'm pretty good at evasive action myself," Genevieve Horne said.

Colonel Downs knew only that a conversation was taking place. He had no idea what was being said. He passed the time composing and relishing the words he would say to MacMillan as soon as they were on the ground at Tachikawa and out of the airplane:

"Captain MacMillan, you will consider yourself under arrest to quarters. You will go directly to your quarters and remain there until you receive further orders."

He would later explain to Genevieve Horne the gravity of Captain MacMillan's offense against good order and discipline; he simply could not ignore it.

Colonel Downs was not given the opportunity to discipline Captain MacMillan for disobedience of a direct order, however. The L-17 was met by a half dozen officers, the senior of them the special assistant to the SCAP chief of staff, a full colonel senior to Colonel Downs and with whom Colonel Downs had previously had personality clashes.

The special assistant to the SCAP chief of staff informed them they were wanted immediately in the G-3 Conference Room at the Dai Ichi Building to render a firsthand report of what they had seen in Korea; they were the first eyewitnesses to be available. The airplane itself would immediately return to Kokura, carrying three SCAP staff officers. The 24th Infantry Division at Kokura had already received an Alert for Movement order, just in case it would be necessary to intervene in Korea.

At the Dai Ichi Building, to Colonel Downs,'s enormous surprise, considering the hour (it was 0415 when they got there), the Supreme Commander, Allied Powers was in the G-3 Map Room, studying a map. He was dressed in a zippered leather jacket and an ancient, washed-smooth khaki shirt and trousers.

"What say you, Mac?" the SCAP said to MacMillan. "Is that the faint rattle of musketry I hear over the far hill?"

"I think we got us a war, General," MacMillan said to MacArthur. "You don't send tanks on a border incident."

"But do we *know* there *are* tanks? Or is this something somebody has heard, and repeated with dramatic amplification?"

"I counted 112 myself, General," MacMillan said. "In just two places."

"Be good enough, MacMillan," the Supreme Commander said, placing a hand on MacMillan's elbow and leading him to an enormous map of Korea, "to show me precisely where they were." And then he remembered Colonel Downs, or very nearly: "Howard, isn't it?"

"Downs, sir," Colonel Downs replied.

"I presume you were with Mac, Colonel Downs?"

"No, sir," MacMillan said. "I asked the colonel to stay behind at Kimpo to make sure we would have fuel to get back here."

"Did you confer with the KMAG staff, Colonel?" MacArthur asked.

"No, sir," Colonel Downs replied. "There wasn't time, sir."

"You have nothing, then, to contribute?" MacArthur replied. He did not wait for an answer. He simply turned his back to Colonel Downs and examined the map while MacMillan showed him where he had seen the Russian-built T34 tanks heading toward Kaesong, Uijongbu, and Ch'unch'on.

II

(One)
The Hotel Continental
Paris, France
28 June 1950

Mr. and Mrs. Craig W. Lowell, their three-year-old son, Peter-Paul, and Mrs. Lowell's father, Count Peter-Paul von Greiffenberg (who had, only a few days earlier, been released from a Siberian concentration camp) had been placed in a four-room suite on the fourth floor of the hotel. The master bedroom's windows opened on both the Rue de Castiglione and the Rue de Rivoli. The other rooms, a sitting room and two bedrooms, opened on the Rue de Rivoli and the Tuileries beyond.

When the telephone rang, Mr. and Mrs. Lowell were asleep in their bed. Mrs. Lowell, a blond, pert-breasted woman of twenty-one, was naked save for a pair of flimsy pale blue underpants. Mr. Lowell, a large, smoothly muscled, mustachioed man of twenty-three, was completely naked. During the night, the sheet that had covered them had been kicked to the bottom of the bed, and in her sleep, Mrs. Lowell had turned on her side and curled up for warmth. Her husband lay sprawled

21

on his stomach, one hand resting possessively on his wife's leg.

He was instantly awake when the telephone rang, rolling over on his back and reaching out for the old-fashioned telephone on the table beside the canopied bed. As he brought the instrument to his ear, he sat up and swung his legs out of bed.

"Yes?" he said, and then remembering where he was, added, *"Oui?"*

"Did I wake you up?" his caller asked, concern in his voice.

"Hold on, Sandy," Lowell said. "I want to change phones. Ilse's asleep."

He placed the ornate handset gently on the bedside table and stood up, crossing the room to a chaise longue, where the maid had laid out his dressing gown. The dressing gown was silk, and there was a large monogram embroidered over the breast. It had come from Sulka's, across the Rue de Castiglione from the Hotel Continental. But the monogram was not Craig Lowell's, and the first time that he had ever been in Sulka's was late the previous afternoon, when they had arrived in Paris, and had gone there—mainly because it was the closest store— to get his father-in-law some underwear and some off-the-shelf shirts.

The dressing gown had belonged to Lowell's father. Like the five-piece matched set of leather luggage stacked by the door awaiting a porter to carry it off for storage, it had just been too good to give to the Salvation Army, although the Salvation Army had been given his father's shirts and shoes and underwear.

At home he never wore a dressing gown, or even a bathrobe. So far as he was concerned, a man was either dressed or he wasn't, and there was no reason for an intermediate step. Ilse had packed the dressing gown for him, so that his barbarian beliefs would not be evident to the people who worked in hotels. Ilse was concerned about things like that, he had come to decide, not because she was concerned what anyone would think about her, but about him.

As he jammed his arms into the sleeves of his father's dressing gown, he was glad that she had packed the damned thing. Otherwise, he would have had to get dressed before going to the phone in the other room. Either get dressed, or run the risk of giving the shock of her young life to Mademoiselle Whatsername, the nurse the bank had arranged to meet them in the hotel.

It was not that he believed that Mademoiselle had never seen the undressed male form. It was the zippers and extra assholes that upset people the first time they saw him.

The zippers and the extra assholes, so called because that was what they resembled, were the result of what the official medical records had termed "moderate to severe lacerations of the torso and upper arm, caused by shrapnel from artillery and/or mortar projectiles" and "two (2) penetrating entrance and exit wounds, in the upper left arm and extreme upper left torso, at the arm juncture, caused by small arms fire, either rifle or light machine gun."

The wounds had long since healed, but his body would be marked forever.

He started for the door, but then stopped. He went back to the bed and very tenderly pulled the sheet on the bed over his wife. He thought again, as he had the very first time he had ever looked at her asleep in his bed, that she looked like a child, much too young, too innocent, to be in bed with a man.

He walked into the sitting room, and was surprised, almost startled, to see his father-in-law sitting on the floor with his son. The older man was wearing one of the shirts they'd bought at Sulka's the day before. Its collar was opened and the sleeves rolled up.

Christ, Lowell thought, he looks like a fucking cadaver.

"Good morning," he said.

"I hope we didn't wake you up," his father-in-law replied.

P.P. smiled at his father.

You don't have to talk, Squirt, his father thought. That smile of yours would charm the balls off a brass monkey.

"No, I have a call," Lowell said. "I'm going to take it out here."

He sat down on one of two opposing couches and picked up the telephone on the coffee table between them and told the operator to put through the call on the bedroom phone.

"Where are you?" he asked.

His caller told him.

"OK," he said. "You're nearly here. Look out the window, and you can see the Opera. It's a straight shot from the Opera here. You'll see a big thing in the middle of the street about two blocks away. That's right in front of the Ritz. Go around it. The street dead-ends on the Rue de Rivoli two blocks beyond. And that's it. We're on the right side, on the corner. I'll order up some breakfast."

He hung up the telephone.

"Captain Felter," he explained to his father-in-law. "He's at American Express."

His father-in-law nodded. Lowell went into the bedroom, hung that phone up, and then returned and picked up the extension and asked for the desk.

"This is Mr. Lowell," he said. "Captain Felter and his family are about to arrive. They're my guests. I don't want them given a bill for anything, including gratuities. You understand?"

When he hung up the phone again, his father-in-law said, "You are very gracious. Perhaps even generous to a fault."

"I'm rich," Lowell said. "It's easy to be gracious and generous if you're rich."

They smiled at each other.

"Besides, I owe Sandy a lot, and he's a hard guy to pay back."

"I owe him a great deal, too," his father-in-law said.

Lowell walked to the door and examined a box with five porcelain buttons, and selected one and pushed it, to summon the floor waiter.

He turned and looked at his son and his father-in-law. P.P. had gotten off the floor and was standing behind his grandfather, with his arms locked around his neck.

"Found yourself a new pal, have you, Squirt?"

"Grosspapa," the child said.

The old count smiled.

"Yeah," Lowell said. "Grosspapa." He looked at his father-in-law. "What am I going to call you?" he asked.

"Whatever you like," the count replied.

"To Ilse," Lowell said, "you're 'Papa.' To the squirt, you're 'Grosspapa.' But how about us? I'd feel a little uncomfortable with 'Dad,' and I don't think you'd like calling me 'Son.'"

"You say what you think, don't you?" his father-in-law replied.

"How about 'Colonel'?" Lowell asked.

"'Colonel' would be fine. And you?"

"How about calling me 'Craig'?"

"Whatever you like," the older man said, adding, "Craig."

"Grosspapa," P.P. said.

"He's your Mama's papa," Lowell said. "And your Grosspapa. And to me, he's the Colonel. How's that grab you?"

"He's Mama's papa?" the boy said, as if surprised.

"Right," Lowell said.

"And *my* Grosspapa," the boy said, possessively.

The Colonel looked on the edge of tears.

The floor waiter knocked discreetly at the door, and was told to enter.

"Good morning, gentlemen," he said.

"What we're going to have to have," Lowell said, "in about fifteen minutes, is breakfast for, let me see," he counted on his fingers, "six. Plus two children. An American breakfast. The Felters are Jews, so we'll skip bacon and ham. How about rump steaks? Fried eggs, pommes frites, steaks. Orange juice. Milk for the kids. Bread, as well as croissants. And coffee. Bring some coffee and croissants right now, would you please?"

"Thank you very much," the floor waiter said, bowed, and left.

Lowell glanced at his father-in-law. There were tears in his eyes, and a tear ran down one cheek.

"Take it easy, Colonel," Lowell said, gently.

"Everything has happened too quickly," he said.

"Yeah," Lowell said, uncomfortably.

"I keep wondering if I have gone mad," the colonel said. "Or if I will wake up."

"There's a corny American expression, Colonel," Lowell said. "'All's well that ends well.'"

"'Corny'?" the colonel asked.

"Trite," Lowell said.

"You learn to lower your expectations," the colonel said. "Until you are pleased that your dream of being warm, or not hungry, has come true."

"I expect," Lowell said, uncomfortably.

"I don't mean to make you uncomfortable, Craig," the colonel said.

"Don't be silly," Lowell said.

"I used to dream of food," the colonel said. "Of beef and butter. Of real coffee."

Lowell said nothing.

"I'm hungry!" P.P. announced. "When do we eat?"

"Are you really hungry?" Lowell said.

"I'm really hungry."

"We'll have some nice liver in just a few minutes," Lowell said.

"You will not! I heard you! You said steak!"

"Do you like steak for breakfast, P.P?" the older man asked.

"It's all right," the child replied, having considered it.

"Steak for breakfast," the colonel said. "My God!"

Lowell said nothing.

"When I came back," the colonel said to Lowell, "I got off the train in Bad Hersfeld, and saw an old comrade of mine. He told me that my wife had taken her life and that he believed my daughter had gone to East Germany to look for relatives. He tried to encourage me by saying the Red Cross was very good about finding people in such circumstances."

"Well, that's all behind you, Colonel," Lowell said.

"I told myself that I would do what I could to find her, to do what I could for her," the colonel went on. "And then, this . . ."

"Yeah, well, what the hell," Lowell said.

He was relieved when the floor waiter rolled in a tray with a coffee service and a plate of croissants on it.

"You get one croissant, P.P.," Lowell said to his son. "To hold you until breakfast comes."

"Why can't I eat now?"

"Because Uncle Sandy and Aunt Sharon are coming, and we're going to wait for them."

He watched as his father-in-law very carefully buttered a croissant and ate it with tiny bites, savoring each morsel.

There came another knock at the door.

"Entrez!" Lowell called.

The door opened.

A slight, balding man pushed the door open and peered cautiously in.

"Come on in, Sandy," Lowell said, walking up to him, and putting his arm around his shoulder.

"Guten Morgen, Herr Oberst Graf," the little man said, in fluent, vaguely Berliner-accented German.

When Peter-Paul von Greiffenberg had returned to Marburg an der Lahn after five years of Soviet captivity, Sanford Felter had been waiting for him at the railroad station. Not, as the count had first believed, as one more policeman to take away his freedom again, but to take him to a reunion with his daughter, and a son-in-law and grandchild he knew nothing about.

Lowell stepped behind Sandy Felter, kissed his wife, and snatched Sanford T. Felter, Jr., aged two, from his mother's arms.

"Thank God, he looks like you, sweetheart," he said.

"Craig!" Sharon Felter said. She was a dark-haired, light-skinned, slightly built woman with large dark eyes.

"One ugly bald man in a family is enough," Lowell said.

"Herr Oberst Graf," Felter said. "May I present my wife?"

"You must forgive my appearance, Mrs. Felter," the older man said, bowing over her hand. "I am honored."

"Oh, we've heard so much about you," Sharon said. "Oh, forgive me. I didn't say it. Welcome home!"

"Thank you," he said.

"Ilse's asleep," Lowell said. "Go throw her ass out of bed, Sharon."

"I will not!" Sharon said. "Craig, really, sometimes . . ."

He walked to the bedroom door.

"Hey, Ilse! Up and at 'em! Sandy and Sharon are here."

"You didn't have to do that," Sharon said, walking to the bedroom door. "Ilse, I told him not to."

And then she went into the bedroom and closed the door after her.

"Breakfast is on the way," Lowell said. "Or it's supposed to be. Help yourself to some coffee."

"We ate before I called," Felter said.

"Well, you're just going to have to eat again. I know your idea of breakfast. A hard-boiled egg and a stale roll."

Felter shook his head, and then opened a briefcase. He took
out a manila folder and handed it to Lowell.

"What's this?"

"The colonel's service record," Felter said. "A certified
copy, anyway, and the findings of the Denazification Court."

"I don't understand," the colonel said.

"American law forbids the immigration of Nazis, Colonel,"
Felter explained. "You have to be cleared. This will clear you."

"How the hell did you get that overnight?" Lowell asked.

"I didn't get it overnight," Felter said. "I worked on that
damned thing for years."

"Hey, buddy," Lowell said. "Thanks."

"You're welcome," Felter said.

"Captain Felter suspected for some time that you were alive,
Colonel," Lowell said to his father-in-law. "He's really the one
who got you out."

"How does one express his gratitude for something like
that?" the colonel asked.

"As briefly as possible, please," Felter said, with a smile.

"Take off your coat and stay a while," Lowell said.

"Your thugs grabbed our luggage the minute we pulled up
outside," Felter said. "At least I hope they were your thugs."

"Meaning what?"

"Meaning I hope you know where to find our luggage, what
room we're in, that sort of thing."

"I think you're down the hall. Get on the phone and ask."

"What do I say? 'This is Mr. Felter, where am I?'" Felter
asked, and chuckled.

Lowell laughed. Felter took off his coat and hung it on the
back of a chair. Then, as discreetly as he could, he reached
in the small of his back, withdrew a Colt .45 pistol, which he
slipped into the briefcase, and then set the briefcase on the
floor beside the couch.

"You've heard of the Mafia, Colonel?" Lowell asked.

"The Mafia?"

"The fraternal order of Sicilian gangsters? They always go
around carrying guns."

"I don't believe Captain Felter is a gangster," the colonel
said.

"Captain Felter is a spook," Lowell said.

"I don't know what a spook is," the colonel said.

"He's an *intelligence* officer," Lowell said, with mock awe. "Which is not quite the same thing as an intelli*gent* officer."

"Oh, Christ, Craig!" Felter said, exasperated.

"I think you're embarrassing the Captain, Craig," the colonel said.

"I'm used to it, Colonel," Felter said. "He has been embarrassing me from literally the first day I met him."

"You'll have to pardon my near total ignorance of my son-in-law," the colonel said. "When was that?"

"We were on our way to Greece," Lowell said. "In 1946. I was being sent there in disgrace, and Felter, demonstrating that he is indeed fit to march in the Long Gray Line, had volunteered for the assignment."

"The Long Gray Line?" the colonel asked, and then remembered. "Oh, yes, of course. West Point. You're a West Pointer, Captain?"

"I went there for a while," Felter said.

"And you, too, Craig?"

Lowell laughed. "Good God, no. I was a reserve officer, just long enough to do my time and get out. Sandy's the one who has the Pavlovian response to the sound of a trumpet. As anyone who knows will tell you, Colonel, I was a lousy soldier."

"Well, some men take to it, and some don't," the colonel said, graciously.

"The military establishment heaved an enormous sigh of relief when they were finally able to kick me out the gate," Lowell said.

Felter looked between the two of them, and saw that Colonel Count Peter-Paul von Greiffenberg, three wound stripes, recipient of the Iron Cross with Swords and Diamonds, the eleventh of his line to go to war for his country, accepted what Craig Lowell had said about his military service at face value.

"I'm sorry, Craig," Felter said. "I can't let that stand."

"What?" Lowell said.

"Colonel, when your son-in-law was nineteen years old, attached to the Greek Army as an advisor, the unit with which he was serving . . ."

"Knock it off, Sandy!" Lowell interrupted him.

"The unit with which he was serving," Felter went on, relentlessly, "Number 12 Company of the 27th Royal Greek Mountain Division, was attacked by a reinforced regiment of Russian-trained Albanian and Greek troops. All the Greek officers were killed. This 'lousy soldier' your daughter married assumed command, although he was at the time shot full of holes. When the relief column reached his position, there were only twelve men left alive. But they held their position, inspired by this 'lousy soldier.' He's such a 'lousy soldier' that they gave him the Order of St. George and St. Andrew."

"You've always had a fat mouth, you little shit," Lowell said.

"Craig!" Ilse von Greiffenberg Lowell said, shocked as she came in the room. "What's the matter with you? After what Sandy's done for us, how dare you talk to him that way?"

"It's all right, Ilse," Sandy Felter said. "It sounded worse than it really was."

"They're always saying cruel things to each other," Sharon Felter said. "They sometimes make me sick to my stomach. You'd never know how much they love each other, the way they talk to each other."

"Oh, shit," Lowell said. He walked quickly to Felter, wrapped his arms around the smaller man, hoisted him off the ground, and planted a wet and noisy kiss in the middle of his forehead.

"Put me down, you overgrown adolescent!" Felter demanded.

"Say 'pretty please,' you little prick," Lowell said. He squeezed Felter in his arms until Felter gave in.

"Pretty please, you big bastard!" he said. Lowell, laughing, set him down.

"Now, if that doesn't prove I love him, what does?" Lowell asked.

"I'm ashamed of you, Craig," Ilse said, but she was smiling.

The floor waiter, trailed by three busboys, arrived with the breakfast, and started to set up the breakfast table.

Felter watched them, and then, out of the blue, said: "Speaking of war, I just heard on AFN that that's not a border incident in Korea, but a real invasion."

"What's not a border incident?" Lowell asked.

"According to AFN—" Felter said, and then digressed to explain. "AFN is the U.S. radio station in Germany, Colonel, and according to the news broadcast I heard just now, what they first said was a border incident is now a real invasion. Seoul is about to fall."

"Have a nice war, Sandy," Lowell said.

"What a terrible thing to say!" Ilse snapped.

"He doesn't mean half the things he says," Felter said. "If you understand that, you can learn to put up with him."

"Can we eat now?" P.P. asked.

(Two)
Washington, D.C.
5 July 1950

By direction of the President, the Secretary of the Army was authorized and directed to call to active duty for the duration of the Korean police action 2,500 company-grade officers of the various arms and services then carried on the rolls of the inactive reserve.

The officer corps of the United States Army is composed of four components. There is the regular army, those officers whose profession is arms, who meet the criteria established by the Congress for the regular army, and who plan to serve until retired. The number of regular army officers is provided by law. Before World War II, the number of officers on active duty who were not regular army was minuscule. During World War II, the percentages were reversed, and only a few officers could be recognized—by their shorter serial numbers—as regular army.

The bulk of regular army officers come from the United States Military Academy at West Point, and from the other service academies: Virginia Military Institute, Norwich, the Citadel, Texas A&M, and a very few others. But it is possible for individuals, normally reserve officers on active duty, to apply for integration into the regular army, and some are accepted.

The second component of the officer corps of the United

States Army is the corps of officers assigned to the National
Guard. Technically, these officers hold commissions granted
by the governors of the various states, since in peacetime the
National Guard is under the control of the various governors.
These officers simultaneously hold reserve commissions in the
United States Army.

The third component is the reserve officer corps, which is
in turn composed of four components:

1) Reserve officers on extended active duty: those who plan
to remain in uniform until retired. These officers serve at the
pleasure of the Congress, and they enjoy no guarantee of service
until retirement (as do officers holding a regular army commission).

2) Reserve officers on active duty: generally involuntary,
such as those officers called to active duty after graduation
from a Reserve Officer Training Corps program at a college
or university. They serve on active duty for a specified period
of time.

3) Reserve officers of the organized reserve: those officers
assigned to a reserve unit, which meets one evening a week
or one weekend a month. They also serve two weeks of active
duty for training in the summertime. These officers receive a
day's pay and allowances for each training session and earn
retirement credit for such service.

4) Inactive reserve officers: those reserve officers who hold
commissions, but are not members of the active army, the
National Guard, or the organized reserve. They undergo no
training and receive no pay.

The officers the army wished to call to duty for the Korean
peace action were officers in the last category, the inactive
reserve.

Whenever possible, such involuntarily recalled officers were
to be given a thirty-day notice so that they could wind up their
personal affairs. It was recognized, however, that due to the
critical situation in the Far East, this would not always be
possible.

A critical shortage of company-grade officers existed in the
combat arms. In the absence of a pool of officers recently
graduated from the various service schools, who could be assigned to troop units, it was decided that a pool should be

formed from the ranks of the inactive reserve of officers meeting the following criteria:

(a) Of appropriate grade and age. (You need young men in the line units.)

(b) Combat experience. (When you get right down to it, somebody who has heard a gun go off in his ear is really the best guy to lead troops in combat; there's no substitute for combat experience.)

It was argued that calling such officers to active duty, particularly when it was not going to be possible to give them even thirty days to wind up their personal affairs, was not really fair to the officers in question. For one thing, they had already been shot at. For another, not only had they not been getting paid the way other reserve and National Guard officers had been paid (a day's pay for two hours' "training" once a week), but they had been specifically assured that if they kept their commissions in the inactive reserve, they would be called to duty only in the event of an all-out war, and only after the National Guard and active reserve had been called to duty.

It was one of the tougher decisions the Commander in Chief was forced to make. He made it based on his own experience as a captain of artillery. It was a goddamned dirty trick on the officers involved, and he knew it. But there was another side to the coin. Sending troops into battle under inexperienced officers when experienced officers were available was inexcusable. The first duty of an officer—whether a lieutenant or a captain or the Commander in Chief—is to the enlisted men. That was a basic principle of command. He could not justify not calling up the best qualified officers simply because they had already done their duty. They were needed again. They could save some lives. It was a dirty goddamned trick on them, but that's the way it was going to have to be.

(Three)
Kokura, Japan
7 July 1950

The well worn but immaculate jeep of First Lieutenant Philip Sheridan Parker IV, the commander of the third platoon of Tank Company, 24th Infantry Regiment, 24th Infantry Division, rolled up before the barracks housing his platoon. Parker slid gracefully out of the vehicle.

The lieutenant, whose skin was flat black and whose features brought to mind an Arab in a flowing robe, was six feet, three inches tall and carried 225 pounds without fat. He walked quickly up the walkway to the barracks. He was dressed in stiffly starched fatigues and wore a very small fatigue cap squarely on the top of his head. Around his waist was a World War I pistol belt, from which dangled a swiveled holster holding a Model 1917 Colt .45 ACP revolver.

He had just learned that his platoon would not deploy to Korea with the rest of the company, but would take possession of some new tanks first. The division ordnance officer had learned of the presence of eight M4A3 medium tanks in the Osaka ordnance depot, where they had undergone conversion of their main armament from a 75 mm cannon to the new, high-velocity 76 mm cannon. In addition, the tanks had undergone Depot Level IRAN, or Inspect and Repair As Necessary. This had meant an almost complete rebuild. Thus, in their moving parts, they were new tanks.

The ordnance officer, after first receiving assurance that he was welcome to the M4A3 tanks, had made his discovery known to the division commander. The division commander had first told the ordnance officer to send someone to Osaka to take physical possession of the tanks. He then decided to assign them to the tank company of the 24th Infantry Regiment, the other two regiments of the division already being in the process of deployment to Korea. The regimental commander of the 24th Regiment had told the tank company commander of the availability of the tanks.

The tank company commander had decided to give the medium tanks to the third platoon. For one thing, Lieutenant Parker had recently come onto the promotion list for first lieutenant, having completed the requisite time in grade. For another, the company commander was of the opinion that Lieutenant Parker was the best of his three platoon leaders. And finally, Parker had had experience with the high-velocity 76 mm tube at Fort Knox. Having made his decision, he called Parker in and told him.

Parker pushed open the left of the double wooden doors of the barracks and started up the stairway, taking them two at a time. His platoon was housed in two twenty-five-bed squad bays on the third floor of the tank company barracks. He knocked on the door of the private room of the platoon sergeant, Sergeant First Class Amos Woodrow, and when Woodrow came out, followed him into the nearest of the squad bays.

"Atten-hut!" Sergeant Woodrow called, and the troops, who had been reluctantly packing their personal equipment in foot-lockers (which would be stored by the quartermaster during their Korean deployment), came to attention.

"Go next door and get the other guys," Woodrow ordered, pointing his finger at the trooper nearest him. The trooper, a slight little man who lived in mingled fear and awe of both his platoon sergeant and his platoon commander, scurried out of the room.

Parker thought that Sergeant Woodrow would be a good man to have along with him. He wasn't overly impressed with many of his troops, and some really worried him, but Woodrow was obviously a first-class noncom.

Sergeant First Class Amos Woodrow also approved of Lieutenant Parker. Sergeant Woodrow was thirty-eight years old, and had been a soldier since 1942. He had served with the 393rd Tank Destroyer Battalion in the Normandy campaign, had been wounded and hospitalized, and then had served a tour with the only Negro unit in the Constabulary in the Army of Occupation of Germany, the 175th Armored Field Artillery Battalion, where he had been crew chief and section leader of a self-propelled 105 mm howitzer.

Sergeant Woodrow liked Lieutenant Parker's style.

On Parker's fifth day with the platoon, Corporal Ezikiah Lavalier had called Corporal Franklin Roosevelt Taylor a moth-erfucker when Corporal Taylor had accidentally sprayed him with a water hose while washing an M24.

"Well, Taylor," Lieutenant Parker had said, "I must confess that I am both surprised and very disappointed to hear that."

"Suh?" Corporal Taylor had said, popping to rigid attention.

"I would never have thought that of you, Taylor," Lieutenant Parker had gone on smoothly.

"I don't know what the lieutenant's talking about, sir," Taylor had said, uneasily.

"Didn't you hear what Corporal Lavalier called you?" Parker had inquired innocently.

"Oh, that," Taylor, visibly relieved, had replied. "That don't *mean* nothing, Lieutenant, sir. We just talks like that."

"Oh, then, it doesn't *bother* you? You don't mind someone saying that about you?"

"It don't bother me none, Lieutenant," Taylor had reasured him.

"Well, I guess that just goes to show how different people are, doesn't it?" Parker had said, and walked away.

That night, in the regimental NCO club, Sergeant Thaddeus J. Quail, the two-hundred-pound assistant mess sergeant, had conversationally requested of Corporal Taylor: "Motherfucker, hand me them peanuts."

"Watch your mouth, nigger," Taylor replied sharply. "Don't you be calling me no motherfucker."

"Who you calling nigger, nigger?"

"Let me spell it out for you, nigger. You're a nigger, but I ain't no motherfucker. You got that straight?"

Whereupon Sergeant Quail punched Corporal Taylor in the mouth. When the participants in the brawl had been separated and returned to their orderly room by the division military police, Lieutenant Parker had been the officer of the day. The charge of quarters had summoned Sergeant First Class Woodrow from his room.

When he got to the orderly, both Sergeant Quail and Corporal Taylor were standing to attention before Lieutenant Parker's desk. Corporal Taylor had lost a tooth, and there was half-dried blood on his lip.

"Rank has its privileges, Sergeant. You may give me your version of what happened first," Lieutenant Parker had told him, in his dry manner.

"Sir," Sergeant Quail said, uneasily, "me and Taylor had a little argument."

"I see. What about?"

"He called me a nigger, that's what he done, and I ain't taking that from nobody," Quail said righteously, and then remembered to add, "sir."

"What he done," Taylor said, equally righteously, "was to call me a motherfucker. That's what he done, Lieutenant, that's what started the whole thing."

"Is that true, Sergeant? Did you accuse Corporal Taylor of having sexual relations with his mother?" Lieutenant Parker asked.

"I didn't say *that*," Sergeant Quail said. "I just called him, friendly-like, that."

"What's 'that'?"

"You called me motherfucker, and you know you did, and other people heard you, nigger!" Corporal Taylor said.

"See, there he goes again!" Sergeant Quail said, righteously.

"The term 'nigger,'" Lieutenant Parker said, reasonably, "comes from the African country of Nigeria. The way it began was the same way people started calling people from Poland 'Polacks' and people from Hungary 'Hunkys.' It is not very nice, and I don't like it myself. In fact, I become very angry when someone calls me a 'nigger,' and I sympathize with you, Sergeant Quail. Under the circumstances, I have been known to lose my temper myself."

"But he called *me* a *motherfucker*, Lieutenant," Corporal Taylor said, in equally righteous indignation. "A motherfucker is a *lot* worse than a nigger."

"Yes, it is," Lieutenant Parker agreed.

There was a long, long pause, during which Lieutenant Parker appeared to be seriously considering the problem. Then he took the 1928 *Manual for Courts-Martial* from the desk drawer.

He consulted the index until he was quite sure that both sinners knew what the volume he held in his hand was, and then found the applicable Article of War.

"Whosoever shall use provoking language to another in the military service shall be guilty of conduct prejudicial to good order and discipline," he read slowly and solemnly, "and shall be punished as a court-martial shall direct." He looked up at Sergeant Woodrow.

"Sergeant Woodrow," he said, "you're an old soldier. Would you say that calling someone a name that suggests he's having sexual relations with his mother is provoking language?"

"Unless it were true, sir," Woodrow said, "it would be."

"Goddamn, you know that's not true," Taylor said, shocked.

"I didn't *mean* it that way, Lieutenant," Sergeant Quail said. "And Taylor knows I didn't. And anyway, he called me a nigger."

"I'll have to give this matter some thought," Lieutenant Parker said. "I want to talk it over with Sergeant Woodrow, to decide whether a court-martial would be in the best interests of the service. Until we reach a decision, you two stay away from each other, and away from the club."

Thereafter the incidence of one soldier of the third platoon of the 24th Infantry Regimental Tank Company suggesting incestuous activity on the part of another soldier dropped dramatically, although there were several fistfights unreported to official authority.

Sergeant Woodrow thought Lieutenant Parker had class. He had not been surprised to learn subsequently that Parker was one of the old breed, that Parkers in the service went back to the Buffalo Soldiers of the Indian wars.

Other soldiers, all Negro, of shades ranging from Parker's flat black to light pink, came into the squad bay and lined up in a half-circle around Lieutenant Parker.

"Atten-hut!" Woodrow called again. As soon as they were still and quiet, Parker gave them at ease.

"Everybody try to pay attention. I've got some news," he said.

The troops didn't seem to care. Parker saw that at least four of them were quite drunk.

"Hey, Lieutenant," one of the tank commanders called, "Where did you get the go-to-hell six-shooter?"

"My grandfather carried it in France," Parker said. "In World War I."

"While he unloaded ships?" a voice from the rear of the group said. Parker recognized him. Staff Sergeant Sidney, a light-skinned troublemaker.

"Stand to attention," Parker said softly. Slowly, almost defiantly, the soldier, a staff sergeant, stood to attention.

"Your ignorance shows, Sergeant Sidney," Parker said, softly. "So I will take time we should be spending doing more important things to tell you things you should know. My grandfather served as a captain with the 369th Infantry Regiment. They fought at Chateau Thierry. My grandfather was awarded the Croix de guerre by the French government. The regiment, whose troops were all Negro, received the Distinguished Unit Citation. The regiment were soldiers, not stevedores. I will not have them slandered by anyone, especially by anyone with your attitude. Do I make myself clear?"

Sergeant Sidney didn't reply.

"Do I make myself clear, Sidney?" Parker said. There was now menace in his voice, although he didn't raise it.

"Yes, sir," Staff Sergeant Sidney said, after a moment.

"Don't open your mouth again until I give you permission," Parker said, and waited a long moment. Then he said, "You may stand at ease."

The room was now absolutely silent.

"There are eight M4A3 tanks, with the high-velocity 76 mm tube at Osaka," Parker said. "I have been told that if I can guarantee we can use them, the third platoon can have them. Who here besides Sergeant Woodrow has had any M4 experience?"

A dozen hands went up, including Sergeant Sidney's.

"How well do you know the M4A3, Sergeant Sidney?"

"I was school-trained at Knox," Sidney said.

"OK. There will be a bus out in front of the barracks in an hour. Make up a list of the others with M4 experience. And have them ready to go when the bus shows up."

"Sir," Sergeant Sidney protested, "we were told we could have the night off, before going on the ship tomorrow."

"You'll be in Osaka tomorrow," Parker said. "We're going there tonight."

"I've got to say good-bye to my girl, Lieutenant," Sergeant Sidney said.

"I'm sorry," Parker said. "There won't be time for that. We have to go to Osaka, take delivery of the A3s, get them on ship board, and rejoin the rest of the regiment in Korea."

Sergeant Sidney said nothing. But there was a look on his face that annoyed, even angered Parker. But there was nothing he could do about it now.

"We're going to turn our M24s over to the other two platoons," Parker went on. "They'll serve as spares. I'll answer questions, but you're warned that I don't know much more than what I've told you."

Sergeant Sidney was not outside the barracks when the bus came, nor was he anywhere to be found.

"Turn the sonofabitch in as AWOL to miss a movement, Lieutenant," Sergeant Woodrow said. "Let him do six months in the stockade."

"I think Sergeant Sidney would much rather be doing push-ups in the stockade than getting shot at in Korea," Parker said. He was embarrassed that he hadn't thought ahead and had Woodrow keep an eye on him.

"What good would he do us in Korea?"

"He's school-trained on the A3," Parker said. "Can you find him, do you think, Sergeant Woodrow?"

"Yes, sir, I know just where to look."

"I would hate to see the career of a good soldier like Sergeant Sidney ruined by his having missed a shipment, Sergeant," Parker said. "Do you think you could reason with him?"

"Has the platoon sergeant the platoon commander's permission to speak informally, sir?" Sergeant Woodrow asked.

"Yes," Lieutenant Parker said.

"I'll have that nigger motherfucker on the boat if I have to break both his legs," Sergeant Woodrow said.

"Carry on, Sergeant," Parker said.

III

Craig W. Lowell was not surprised to find Andre Pretier's chauffeur waiting for him beyond the glass wall of customs at LaGuardia, but he was surprised when the chauffeur told him that Pretier was in the car.

Andre Pretier was Lowell's mother's husband. Not his stepfather. They had been married after Craig had been drafted into the army in early 1946, following his expulsion for academic unsuitabilit· from Harvard. While the chauffeur collected his luggage, Lowell looked for and found the car.

It was a Chrysler Imperial, with a limousine body by LeBaron, a long, glossy vehicle parked in a TOW AWAY zone. There was an official-looking placard resting against the windshield, bearing the seal of the State of New York and the words

41

OFFICIAL. Craig had often wondered if Pretier had been provided with some sort of honorary official position by some
obliging politician, or whether he or his chauffeur (who had
been with him for twenty-five years) had just picked it up
somewhere and used it without any authority, secure in the
knowledge that airport and other police asked fewer questions
of people in custom-bodied limousines than they did of other
people.

The first Pretier in America had come as a member of the
staff of the Marquis de Lafayette during the American Revo-
lution. He had stayed after the war and founded the shipping
(and later import-export) company which was the foundation
of the Pretier fortune. He had been at Harvard with Lowell's
father, and there, incredibly, become enamored of the woman
who was to become Craig Lowell's mother, an infatuation that
was to last his lifetime. He had proposed marriage precisely
one year and one day after Lowell's father had been buried.

Andre Pretier leaned across the velour seat of the Chrysler
and offered his hand to Lowell as he bent to enter the car.

"I didn't expect this," Lowell said. "Thank you, Andre."

"We had to take your mother to Hartford," Pretier said.

Oh, shit, that's all I need, Lowell thought.

Hartford was the euphemism for the Institute of Living, a
private psychiatric hospital in Hartford, Connecticut.

Pretier handed Lowell a small crystal bowl, a brandy snifter
without a stem.

"Bad?" Lowell asked.

Pretier threw up his hands in resignation.

"She simply can't take strain, or excitement," Pretier said.

"What was I supposed to do, Andre?" Lowell asked,
sharply. "Tell my father-in-law to stay in Siberia?"

"I don't think that had anything to do with it," Pretier replied, not taking offense at Lowell's outburst. Lowell had often
thought that the real reason he disliked his mother's husband
was that Andre Pretier rarely, almost never, took offense at
anything, no matter what the provocation.

"What set her off, then?"

Pretier threw his hands up in frustration again.

"I don't really know. She...uh...had a relapse in the city."

"A spectacular relapse?"

"I'm afraid so," Pretier said. "They had her at Bellevue."

"She's all right, now?" Lowell asked.

Pretier nodded. "I thought you had enough on your hands," he said. "Otherwise I would have called."

"She didn't start asking for me?" Lowell asked.

"She was sedated rather heavily until today," Pretier said.

"Medically, or because I was due in?"

"Both."

"And you think I should go to Hartford?"

"I would be very grateful if you would," Pretier said. "The doctors think it would be beneficial, if you could find the time."

How the fuck can I refuse, when you put it that way? Lowell thought. What decent, true-blue American boy could refuse to go see his loony mother in the funny farm when that would both be beneficial, according to the doctors, and make her long-suffering husband very grateful?

"Of course," Lowell said. "When?"

"I didn't think you would want to take the train," Pretier said. "I've arranged for a plane."

"That's very kind of you, Andre," Lowell said. He reached up and helped himself to more cognac.

His mother, a tall, rather thin, silver-haired woman, didn't seem especially pleased that he had flown to Hartford to visit her, and she didn't ask more than perfunctory questions about what had taken place in Germany and France.

"You said he was a count, didn't you?" she asked. "Didn't I hear that someplace?"

"Yes, he is."

"And lost everything in the war, doubtless, so that we'll have to support him?"

"Actually no, Mother," he said. "The von Greiffenbergs are from Hesse, which is in the American Zone. He didn't have his property confiscated."

"We'll see," she said, closing the subject. She didn't like

being told that the father of the foreign doxy her son had dragged home from Europe wasn't after her money as well as his.

A little ashamed of himself (she was, after all, a sick woman in a hospital), he refused to drop the subject.

"Actually, Mother, the reason I'm here is that he gave me a power of attorney to claim his property here."

"What property here?"

"The government has it, under the Enemy Alien Property Act. Some money, some securities, even some art."

"And you really think the government will give it up?"

"So the lawyers tell me."

"We'll see," she said.

It was after ten when he finally got to his house on Washington Mews, a private alley near Washington Square in Greenwich Village. Andre had suggested that he spend the night at Broadlawns on Long Island, the rambling estate that Craig had inherited from his father, and that he now rented to the Pretiers, because Andre refused to live there without paying. But Lowell wanted to go home to the town house that Ilse had decorated, to sleep in their bed, to be at least that close to her.

There was no one home at 11 Washington Mews. Their servants had been given the time off while he and P.P. and Ilse were in Europe, and he had to go through the complex procedure of first unlocking the door and then racing up the stairs and down the corridor to his bedroom to put another key into the burglar alarm, to deactivate it before it rang both Pinkerton's and the police precinct. Otherwise a platoon of police cars with howling sirens would descend on Washington Mews.

He turned off the burglar alarm and then went back downstairs to get the one suitcase he had with him and which he had dropped at the door. He remembered seeing some mail on the floor, too.

There were five or six letters, which he tossed unread onto the hall table, and the yellow envelope of a telegram. He almost tossed that with the unopened letters, but then decided it might be a cablegram, rather than a telegram, some just remembered bit of information his father-in law thought he should have in order to better handle his affairs in New York.

He opened it. It wasn't a cablegram. It was a telegram.

WASH DC (GOVT RATE) JUL 7 1950
CAPTAIN CRAIG W. LOWELL 0-495302
11 WASHINGTON MEWS
NEW YORK CITY
FONE & DELIVER

BY DIRECTION OF THE PRESIDENT, YOU ARE ORDERED TO REPORT TO FORT GEORGE G. MEADE, MARYLAND, NOT LATER THAN 2400 HOURS 12 JULY 1950 TO ENTER UPON AN INDEFINITE PERIOD OF ACTIVE DUTY IN CONNECTION WITH THE KOREAN PEACE ACTION.

> EDWARD F. WITSELL
> MAJOR GENERAL, US ARMY
> THE ADJUTANT GENERAL

(Two)
Pusan, Korea
12 July 1950

The third platoon of Tank Company, 24th Infantry Regiment, debarked from the USNS *Private Albert Ford* at Pusan four days after the rest of the company had arrived.

Lieutenant Parker had a premonition that he was going to be very much alone in this police action, this show of force, or whatever it was. He was worried, even frightened by the prospect. He had never heard a shot fired in anger, had never issued an order involving life and death. Parker was quite as innocent—as virginal—at war as most of the troops in his platoon.

On the other hand, he had heard a good deal about war, about the unpredictability of human reaction to it. He had often heard that sometimes it was the apparently strong who turned out to be unable to handle their fear; who, if they didn't actually collapse under fire, were unable to think clearly, who couldn't make rational decisions. He wondered if that would happen to him.

There was no question in his mind that so far as junior armor officers were concerned, he was as well trained as any. He was, like his father before him, a graduate of Norwich University, a small institution little known outside Vermont and the army. Norwich had been providing the army with regular cavalry officers for more than a century. Norwich second lieutenants "coincidentally" were given regular army commissions on the same day West Point graduates got theirs; "coincidentally" it had as its president a retired West Pointer general officer of cavalry; and "coincidentally" it had a faculty for the military arts and sciences provided by the army to the same criteria as the faculty to West Point.

There was a gentleman's agreement going back to the time that Sylvanus Thayer had become Commandant of West Point. The cavalry establishment, in and out of uniform (and in and out of uniform, cavalry has been, since the first warrior mounted a horse, the service of the wealthy and powerful), would not fight the Corps of Engineers and the infantry and Sylvanus Thayer and West Point; and the West Point establishment, in and out of uniform, would not only see that Norwich graduates were given regular cavalry commissions but would regard them as professional and social peers.

Similar gentleman's agreements existed between the West Point establishment and the Citadel (assuring that the regular officer's corps of all the arms and services had a fair leavening of well-bred Southerners) and the Texas Agricultural and Mechanical College (assuring that both the regular artillery and the reserve officer's corps were liberally laced with Aggies). The relationship between the West Point establishment and the Citadel and Texas A&M was much better known, because the relationship between Norwich and the West Point establishment was seldom discussed.

After graduating from Norwich and entering upon active duty, Lieutenant Parker had attended the Basic Armor Officer's Course at Fort Knox, Kentucky. He had graduated "with Great Distinction"—that is to say, as the honor graduate of his class—but Fort Knox had not been entirely the beginning he had hoped to make on his career. Socially, it had been a disaster.

He had shared a BOQ suite (two two-room "apartments"

sharing a shower and toilet) with a second lieutenant who had
attracted the wrath of the military social establishment like a
magnet draws iron filings. He was not a West Pointer, nor even
someone commissioned from the Reserve Officer's Training
Corps or Officer Candidate School. The man was Second Lieutenant Craig W. Lowell.

Parker had thought of Lowell a good deal since this Korean
business had started. Lowell was in New York, a civilian, and
working in the family business, which was modestly described
as an investment banking firm. Parker had wondered if Lowell
would be recalled and decided that he probably wouldn't be.
And he'd really wondered, now that he was actually going to
war, if he would be able to function as well as Lowell had
functioned in Greece.

No one would have thought that Lowell would be a good
soldier, a good officer, but he had wound up with the second
highest decoration for valor the Greek government gave. On
the other hand, everyone would expect a Norwich graduate to
at least "do his duty," and possibly serve with distinction—
especially the son of a Norwich graduate who had commanded
a tank destroyer battalion across North Africa and Europe, the
grandson of a colonel who as a captain had commanded a
company of the 369th Infantry in War I, and the great-grandson
of a master sergeant who had fought Indians with the 9th Cavalry and gone up Kettle Hill in Cuba with Teddy Roosevelt.
Philip Sheridan Parker IV told himself he would be satisfied
if he didn't shit his pants and run when he first round came his
way.

(Three)
When the platoon assembled on Pier One in Pusan, Staff
Sergeant Sidney was present and accounted for, although com-
plaining of pain from injuries suffered in a fall in the shower.
Perhaps because of the "fall in the shower," he seemed ready
to do what was expected of him, and Parker put him to work—
still another time—checking the machine guns on the M4A3s
and the personal weapons.

It took about two hours to unload the M4A3s from the hold
of the *Albert Ford* and another hour to fuel and arm them.

Parker found a supply of 76 mm high-velocity rounds in a warehouse directly across from where the *Albert Ford* was tied up; and in the belief that ammunition supply would be a problem (so far as he knew, he had the only medium tanks in Korea), he ordered that as many cases of the ammunition as possible be tied to the outside of the tanks.

Sergeant Woodrow disappeared for thirty minutes during the off-loading procedure and returned with a General Motors six-by-six truck and a Dodge three-quarter-ton ambulance without the Red Cross insignia painted on its sides. The trucks bore bumper markings identifying them as belonged to the 25th Infantry's Headquarters and Service Company. The bumpers were spread with track grease and then covered with dirt from the pier so the markings could not be read. When the platoon moved out, both trucks, loaded as heavily as possible with 76 mm ammunition, were placed in the column after the first two tanks.

Five hours later, coming around a bend in a narrow, tar-covered road, Lieutenant Parker came on the regimental headquarters. It consisted of a tent fly erected by the side of the road to shade the headquarters staff from the hot sun, and the regimental headquarters' vehicles, halfheartedly camouflaged across the road.

There was also one M24 tank. When Parker saw it, he thought he might be in luck; it was possible the company commander was at the command post.

He was not. And the M24 was all that was left of the first and second platoons of the tank company.

"My report to division said that Captain Meadows and the others are missing and presumed dead or captured," the regimental commander said bitterly. "I have, however, been reliably informed that the captain, was seen together with several of his officers and approximately seventy men, on foot headed in the general direction of Pusan."

"I don't quite follow you, sir."

"I mean they bugged out, Lieutenant. They turned tail and ran. Is that clear enough for you?"

"What are my orders, sir?"

"Render what assistance you can to the 3rd Battalion," the

colonel said, pointing out their location on a map laid on the hood of a jeep. "The last time I heard, they were in this general area."

The colonel was obviously distraught. And it was equally obvious that the colonel, if he did not expect Parker and his men to run like the others, at least would not be shocked or surprised if they did.

"I presume, sir, the orders are to hold that line?"

"Those are my orders, Lieutenant," the colonel said.

Parker went back to the road and climbed in the turret of his M4A3. He put on his helmet and adjusted the radio microphone in front of his lips.

He looked around at his force: a few tanks, manned by frightened, inexperienced, inadequately trained black men. And they were supposed to take on the whole North Korean Army? It was absurd on its face. What was going to happen was that they were all going to get killed. Unless they ran.

But then he had another thought. This was not the first time a few black men had faced an enemy superior in numbers—and probably in skill. Master Sergeant Parker of the 9th Cavalry had fought and beaten Chiricahua Apache, and had lived to run up Kettle and San Juan hills with the Rough Riders.

The cold fact was that if he didn't do this right, if he didn't come through now as his heritage and his training required, the men with him would die.

It was clearly better to die fighting than die running.

He pressed the mike button.

"Wind 'em up," he heard himself say. "Charge the machine guns. Load the tubes with a HEAT round. The bad guys are about a mile from here."

He was frightened. He laid his hand on the wooden grips of the 1917 Colt revolver. So this was what it was all about. Not knowing what the fuck you were supposed to do, or how the fuck to do it.

Had his father and his grandfather gone through something like this?

"Move out," he said to the microphone. The M4A3 jerked under him.

Around the next bend, he could see men on foot coming

down both sides of the road. When he got close to them, he told the driver to slow. He put binoculars to his eyes. He could see nothing, except a haze that might be smoke residue from incoming rounds—or which might be haze, period.

A lieutenant flagged him down. Parker ordered the tank driver to stop. The lieutenant climbed with difficulty over the tied-on cases of 76 mm ammo.

"Turn around," he said. "They're right behind me." There was terror in the lieutenant's eyes.

"I don't see anybody back there," Parker said.

The lieutenant looked over his shoulder.

"The colonel told me to tell you to secure your positions," Parker said. "Reinforcements are on the way. We're the first of them."

"I'm not going back up there."

"Tell your men to climb on my tanks," Parker said. "You'll have to show me where to go."

The lieutenant looked at him out of wide eyes.

"Tell them," Parker said, again, softly. "Everything's going to be all right."

For a moment, he thought that he had won.

"Fuck you," the lieutenant said, not angrily. A man who had made his decision. He jumped off the tank.

His men had gathered in a clump around Parker's tank, watching. Paying no attention to them at all, the lieutenant resumed walking toward the rear. Parker pulled the Colt from its holster, pointed it at the sky, and pulled the trigger.

The noise was shocking, hurting his ears.

The lieutenant turned and looked at him.

"Get your men on the tanks," Parker ordered.

The lieutenant looked at him for a long moment, and then deliberately turned his back and started walking.

I'll fire a shot into the ground beside him, Parker thought; but even as he raised the pistol, he knew that wouldn't work. The sights lined up on the lieutenant's back. He pulled the trigger. The old pistol leapt in recoil. The lieutenant fell spread-eagled on the ground, tried to rise, then fell again and didn't move.

Parker looked at the men gathered around his tank. His eyes fell on a sergeant.

"Have your men climb on the tanks, Sergeant," Parker shouted. "You are now under my command."

The sergeant didn't move. Parker tried to put the Colt back in its holster. He missed. He could hear the pistol clattering around in the hull. He hoped it wouldn't land on its hammer and fire. He put his trembling hands on the handles of the .50 caliber machine gun, and—awkwardly—trained it on the infantrymen on the ground.

"Mount your men, Sergeant," Parker ordered.

"OK," the sergeant said, softly, and then raised his voice. "On the tanks," he shouted. "Everybody on the tanks."

Parker touched his throat microphone.

"If anyone jumps off, shoot him," he ordered. "Move out!"

A half mile further down the road, he came on the defense positions. There were twenty men manning them. Another sergeant ran out when the tanks approached.

"Is there an officer here?" Parker asked.

"No, sir, he bugged out," the sergeant said.

"You're in command?"

"I guess so, Lieutenant."

"Put these men to work," Parker ordered. "If any of them try to leave without my specific order to move, shoot them."

The sergeant, a wiry little black with an acne-scarred face, came to attention and saluted.

"Yes, sir," he said.

"I'll see you're decorated for this, Sergeant," Parker said. Then he touched the throat microphone. "Woodrow, put the tanks in a defensive position."

"Yes, sir," Sergeant Woodrow's voice came back.

"Let's take a run up the road a little and see what we can see," Parker said to his driver.

There was no response. Parker looked into the tank interior. The driver was handing the old Colt up to him.

"You really shoot that bastard, Lieutenant?" the driver asked.

Parker looked at him a moment before he nodded his head.

"Get back in the saddle," he ordered. "I want to see what's up ahead."

"Yes, sir!" the driver said. He dropped back into the hull. In a moment his voice came over the intercom. "OK, Lieutenant."

"Scouts forward," Parker said, almost to himself.

"Right up the fucking road, Lieutenant?" the driver asked, as the tank began to move.

"Right up the fucking road," Parker replied.

Another half a mile further forward, they came across six M24 light tanks. Five were facing forward, one toward the rear. They formed a half-circle.

"Maybe they're booby-trapped," the driver said, putting Parker's thoughts into words.

"Yeah, and maybe they're not," Parker replied. "Maybe they were just left here." He thought for a moment. He touched his throat microphone again. "If anybody shoots at me, return the fire," he said. "I'm going to go see."

He hoisted himself out of the turret, climbed down the tracks, and ran to the nearest M24, the one facing to the rear. The hatches were open, but there was no sign of damage at all. He climbed onto the hull, looked down into the driver's seat, and then stood on the hull and looked into the turret. Finally, he climbed into the turret. There was ammunition for the tube, and the machine guns were cocked and ready to fire. Just to be sure, he dropped into the driver's seat and tried to start the engine. It cranked but wouldn't start, and for a moment, Parker thought it was out of fuel. But the gauge showed half full. Perhaps a fuel line stoppage. He wondered if he remembered enough from watching mechanics to clear a fuel line stoppage.

And then the engine caught. It ran roughly for a moment or two and then smoothed out. He put it in gear and drove it to where his M4A3 sat and climbed out.

He ordered the gunner and the loader from his tank. He installed the gunner in the M24 and told him to go back to where the rest of the platoon was in place and to tell Sergeant Woodrow to send four crewmen back, anyone who thinks he can drive an M24.

"You always wanted to be a tank commander," he said to the loader, the junior man in a tank crew's hierarchy. "You go get one of those M24s, and its yours . . . as commander."

"Jesus Christ, Lieutenant!" the loader said, unnerved.

"Go on," Parker said. "I don't see why we should give our tanks to the enemy, do you?"

"No, sir," the loader said, and he ran toward the parked tanks.

Parker climbed into the M4A3 and took the gunner's position. He strapped on the throat microphone.

"You're the commander," he said to the driver. "Until we get some people back up here, I'll have to fire the tube."

He put his eyes to the rubber eyepieces of the gunsight. He moved the turret from side to side. There was nothing out there but a bright summer Korean day.

In fifteen minutes, crewmen from his M4A3 showed up, clinging to the hull of the M24 he had taken over. Five minutes after that, the last of the M24s had driven past him on the way to the defensive positions. He watched the last one depart, and then took a final look through the sight.

He saw movement, and then quite clearly saw crouching figures coming onto the road at a right angle from the left, and then following the road in his direction, in the ditches on either side.

He touched the throat microphone.

"I'm going to fire one round in this thing," he said. "The minute I do, turn it around and shag ass."

"Gotcha, Lieutenant," the driver said. Parker aimed the cannon. HEAT rounds were High Explosive, Anti-Tank, not very effective against personnel. What he needed was a cannister round. But he didn't have a cannister round.

He took aim at a concrete drain abutment and pressed the trigger. The round went whistling over it, to explode harmlessly five hundred yards away. Immediately, the driver spun the tank around on one track and hightailed it for the rear.

Furious, Parker climbed awkwardly into the turret of the lurching tank, skinning his hands and knees. He stood on the seat, grabbed the handles of the .50 caliber machine gun, and spun the turret around to face the rear. By the time the turret swung, they were around a corner in the road; and there was nothing for him to fire at.

When he got back to where he had left Woodrow and the platoon, he didn't know what to do with the M24s. He was unable to raise the regimental CP on any of the tank radio frequencies.

He walked over to Sergeant Sidney's M4A3. Sidney was sitting with his legs straddling the tube.

"Sidney," Parker said, "take one of those M24s and go back to regiment. Tell the colonel we have six of them and ask him what to do with them. And get us a radio frequency."

Sidney looked at him as if he were very sleepy. He nodded without saying a word and climbed off the cannon barrel. It was not, Parker decided, the time to remind Sidney that when sergeants were given an order by an officer, they were supposed to say, "Yes, sir."

Twenty minutes later, the regimental commander showed up, driving a jeep himself.

Parker climbed off his tank, walked to the jeep, and saluted.

"Where did you get the tanks, Lieutenant?" the colonel asked.

"I found them on the road, sir," Parker said. "They had apparently been abandoned. I'm going to need crews for them."

"Who are these other men?" the Colonel replied, not responding to the request.

"I think they're from Item Company, sir," Parker replied.

"That figures," the colonel said. "I recognized the body of Item Company's commander on the road on the way up here."

It took a moment before Parker realized the colonel was talking about the lieutenant he had shot.

"There's no other officer up here?" the colonel went on.

"No, sir."

"OK," the colonel said. "I don't have any communications to give you, but I'll try to get word to you if there's a further withdrawal." He corrected himself: *"When* there is a further withdrawal."

"Yes, sir."

"In the meantime, do the best you can," the colonel said. "You've got the ball."

"Sir, what about crews for the M24s?"

"That's your problem, Lieutenant. You're the company commander."

"Sir?"

"You heard me. You're Tank Company commander, and if that's what's left of Item Company, you're also Item Company commander. Your orders are the same as mine. Do what you can with what you've got."

"Yes, sir."

"I wouldn't spend a lot of time digging in," the colonel said, as he cranked the jeep engine. "Apparently, we're not the only ones suffering from bug-out fever."

Parker saluted, a reflex action, as the jeep pulled away. The colonel was too preoccupied with other matters to remember to return it.

"Sergeant Woodrow!" Parker called. Woodrow came running up.

"What's the word, Lieutenant?"

"I've just been named company commander. This is apparently the company."

"Yes, sir."

"That makes you first sergeant," Parker said. "Of our people and these infantry types. The tanks are ours, but we're going to have to find crews for them."

"I'll get right on it, Lieutenant," Woodrow said. He touched his right hand to his forehead, a sloppy movement of his arm and wrist until the fingers touched the eyebrow, then a crisp movement, almost a jerk of the hand two inches away from the forehead. It wasn't a parade ground salute, but it was a salute rendered with respect, from a first sergeant to his company commander on the battlefield. Their eyes met for a moment.

"Thank you, First Sergeant," Lieutenant Parker said, the faintest suggestion of emotion in his voice. "Carry on."

(Four)
Tokyo, Japan
18 July 1950

The assignment of officers in the grade of captain rarely

comes to the attention of very senior officers. But there are exceptions.

"Is there something else, VanAntwerp?" the Supreme Commander, Allied Powers asked of one of his colonels, who lingered momentarily after the other officers had left the SCAP conference room after the reading of the daily communiqué.

"Sir," the colonel said, "I'm concerned about MacMillan."

"Oh? Where is he? I haven't seen him about lately."

"In Korea, sir, flying an L-5."

"'General,'" the SCAP quoted Captain MacMillan on his return from Korea immediately after hostilities began, "'I think we got us a war.'" The SCAP smiled. "MacMillan is a warrior, Colonel. He lies dormant, like a hibernating grizzly, until he hears the blare of the trumpet and the roll of the drum, and then he comes alive again."

"General, MacMillan has the Medal," the colonel said.

"You are implying?" SCAP asked.

"That there would be a good deal in the press in the event Captain MacMillan should be killed, or turn up missing, or fall into the hands of the enemy."

SCAP thought that over for a moment.

"Yes," he agreed, nodding his head. "Recommendation?"

"That Captain MacMillan's contribution to the tactical situation as an L-5 pilot is no greater than any other pilot's. His loss at this time would have unfortunate public relations aspects."

"Recommendation?" SCAP asked again.

"That he be assigned other duties."

"Recommendation?"

"That he be returned to the Zone of the Interior for training as a helicopter pilot. Initially, particularly if the general saw fit to decorate him for his services, specifically his rescue under fire of the three KMAG officers from the Ongjin peninsula, he would have a definite public relations value."

"Order him home, Colonel," SCAP said. "Silver Star, you think?"

"'General of the Army Douglas MacArthur,'" the colonel quoted from the photo caption he would release, "'himself holder of the Medal of Honor, is shown awarding the Silver

Star to Captain Rudolph G. MacMillan. It was the third award of the Silver Star to MacMillan, who won the Medal of Honor in World War II. MacMillan was decorated for his heroic service as an army aviator in the opening days of the Korean conflict . . .'"

"Yes," the SCAP said. "Arrange it, Colonel."

"Yes, sir."

IV

(One)

Captain Craig W. Lowell, Armor, U.S. Army Reserve, 11 Washington Mews, New York City, having been ordered—by telegram, by direction of the President of the United States—to report to the United States Army Reception Center, Fort George G. Meade, Maryland, not later than 2400 hours on 12 July 1950 for an indefinite period of active duty in connection with the Korean conflict, rolled up to the MP shack at the gate at 2330 hours.

He had checked into the Lord Baltimore Hotel in Baltimore shortly after two that afternoon, after driving down from New York City in his Jaguar XK120 convertible coupe. Someone from the office had called, and when he walked up to the desk and gave his name, an assistant manager appeared almost instantly, introduced himself, said how pleased they were to have him in the house, that they had a nice, quiet little suite for him, and if there was anything, anything at all he could do to make Mr. Lowell's stay more pleasant...

"Thank you," Lowell had said. "There is."

"How may we be of service?"

"That's full of uniforms," Lowell said, pointing to the canvas Valv-Pak at the feet of the hovering bellman. "I'm going to need everything washable in it washed and everything else pressed, practically immediately."

"It will all be ready for you in the morning," the assistant manager said.

"I need it by eight o'clock tonight," Lowell said.

"That may be a little difficult," the assistant manager said.

"I'm sure you'll be able to manage," Lowell said. "I'll keep the suite, even if I don't get to stay in it, until I tell you otherwise. Bill it to the firm, marked for my personal account."

"Certainly, Mr. Lowell," the assistant manager said.

Lowell motioned the bellman over, gave him ten dollars, and told him to take care of the uniforms that needed washing and pressing. And then he went in the bar and had a couple of drinks and tried to work up enough courage to call the Hotel D'Anglais in Monte Carlo, where Ilse, P.P., and the colonel were waiting for him, and to tell Ilse what had happened.

He had talked to her three times since he'd been in the United States and hadn't been able to tell her. He knew that not having told her posed another problem. She would be hurt.

He decided, again, that he would wait until he knew something. When he realized he was getting as tight as a tick tossing down the scotches, he left the bar and went down Baltimore Street and went in the first movie theater he came to.

He fell asleep and woke up with a stiff neck and his right leg painfully asleep.

He went back to the hotel, went into the hotel dining room, and had a split of California burgundy with a large slice of rare roast beef and then went to the desk and got the key to the suite.

There were two message slips under the door. Both said the same thing. He was to call Porter Craig in New York City. Porter Craig was his cousin and chairman of the board of Craig, Powell, Kenyon and Dawes, Investment Bankers. Porter Craig was ten years older than Craig Lowell. He was Groton and Harvard and the Harvard School of Law. He did not get as much exercise as he would have liked, and was getting a little thick at the middle. He was also getting a little thin on top, and there was the suggestion of the jowls he would have in later life. If it were not for the coldness in his eyes, Porter Craig might have looked kindly.

Porter Craig's reaction to Lowell's telegram from the adjutant general of the United States Army was contemptuous anger. He would have a word with the senator, and that would be the end of it. It was absolutely outrageous that they should ask him to serve again. He had done his share.

The truth of the matter, Lowell knew, was that Porter was overreacting. In his heart of hearts, he would much prefer that Craig Lowell be gone from Craig, Powell, Kenyon and Dawes. Knowing that had shamed Porter, and his reaction had been to demand that Lowell accept the influence he could bring to bear against the army.

"You're going to have to let me do this, Craig, before you report. Once you report, getting you out will be infinitely more difficult than keeping you out. You understand that?"

"I'll let you know when I need you, Porter," he had told him.

He did not return Porter's calls now.

He undressed, showered, and shaved, aware that it was something of a symbolic ritual, and then he dressed in his uniform, except for the green tunic. He laid this on the bed and pinned the twin silver bars of a captain on the epaulets, the U.S. and armor insignia on the lapels. He looked at his ribbons, and replaced them in the leather insignia box. And then he took from the insignia box a miniature, unauthorized, and thus very popular version of the Expert Combat Infantry Badge and pinned that over the breast pocket.

He put the tunic on, buttoned it, and closed the belt, then took an overseas cap and put that on. He examined himself in the mirror. He saluted his image.

"Captain Lowell," he said. "Reporting for duty, sir." And then he said, "Shit!"

Then he called the desk and told them to have the car brought around and to send a bellman to his room. A moment after he hung up, he called back and told them to send up a bottle of Haig and Haig Pinch with the bellman.

When the bellman showed up, Lowell told him to take the uniforms on their hangers and to lay them out either in the trunk of the Jaguar or behind the seat, so they wouldn't get mussed, and to put the Valv-Pak and the briefcase on the passenger side seat.

"I'll be in the bar," Lowell said. "Acquiring some liquid courage."

"My brother-in-law got called up, too," the bellman said. "Poor bastard."

"Your brother or me?" Lowell asked.

"Both of you," the bellman said.

Lowell thought again of calling Ilse and decided against it, then had two drinks in the bar before walking out of the hotel lobby and getting directions to Fort George G. Meade from the bellman. After that he got in the car and drove off.

The MP at the gate came to the car, saluted, and bent over.

"Reception center," Lowell said.

"Stay on this road, sir," the MP said. "One point three miles. You'll see a sign."

"Thank you."

"That's a real fine set of wheels, Captain," the MP said, and saluted again.

It was, Lowell thought, his second visit to Fort George G. Meade, Maryland. He had previously reported here after a postcard had informed him that his friends and neighbors had selected him for induction into the armed forces of the United States. That was so much bullshit. He had been drafted because he'd been given the heave-ho from Harvard, cancelling his academic exemption.

He had arrived the first time by chartered bus, after a train ride from New York. He remembered the sergeant who had been waiting for them at the reception center, who had been displeased with the speed with which Private Lowell had gotten off the bus and into ranks, whose spittle had had sprayed Private Lowell's face as he screamed in his ear that he personally doubted that such a pile of shit could ever be turned into a soldier.

This time, when he reported to the reception center, a sergeant got to his feet when he walked in the building and actually smiled at him. He then assigned a corporal to take him to the BOQ. The corporal collected five dollars for BOQ fees, to pay for the orderly who had made up the bunk and who would sweep the floor and clean the latrine he was to share with the three other officers in the two bedroom, one latrine suite.

No bugles were blown the next morning, and neither did some bull-chested cretin amuse himself by lifting the end of his bunk and letting it slam back to the floor. No one screamed, "Drop your cocks and pick up your socks, it's reveille!" at the top of his lungs.

A sergeant came in and turned on the lights.

"There will be an orientation formation at 0800, gentlemen," he said. "If you want breakfast, the officer's open mess feeds from now on. The big white building the other side of the parade ground."

But there were other painful similarities. The impersonal physical examination, so much meat on the hoof being examined by bored doctors. The arm stiff from the tetanus shot, like seven others administered whether or not it was needed, because that speeded up the processing.

The forms to be filled out.

The false hopes: "They can't send all of us to Korea. When this bullshit is over, we'll be assigned somewhere counting mess kits."

"Shit, I haven't been near the army for five years. I'm not qualified to command a squad, much less a company."

"I've been working for the Chase Manhattan bank. I'd be of much greater use as a finance officer than in a line company. I don't know anything anymore about a line company."

"That fucking war is going to be over in six months. Just as soon as Truman gets the balls to drop the A-bomb on them."

The first thing that the Adjutant General's Corps captain (who would interview Captain Lowell and determine his assignment) thought when he saw him was that, if he were not wearing the "Bloody Bucket" shoulder patch from the 28th Infantry Division, Pennsylvania National Guard, Lowell could have easily been mistaken for a regular, or what was known as a "career reserve" officer. He *looked* like a soldier, not like most of the other recalls, who generally showed up in a uniform that looked as if it had been stuck in an attic trunk for a half decade—if, indeed, they showed up in uniform at all.

Captain Lowell's Class "A" green tunic and pink trousers were immaculate and perfectly tailored. His feet were shod in the highly polished, pebble-grained jodhpurs normally worn only by regular armor—or armored cavalry—officers who felt their appearance justified the extraordinary cost. He wore no ribbons on his breast; it was bare save for the miniature, unauthorized version of the wretched silver flintlock on a blue background, the Expert Combat Infantry Badge.

"You're one of the unfortunates, Captain Lowell," the AGC captain said to him with somewhat forced joviality. "Your service record seems to have been mislaid between here and Fort Benjamin Harrison."

At Fort Benjamin Harrison, in Indiana, in enormous, file-filled warehouses, the army maintains the records of officers and enlisted men not on active duty.

"Where does that leave me?" Captain Lowell asked.

"Well, what we're going to do for you fellows is make up a temporary service record, and 201 file, and then correct it when the real thing catches up with you. I don't suppose you've kept your own 201 file?"

"As a matter of fact, I have," Lowell said. He reached onto the floor beside him, picked up a softly gleaming, saddle-leather attaché case bearing his initials in gold. "May I?" he asked, placing it on the captain's desk and opening it. He took out two inch-thick folders, their contents held in place by metal clips. "Everything's in there," he said.

The AGC captain flipped quickly through them.

"May I have these? They'd certainly be a help."

"You may make certified true copies of anything you want," Captain Lowell said, "but you can't have them."

The AGC captain didn't like that at all. He spent the next fifteen minutes reading through the files.

"You've had a very *interesting* career, haven't you?" he said, finally.

Lowell didn't reply.

"Captain, how would you feel about a detail to infantry?" the AGC officer asked.

"I wouldn't like that at all, Captain," Captain Lowell said, flatly.

"You've got to look at the big picture," he said. "There aren't that many vacancies for armor officers of your grade."

"Great, send me home."

"You've had service—according to your record, distinguished service—as an advisor to an infantry unit. And we need infantry company commanders. You have the Expert Combat Infantry Badge."

"Cut the bullshit," Captain Lowell said, unpleasantly.

"Now wait a minute!"

"I'm not going to take a voluntary detail to infantry. If I'm detailed to infantry, I will make a stink you wouldn't believe. I'm a qualified armor officer."

"Not as a captain, you're not. You're not a graduate of the Advanced Armor Officer's Course."

"Neither am I of the Advanced Infantry Officer's Course," Lowell said.

"I don't really need your permission, you know."

"Yes, you do, you chair-warming sonofabitch, or else you wouldn't have called me in here to feed me your line of bullshit."

"Have a seat, Captain Lowell," the lieutenant colonel in charge of Recalled Officer's Classification and Assignment said, and then he said to the AGC captain, "I'll handle this, Tom."

He spent fifteen minutes going over Captain Lowell's personal 201 file.

"You're very young to be a captain, you know," he said, finally.

"Yes, sir, I suppose I am," Lowell said.

"We need infantry company commanders," the lieutenant colonel said.

"I hope you find them, sir," Lowell said.

"What have you been doing as a civilian, Captain?" the colonel asked.

Lowell took a moment to reply. The colonel looked up at him.

"I'm an investment banker," Lowell said.

"I'm not entirely sure what that means," the colonel said.

"Did you have a title of some sort?"

"Vice-chairman of the board," Lowell said, distinctly.

"The name of the firm?"

"Craig, Powell, Kenyon and Dawes," Lowell said.

"I don't know the name," the colonel said. Lowell didn't reply.

"In New York City?"

"Twenty-three Wall Street," Lowell said.

"Paid pretty well, I suppose," the colonel asked, idly.

"Is that an official request for information, Colonel?" Lowell asked.

"Yes," the colonel said. "I guess it is."

"I drew a hundred thousand," Lowell said.

"Captain," the colonel said, more in resignation than anger, "if I have to tell you this, I will. It's a court-martial offense, the uttering of statements known to be false in response to an official inquiry. According to your own 201 file, you were graduated from the Wharton School of Business just about a year ago. And now you're telling me . . ."

Lowell reached forward slightly and nudged the telephone toward the colonel. "Use my name and call collect, Colonel," he said. "You asked for the information and I gave it to you. I inherited half the firm from my grandfather."

The colonel looked at Lowell for a long moment.

"You were originally commissioned in the Finance Corps," he said. "Is that what this is all about? You want to go back to the Finance Corps?"

Lowell chuckled.

"Colonel," he said, "I would be outright disaster in the Finance Corps."

"But you were originally commissioned in the Finance Corps?"

"That was simply an expedient means of getting me into an officer's uniform," Lowell said. "I never stepped behind the counter of a finance office."

"You won a battlefield commission?" the AGC lieutenant colonel asked.

"First they handed me a commission," Lowell said. "The battlefield came later."

"I think that needs an explanation," the lieutenant colonel said.

Lowell hesitated a moment before replying.

"You know who General Porky Waterford was, I presume, Colonel?"

"Yes, of course. He had the 40th Armored Divison, 'Hell's Circus,' during War II. You were with 'Hell's Circus'?"

"I wasn't in the Second World War," Lowell said. "I was drafted after the war and sent to the Army of Occupation in Germany. To the Constabulary, which Porky Waterford commanded."

"And?"

"It was important to the general that his polo team play the polo team of the French Army of Occupation, and win."

"I don't quite follow you," the lieutenant colonel said.

"I play polo, Colonel," Lowell said. "In those days I had a three-goal handicap. The general wanted me to play on his team against the French. I could not play because French officers will not play with enlisted men. I was a PFC."

"And you're telling me you were commissioned just so you could play polo?"

"I made a deal with Waterford's aide, a captain named MacMillan. I would take the commission, as a Finance Corps second john, and play polo, and within six months I would be out of the army."

"There was an officer named MacMillan who won the Medal," the lieutenant colonel said.

"That's Mac," Lowell said. "But that well-laid plan didn't quite work out the way it was supposed to."

"What plan?"

"To get me out of the army," Lowell said. "While we were playing the French at Baden-Baden, General Waterford dropped dead. He had a heart attack in the saddle, going for a goal. So that ended the polo, and that ended my chances to get out of the army the same way I got my commission, in other words, somewhat irregularly."

"Frankly, Captain, if this incredible yarn of yours is true, I don't understand why they wouldn't have been happy to separate you. As quickly as possible."

"I hadn't been an officer long enough to be given an efficiency report," Lowell went on. "So they got rid of me. They sent me to the Military Advisory Group in Greece, apparently in the belief that if luck failed them, and I didn't get killed, the Advisory Group would get stuck with throwing me out of the army."

"What did they do with you in Greece?"

"I wound up as advisor to Greek mountain infantry company. For all practical purposes, I commanded it."

The lieutenant colonel looked closely at him. Lowell met his eyes.

"Then I got hit," Lowell said. "And they sent me home. To the Basic Armor Officer's Course, where officers who had never heard a shot fired in anger told me all about what I could expect if I should ever get in combat. But I came out of Knox, out of the army, trained as tank officer."

"What do you want, Captain?" the AGC lieutenant colonel asked.

"If I have to go to war again, I want to go as an armor officer."

"You have been around the army long enough to know that what counts is what the army needs, not what the individual would like."

"I have no intention, sir, of taking a detail to infantry," Lowell said.

"What's wrong with the infantry?" the colonel asked.

"Right now, the infantry in Korea is being sacrificed for time. I don't intend to be part of that sacrifice."

"That could be interpreted as an admission of cowardice," the colonel said.

"I readily admit to being a coward," Lowell said. "But I'm not a fool."

"Captain Lowell," the colonel said, "the personnel requirements of the army are such at the moment, due to the situation in Korea, that there is a surplus of armor officers, and a shortage of infantry officers. To meet the requirement for infantry officers in Korea, the army is detailing a number of armor officers to infantry, selecting those who have infantry experience, and

for whose service as armor officers there is no projected need.
You have been selected as one of those officers, Captain Lowell. That is all, you are dismissed."

HEADQUARTERS

U.S. ARMY RECEPTION CENTER

FORT GEORGE G. MEADE, MARYLAND

SPECIAL ORDERS

NUMBER 187   14 July 1950

EXTRACT

****

18. CAPT Craig W. LOWELL, ARMOR, 0–495302,
Co "B" USARC, Ft Geo G Meade, Md, is detailed IN-
FANTRY trfd and will proceed USA Inf Sch Ft Benning,
Ga, for purp of attending Spec Inf Co Grade Off Crse
50–5. On completion trng off will report to CG Ft
Lawton, Wash, for air shpmt to Hq Eight US Army,
APO 909 San Fran Calif for asgmt within Eight US
Army. Five (5) Days delay-en-route leave authorized
between Ft Benning and Ft Lawton at Home of Record,
11 Washington Mews, New York City NY. Off is *not*
entitled to be accompanied by dependents. Off auth stor-
age of personal and household goods at Govt Expense.
S–99–999–999. Auth Ltr, The Adj Gen dtd 1 Jul 50,
Subj: Detail of Surplus to Needs Armor, Artillery and
Signal Corps Officers to Infantry.

****

BY COMMAND OF
MAJOR GENERAL HARBES
Morton C. Cooper
Lt. Col, AGC
Acting Adjutant General

(Two)
Fairfax, Virginia
15 July 1950

Lt. Colonel Robert F. Bellmon, Armor (Detail, General Staff Corps), Chief of the Tank and Armored Personnel Carrier Section of the Tracked Vehicle Division of the Office of the Assistant Chief of Staff for Operations, had caught himself making six stupid mistakes in a two-hour period in his office in the Pentagon, and had decided to call it quits.

He knocked at the office door of his boss, a brigadier general, who looked up and smiled, but did not speak.

"With your permission, sir," Bellmon said, "I'm going to hang it up. I'm spending more time correcting the stupid mistakes I'm making than I am doing anything worthwhile."

"You've been reading my mind, again, Bob," the general said. "Honest to God, I was just about to get up and run your ass out of there. You've been putting in too much time."

"Thank you, sir," Bellmon said. "I'll see you in the morning, General."

"No, Colonel. You will see me Friday morning. You will take tomorrow and the day after tomorrow off."

"I'll be all right in the morning, General," Bellmon protested.

"Indulge me, Bob," the general said. "Take a couple of days off. Get drunk. Charge your batteries."

"I'll really be all right in the morning, General."

"Splendid," the general said. "Then you will be able to enjoy your morning ride through the Virginia hills, or your golf game, or for that matter, whatever indoor sport strikes your fancy. Goddamn it, I told you Friday."

"Yes, sir," Bellmon said. "Good afternoon, General."

"You tell Barbara what I said," the general said.

"About indoor sports, General?" Bellmon asked, with a smile.

"Leave, Colonel!" the general said, and pointed his finger out the door.

Bellmon went to Pentagon Parking Lot A64-B and found his 1948 Buick convertible (as far as he was concerned, the last of the good ones) and started home.

He started to plan, for he was by nature a planner. The statement of the problem was that he was exhausted, physically and, more important, mentally. Since he had returned from Europe, summoned off leave when the Korean balloon went up, he had been putting in eighteen-hour days of logistic chess. He had been trying to find and move and arrange for the inspection and repairs of sufficient tanks to equip the forces presently in Korea, those in Japan about to go to Korea, those in Hawaii about to go to Japan and/or Korea, those in the United States about to go to Hawaii, Japan, and/or Korea, and those about to be formed.

He loved the challenge. Not as much as he would have loved to command one of the tank battalions, of course, but as the next best thing. It was a bona fide intellectual challenge, even more fascinating than chess, because the available supplies and the requirements for them changed literally hourly.

He had done a good job, shuffling around literally billions of dollars' worth not only of tanks and personnel carriers, but the support for them, human and materiel. This had exhausted him. He'd reached his limits.

He would be all right in the morning, but the general had been dead serious. He was not to report back to work before Friday.

With a little bit of luck, he could get the kids to go to bed early, and then he'd feed Barbara a couple of martinis, and they could make whoopee tonight. That's what he needed. Dr. Bellmon's prescription for Colonel Bellmon's exhausted condition: three martinis and a piece of tail.

Twenty minutes after he left the Pentagon, he reached the split rail and fieldstone fence of "the Farm." There was no name on the mailbox by the drive and no sign. There was only an old mule-drawn plow, painted black, sitting on the fieldstone fence, clearly visible.

It was a question of being discreet. The Farm was far too luxurious a place for a lowly lieutenant colonel to live in without comment. Unless, of course, one knew the circumstances. The truth was that it was indeed a farm. It had been a farm in great financial distress when Bellmon's grandfather had bought it, when he was a major assigned to the War Department in 1909. Major (later, Lieutenant General) Thomas Wood Bellmon had seen the place as a good investment. Its lands could be farmed on shares, or rented out, and the income would pay the mortgage. In effect, it gave him a rent-free place to live while stationed in Washington, at the expense of having to drive an hour each way to the State, War and Navy Building on Pennsylvania Avenue next to the White House.

The Farm had long since been paid off (it had twice changed hands by inheritance) and it now contained 480 acres more than it did when Major Bellmon had bought it. It was more than self-supporting. All but the seven acres around the house itself, these in woods, were rented out.

When a Bellmon (Bellmon's two older brothers were general officers) or a Waterford (Bellmon's wife was the daughter of the late Major General Peterson K. Waterford and she had two brothers who were officers, one army, and one, God forgive him, a flyboy) was stationed in the Washington area, he occupied the house. When none was in the area, it was rented out to old friends. The rent charged was the housing allowance, which wouldn't come close to paying what the Farm was worth, but did pay for repairs, taxes, and upkeep, more important, it kept somebody in the house to see that the pipes didn't burst or that someone didn't steal all the furniture.

The house itself was three or four times as large as the original Virginia farmhouse Major Bellmon had bought forty-one years before. Additions had been made. The original house, now the left wing, was converted into a study. The house now had nine rooms, four baths, a swimming pool, a garage, an outbuilding where the kids played, and even a trap range overlooking a valley.

There was a similar establishment, Casa Mañana, owned by the family in Carmel, California. There was no rule that said that simply because you were an officer you had to raise your family in the really dreadful family housing found on most camps, posts, and stations. There was an unwritten law that you could live comfortably—in keeping with your means— and discreetly. Hence, no sign at the gate to the estate. Just the old plow, painted black.

"Turn in, General, at the old plow on the fence. The house is a quarter mile down the dirt road. We generally have a nip about seven, and eat around 2000."

Bob Bellmon blew the horn as he approached the house. This annoyed Barbara greatly, but the kids liked it. He parked the Buick convertible beside Barbara's Ford station wagon and the jeep, and got out. He was surprised and pleased to see her, and the kids, a boy and a girl, waiting for him at the door.

Just like a Norman Rockwell cover on the *Saturday Evening Post*, he thought, and then was annoyed with himself for being a cynic.

"You and that damned horn," Barbara said, as she gave him her cheek to kiss. He quickly squeezed her buttocks.

"I am ordered to take two days off," he said.

"It's about time he saw how exhausted you were," Barbara said, in reference to the general.

"I don't know if he did or not," Bellmon said. "I asked for the time."

"Well, either way," she said.

They went into the house. He hung the tunic carefully on a hanger in the hall closet, and put the brimmed cap on the shelf above.

"Make me a very cold, very large martini," he said. "While I change."

"Drink now, change later?" she asked.

"No, change now, drink lots later," he said.

"Is it going to be one of those days off?"

"And aren't you glad?" he said.

"Uh huh," she said. "And guess who's going to choir practice?"

"God loves me," Bellmon said, and went upstairs to change. What more could a man ask, he asked himself rhetorically, than for two days off, a cold martini, a wife who likes to fool around, and a priest of the Episcopal Church who schedules children's choir practice at precisely the right time.

When he came down, the kids and Barbara were gone. She had taken them early to choir practice, he realized, or had in some other manner gotten rid of them. He would have to make his own martini. That seemed a small enough price to pay.

Ten minutes later, he heard the crunch of automobile tires on the road and decided it was Barbara coming home. If he had planned ahead, he thought, he could have greeted her at the door starkers and played "Me Tarzan, You Jane" with her on the living room floor.

It was probably better this way, he thought. Drag it out a little.

The bell—a real, old-fashioned, hand-twisted door bell— rang.

"Christ!" he said. "Who the hell?"

He opened the door.

Craig W. Lowell stood outside his door. He wore gray flannel slacks, a white shirt, and a cravat, like an English duke in the country.

This was bound to happen, Bellmon thought. Something— something like Craig W. Lowell showing up out of nowhere— was bound to fuck up his fun.

"Hello, Craig," he said, forcing himself to smile. "What brings you traipsing down my country lane?"

"I heard that beggars are offered booze," he said.

"Come on in," Bellmon said, putting his hand on his arm. He didn't like Craig W. Lowell. Barbara did. For reasons he couldn't begin to understand, Barbara automatically forgave Lowell for things that would have seen her terminate a lifelong friendship with somebody else. Barbara's father, General Waterford, and Lowell's father-in-law, just returned from Russian imprisonment in Siberia, had gone to Samur, the French cavalry school, together before War II.

Lowell's father-in-law, Colonel Count Peter-Paul von Greiffenberg, had also been the commandant of the POW camp where Bellmon had been confined. Von Greiffenberg and Bellmon had become friends, separately from the colonel's relationship with General Waterford.

Until von Greiffenberg had shown up alive in Marburg a month before, Bellmon had believed that he was dead. Bellmon was delighted that von Greiffenberg had survived, not only for himself, but for the colonel's daughter. Bellmon liked Ilse von Greiffenberg Lowell very much.

It was Craig W. Lowell that he disliked.

"What can I make you?" Bellmon asked.

"Scotch," Lowell said. "Please. Barbara home?"

"Not at the moment," Bellmon said, going behind the bar in the living room to make Lowell a drink. "How's the colonel making out?" he asked.

"He's taking the waters in Monte Carlo," Lowell said, dryly, "while I work on his financial affairs."

"When did you come back?"

"On the seventh," Lowell said.

"And when are you going back to Europe?"

"I wish to hell I knew," Lowell said. He took the scotch from Bellmon and raised the glass to him. "Mud in your eye, Herr Oberstleutnant," he said.

"Who's here?" Barbara called from the front door.

"Come and see," Bellmon called back.

Barbara took one look at Craig W. Lowell and squealed with pleasure. "You look like an advertisement for fairy cigarettes in *Town and Country*," she said. She went to him and kissed him on the cheek. "I thought you'd be in the south of France."

"Obviously, no," Lowell said. "I have the strangest feeling that I walked in here in the middle of Bob's Day."

You sonofabitch, Bellmon thought, furiously. How dare you say something like that to me in the middle of my living room?

Barbara collapsed in laughter, infuriating her husband even more.

"How could you tell?"

"He was pawing at the ground when he opened the door," Lowell said. "And then he seemed even less joyous to see me than he usually does."

Barbara laughed.

"What brings you way the hell out here?" she asked. "I'm delighted to see you, of course, and we insist you stay for dinner and the night...(Goddamnit, I knew she'd do that, her husband thought)...but I'm surprised."

"I couldn't stay the night," Lowell said. "Thank you just the same."

"You tell me why not," Barbara insisted, taking her husband's martini glass and sipping from it.

"That would put Bob in the awkward position of harboring a deserter," Lowell said. They looked at him in confusion.

"If that's supposed to be funny, I missed the punch line," Barbara said.

"It's not funny. I've deserted."

"Deserted what?" Bellmon asked.

"I've been ordered to Benning," Lowell said. "To go through some quickie course for reserve officers they're going to send to Korea to get slaughtered, and I've decided I'm not going."

"You're serious, aren't you?" Barbara asked.

"You were recalled?" Bellmon asked.

"There was a telegram waiting for me at the house," Lowell said.

"Ordering you to Benning?"

"Ordering me to Meade, where some pencil-pusher told me that I was now in the infantry."

"There's a shortage of infantry officers," Bellmon said.

"So I'm told."

"You're not serious about not reporting, are you?" Bellmon asked.

Lowell took an airlines ticket folder from his pocket.

"Ten forty-five to London, with connections to Monte Carlo," he said.

"They'll court-martial you, you realize?"

"Possibly."

"What do you mean, 'possibly'?" Bellmon snapped. "That's absence to avoid hazardous service. They can shoot you for that."

"Come on, Bob," Lowell said. "I'm not much of a soldier, I admit, but I know better than that. They haven't, at least officially, shot anybody since they blew away that Polack, Slovik."

Lowell looked at Barbara, and handed her his glass.

"I could use another one of these," he said.

"Sure," she said. "I'm sorry you had to ask."

"Why are you telling me all this, Craig?" Bellmon asked.

"You don't think there's anything I can do to help you, do you?"

"Yeah, as a matter of fact, since you ask, Colonel, I do," Lowell said.

"And what would that be?"

"You could get on the telephone, and convene an ad hoc meeting of the West Point Protective Association, and find somebody to cancel that detail to infantry."

"What makes you think I could do something like that, even if I wanted to?" Bellmon demanded angrily.

"Because otherwise, I'm gong to make a big stink."

"That sounds like a threat," Bellmon said.

"No threat. Statement of intentions."

"I'm trying to control my temper," Bellmon said. "I think you had better leave before I no longer am able to."

"Hear him out," Barbara said, her voice flat. She handed Lowell the drink he had asked for, and when her husband said nothing else, she went on: "What do you want from Bob, Craig?"

"I don't want to be sent to Korea as an infantry officer, and get myself killed."

"The killing of officers comes with war, Lowell," Bellmon said, icily.

"Killing and slaughter are two different things," Lowell said.

"What kind of a stink are you going to cause?" Barbara asked, sounding as if she were idly curious.

"'Craig W. Lowell, New York banker, charged with desertion,'" he said. "'Decorated hero says he is will not go to Korea as untrained cannon fodder.'"

"You'd do that, too, wouldn't you, Lowell?" Bellmon asked, the contempt in his voice shocking even his wife.

"You bet your sweet ass I will," Lowell said.

"I can't pretend to understand what you're thinking," Bellmon said. "What made you think you should bring me into this."

"It's not that hard to figure out," Lowell said. "I figured it out between Fort Meade and Washington. I fucking near . . . sorry,

Barbara, that just lipped out..."

"I've heard the word before," Barbara Bellmon said.

"I was nearly killed in Greece, you will recall."

"And returned a decorated hero," Bellmon said.

"I shouldn't have been on the goddamned mountaintop, Robert," Lowell said. "One of you professionals should have been there."

"I grant the point, but so what?"

"So once is enough," Lowell said. "I came through that. But I am not going to put myself in a position again where I am unqualified to lead untrained troops. And get my ass blown away at the same time."

"I'm beginning to understand your warped thinking," Bellmon said. "But you had better understand, Lowell, that the army is bigger than you, or me, and that individual desires have nothing to do with anything. You better get back in your car and proceed as ordered, to Benning."

"You're not refusing to go to Korea, are you, Craig?"

"As an infantry officer, I am."

"He's bluffing," Bellmon decided, and announced, "He's desperate and bluffing. You're really despicable, Lowell."

"Certainly desperate and probably despicable, but not bluffing," Lowell said. He drained his glass and laid it on the bar. "Sorry you had to get involved in this, Barbara," he said.

"Where are you going?" Barbara asked.

"I'll send you a postcard from the Riviera," Lowell said.

Barbara pushed the lever on a flop-open telephone directory.

"What are you doing?" Bob Bellmon asked.

She dialed a number.

"Colonel Bellmon calling for General Davidson," she said. She handed the telephone to her husband. "You can either tell him to send the MPs to Washigton National," Barbara said, "to stop a deserting captain. Or that you found out that the system grabbed an armor officer who's badly needed in Korea and threw him into the infantry."

He took the phone from her without thinking.

"I'll do nothing of the kind," he said.

"Who's Davidson?" Lowell asked.

"Deputy Chief of Staff, Personnel. He was my brother's

roommate at the Academy," Barbara Bellmon said.

"General," Lt. Col. Bellmon said to the telephone, "I really hate to bother you personally with this, but I don't know how else to handle it. And it's further made delicate because the officer involved is a close friend of my wife's. The point, sir, is that the net you threw out to snag infantry officers snagged an armor officer we really need."

Barbara Bellmon and Lowell watched Bob Bellmon as he spoke. Then he said, "One moment, please, sir," and turned to Lowell. "Let me have your orders, Lowell."

Lowell handed him his orders. Bellmon read them over the telephone.

"Thank you very much, sir," Bellmon said, finally. He handed Lowell his orders back. "I'll have Captain Lowell remain at Fort Meade until the paperwork comes through."

"Now," Barbara Bellmon said, "let's have a friendly drink."

HEADQUARTERS

U.S ARMY RECEPTION CENTER

FORT GEORGE G. MEADE, MARYLAND

SPECIAL ORDERS

NUMBER 191   18 July 1950

EXTRACT

****

1. So much of Para 18, Spec Orders 187 this Hq dtd 14 July 1950, pertaining to the detail of CAPT Craig W. LOWELL, ARMOR, 0–495302 to INFANTRY is rescinded. AUTH: Telecon, Deputy, the Asst Chief of Staff, Personnel, Hq Dept of the Army & Acting Adjutant Gen, this Hq, 17 July 1950.

2. So much of Para 18, Spec Orders 187 this Hq dtd 14 July 1950, pertaining to the trans of CAPT Craig W. LOWELL, Armor 0–495302 to the USA Inf Sch, Ft Benning Ga for tng, and for trans to Hq US Army Eight is rescinded. AUTH: Telecon Asst Chief of Staff, Per-

sonnel, Hq Dept of the Army & CG, US Army Reception Center & Ft Geo G Meade, Md. 16 July 1950.

3. CAPT Craig W. LOWELL, ARMOR, 0–495302 Co "B" USARC, Ft Geo G Meade, Md., is trfd and will proceed US Army Outport, San Francisco Calif International Airport, San Francisco Calif by the most expeditious military or civilian air transport for further mil or civ air shipment (Priority AAAA-1) to Hq 73rd Med Tank Bn, 8th US ARMY in the field (Korea). This asgmt is in response to TWX Hq SCAP re critical shortage Co Grade Armor Officers dtd 3 July 1950. The exigencies of the service making this necessary, off is *not,* repeat *not,* auth delay en route leave. Off is *not* entitled to be accompanied by dependents. Off auth storage of personal and household goods at Govt Expense. S–99–999–999. AUTH: Telecon Asst Chief of Staff, Pors, Hq Dept of the Army Wash DC & Acting Adj Gen this Hq 17 July 1950.

****

BY COMMAND OF
MAJOR GENERAL HARBES
Morton C. Cooper
Lt Col., AGC
Acting Adjutant General

(Three)
The Naktong River
South Korea
24 July 1950

Lowell took the Pennsylvania Railroad to New York, a TWA triple-tailed Lockheed Constellation to San Francisco, a United DC-6 to Honolulu, and another DC-6—this one Pan American—to Tokyo via Wake Island.

He called Ilse from New York and told her what had happened; and when he hung up, he went to the VIP lounge and got wordlessly as stiff as a board before boarding the plane. When he called her again from San Francisco, it was ten hours later, and her father had apparently talked to her, because she was not hysterical, only weeping and trying to be brave. He got the colonel on the line, and the colonel said that whatever he did, he was not to worry about Ilse and Peter-Paul. He would take care of them. The colonel wished him God speed.

He called Porter Craig from San Francisco and told him what was happening, and asked him to personally make sure (which meant getting on a plane and going to Europe) that Craig, Powell, Kenyon and Dawes was doing everything possible to get the colonel's affairs straightened out as quickly as possible. He told Porter to personally make sure that Ilse understood that his army pay would be more than adequate for his needs, and that his salary from the firm would continue.

"I don't want her skimping and scraping, Porter, you understand?"

"Good God, Craig, don't worry about her. She's family, for God's sake!"

For some reason, that short sentence from Porter Craig, whom he generally thought of as a three-star horse's ass, reassured him.

"Yeah, Porter, she is," he said, his voice tight.

"You take care of yourself, old boy," Porter said. "Since you insist on going through with this, the least I can do is put your mind at rest about your wife and child. Andre does very well with your mother. You're the one we're all concerned about."

"Yeah, well, you keep your sticky fingers out of the till, Chubby," Lowell said and hung up because he was afraid he was going to start crying.

An army bus met them at Tachikawa Airport outside Tokyo and drove them through really stinking rice paddies and sooty industrial areas to a military base, Camp Drake. He was assigned a BOQ, issued a footlocker for his Class "A" pink and green and tropical worsted and khaki uniforms (which would be stored at Drake while he was in Korea), then issued a steel helmet, a .45 Colt pistol with a web belt, a holster, three magazines, a magazine holder, a first aid pouch, and, for reasons he didn't understand, a compass. He was told that in the morning he would be issued new fatigues and combat boots and taken to the range to fire the .45. In the meantime, he was restricted to the BOQ and the officer's open mess.

There was a telephone center in the mess, and he put in another call to Ilse. While he was waiting for it to go through, at 0310 Tokyo time, a sergeant came and found him.

"I thought you'd gone over the fence to Tokyo for the night, Captain, when I couldn't find you in your BOQ."

"I'm trying to call my wife," Lowell said.

"I got a car outside, Captain," the sergeant said, uncomfortably. "There's a C-54 going to K1—that's Pusan—at 0400. With that priority of yours, you've got to be on it."

The C-54 was an old and battered cargo plane. He rode to K1 airfield, on the southern tip of the Korean peninsula, stretched out on the pierced aluminum floor.

There was no one to meet him, and the air force types in the crowded terminal had only a vague idea where he might find the 73rd Medium Tank Battalion.

"If you can't get them on the phone, Captain, there's no fucking telling where the fuck they are."

Lowell picked up his now nearly empty Valv-Pak (it held only four sets of fatigues, underwear, a second pair of tanker's boots, his toilet kit, and the 9 mm Pistole-08, the German Luger he'd carried in Greece) and walked out of the terminal.

His first impression of Korea was that it stank. Later that day he was to learn it stank because the Koreans fertilized their rice paddies with human waste. His second impression was that the U.S. Army in Korea was in shitty shape. There was an aura of desperation, of frenzy, even of fear. They were getting the shit kicked out of them, and it showed.

He hitchhiked a ride in a three-quarter-ton ammo carrier into Pusan itself, and asked directions of an MP.

"They're somewhere up near the Naktong, I think," the MP told him. "Everything's all fucked up."

The MP flagged down an MP jeep for him, and they carried him to the outskirts of town to the main supply route, a two-lane, once-macadamized road now reduced to little more than a rough dirt trail by the crush of tanks and trucks and artillery passing over it.

Lowell tried vainly to catch a ride with his extended thumb and finally stopped another three-quarter-ton ammo carrier by stepping into the middle of the road and holding up his hand like a traffic cop.

Two hours later, he was at the command post of the 73rd Medium Tank Battalion (Separate), on the south bank of the Naktong River.

The command post was new; it wasn't even completed. Soldiers, naked to the waist, sweat-soaked, were filling sandbags with the sandy clay soil and stacking them against a timber-framed structure built into the side of a low hill.

The unfinished structure, however, was already in use. When Lowell walked inside, a very large sergeant was marking on a celluloid-covered situation map with a grease pencil; a GI manned a field switchboard; and, most importantly, a wiry lieutenant colonel and a plump major were crowded together at a tiny, folding GI field desk, examining what Lowell thought was probably an inventory of some kind.

He walked up to the desk and waited until they became aware of his presence. The major spoke first.

"Something for you, Captain?"

Lowell came to attention, saluted, and said: "Captain C. W. Lowell reporting for duty, sir."

The wiry little lieutenant colonel returned the salute. "Got your orders, Captain?" he asked, and Lowell handed them over. The lieutenant colonel read them carefully, and then passed them to the major.

"You have a personal copy, Captain?"

"Yes, sir."

"Let's take a little walk," the lieutenant colonel said. He stood up and put his hand out. "I'm Paul Jiggs," he said, dryly. "Commander of this miraculous fighting force."

Lowell shook his hand.

"Major Charley Ellis," Jiggs continued. "S-3. We don't have an exec at the moment. He got blown away before he got here." Lowell was aware that Colonel Jiggs was watching his face for his reaction to that somewhat cold-blooded announcement. He tried to keep his face expressionless. Major Ellis offered his hand and gave Lowell a smile.

"We won't be long, Charley," Colonel Jiggs said. "Do what you think has to be done."

"Yes, sir," Major Ellis said. Colonel Jiggs put his hand on Lowell's arm and led him out of the half-finished bunker, around it, and to the crest of the hill against which it was built.

"That's the Naktong," he said, indicating the river. "If they get across that, it'll be Dunkirk all over again, except that we're not twenty miles from the White Cliffs of Dover. It will be a somewhat longer swim across the Sea of Japan."

"And are they going to get across?" Lowell asked.

"Of course not," Jiggs said, sarcastically. "If for no other reason than my magnificent fighting force is digging in to repel them. I say magnificent, Captain, because the 73rd Medium Tank Battalion, Separate, didn't even exist a month ago. It sprang miraculously from the ground to do battle for God and country, manned with rejects, clerks, gentlemen from various Army of Occupation stockades, and equipped with junk from various abandoned ordance depots. Do you get the picture?"

"Yes, sir, I think so," Lowell said.

"You will forgive me, Captain," Colonel Jiggs said. "There is nothing personal in this. But I confess a certain disappointment in what I got in response to a desperate request for experienced company commanders. In my innocence I was hoping to get a battle-experienced company commander. And what I get is a National Guardsman, to judge by that Bloody Bucket patch on your sleeve. And—forgive me, Captain—a captain who doesn't look either old enough to be a captain, or to have earned that CIB he's wearing."

Lowell flushed but said nothing.

"And who is, moreover, to judge by his orders, either someone with friends in high places, or a fuck-up, and most probably both." When Lowell didn't reply, Colonel Jiggs went on. "I solicit your comments, Captain. And please don't waste my time."

"What would you like me to say, Colonel?" Lowell asked.

"For example, tell me how old you are?"

"Twenty-three, sir."

"How the fuck did you get to be a captain at twenty-three?"

"The truth of the matter, Colonel, is that I made a deal with a regimental commander in the Pennsylvania National Guard. If he would make me a captain, I would get his M46s running. He did, Colonel, and I did."

"That figures," Colonel Jiggs said. "The goddamned National Guard has M46s, and here I sit with a motley collection of M4s!" Then he looked at Lowell. "How did you get to be an expert with the M46s?"

"I was assigned to the Armor Board. I was project officer on the 90 mm tube project."

"How the hell did you get an assignment like that?"

Lowell didn't reply.

"Not important. I'll take your word about that. I have been promised, in the oh, so indefinite future, that we'll be given M46s. If we're both alive when that happens, we'll be able to see if you're an expert or not. Tell me about that CIB you're wearing. Did you get it in War II? That would mean, if you're twenty-three, that you are a very young veteran indeed of War II."

"I came in the army in 1946," Lowell said. "I got the CIB in Greece."

"Doing what?"

"I was an advisor to the 27th Mountain Division."

"They didn't have tanks in Greece," Jiggs said.

"I didn't say they did, Colonel," Lowell said.

"You want to explain those fascinating orders of yours? How come the Assistant Chief of Staff, Personnel, took a personal interest in your assignment?"

"No, sir, I do not," Lowell said.

"Are you influential, Lowell, or a fuck-up?"

"Both, sir," Lowell said.

For the first time, Colonel Jiggs smiled at him.

"Do you think you're qualified to command a tank company, Lowell?"

"No, sir," Lowell said. "I can probably command a platoon all right, but a company would be more than I can handle."

"Is that so? Are you modest, Captain Lowell?"

"A realist, sir."

"You're a captain. Platoon leaders are lieutenants."

"You can have the railroad tracks," Lowell said. "I think I can hold my own with a platoon, if you'll give me one."

"It doesn't work that way, Lowell," Colonel Jiggs said. "It doesn't work that way at all. Captain, you now command Baker Company. Get your ass up there, look around, get settled, and I'll be up either later today, or in the morning, and we'll have another little chat."

"Yes, sir."

"That's all, 'Yes, sir'?" Jiggs asked.

"Yes, sir," Lowell said.

(Four)
Company "B" 73rd Medium Tank Battalion (Separate)
The Naktong River, South Korea
24 July 1950

The jeep driver who came from Baker Company to pick him up was a staff sergeant who needed a shave and whose fatigues were streaked under the arms, between the legs, and down the back with grayish-white. At least they were taking salt tablets, Craig Lowell thought; at least they *had* salt tablets to take.

He was aware that the staff sergeant was examining him with contempt and resignation. The staff sergeant had seen the Bloody Bucket patch of the 28th Infantry Division, Pennsylvania National Guard, sewn to Lowell's now sweat-soaked fatigue shirt.

"You taking over, Captain?" the staff sergeant asked. When enlisted men dislike officers, they address them by their rank and avoid the use of the term "sir."

"Yes, I am," Lowell said.

"Just get in from the States?"

"'Just get in from the States, *sir?'*" Lowell corrected him. "Yes, Sergeant, I just got in from the States, and I'm a chickenshit candy-assed National Guardsman who will bust your ass down to private the next time you fail to call me 'sir.' 'Captain' will not do."

"Shit," the sergeant said, and Lowell turned, surprised, to glower furiously at him. The sergeant was smiling at him. "You a mind reader, Captain? *Sir*."

"You can bet your regular army ass I am," Lowell said.

"Most of the replacement officers show up in brand-new fatigues," the sergeant asked. "Did they run out of them over there, too?"

"I don't know. They didn't issue me any."

The sergeant nodded his understanding. He had not called Lowell "sir," but there was no longer surly disrespect in his tone of voice. Lowell let the failure to call him "sir" pass.

"The company's short of clothing?" Lowell asked, as the jeep bounced up a narrow, rocky road.

"We're short of everything," the sergeant said, and this time he remembered and added, "sir."

"What do you do?" Lowell asked.

"I lost my tank," the sergeant said. "Sir."

"What happened?"

"Sonofabitch collapsed of old age," the sergeant said, "Engines won't take this fucking heat. Nothing takes this fucking heat long."

"What's the company doing?" Lowell asked.

"Sitting on this side of the Naktong, waiting for the gooks to cross it."

"Using the tanks as pillboxes?" Lowell asked.

"That's about it, sir," the sergeant said, seemingly surprised that a replacement officer would know enough to ask that kind of a question.

"Have the tracks been exercised? Will they run if they have to?" Lowell asked.

"Some of them," the sergeant replied. "And some of them won't."

"Maintenance?"

"Shit!" The disgust and resignation was infinite in the single word.

They came to the command post. As at the battalion CP, a sandbag bunker was being built against the side of a hill. There was a field kitchen set up under a canvas awning, called a "fly," and behind it was a grove of tall, thin poplars. There

was an enormous mound of fired 75 mm shell casings and
beside it an equally large mound of the cardboard tubes and
wooden cases in which the shells had been shipped from the
ammo dumps. There were three eiqht-man squad tents set up
on the bare, baked ground; and sandbag-augmented foxholes—
one-man, three-man, and one large enough for eight people—
had been dug around them. They were intended to provide
protection during mortar and artillery barrages, Lowell realized;
but they were dug in the wrong places.

The realization that he had spotted something wrong pleased
him. It was a suggestion, however faint, that he knew more
than whoever was presently in charge here.

"The lieutenant's in there, probably, Captain," the staff
sergeant said. Lowell looked at him. When Lowell's eyebrows
raised in question, the staff sergeant added the required "sir."

"You're learning," Lowell said, smiling at him. "You're
learning."

The staff sergeant had indicated the sandbag bunker, but
Lowell didn't go there when he got out of the jeep. He walked
first to the eight-man tents and stuck his head inside them, one
at a time. In each were sleeping men, stretched out on folding
canvas cots. There was a strong smell of sweat in each tent.

Lowell then walked up the gentle slope of the hill against
which the CP bunker was being built.

At the military crest (just below the actual crest) of the hill,
eight M4A3 Sherman tanks had been emplaced so that in their
present position, or by moving them no more than ten feet,
their tubes could be brought to bear down the far side of the
hill, which sloped gently down to the banks of the Naktong
River. Four hundred yards to his left, Lowell saw a bridge,
both rail and road, that had been dropped into the river.

He walked to the nearest M4A3. Its crew members, sweat-
soaked, were either sitting or lying on the ground in its shade.
Two of them were shirtless, and all of them were dirty, tired,
and unshaved. None of them moved when he walked up. He
looked down at one crewman until he reluctantly got to his
feet.

"What shape is this thing in?" Lowell asked.

"It overheats," the crewman said. Lowell looked at him curiously as if he didn't understand.

"It overheats," the crewman repeated. "Gets hot. Fucking filters are all fucked up, and so's the radiator."

"From now on, you say 'sir' to me, soldier," Lowell said.

"It overheats, *sir*," the soldier said. "You some kind of inspector or something? *Sir?*"

"I'm your commanding officer," Lowell said. "What do you plan to do about cleaning the filters? About flushing the radiator?" Lowell went to the tank and stood on the bogies and ran his hand into the slots in the armor over the engine. "And about getting the mud and crud out of there?"

"You work on it in this heat, *sir*," the crewman said, impatiently explaining something quite obvious to a moron, "you either burn your hand, or you get heat stroke."

"Have you checked the water in the batteries today?" Lowell asked.

"Yes, sir," the crewman said.

"Then it could be reasonably expected to start?" Lowell asked.

"It would probably start, yes, sir."

Lowell quickly climbed onto the side of the tank and then dropped into the hatch over the driver's seat. The temperature inside the tank, which had been exposed to the sun all day, was probably 120 degrees, possibly even higher. His body was instantly soaked in sweat. The batteries sounded weak when he started the engine. By the time he had it running and the engine smoothed down enough to move it, the lever—exposed through the open hatch to the direct rays of the sun—was too hot to hold. He squirmed around and got a handkerchief from his pocket and used it to keep his hand from being burned.

Then he raced the engine to signal he was going to move, locked the left track, and threw the right into reverse. The M4A3 backed out of its position. When he had it pointing in the right direction, he drove it quickly down the hill, past the field kitchen, and ten yards into the grove of poplars, crushing them under the tank. Then he got out of the tank.

By the time he walked back to the field kitchen, his presence had been made known to the acting company commander, who was waiting for him. The acting company commander was a thin first lieutenant in salt-streaked fatigues. He needed a shave.

"Are you Captain Lowell, sir?" he asked.

"Get yourself a shave and a clean uniform, Lieutenant," Lowell said, cutting him off in midsentence. "And then report to me properly."

He turned his back on him and looked up the hill to the revetment from which he had driven the M4A3. The crew was standing up now, looking down to see what the hell was going on. Lowell pointed at them, finger and arm extended, and then made a fist with his hand and pumped it up and down over his head, the signal to "form on me." Hesitantly at first, the crew of the M4A3 started down the hill, eventually breaking into a little trot.

"Yes, sir?" the man he had spoken to on the hill said.

"You're the tank commander?"

"Yes, sir."

"Do you know in which of those squad tents the mess sergeant is asleep?"

"Yes, sir," the tank commander said, baffled by the question.

"Ask the mess sergeant to report to me, please, Sergeant," Lowell said. "And then take those tents down, slit the seams, and rig a sunshade where I parked your tank. Then flush the radiator and the filters. When you've done that, you and your crew can get some sleep."

"Rip the tent up?" the tank commander asked, incredulously.

"A fightable tank is liable to keep us all alive, Sergeant," Lowell said. "That makes more sense to me than providing a place for the mess sergeant to sleep."

"Yes, sir," the tank commander said, more than a little pleased that this new company commander was going to throw the mess sergeant's ass out of bed.

The mess sergeant, a fat, heavily sweating, nearly bald man in his middle thirties, his fatigue shirt unbuttoned, his feet jammed into laceless combat boots, approached Lowell a few minutes later, his bluster fading as Lowell met his eyes.

"The captain's got to understand that other people, I mean not just the cooks and KPs, use them tents."

"Not anymore they don't," Lowell said. "What have you got cool to drink, Sergeant?"

"We ain't got any ice or anything like that, Captain," the mess sergeant said, "if that's what you're asking."

"Get me what you have, please," Lowell said, coldly.

The mess sergeant waddled to a Lister bag and returned in a moment with a canteen-cup full of water. Lowell took it, tasted the water, and spit it out.

"That's the purifier, Captain," the mess sergeant said. "Can't do nothing about that."

"You can purify drinking water by boiling it," Lowell said. "Water purification pills are intended for use only when there's no other means available. Why is it that I don't see water boiling?"

There was no reply that could be made to that. The mess sergeant flashed Lowell a wounded look.

"You do know how to make GI strawberry soda, don't you?" Lowell asked.

"Sir?" the mess sergeant replied, baffled by the question.

"You heat cans of strawberry preserves and gradually add water which has been boiled," Lowell said. "It's not much, but it's a hell of a lot better than that chemically flavored horse piss you're handing out. Put someone to work on that right away."

"Sir, I don't know if we got any strawberry preserves," the mess sergeant said.

"Then make it out of what preserves you do have," Lowell said, icily. "And if you don't have any preserves, Sergeant, then go steal some."

The acting company commander returned, in a clean, unpressed fatigue uniform. His face was bleeding from his shave. He walked up to Lowell and saluted, holding the salute as he recited, "Sir, Lieutenant Sully, Thomas J. I've been acting company commander."

Lowell returned the salute, very casually.

"My name is Lowell, Lieutenant," he said. "I herewith assume command. Please see that a general order so stating is prepared for my signature."

"Captain, we was never even issued a typewriter," Lieutenant Sully said.

"In that case, Lieutenant," Lowell said, "find someone who prints very neatly. Where is the first sergeant?"

"Captain, we've been taking turns, twelve hours on and twelve off. He's sleeping."

"Where?"

"In the bunker, sir."

"Have we got a field first?"

"Staff Sergeant Williams, sir. The man who picked you up at battalion."

"Oh, yes," Lowell said. He looked around and located Staff Sergeant Williams, and made the "form on me" signal to him by pumping his fist over his head.

"Yes, sir?" Sergeant Williams said.

"You've heard what I want done with the squad tents?"

"Yes, sir. Ripped up into sunshades."

"Colonel Jiggs will be here either later today or in the morning," Lowell said. "By the time he gets here, I want the tents gone, and I want those latrine holes somebody dug where the tents are, filled up. You got that?"

"Yes, sir."

"I'm now going to see the first sergeant," Lowell said. "I want to see him privately. I'm curious to see if he's as fucked up as everybody else I've seen around here."

He walked to the sandbag bunker and disappeared inside.

"Jesus Christ!" Lieutenant Sully said. "Who the fuck does he think he is? Patton?"

"I don't know, Lieutenant," Staff Sergeant Williams replied thoughtfully. "I got the feeling he knows what he's doing. Maybe a little inspired chickenshit is just what this outfit needs." Then he realized what he had said. "No offense, Lieutenant."

The mess sergeant reappeared.

"Lieutenant," he said. "The only preserves we got is little bitty cans, one to each case of 10-in-1's. You really want me to open all them cases like he said?"

"What I want, Sergeant Feeny," Lieutenant Sully said, "is beside the point. What's important is that the company commander told you to boil water and make drinks out of preserves. If I were you, from what I've seen of our new company commander, I'd get the lead out of my ass and do what he told you to do."

At first light the next morning, Lt. Col. Paul T. Jiggs got in a jeep and drove to Baker Company.

Baker Company's troops were shaving, using their helmets as wash basins. They were all wearing their fatigue jackets, and they were all wearing their .45 pistols in their shoulder holsters. Canvas flys protected all the tanks on the line from the sun.

When he saw Captain Lowell, the Bloody Bucket of the Pennsylvania National Guard was gone from his fatigues. Captain Lowell was standing in the mess fly, watching the mess sergeant (significantly, the mess sergeant himself, not one of the cooks or one of the troopers in KP) scramble powdered eggs. Lowell was bareheaded. He had a German Luger stuck in the waistband of his trousers. He was puffing on a large, black cigar.

When he saw Colonel Jiggs, Lowell took the cigar from his mouth and, smiling broadly, threw him a salute that was cocky to the point of insolence.

"Good morning, sir," he said. "Would the colonel care for some breakfast?"

"I've eaten, thank you," Jiggs said.

"Then how about a cool glass of GI strawberry soda? I regret we have no orange juice, but the sergeant's working on that."

"I think that would be very nice," Colonel Jiggs said.

I'll be damned, he thought, if this kid doesn't seem to know exactly what he's doing.

V

(One)
Frankfurt am Main, Germany
30 August 1950

The black Buick Roadmaster (carefully waxed and polished from the day, six months before, it had been delivered at the European Exchange Service Automobile Center) signaled for a right turn, slowed, and turned off the northbound lane of the autobahn and into the EES service station at the Frankfurt am Main turnoff.

It rolled slowly up to the pumps. The driver, already balding though still a young man, operated the electrically powered windows and told the attendant to fill it up with high test and to please check under the hood. He operated the hood release latch, and then put his uniform cap on, opened his door, and got out. There were captain's bars on the epaulets of his green tunic and the crossed rifles of infantry on the lapels. There was the flaming sword on a blue background shoulder patch, the insignia of the European Command. But there was no fruit salad on his breast, nor parachutist's wings, nor other qualification badges. He was a small man, short and small-boned, obviously Jewish.

There was fruit salad in a drawer in his dresser in his quarters. There was a Bronze Star for his performance as a POW interrogation officer, and a second Bronze Star for his participation in Task Force Parker, which had liberated several hundred officer prisoners in the closing days of World War II. There was a set of silver parachutist's wings, and a small strip of cloth with the word "Ranger" embroidered on it. There was even a ring, a ring-knocker's ring, with USMA 1946 cast in gold around an amethyst.

But the captain was in the intelligence business, and a balding little Jew wearing a Ranger patch and jump wings and a West Point ring and a couple of Bronze Stars would stand out in a crowd. Intelligence officers try very hard not to stand out in a crowd.

A woman, smaller even than the captain, opened the right rear door of the Roadmaster and emerged with an infant in her arms. She wore black pumps, a small black hat, and a simple black dress. There was a brooch on her breast, and a gold Star of David hung from a thin gold chain around her neck.

The captain opened the right front door of the Roadmaster and plucked a male child from a steel-and-plastic seat hooked over the automobile seat. He sniffed.

"He didn't wait," he said.

"He's still a baby, Sandy," the woman said. "And it was a long ride."

She took the boy from him and with a child in each arm walked to the ladies' rest room. The captain went around to the trunk and took out a rubber and canvas bag used to store soiled diapers. Sharon did not believe in the new disposable diapers. Not only were they criminally expensive, she believed they irritated the baby's skin. She would flush the diapers in the toilet, then put them in the rubber bag to take home. After the bag had been removed from the trunk, the captain would leave the trunk open for at least an hour, and then spray the interior with an odor killer.

The captain carried the diaper bag to the door of the ladies' rest room. He set it outside the door, knocked at the door to let Sharon know he'd brought her the bag, and then went into the men's rest room. When he came out, he went out to the service island, watched the attendant check the oil, the water in the window washer reservoir and the radiator, and the hydraulic fluid in the transmission, power brakes, and power steering. He took a notebook with an attached pencil from the glove compartment and made precise entries regardinq the servicing of the Buick, including a computation (to two decimal places) of miles per gallon.

Except for his uniform and the fact that they were on the autobahn outside Frankfurt, Germany, they could have been a typical American couple out with the children for a ride, and stopping for gasoline on the highway.

Sharon finished the necessary business with the children in the rest room. As she put the older child in the front seat, and then got in the back seat with the baby, the captain paid for the gasoline with both U.S. Forces of Occupation scrip (used in lieu of "green dollars") and gasoline ration coupons. Then he got behind the wheel, and they drove into Frankfurt am Main.

The parking lot behind the Frankfurt Military Post chapel was half full of cars, many of them (like the Buick Roadmaster, which carried a MUNICH MILITARY POST tag) with tags from outside Frankfurt: Nuremberg, Heidelberg, Bad Tolz, Berlin, Stuttgart, even Salzburg and Vienna.

It was a gathering of American Army Jews, a regular, every other month affair, held in rotation by every group of Jews large enough to be entitled to the services of their own rabbi, and functioning as a sort of unofficial congregation.

There were services, of course, and tours of the areas where they met, but the real purpose was fellowship, to be with their own kind. The captain had told his wife that actually the real purpose was gluttony. She had pretended shock, but giggled, for the captain was close to the truth. Each "congregation" tried valiantly to outdo the other in the kind and variety and, of course, quality of the food served during the two-and-a-half-day "get-togethers." Stuttgart, at the moment, was the undisputed victor. At the Stuttgart get-together, in addition to the roast chicken and the chopped liver and the gefilte fish and all the rest, there had been fresh orange juice and a fruit salad and two kinds of wine . . . all imported, who knew how, from Israel.

As the captain parked the Buick, three GI buses, former six-by-six trucks with buslike bodies fixed on them, pulled into the parking lot. That was for the cultural tour of Frankfurt, scheduled for this afternoon. After sundown the services would begin.

As soon as they were out of the car, women from the Frankfurt congregation converged on them to take the children and turn them over to the care of the *goyim*, more formally known as the Frankfurt Military Post Protestant Women's Fellowship, who ran an around-the-clock nursery for the Jews when they got together, in exchange for similar services from the Jewish women.

Sharon went off with the women and the suitcases full of clothes and diapers. The captain stood by the Buick, not quite knowing what to do. The Chaplain (Major) Rabbi of Frankfurt Military Post, a large and jovial redheaded man, went to rescue him.

"Welcome, welcome," he said. "I'm Rabbi Felter."

The captain looked at him and laughed.

"I'm Captain Felter," the captain said. "How have you been, Cousin?"

The rabbi laughed. "I wondered what you would look like," he said. "I saw your name on the roster. Munich, right?"

"Right," Felter said.

"Mrs. Felter get taken care of all right?" the rabbi asked. Captain Felter nodded. "Well, come on, we'll get you your name tag, and then I'll get you, kinsman, a special treat. Some bona fide Hungo-Israeli Slibbovitz. One up on Stuttgart."

The rabbi, a demonstrative man, put his hand on the small of Captain Felter's back. And then he withdrew it as if he had been burned. The smile on his face changed from happy to strained. He looked down at Captain Felter.

"You really think you need that here, today?" he asked. Felter met his eyes.

"You said something about Slibbovitz, Rabbi?" he replied.

"Right, just as soon as we get you your name tag."

A large-breasted woman sat behind a folding table.

"Who do we have here, Rabbi?" she asked.

"This is Captain Felter," the rabbi said. The woman flipped

through a box and came up with two neatly lettered name cards, with safety pins on their backs.

"Captain Sanford?" she said. "And Mrs. Sharon?"

"Right," Captain Felter said. "Thank you."

Rabbi Felter took the captain's name plate and pinned it on the flap of his breast pocket. He examined it to see it was straight, and he read it:

> CAPT Sanford T. 'Sandy' Felter
> (Sharon)
> Office of Agricultural Evaluation (Bavaria)
> Hq, EUCOM

Bullshit, the rabbi thought. Office of Agricultural Evaluation, my ass. Not with a .45 automatic under his tunic; not with that icy look he gave me when he knew I had felt it. The rabbi smiled.

"On to the first authentic bona fide Hungo-Israeli Slibbovitz ever exported from Israel. Stuttgart, eat your heart out!"

(Two)

Two hours later, after an enormous lunch that he knew would give him indigestion for the rest of the week, Captain Felter detached himself from the group being given a tour of the just reconstructed Temple Beth-Sholem. Before Hitler (and now, again) it was the most beautiful synagogue in Frankfurt.

He walked down the wide steps and started toward the corner. And then a taxi appeared, a Mercedes sedan with a checkered border running around its middle. He flagged it, and it pulled to the curb. The driver rolled down the window.

"Will you take me to the Farben Building?" Felter asked, in English.

"Get in," the driver said, and reached over the seat back and opened the door. The cab headed for the I.G. Farben Buildinq, but when it reached Erschenheimerlandstrasse, it turned left rather than right.

"How have you been, my friend?" the driver asked, in German.

"Until I had lunch, I was doing fine," Felter replied, in accentless German. "And you, Helmut?"

"We just came back from holiday," the driver said. "Went to a little country hotel outside Salzburg. Got some clean air."

The taxi drove to a recently refurbished office building overlooking the Main River. There was an underground garage. The taxi drove to the door of an elevator and stopped, and Felter quickly got out and entered the elevator. He pushed the 8th floor button, and when the elevator began to rise, said, rather loudly: "The Baker's Boy just got on."

A female voice came over a hidden speaker: "Good afternoon. Isn't it lovely out?"

The elevator stopped, and the door opened. Felter saw a pleasant-faced, gray-haired woman sitting behind a receptionist's desk. A sign hung on the wall behind her, the legend engraved in either glass or lucite: "The West German Association for Agronomy".

"Go right in," the woman said. "He's been waiting for you."

She pushed a button beneath her desk, and there was the sound of a solenoid receiving an electrical impulse. When Felter pushed on a steel door covered with a wooden veneer, it moved effortlessly inward, permitting him to pass, and then closed with a clunk like a bank vault after him. Inside were two other doors, again sheathed in wood veneer. As he approached one, there came again the sound of a solenoid being activated. Beyond the second door was a large, sunlit room furnished in light oak.

A bald, stout, benign-looking man in his shirt-sleeves crossed the room to shake Felter's hand, and to offer him a drink or coffee.

"I've just had some of the first Hungo-Israeli Slibbovitz ever exported," Felter said. "What I need is an Alka-Seltzer."

"How about some peppermint schnapps?"

"God, no. That would make it worse."

"Try the schnapps, Sandy," the bald man said. "The peppermint is good for you."

He went to a bar, concealed in a cabinet, and poured a long-stemmed glass three-quarters full of peppermint schnapps and handed it to Felter.

"This is going to take some time," the bald man said. "You want to take off your coat?"

Felter unbuckled his tunic belt, and then unbuttoned the tunic and took it off and hung it up. The bald man waved him into a chair, and handed him a two-button switch.

"Left stops the projector," the bald man said. "Right operates the dictating machine."

"I remember," Felter said. He sat down in the chair and then sat up and reached behind him and laid the .45 automatic on the table beside the dictating machine.

"Der kleine Kaptain und die grosse Kanone," the bald man chuckled. "Do you really need something that large, Sandy?"

"I can't hit the broadside of a barn with a snub-nose," Felter replied, "and if you hit something with a .45, that's it."

The bald man went to his desk and pushed several buttons. Heavy curtains closed over the windows, and a beam of light from a motion picture projector flashed on the wall. The frozen image of a railroad station appeared on the wall.

"It's all yours, Sandy," the bald man said. Felter pushed one of the buttons on his control. The frozen images began to move. The camera focused on a man coming out of the station. Felter froze the image, stared at it for a moment.

"That's him," he said. "No question about it." He said the man's name and then pushed the button which sent the images into motion again. It took half an hour for all the film, generally in segments no longer than sixty or ninety seconds, to be shown.

"Very interesting," he said, when the projector died, and the curtains whooshed open again. "What the hell do you think it is?"

"Obviously," the bald man said, "I was hoping you could tell me."

"Off the top of my head," Felter said, "what it looks like to me is that somebody needs to be convinced he's playing with the big boys. Step Two is that if they are willing to send him in to convince that somebody, then that somebody is somebody worth convincing. I don't like that."

"What do you think of Karl Neimayer?" the bald man asked.

"I was afraid to bring his name up to you," Felter said.

"Have you got somebody on him?"

"That would violate the solemn agreement between the United States and the Federal Republic of Germany," Felter said.

"Have you got somebody on him, Sandy?"

"Next question, Gunther?"

"I have been reluctant to really watch him, Sandy," the bald man said. "Especially since I know other people are watching him, too. I can't afford to have a parade following him around. And, I submit, neither can you. We have a certain commonality of interest here, Sandy."

"Not admitting, of course, that I have anybody on Neimayer, what do you propose?"

"Simply that it would make a lot more sense to have one of yours on Neimayer alternating with one of mine, than to have both of ours on him at the same time."

"It would be our ass if we were caught," Felter said. "You know that."

"I can really trust my man," the bald man said. "Can you really trust yours?"

Felter thought that over a moment.

"Yes," he said. "He reports that he's had to break it off several times, for fear Neimayer would be too suspicious. I could put it to him that this would be a solution. They'd have to know each other."

"Deal?" the bald man asked. "They can take turns watching him?"

"Deal," Felter said.

He wrote a name and a telephone number on a scrap of paper and handed it to the fat man. "He knows my handwriting. Have your man give him this."

"Dieter Stohl," the bald man said, "is my man."

"Jesus," Felter said. "I never would have guessed."

"Thank you," the bald man said. "I thought you would have. Or are you attempting, again, to convince me how inept you are?"

"Gunther . . ." Felter said, mockingly, holding his hands out before him in a gesture of helplessness.

"You almost got away with it," the bald man said. "As long

as I have been in this business—and theoretically should know better—I constantly have to remind myself that you generally know three times as much as you want me to think you know."

"You overestimate me," Felter said. "All I am, Gunther, is an American *schlemiel* playing spy."

"Sure, you are," Gunther said and smiled. "And I am the Virgin Mary."

"If there's nothing else, I have to get back," Felter said. "Do I get a cab ride?"

"There's one other thing," the bald man said. He laid a pinkish manila folder in Felter's lap. Felter read it.

"Oh, shit!" he said.

It was an extract of criminal police records, from Kreis Marburg and Kreis Bad Nauheim, of Land Hesse. It detailed the arrest for soliciting for the purposes of prostitution, and for frequenting premises known to be used for prostitution, of Ilse von Greiffenberg, also known as Ilse Berg.

"There's no record of conviction for prostitution," Felter said. "All this means is—"

The bald man interrupted him: "That she was picked up for hanging around the Tannenburg Kaserne in Marburg and the officer's hotel in Bad Nauheim, where she was trying to keep from starving. The countess had just killed herself. She was sixteen. I'm not condemning her, Sandy."

"Yes," Felter said, "that's all it means." Then he looked at the stout German and met his eyes. "You owe me, Gunther," he said. "I want this, every last goddamned copy of it, jerked from the files and burned."

"This is the next to the last copy of it," Gunther said. He took it from Felter, walked to one of the cabinets along the wall, slid it open, and dropped it into the open mouth of a small gray machine. There was a whirring noise, and from the bottom of the machine, tiny chips of paper, no larger than a character on a typewriter, poured out in a stream into a paper bag with BURN printed in two-inch-high red letters on it.

"'The next to the last copy,' is what you said," Felter said.

"You have it," the bald man said.

"*I* have it?"

"The Americans. An application on behalf of the lady in question for accreditation as an authorized dependent was made."

"I made it," Felter said. "Or I had it made. Her husband, who incidentally is my best friend—"

"Then a very fortunate man," Gunther interrupted him.

"—is a reserve officer," Felter went on, "who was recalled and shipped almost immediately to Korea."

"So I understand," Gunther said. Felter looked at him in surprise.

"How did you get involved?" he asked.

"I must confess—and don't be angry, Sandy—that I decided, from the way you got the count out of Germany, the rapidity with which he was given an entry visa to France, that you knew something about him that we didn't."

"I explained that to you, Gunther," Felter said. "He has high-placed friends. My involvement was personal, not in the line of business."

"So you told me. But you must admit that it is rather unusual for someone released from a Russian POW camp who crosses the East German border at four one afternoon, to be in a suite in the Hotel Continental in Paris at five thirty the next day."

"Do you also know what time I arrived?" Felter asked, dryly.

"At eight twenty-five in the morning, the next day," Gunther said.

"I'm impressed," Felter said. And then went on: "Ilse's husband is a very wealthy, very powerful man, who generally gets what he wants, when he wants it. He wanted his wife reunited with her father in relaxing circumstances, and he was able to arrange that. That's all there is to it. We're not interested in the colonel, Gunther, really, we're not."

"We are," Gunther said.

"Why? Will you tell me?"

"He was about the only active participant in the von Klaussenberg bomb plot who wasn't even suspected. A very clever man, Oberst Graf von Greiffenberg."

"Why are you interested?" Felter asked. He was surprised. He hadn't known that von Greiffenberg had been in on the plot to blow up Hitler. Now that he heard he was and thought about it, he wasn't surprised. But he was surprised that he didn't know about it.

"People like you and me and the count, my friend, are always in demand," Gunther said.

"I don't think he'd be interested," Felter said.

"You can never tell, though, can you, until you ask? I don't think he came home from five years in Siberia with a profound admiration for Marx, Lenin, or Peace Through Socialism."

"As you say," Felter said, "you never can tell."

"Just as a precautionary measure, we flagged the count's file," the bald man said, "asking that we be notified of any activity. We have a reliable man in the Kreis office in Marburg an der Lahn. A devoted pensioner."

"And he's the sonofabitch who dragged this out of the sewer?"

"Your army, my friend," the bald man said. "Your CID, Criminal Investigation Division, seems fascinated with prostitution and vice. They're the ones who requested a records check on Frau von Greiffenberg-Lowell."

"And your sonofabitch self-righteously gave it to them."

"No, my sonofabitch found out about it, and sent me the copy we just shredded, and checked carefully to see that was all of it."

"Sorry," Felter said. "I just . . ."

"I think when the Graf gets his affairs in order, he'll find that the man who has been so obliging to your CID has been helping himself to the Graf's assets while the Graf was in Siberia. His motivation, apparently, was to keep the Graf from prosecuting and making public his daughter's shameful past."

"Are we sure there's only one copy left?"

"There are no copies anywhere in German files," the bald man said, flatly, so there could be no chance of misunderstanding him.

"Now, I owe you one, Gunther," Felter said. He reached over and picked up the .45 automatic and slipped it into the skeleton holster in the small of his back. He put his tunic on, and then his hat, and shook the bald man's hand. "Thanks again, Gunther."

In English, the bald man said, "It's always a pleasure doing business with you." He wrapped an affectionate arm around Captain Felter's shoulders, and walked with him through the two steel doors to the elevator.

(Three)

The Mercedes taxicab took Captain Felter to the former headquarters of the I. G. Farben chemical cartel, carefully spared from wartime bombing in order that it might serve as an American headquarters. A WAC sergeant at the visitor's desk directed him to the Office of the European Command Provost Marshal General.

From the relaxed attitude of the personnel in the provost marshal general's outer office, he sensed the PMG was not in his office.

"I'd like to see the provost marshal general, please," Felter said to the Military Police Corps lieutenant colonel.

"I don't think you have an appointment, Captain," the lieutenant colonel replied, almost gaily. "The PMG only makes appointments when he plans to be here."

Felter took a leather folder from his breast pocket and held it before the lieutenant colonel's face.

"Who is the most senior officer I can see?" he asked.

"We don't see very many of those around here," said the lieutenant colonel. Unconscious that he was doing so, he stood up and nearly came to attention. "If you can tell me what you're after, perhaps I could help you," he said.

Ten minutes later, a florid-faced man in uniform, but wearing the insignia of a Department of the Army civilian employee, carried a thick manila folder into the outer office of the provost marshal general.

"Is this the entire file?" Felter asked. The florid-faced man looked to the lieutenant colonel for guidance. "I mean, is this all the notes, the drafts, leads, whatever?"

"Answer the man," the lieutenant colonel said. "He has reasons for asking."

"No, sir," the florid-faced man said. "That's not all. That's as far as we got. I mean, we're not finished."

"Get me the rest," Felter said. "Everything. And if you

prepare a receipt, Colonel, I'll sign it."

"You're taking the file with you?" the florid-faced man asked, surprised.

"Yes, I am," Felter said.

"Colonel," the florid-faced man said, "that's a working file." He looked at Felter. "You know what's in it?"

"Yes, I know what's in it," Felter said. "That's why I came for it."

"Well, then, look. It's not just one of those routine things where we don't give this dame a clean bill and a PX card. The guy that married her's an officer. We have to bring the CIC in on this. They're going to want to see that file, too. To make their determination. In case he goes for a Top Secret clearance."

"And the CIC would bring it to our attention in good time," Felter said. "The problem being that their good time would be far too late to do us any good."

"I see what you mean," the lieutenant colonel said, solemnly.

"Well, what do we do about not giving her a PX card?" the florid-faced man said.

"If it would make things any easier for you, I'll give you a memorandum—presuming you can have someone here type it up for me—"

"Of course," the lieutenant colonel said.

"Stating that I have the file, and that there is nothing in it of a detrimental nature which would preclude the issuance of dependent credentials," Felter went on.

"And you'll deal with the CIC?" the lieutenant colonel asked.

"Yes, of course."

"But there *is* detrimental material," the florid-faced man insisted.

"No," Felter said, slowly, carefully. "There is not."

"For Christ's sake, Dannelly," the lieutenant colonel said, "can't you see there is more to this case than some fraulein peddling her ass before she got some stupid jackass to marry her?"

Felter looked at Dannelly's florid face and solemnly nodded his head.

"I'll go get the notes and stuff," Dannelly said.

Felter went directly from the Office of the Provost Marshal General to the basement of the Farben Building, to the Classified Documents Vault. They knew him there, but even though he was not seeking access to the vault itself, just to the general area, they first compared his signature and thumb print with the signature and thumb print on file.

"We don't see much of you guys," the lieutenant colonel on duty said. "What can we do for you, Felter?"

"I want to use your shredder," Felter said, "and get rid of some stuff that's overclassified."

"You need a witness to the destruction?"

"No," Felter said. "But I would like to witness the burning."

He walked to the shredder, a larger, noisier one than the shredder in the bald man's office. He put a fresh burn bag under it, and fed the CID's report on Lowell, Ilse Elizabeth (B. von Greiffenberg), German National (Dependent Wife of Captain LOWELL, Craig W. 0–495302 Armor, USAR) into the shredder. When it was shredded, he took the burn bag out behind the Farben Building and handed it to a burly uniformed MP who threw it into a raging fuel-oil incinerator.

Then he walked over to the Frankfurt Military Post chapel and sat in the Buick and waited for Sharon and the others to come back from their tour of the rebuilt synagogue and the other cultural attractions of Frankfurt am Main.

(Three)
Sangju, South Korea
11 September 1950

The company clerk of Tank Company, 24th Infantry Regiment, 24th Infantry Division, walked into the Old Man's office and laid two thin stacks of paper in front of him, the white original and the yellow carbon.

"Here the sonofabitch is, sir," he said.

"Sit," the company commander ordered. "I will read it. If there are no mistakes, strike-overs, or other manifestations of your gross incompetence as a company clerk, you may then have a beer, like the rest of those who are righteous and efficient in our assigned tasks."

The young, light-tan sergeant smiled at his huge company commander. The Old Man knew how much he hated being drafted to be company clerk.

"You understand, of course," the Old Man went on, "why you have to wait for your beer? If you can't do it sober, what would it look like . . ."

"That sonofabitch is perfect, sir," the young tan sergeant said.

The Old Man read it very carefully.

MORNING REPORT TANK COMPANY 24TH INFANTRY REGIMENT 11 SEPT 1950

PRESENT FOR DUTY: OFFICERS	WARRANT OFFICERS	NONCOM OFFICERS	ENLISTED
1	0	16	102
ABSENT IN HOSPITAL		2 OFF 0 WO	54 EM
ABSENT WITHOUT LEAVE		0 OFF 0 WO	36 EM
ABSENT AND PRESUMED KILLED IN ACTION OR MISSING		4 OFF 1 WO	104 EM
CONFINED PENDING COURT-MARTIAL		1 OFF 0 WO	3 EM

ORGANIZATION RELIEVED VICINITY SANGJU KOREA AND PLACED IN EIGHTH ARMY RESERVE EFFECTIVE 0001 HOURS 11 SEPT 1950

ABRAHAM, CHARLES W SGT RA 12379757 PREV REPORTED MIA CONFIRMED KIA 30AUG50

FOLLOWING BREVET PROMOTION VERBAL ORDER COMMANDING GENERAL 24TH INFANTRY DIVISION CONFIRMED AND MADE MATTER OF RECORD:
1ST LT PARKER, PHILIP S IV 0-230471 TO BE CAPT EFFECTIVE 10SEP50 THE EXIGENCIES OF THE SERVICE MAKING IT NECESSARY AND THERE BEING NO OTHER QUALIFIED OFFICER AVAILABLE, UNDER THE PROVISIONS OF AR 615-356

FOLLOWING TWO BREVET PROMOTIONS VERBAL ORDER COMMANDING OFFICER 24TH INFANTRY REGIMENT CONFIRMED AND MADE MATTER OF RECORD:
SFC WOODROW, AMOS J RA 36901989 TO BE 1ST SGT EFFECTIVE 29JUL50

S/SGT SIDNEY, EDWARD B RA 16440102 TO BE M/SGT EFFECTIVE
29JUL50

FOLLOWING FIFTY-THREE BREVET PROMOTIONS VERBAL ORDER
COMMANDING OFFICER TANK COMPANY 24TH INFANTRY REGI-
MENT CONFIRMED AND MADE A MATTER OF RECORD SEE AT-
TACHMENT ONE HERETO

FOLLOWING OFF ATTACHED AND JOINED FROM 8TH US ARMY RE-
PLACEMENT COMPANY 11SEP50
1ST LT STEVENS, CHARLES D 0-498566
1ST LT DURBROC, CASPAR J 0-3490878
1ST LT PORTERMAN, JAMES J 0-4017882
2ND LT WITHERS, ALLAN F 0-4119782
WOJG KENYON, ALGERNON D RW-39276

FOLLOWING 102 EM ATTACHED AND JOINED FROM EIGHTH ARMY
REPLACEMENT COMPANY 11SEP50 SEE ATTACHMENT TWO HERETO

> PHILIP SHERIDAN PARKER IV
> CAPTAIN, ARMOR
> COMMANDING

The large black man looked at the small tan man.

"I'm awed," he said. "I am awed."

"Thank you, sir."

"But no beer," Captain Parker said.

"No beer?"

Captain Parker reached into a duffle bag.

"A literary type such as yourself deserves more than common beer," he said. He handed him a bottle of scotch.

"Ah, hell, I couldn't take that, Captain. I know they only
gave you three bottles."

"Don't argue with me, Sergeant," he replied. "I'm a captain
now, you know."

As this exchange was taking place, the officers listed in the
morning report were gathered in the Operations Room of the
S-3 section of the 24th Infantry Regiment.

"I wanted to have a word with you gentlemen before your
transport arrives," the regimental commander said to Lieutenants Stevens, DuBroc, Porterman, and Withers.

They were dressed identically in brand-new fatigue uniforms, still showing the creases from packaging. They also wore brand-new combat boots, and each carried a .45 Colt Model 1911A1 automatic pistol in a shoulder holster.

"I'll begin by saying that what I have to say to you is not to go any further than these walls." The walls to which he referred were those of a stuccoed frame building, three stories high, which four months before had been the Pusan Normal School.

"An officer, during his career, serves in many challenging assignments. There is no assignment more challenging, however, than service with colored troops. I can think of no test better designed to test the leadership qualifications of an officer. You may consider yourselves fortunate to have been given such an assignment, no matter what you may be thinking at the moment.

"You may have heard certain rumors about the combat effectiveness of this regiment. Unfortunately, most of what you have heard, discounting the inevitable exaggeration as a story makes its way around, are true.

"Some of our troops have run in the face of the enemy. Some of our troops have abandoned their positions and their equipment and given in to panic. There have been instances of outright cowardice. I will not deny there is a good deal of mud on the regiment's colors.

"Which brings us to the basic question, why? And the answer to that, gentlemen, not to mince words, is leadership. This regiment has been poorly led, from the platoon level to the command level. I am the fourth commander of this regiment since it was committed to this conflict, so the failures of leadership fall as heavily on senior officers as junior.

"It is my intention, gentlemen, to restore the good name of this regiment. I regard my assignment here as a challenge, almost as a compliment to me. My superiors apparently feel that I am capable of leading this regiment in such a manner that what has happened so far will be ascribed by the historians to the confusion that is an inevitable by-product of turning a garrison duty unit into a combat unit.

"The regiment has been badly mauled in the opening days

of this conflict. Average unit strength is approximately sixty percent of the authorized table of organization and equipment. Until the last couple of days, requirements elsewhere have denied us replacement personnel.

"You gentlemen are the vanguard of the new and revitalized 24th Infantry. In one way, the fact that the unit to which you will be assigned will have an entirely new complement of officers and have as replacements more than fifty percent of its strength, may be viewed as an advantage. You will have the opportunity to mold it in your image, gentlemen. I am sure you will rise to the challenge. Are there any questions?"

"Sir, you said, 'an entirely new complement of officers'?" Lieutenant Stevens asked. He had already determined that he was the senior officer. He had interpreted that to mean he would be the company executive officer, but with "an entirely new complement" he might be company commander. If you served in combat with a company for thirty days in a position senior to your rank, you could be promoted to that rank.

"A slip of the tongue. There is one officer presently assigned to Tank Company," the colonel said. "I'm sure that at least one of you will outrank him. He made first lieutenant in May."

Lieutenant Stevens found this very fascinating information indeed.

It had been the division commander's intention to call the regimental commander to inform him of his decision to make Parker a captain, which would permit him to remain in command. From everything he'd heard about Parker, he was a first-class officer and not only deserved the promotion but was obviously qualified to command (he had lived through the last two months). But something had come up every time he was about to reach for the telephone and tell him of his decision.

Lieutenant Stevens rode in the front seat of the ambulance without Red Cross markings, wondering if that wasn't somehow illegal. An ambulance was an ambulance. Taking one . . . it was probably stolen . . . and painting the red cross over and using it like a truck was something you could expect from a bunch of niggers.

One of the first things he would do in command would be to get rid of it. If they wanted to be treated like white men, it was time they understood they would be expected to behave like white men.

Tank Company was located six miles from the regimental command post, in a village called Chinhae. Lieutenant Stevens was momentarily pleased when he saw the first sergeant, a tall erect colored man in a crisply starched uniform, who approached the ambulance, came to attention, and saluted.

"Sir, may I welcome you to Tank Company?" the first sergeant said. "We've been waiting for you gentlemen for a long time."

"Thank you, Sergeant," Lieutenant Stevens said. "Will you have someone take care of our personal gear? Is that the way to the orderly room?"

"Yes, sir," the first sergeant said. Stevens knew that he had zinged him. Good. The important thing to do was establish your control. Then you could be a nice guy. Within reason, of course. Give a nigger an inch and he'd take a mile.

Tank Company had apparently taken over some sort of Korean country inn, something like a hotel. The floor was of woven straw. There was a sign lettered with a wax crayon, tacked to the wall. SHOE LINE. BARE FEET BEYOND THIS POINT.

Some nigger's sense of humor, obviously mocking the sign erected at regimental boundaries: HELMET LINE. HELMETS WILL BE WORN BEYOND THIS POINT.

Well, he had no intention of paying a bit of attention to that. He marched down the tatami-covered corridor until he came to another sign. CP.

He slid a sliding door open. There was a nigger buck sergeant sitting in front of a typewriter, his face making it perfectly obvious that the device was entirely too complicated for him to grasp. He looked up at Lieutenant Stevens and the other officers and his eyes widened.

"Don't you come to your feet, Sergeant, when you see an officer in here?" Lt. Stevens demanded. He was rather pleased with himself. He was establishing his position on military courtesy much sooner than he thought he would have an opportunity to do so.

The sergeant jumped to his feet. "Sorry, sir," he said. "The Old Man says not to, and we haven't had many officers around here." He paused, smiled, and added, "We ain't been inside all that much, either."

"Watch it in the future, Sergeant," Lieutenant Stevens said, with what he thought was just the proper mixture of sternness and paternalism. "Where is your officer?"

"In his office, sir," the sergeant said, nodding to another sliding door.

Lieutenant Stevens slid the door open. He saw a very large, very black man, naked to the waist, sweating, standing looking out the window. He held a can of beer in his hand.

"Ah, you must be the replacement officers," he said. "Come on in and have a beer." He waved at a metal container on the floor. It bore a red cross on all of its visible sides, and the words HUMAN BLOOD—RUSH.

"Just what the hell is going on around here?" Lieutenant Stevens asked.

"I beg your pardon?" the half-naked nigger asked in that phony Harvard a lot of them, in Lieutenant Stevens's experience, affected.

"Are you by any chance an officer?" Lieutenant Stevens demanded.

"Yes, I am," the nigger replied, amused. "Who are you?"

"I'm Lieutenant Stevens," Stevens said.

The half-naked black man with the can of beer stopped smiling. He looked Stevens up and down, and then looked beyond him at the other officers.

"Is that a West Point ring I see on your hand, Lieutenant Stevens?"

"As a matter of fact, it is," Stevens said. "But I asked who the hell you are."

"I find it difficult to believe," the half-naked nigger said, in his Harvard accent, every syllable precisely pronounced, "that an officer exposed to all the opportunities afforded by the United States Military Academy at West Point is unaware of the protocol involved in reporting to a new command. I presume, therefore, there is some excuse for your lack of military courtesy."

"I believe I'm in command here, Lieutenant Parker," Lieutenant Stevens said.

"Oh?" Parker said, his tone of voice suggesting idle interest. "I haven't been informed of my relief."

"I'm informing you now," Stevens said.

"I see," Parker said. "And where am I supposed to go? Regiment? Did you happen to bring me a copy of my orders?"

"You'll stay here, so far as I know," Stevens said. "What I'm saying, Lieutenant, is that I'm senior to you."

"I was promoted captain today," Parker said. "Were you promoted captain before that?"

Stevens felt his stomach contract into a knot.

"There's apparently been some sort of mix-up," he said.

"Sir," Parker said.

"Sir," Stevens said.

"Well, now that the air is cleared," Parker said, "have these officers sit down, lieutenant, and remove their foot gear. There's a sign outside that you should have read."

Stevens and the others just looked at him.

The sergeant who had been behind the typewriter came into the room without knocking.

"Here's your shirt, Captain," he said.

"One of the beer cans was frozen," Parker said, conversationally. "It exploded." He turned his back on the others and tucked his shirt in his trousers. "And when you have removed your shoes, gentlemen," he went on, "you can go back out and try reporting to your new commanding officer as the customs of the service dictate."

Stevens heard the nigger warrant officer chuckle. His face flushed, he sat down on the woven straw tatami and took off his boots. Deeply humiliated, carrying his boots in his hands, he went back down the corridor past the SHOE LINE sign, dropped off his boots, and then made his way back to Parker's office.

When the four officers and the warrant officer were shoeless, Stevens marched them into Parker's office.

"Sir," he said, saluting. "Lieutenant Stevens and other replacement officers reporting for duty."

Parker casually returned the salute.

"Stand at ease, gentlemen," he said. "Welcome to Tank Company, 24th Infantry." He met the eyes of each man. "As we have just established, I am Captain Philip Sheridan Parker IV, the commanding officer. There are some things I think you should know. First of all, about me. I am not only regular army, but I am a fourth generation army brat. For the past two months, I have been the only officer physically present for duty. I am still alive, and in command, and that should impress you as de facto proof that I am qualified to command this unit.

"Secondly, Tank Company has the distinction of being the only unit in the regiment which has not, at least since I've been in command, run in the face of the enemy. Through a process of attrition, our strength, until Eighth Army saw fit to send us replacements today, was down to one officer, sixteen noncoms and 102 enlisted men. Each of these men, and especially the noncoms, has been tried in battle and found worthy. The first sergeant pointed out to me this morning that none of our platoon sergeants or tank commanders held a rank higher than corporal when we entered combat. The majority, in fact, were privates first class.

"I have no way to judge the quality of the replacements, officer or enlisted. I have full confidence in the men I had before you and the enlisted replacements arrived. Having seen here what the effects of poor leadership are, I have no intention of seeing either the combat effectiveness of this unit destroyed, or equally important, losing the lives of any of my men by placing in a position of command any officer until I am satisfied that he is, indeed, qualified to take command.

"I am, therefore, going to turn each of you over to a platoon sergeant. You, Lieutenant Stevens, will be turned over to First Sergeant Woodrow. Until such time as they, in their exclusive judgment, decide that you are qualified, you will, with the insignia of rank removed, function as a tank crewman, and perform such other duties as you may be assigned."

"You can't do that!" Stevens protested.

"Any officer who fails to measure up will be relieved. There is a pool of officers who have been relieved in Pusan. I understand they are engaged in unloading ships, as stevedores," Parker went on.

"What about me, Captain?" the warrant officer asked.

"Were you a company clerk before you got your warrant?"

"I was a battalion personnel sergeant," he said.

"OK. You can relieve Sergeant Foster," Parker said. "If you can find a typist in the replacements, you can have him. All of our morning reports for the past two months have to be redone. Foster can help you do that. When he's finished, I promised him a tank."

He looked at each of them again, one at a time, slowly.

"With the exception of Lieutenant Stevens, you are dismissed," he said. "Tell Sergeant Foster I said to turn you over to Sergeant Woodrow."

Confused, shaken, angry, they saluted awkwardly in sort of a contagious reaction, and filed out of the office. Stevens remained.

"I presume, Lieutenant," Parker said, "that in addition to being regular army, you are a career soldier?"

"Yes, sir," Stevens said.

"You won't have much of a career if I relieve you, Lieutenant," Parker said. "Oh, eventually, I'm sure the West Point Protective Association would take care of you. They would have the records changed. But you and I know, Lieutenant, don't we, that you would forever be identified as the guy who was relieved in the nigger tank company? Officers who are relieved while serving with a nigger tank company very seldom make general, Lieutenant." Parker let that sink in a moment, and then he went on.

"If you cross me, you'll be lucky to make light bird in twenty years. I know the rules of this game, and I know them better than you do." Parker paused. "I don't expect a reply, Lieutenant, and you are dismissed."

VI

(One)
Company "B" 73rd Medium Tank Battalion (Separate)
Pusan, South Korea
2 September 1950

The Old Man, also known as "the Duke," and sometimes as "Deadeye"—none of these appellations ever to his face although he was fully aware of and rather pleased by what the troops called him—walked down the trench to the command post. He had a cigar jammed into the corner of his mouth, and he carried an M1 Garand rifle in the crook of his arm, for all the world like a hunter out for an afternoon's sport.

Forty-five minutes before, a six-by-six had deposited replacements—one lieutenant and four troops, two sergeants and two privates first class—at the CP, and they were nervously waiting to meet their new commanding officer.

Baker Company was in the hills, north and west of Pusan, its M4A3s dug into the shale of the mountains, surrounded by sandbag revetments. Where possible, a roof of logs and sandbags was built over them. They were, for all practical purposes, pillboxes. Their function was to protect the line with direct fire from their 75 mm cannons and their machine guns.

The M4A3s seldom moved from their positions. The engines were regularly run, and they received regular maintenance, and the tanks were moved a few feet once or twice a day to keep the tracks lubed; but the troops had been fighting more as infantrymen than as tankers, the distinction between them being primarily that the infantrymen were periodically relieved, if only for a brief period, while the tankers had yet to leave the lines. The heat was brutal, and there was little ice.

S/Sgt William H. Emmons, Jr.:

We had ice. God knows where the Duke got it, but he got it; and we had enough to cool, if not chill, our drinking water, and the strawberry preserve soda, and the daily booze ration. It was so fucking hot that sometimes the beer cans exploded before we could get them cooled. The food was C and 10-in-1 rations, high protein, left over from World War II and generally inedible. When the Duke took over, the company was suffering from dysentery, heat rash, heat exhaustion, and low morale, primarily because we were under intermittent fire twenty-four hours a day (not continually, just enough to keep our nerves taut, or to drive us over the edge) and the only thing we had to look forward to was more of the same.

When the Duke walked in the CP bunker, the first sergeant called "Atten-hut!" and the replacements stood straight and tall.

"Rest," the Duke said, and then: "What have we here? Visitors?"

"Sir," the lieutenant said, saluting, "Lieutenant Monahan reporting for duty with a detail of four."

The Duke returned the salute.

"What about that, First Sergeant?" the Duke said. "The lieutenant has manners."

"Yes, sir," the first sergeant said. "I noticed that."

"But you don't," the Duke said. "You haven't offered these gentlemen a libation, have you? Shame on you, First Sergeant."

"I beg the captain's pardon, sir," the first sergeant said, as if he was all shook up by the criticism. Then he turns to the replacements: "May I offer you gentlemen a small libation?"

I admit, I didn't know what a fucking libation was until I met the Duke, but the buggy look they gave the soldier was because you don't expect first sergeants to pass out booze anywhere, much less in a bunker about fifty yards from the fucking front line.

"Sir?" the replacement lieutenant asked, baffled.

"We have martinis, scotch, bourbon, and some really dreadful rum," the Duke said.

"Not for me, thank you, sir," the replacement lieutenant said. He was not about to make a fool of himself. The troops shook their heads and mumbled, "No, thank you, sir."

"I think I'll have a martini, First Sergeant, if you please," the Duke said.

"I just happen to have some made, sir," the first sergeant said. "And with the captain's permission, I will have one myself."

"Of course," the Duke said.

Then he asked the replacements for their orders, and by that time the first sergeant had taken a blood flask from a Medical Corps insulated cooler. He also took two martini glasses from the cooler. The blood flask, which had a rubber gasket sealer, was filled with a transparent fluid. which the first sergeant carefully poured into the martini glasses.

The replacements watched this wide-eyed.

"I regret, sir," the first sergeant said, like an English butler, "that we seem to be out of both olives and onions."

"The exigencies of the service, First Sergeant," the Duke said.

They raised their glasses to each other.

"To Baker Company, 73rd Medium Tank," the Duke said.

"You play ball with Baker Company," the first sergeant replied.

"Or you get the bat stuck up your ass," the Duke finished. They sipped their martinis.

The Duke turned to the replacements.

"We give you an option around here, gentlemen," he said. "You get two drinks, or two beers, a day. You may take less, but no more. Would you like to know what happens to anyone, but especially noncoms and officers, who take more than their daily sauce ration?"

"Yes, sir," the replacement lieutenant said, after he realized he was expected to reply.

"Pray tell the lieutenant, First Sergeant," the Duke said.

"You get the bat stuck up your ass," the first sergeant said. And then it was too much, and the Duke broke up and laughed, and the first sergeant laughed, and that made it all right for the rest of us to laugh.

"Welcome to Baker Company," the Duke said. "I'm the Generalissimo of this ragtag rolling circus. My name is Lowell. You may call me 'sir.'"

The goddamned Duke had class, there was no question about that. That regular business of giving the replacements a drink (some took it and some didn't know what the fuck was going on and didn't) did a couple of things. It made them feel at home; it made them feel they were in sort of a special outfit; and it got the Duke's point across, that nobody could afford to get sauced.

That fucking M1 he carried was one more proof. The .30 caliber M1 Garand was the standard weapon of the infantry soldier. It was looked down upon by tankers, both as a tool of the infantry dogfaces and as a heavy unwieldy weapon which kicked like a fucking mule. Very few noncoms, and even fewer officers, even in the infantry, carried one.

They were practically fucking unknown in a tank company, for Christ's sake, except for such shits and feather merchants as the cooks and the truck drivers. The basic weapon for tank crews was the .45 caliber M3 submachine gun, called the grease gun because that's what it looked like. Tank crewmen were also armed with the Colt Model 1911A1 automatic pistol. If they could get one, the tankers, officers, noncoms, and troopers armed themselves with the Thompson .45 caliber ACP submachine gun, "the Thompson" or "tommy gun," which was sometimes available for purchase at a going rate of $100; or with a carbine, either the M1, which was a semiautomatic shoulder weapon firing what was really a pretty hot pistol cartridge, or the M2 carbine, which had a lever permitting full automatic fire. Both versions were generally equipped with two curved, 30-round "Banana" clips, taped together upside down, *so that as soon as you blew away thirty rounds, all you had to do was pull the empty magazine out, turn it over, and slam the other, loaded magazine back in.*

Comes the Duke, comes Deadeye, right out of the National Fucking Guard, and just about as soon as he had the mess sergeant's fucking tent torn down to make sunshades for the tanks, he takes a Garand away from one of the assholes in the kitchen, and gives him his Grease Gun for it.

And then he zeroes the sonofabitch, just like he was on some fucking basic training rifle range back in the land of the big PX, getting down on his goddamned belly, doing everything but wrapping the strap around his arm, and zeroes the sonfabitch, shooting holes in a fired 75 mm casing he set up by pacing off two hundred yards right behind the line.

There's the company, tearing down tents, and ripping them up, and filling in latrines and foxholes that had been dug someplace he don't like, and here's the mess sergeant boiling a thirty-gallon pot of water and stirring strawberry preserves around in it, and here's practically everybody else working on the tanks (and the fucking gooks are going to hit us for sure, just as soon as it gets dark) and here's the Duke on his belly like some basic trainee, going through that up-two-clicks, right-three-clicks, zero bullshit with a fucking Garand.

For reasons of their own, the gooks didn't hit us that first night the Duke took over. They hit us the next night.

The way it worked, back then, was that they would wait until it got dark, or as dark as it was going to get, and then they'd throw mortars at us, and some artillery—not much, they weren't in much better shape, supply-wise, than we were, and I guess maybe they knew they were pissing in the wind, since we had the bunkers and the tanks.

So they'd lay in a barrage, and then they'd lift it, and then they'd start down to the edge of the river from their positions on the other side. Some of them had boats and floats, but you could practically walk across the Naktong River where we were.

Once they lifted the mortars, they wouldn't shoot their small arms until they were across the river. I guess they knew it wouldn't do them any good. And we didn't shoot back, either, until they were across the river and actually starting to come up the slope to our positions.

We were in pretty shitty shape as far as ammo went. We needed what they called "canister," which is sort of a super shotgun shell. Sonofabitch is filled with ball bearings; and when it goes off, it really blows troops away. Naturally, since we needed canister, what the bastards sent us was HEAT, which means High Explosive, Anti-Tank, and which is great if you're shooting at tanks but is next to fucking worthless if you're shooting at people. I mean, using HEAT against troops is like shooting fucking flies with a .45, you get my meaning?

So what we did was call in artillery, and sometimes we got it and sometimes we didn't, so what we usually wound up doing was firing the light weapons on the tanks. Thirty and fifty caliber machine guns. Now, the machine guns on a tank are air-cooled, which means that when you start firing one of them steady, the barrel heats up—I've seen them glow like coals—and pretty soon you have to change the sonofabitch, which is a pain in the ass when it's cold, not to mention glowing red goddamned hot, and when people are coming up the hill shooting at you.

So the way it worked was we waited until they were across the river and then opened fire. If we got artillery, fine. And if we didn't, we did pretty well just with the machine guns and with what canister rounds we did have.

Like I said, the first night that the Old Man had the company, the gooks didn't hit us. So we knew they would the second night.

So right after dark, the Old Man shows up in the positions. He's puffing on this big black cigar, he's got this fucking Garand in his arms, with a couple of extra clips to the strap, and, so help me, Christ, he's got a hand grenade in each pocket of his fatigue jacket. And he's dragging Lieutenant Whatsisname? The little fucker who got blown away two, three days later. The one who had been acting CO, after Captain Dale got it, until the Duke showed up. Sully was his name. Thomas J. Sully.

Anyway, the Duke's got Sully with him, and Sully explains

what usually happens, and the Duke listens, and asks a couple of questions, and then Sully says that maybe it would be a good idea if they went back to the company CP, so they could be there when the gooks start coming.

The Duke looks at me—we were standing by my tank, you see—and he says, "The radios in that rusty tub work, Sergeant?" and I tell him. "Yes, sir, most of the time," and he asks me can I come up with enough wire to run an extension between the commander's cupola commo panel and the platoon bunker, and I tell him sure.

"Do it," he says, and then he tells Sully he thinks he'll stick around up here, and if Sully wants to go back to the CP, he can. Sully thinks it over, decides the Duke is out of his fucking mind, and shags his ass off the hill.

So then we sat and waited for the gooks. The Duke asks us about where we come from, and whether we're married or not, the usual officer bullshit, and sure enough, thirty, forty minutes later, the gooks start throwing mortars at us, the way we knew they would.

It lasted maybe five, ten minutes, and then it lifted. And when it lifted, no Duke. I figured he got smart and went down the hill. I had a BC scope, you know what I mean? They're like binoculars and a periscope put together? You can see over the edge of someplace without exposing your head. It stands for Battery Commander's scope, I think. Anyway, I had a BC scope set up in the bunker, and I was looking through it. It was full moon, or nearly, and I could see pretty good.

Sure enough, down their hill they came, first their point men, and then two guys maybe ten feet behind him, and then four, five guys behind them. Making sort of a triangle, and heading toward us.

The gook point man was a good three hundred, maybe three hundred fifty yards from us.

And then I hear, right over my head, three shots. Bang Bang Bang. Thirty caliber, but too far apart to be a machine gun. I am just wondering what the fuck our new National Guard commander is up to when I notice that the gook point man and one of the two guys behind him is down.

That sort of upsets the gooks, and they all fell down, and started shooting up the other side of the river, the bank, I mean, right across from them, where they figure we stuck an outpost. They blow the shit out of it with their small arms, and even call mortars in on it. Now I know we don't have anybody down there, so it has to be the Duke. So I go outside, and there he is, sitting on top of the bunker, this time with the strap of the M1 around his arm, and wearing a shit-eating grin.

"I think they see ghosts, Sergeant," he said. "Better they battle ghosts than us, wouldn't you say?"

So I told him he was pretty good with the Garand, and he said, " 'Pretty good'? Sergeant, I'm magnificent!" You see what I mean, class?

So what happened after that was that we picked one guy, the best shot, from each platoon, and made him a sniper, and the Duke actually came up later with real sniper's rifles, '03A4 Springfields, and M1Cs, which is an M1 with a cheek piece on the stock and a four power scope. And after that, let me tell you, the gooks didn't walk across the Naktong like it was a fucking street. They still came, but by Christ, they came careful!

Sgt. Jared Mansfield:
The Old Man had been called to battalion, and they talked about what was going on, even though he was called to battalion at least once a day. The Old Man, for all practical purposes, was the battalion S-3 (Plans and Training Officer). The S-3 was an ineffective old fart who couldn't find his ass with both hands. If he didn't have the Old Man showing him how to pour piss out of a boot, the outfit would be as fucked up as that nigger division had been. But they talked about the Old Man being at battalion again because there was nothing else to talk about. They wondered if he would be able to steal some more beer, or if there would be mail.

The Old Man returned from battalion at 1530. In his jeep were three bags of mail, six cases of beer, and one case of Coca-Cola. He carried one of the cases of beer into the CP himself, and the first sergeant and the clerk and the radio operator went out to collect the rest.

The Old Man walked to where the executive officer was sleeping. It was a bed made from an air mattress suspended on communications wire woven between the tree trunks that also served as pillars to hold up the plank-and-sandbag roof of the bunker. He gently touched his arm.

"The mail is here," he said. The XO swung his feet off the bed, and got to his feet.

"Send for runners for the mail," the Old Man said. "And then we'll have an officer's call. Noncoms are invited, but I want at least a sergeant left in each platoon."

"Yes, sir."

"There's a little beer, and one lousy case of Coke," the Old Man said.

Runners from the platoons came quickly and stood impatiently as the company clerk went through the first-class mail pouch, breaking the mail down into platoons.

The three platoon leaders and the chief warrant (who was supposed to be the administrative officer, but who had been a motor sergeant before taking the warrant exam and was now happily functioning as the motor officer) drifted into the command post as soon as they had determined if they had, or didn't have, mail in the bag.

"You, Tommy," the Old Man said to the second platoon leader, "are a fucking disgrace to the officer corps."

"Yes, sir," the second platoon leader replied, "I am. Does that mean, I hope, that the captain is thinking of sending me home in disgrace?"

"Where the hell have you been, anyway? What have you been rolling in?"

"We pulled the power package on Twenty-Two, sir. The transmission was losing fluid. When we pulled it, we found out why. The housing was cracked."

"All over you?"

"Yes, sir."

"Have you got it running?"

"Yes, sir."

"Is everything else running?" the Old Man asked and looked at each officer in turn and finally at the chief warrant. The chief warrant reported that everything was running, and that he had managed to get three complete, in-the-crate, power packages and three complete, in-the-crate, sets of tracks.

"Not individual tracks, Captain. Complete sets. Two complete tracks in a box. Christ only knows where they found them."

"I don't suppose," the Old Man said, innocently, *"that they'd fit an M46?"*

"No, sir," the warrant officer replied, and looked curious.

"OK, then," the Old Man said, *"sometime in the next four days, put them on the tanks that need them most."*

"I thought about that, sir," the warrant officer said. *"I thought I'd wait until we lose one. What the hell, there's no sense in replacing a track until it goes."*

"Make up your mind where you want to put them, but I want them put on the tanks that need them most, and as soon as you can get to it. What about the wheels?"

"The jeeps are all running, sir, and in good shape. The both of them," the warrant officer said. There were four jeeps in Company "B." Two were authorized. Two had been "borrowed" when their drivers had left them momentarily unattended. The Old Man obviously knew about the two stolen jeeps, but said nothing about it.

"We're being relieved," the Old Man announced.

"Jesus, it's about time," one of the platoon leaders said.

"As soon as it gets dark," the Old Man went on, *"a Korean captain and a platoon leader, and one platoon, will come up. They'll be sneaked up. The idea is not to let the bad guys know we've been relieved by Koreans. They will be followed by another platoon tomorrow, and the third platoon the day after tomorrow. As soon as they have been checked out to my satisfaction, our platoons, one at a time, can come off the hill."*

"What about the equipment, Captain?" the chief warrant officer asked.

"We'll turn our tanks over to them," the Old Man said.

"And go through the whole business of getting everything in fairly decent shape again? Why the hell can't the slopes bring their own tanks, and let us keep ours?"

"I made the same passionate speech to Colonel Jiggs," the Old Man said. *"He heard me out, and then he said, 'OK, if you feel that strongly, you can keep your tanks, and I'll give the M46s to the Koreans.'"*

"M46s? No shit!"

"So I said, 'Yes, sir, I know the stalwart men of Baker Company would much prefer their spotless and shining M4A3s to dirty new M46s.'"

There was laughter, and then the lieutenant that the Old Man had jumped on spoke up.

"What's the catch, Captain?"

"My orders are to insure that everybody is checked out in the M46, and to prepare for an attack," the Old Man said.

"Attack? Whose stupid idea is that? Walker's?"

The reference was to Lt. Gen. Walton "Bulldog" Walker, the Eighth Army commander, who shared a surname with a Company "B" cook.

"It came to him when he was slicing Four Ways," the Old Man said, referring to the field ration meat, which could be used in four ways.

There was more easy laughter.

"Goddamn, Captain, every other slant-eye in the world is out there. And what are we supposed to do for support? They even pulled the Third Marines out of here."

"I will bring your solemn assessment of the situation to the colonel's attention," the Old Man said. "But in the meantime, at least until he sees the error of his ways, I'm afraid we're just going to have to go along with him."

There was laughter.

"Tell the troops," the Old Man said, "but make sure you also tell them I'm going to be the judge of whether or not the Koreans are capable of relieving us. That's all."

(Two)

They left the bunker. The Old Man made a levitating signal with his hand to the company clerk, who had sat down again behind the typewriter.

"Yes, sir," he said.

"I would be profoundly grateful for a sheet of paper and an envelope," the Old Man said.

The executive officer gave him some with *Officer's Open Mess, Fort Shafter, Hawaii* printed on it in golden ink. The

Old Man rolled the paper into the typewriter, carefully X-ed out Fort Shafter, Hawaii, and typed in "Fortress Lowell, South Korea.

Then he typed, very rapidly, as if he had been thinking for some time about what he was going to say.

> My Darling Ilse,
>
>   I have a few moments between golf and the cocktail hour, and I thought I would pass it dropping you a note instead of dancing with the ladies, although I know my actions will break their hearts.
>
>   There was no mail from you today, and I could cheerfully boil in oil the bureaucrat who decided that since we can mail letters post-free from here to America, there was no point in sending any stamps here. My letters, as you've noticed, have to make a stop at the firm, so that they can be remailed to you. God only knows what has happened to your letters to me. I have had only one, the one you sent to Fort Lawton, since I got here. The others are probably en route by sea, via the Suez Canal and mysterious India.
>
>   Despite that, my morale is reasonably high, as high as any man denied the pleasure of the company of his wife and son can be. I have a fine company, as I've written before, good officers, good noncoms, and a few unmitigated sonsofbitches.
>
>   They've apparently finally gotten the supply system into gear, for today I was informed that we will be reequipped with M46 tanks starting tomorrow. Your father will be able to explain that they have a 90 mm tube, as opposed to the 75 mm on the M4A3s, a lower profile, and are generally a far better tank all around.
>
>   What I suppose I'm leading up to saying, *Liebchen*, and please don't misunderstand me, is that although I bleed at being separated from you and P.P., I really would much rather be here, doing

what I'm doing, than I would be at the firm. In some strange, perverse way (and I wouldn't tell anyone else this), I feel as if I belong here, in the sandbags, surrounded by weapons, and the sometimes really ghastly smell of the army.

I'm a good officer. I say that with all modesty. I don't think it's anything that I do. I just seem to be able to understand the system, and the people that make it up, and to make the whole thing fit together like a jigsaw puzzle or a well-oiled clock. There is no question in my mind (or in the colonel's either; he as much as told me) that Baker Company is the most efficient in the battalion. We seem to work together. The company is alive. I'm proud of it and of being part of it, and most of all for knowing that I'm responsible for it.

So, *Liebchen*, I'm going to take up the offer you made me in Philadelphia, when you said I could go back in the army. We'll be here about a year, I would judge, and then I'll be coming home to you. I'll take a month's leave in Germany.

I won't write how much I miss you and P.P., because I'm a big boy now and big boys aren't supposed to cry. You won't mind me saying that I adore you, though, will you?

All my love.

He signed his name with a grease pencil, licked the envelope, and only then remembered he hadn't addressed it. The address still tore him up.

Mrs. Craig W. Lowell
Schloss Greiffenberg
Marburg an der Lahn, Germany.

Schloss meant castle in German; it sounded as if the mailman rode a horse and wore a suit of shining armor.

He folded that envelope smaller, so that it would fit inside the envelope which would take it to the firm, for remailing to Germany.

"I have to beg one more envelope," he said. He looked at

the company clerk. "You got one I can have, Stu?"

"What's the postage to Germany, Captain?" the company clerk replied.

"I have no idea."

"I wrote my mother, Captain, about the trouble you were having writing to Mrs. Lowell, and she sent me a bunch of stamps for you. They're fifteen-cent ones. I'll put two of them on, to make sure." He reached out his hand for Lowell's envelope.

"Why, thank you very much," the Old Man said. "And thank your mother for me, too, please, Stu." The Old Man turned, so that neither the exec nor the company clerk would see that his eyes, for some reason, had suddenly started to water.

(Three)
Washington, D.C.
6 September 1950

Rotary Wing Course 50–4 (Special) had been established at Fort Sam Houston, Texas, by verbal order of the Secretary of the Army in order to meet a requirement of the highest priority from Eighth United States Army, Korea (EUSAK). From the very first days of the Korean conflict, it had been quite clear that rotary-wing aircraft, specifically the Bell H13 and the Hiller H23, were ideally suited for use as battlefield ambulances. They saved lives.

Within two weeks of the commencement of hostilities, enterprising army aviators had fitted locally fabricated litter racks to the skids of the few helicopters available, turning them into aerial ambulances.

Technically, such modifications were aerodynamically unsound, for with a pilot, and two wounded men in the litter racks, both aircraft were over maximum gross permitted weight. They were also illegal, because they had not been approved by the air force, which had, under the Key West Agreement of 1948, sole engineering responsibility for army aircraft.

The aerial ambulances worked. To hell with the engineers, and screw the air force.

Both the H13 and the H23 helicopters were designed to carry a pilot and a passenger, each with an estimated weight of 180 pounds. It was believed, furthermore, that carrying an approximately 180-pound weight in the only position the litter racks could be fitted would severely affect the weight and balance characteristics of the aircraft. Carrying two such weights would not only further increase the imbalance, but would raise the aircraft's gross weight beyond the point where it could fly safely, if indeed at all.

On the other hand, loading a critically wounded soldier onto a helicopter litter rack meant that he could be flown quickly, and in relative comfort, to a Mobile Army Surgical Hospital (MASH) where his life, 95 times out of 100, could be saved. That statistic stood out: If a wounded soldier arrived alive at a MASH, the odds were 95–5 that he would live.

Too many wounded men had arrived dead at the mobile hospitals after a two-hour-long ride over battered and potholed roads in the standard army ambulances—Dodge three-quarter-ton truck frames with square bodies capable of carrying five litters.

Notwithstanding the established principles of aerodynamics and the Key West Agreement of 1948, which forbade the army to do much more with airplanes than use them as aerial jeeps, the H13s and the H23s shuttled back and forth between the battlefield (known now as the main line of resistance, or MLR) and the mobile hospitals and saved lives. The call went out for many more helicopters, and the pilots to fly them, as quickly as possible.

The aircraft themselves were easier to come by than the pilots to fly them. Bell and Hiller went on a three-shift, twenty-four-hour-a-day production schedule. It was decided that for convenience in maintenance and parts supply, Hiller H23s should be used exclusively in Korea, at least until things straightened out. As a result, H23s from the army worldwide were hastily shipped to the Far East. They would be replaced, according to plan, by Bell H13s as they came off the production line.

Pilots posed a greater problem. There were few helicopter pilots in the army when the war broke out, and the pool of chopper pilots available in the reserve was negligible or nonexistent. An unusually well-qualified pilot is required to teach someone else how to fly, and the few highly qualified pilots around had quickly been ordered to Korea.

Contracts were let to engage the relatively small number of civilian helicopter pilots as instructors, and applications for helicopter pilot training, from commissioned and warrant officers, were quickly processed and approved, the criteria being essentially that the applicant could pass the rigid standards of a flight physical.

The Medical Corps, to spare its physicians from administrative matters, had established a corps of administrators, called it the Medical Service Corps, and issued them caducei with the letters MSC superimposed on them as lapel insignia. When the first medical evacuation helicopters were assigned to the Medical Service Corps, so were the pilots that came with them.

Then the Medical Corps, which had always been admired, but had never had much of a dashing military reputation, entered the political arena. The surgeon general received permission to gather together at the Army Medical Center, at Fort Sam Houston, in San Antonio, Texas, sufficient numbers of its helicopter pilots to train *other* Medical Service Corps officers to be helicopter pilots. It also received authority to increase the number of Medical Service Corps officers it was permitted to have. Care of the wounded has always been given the highest priority within the army, and it was given here.

Almost immediately, however, it became apparent that if the Medical Corps got all it asked for in the way of instructor pilots and training helicopters, there would be an insufficient number of either available elsewhere in the army to train the helicopter pilots required for other missions. It was decided to return helicopter training to the artillery, where it had been before Korea, and to make available to the Medical Corps as many spaces as possible in the classes.

It was also decided that the training underway at San Antonio would be permitted to continue until such time as the Artillery School at Fort Sill was prepared for the massive influx of student pilots. In the meantime, a certain small number of officers of other arms and services would be sent to Fort Sam to undergo flight training with the medics.

Despite what he had been told in the Far East (that he was being sent home in order to go to chopper school), Captain Rudolph G. MacMillan quickly learned by phone what the candy-asses in the Pentagon really wanted to do with him. First, they wanted to put him on display for a couple of months as a hero. Then, maybe, they could talk seriously about "finding him a space" in a rotary-wing transition course.

Well, screw that! He wanted to get back in the goddamned war before it was over.

He hung up the telephone, went upstairs in Roxy's mother's row house on Railroad Street in Mauch Chuck, Pennsylvania, and took a green tunic from the closet. He laid it on the bed, pinned his ribbons on it—all of his ribbons, including the one which sat alone and on top of all the others, the blue-silk, star-spotted ribbon of the Medal—and then hung the tunic on the hook in the back seat of his brand-new 98 Olds "Rocket" and started out for Washington.

Lt. Colonel Robert F. Bellmon, who had been in the Polish stalag with him, was assigned to the Office of the Assistant Chief of Staff for Operations. If Bellmon couldn't do him any good, there were other people. Before he became a talking dummy for the assholes in PIO, he would complain right up to the top, as far as the Chief of Staff, if that was necessary.

Bellmon laid it on the line, and told MacMillan what he suspected. They wanted him out of the Far East because of the Medal. They didn't want anybody with the goddamned Medal to get blown away. A dead hero is worse, public relations-wise, than an ordinary dead soldier. He had been sent home to get his ass out of the line of fire, not to become a chopper jockey.

"I can probably get you out of the hands of public relations, Mac," Bellmon told him. "But you better get used to the idea that you're going to sit out the rest of this war. They're not going to send you back to the Far East, period."

Colonel Bellmon walked MacMillan down the labyrinthine corridors of the Pentagon to the office of a classmate assigned to the Office of the Assistant Chief of Staff, Personnel. He introduced Mac to him as an old and dear friend, who had been in the stalag with him, who had been in the Far East, and who was now in the clutches of the people in public relations.

Bellmon seldom asked for favors. Colonel Bellmon's class-mate was prepared to do anything within reason for an old and dear friend of Bellmon's, particularly one with the Medal, short, of course, of sending him back to the Far East.

It posed no problem at all. An infantry captain at Benning, an assistant instructor in the Department of Tactics, would receive notification that because of space limitations, his orders to attend helicopter flight training at Fort Sam Houston had been cancelled, and that he was being rescheduled for a sub-sequent class, details to follow.

Captain Rudolph G. MacMillan would receive orders di-recting him to report for helicopter pilot training at the U.S. Army Medical Center, Fort Sam Houston, San Antonio, Texas.

Afterward, Bob Bellmon insisted that Mac spend the night at the Farm. Barbara, Bellmon said, would not forgive Mac for not bringing Roxy with him to Washington, but he would just have to face up to that.

They stopped and bought steaks on the way to the Farm, and grilled them, and talked about how General Waterford, despite the long hours he had spent concealed by charcoal smoke, was probably the world's worst steak broiler, personally responsible for the destruction of more good meat than any other human being.

"Good God, Mac!" Bellmon said, suddenly. "You don't know about Colonel von Greiffenberg, do you?"

"What about him?"

"He's back," Bellmon said.

"I thought he was dead," MacMillan said. "I heard—*you* told me—that the Russians blew him away just before you got liberated."

"That's what I thought. So did everybody else. But he showed up alive. The Russians had him in Siberia."

"Well, I'll be goddamned," MacMillan said, pleased. "That's damned good news." And then his face clouded. "And what about Lowell?"

Craig W. Lowell was not one of Captain Rudolph G. MacMillan's favorite people. Despite what Lowell had done in Greece, in MacMillan's judgment Lowell was a candy-ass who should never have been commissioned.

"I've seen him twice lately," Bellmon said, looking at his wife to signal her to keep her mouth shut.

"And?" MacMillan asked.

"Once, in Germany. He was there, of course, to meet the colonel when he came across the border," Bellmon said.

"I'm glad for Ilse," Mac said. "Roxy and I always liked her. I never could figure what she saw in Lowell, but she was all right."

"And then we saw Captain Lowell," Barbara said. "When he stopped by on his way to the Far East."

"*Captain* Lowell?" Mac asked, disbelieving.

"What do you think about that?" Bellmon asked.

"How the hell did he arrange that? He can't be more than twenty-four or twenty-five years old?"

"Twenty-three, actually," Bellmon said. "He went in the National Guard, and arranged to get himself promoted. He's good at that sort of thing, you may have noticed."

"Ah, that makes me sick. He's got no more right to be a captain than Roxy does. What's he doing? Playing golf at Camp Drake?"

"There is a pool of misfit officers, relieved officers, incompetent officers, in Pusan," Lieutenant Colonel Bellmon said. "They are engaged as stevedores, I understand. I devoutly hope that Lowell is among them."

"That's a filthy, rotten thing to say!" Barbara said, furiously.

"Your friend Lowell is a thoroughly rotten man," Bellmon said.

"You've got no right to say anything like that," she said.

"After his coming here the way he did," Bellmon said, as angrily, "I have the perfect right."

"The reason you don't like Craig, darling," Barbara Bellmon said, icily, "is because he has the balls to do things you don't. He won't let the system crap on him, and call it 'cheerful willing obedience to orders.' You don't like Craig, darling, because he makes you realize that you're more of a clerk than you like to admit."

She jumped to her feet, spilling her drink in the process, and stormed inside the house.

"Jesus, what was that all about?" Mac asked.

"I was just thinking," Bellmon said, "that my wife, when she is angry, is really her father's daughter."

"Jesus, yeah," MacMillan said. "That sounded just like one of the general's tantrums, didn't it?"

"I'll give her a couple of minutes to cool down," Bellmon said. "And then I'll go get her."

Goddamn that bastard Lowell, he thought. He can cause trouble when he's ten thousand miles away.

(Four)
Brooke U.S. Army Medical Center
Fort Sam Houston, Texas
10 September 1950

When he reported for duty at Fort Sam, MacMillan's breast pocket was bare of all ribbons and qualification badges except his aviator's wings. He did not want to call attention to himself at all, just get through this bullshit as quickly and as smoothly as possible. If his orders had not identified him as a fixed-wing, instrument qualified aviator, he would not have worn his wings either.

Fixed-wing aviators, he learned on arrival, had no set program. They would be rotary-wing students until such time as they had been adjudged competent, entry-level helicopter pilots, or until it became clear that they were never going to master safe flight in rotary-wing aircraft.

Fixed-wing qualification is no indicator at all of an individual's potential as a chopper jockey. Helicopter piloting is the most difficult of all flying in terms of coordination; and numbers of splendid fixed-wing pilots have never been able to make the transition.

MacMillan's instructor had long before learned that it was quite necessary to destroy the ego and self-confidence of a fixed-wing pilot about to undergo rotary-wing training in order to make him pay attention. The quickest and surest way to do that was to take him for an orientation ride and let him see for himself how difficult it was and how embarrassingly inept he was at it.

A fixed-wing aircraft is controlled, simplistically, by the stick and the rudder pedals. Climbing is accomplished by pulling back on the stick, descending by pushing forward on it. Turns are accomplished by moving the stick from side to side and by depressing one of the rudder pedals. Straight and level flight can often be accomplished simply by removing one's hands and feet entirely from the stick and rudder pedals, and letting the plane fly itself.

Helicopter flight is somewhat more complicated. There are pedals which function essentially like rudder pedals, but they are *not* rudder pedals, and taking one's feet off them entirely will immediately start the helicopter's fuselage spinning. It is necessary, using the "rudder pedals" (which actually control the small, counter-torque rotor mounted vertically in the tail), to maintain an equilibrium between opposing forces.

There is a "stick" between the legs, and it too has major differences from the stick on a fixed-wing aircraft. What it actually does is tilt the "rotor cone" in the direction it is moved. The rotor cone is the arc described by the rotor blades as they revolve. Imagine an empty, very wide-mouthed, very shallow ice cream cone. If the cone is tilted forward, it tends to move the helicopter forward; tilted to the rear, it tends to move the aircraft to the rear. It can be tilted in any direction.

The helicopter pilot's left hand is simultaneously occupied by a third control. A motorcycle-like rotary throttle is held in the curled fist. The straight piece of aluminum tubing on which it is mounted also controls the angle of the blade. In other words, it adjusts the "bite" the rotor blades take of the air as they spin around the rotor head. The steeper the bite (angle of attack), the more lift is provided. And the steeper the angle of attack, the more power is required. Constant throttle adjustment is required. An instrument in front of the pilot has two separate needles, one indicating rotor speed, and the other engine rpm. The needles are supposed to be superimposed, within a small range indicated by a green strip on the dial.

For purposes of comparisons, when the pilot of a fixed-wing aircraft is poised for takeoff, he simply pushes the throttle forward to "take off power." Then he steers the airplane, as it gathers speed down the runway, by use of the rudder pedals and stick. At a certain point, the speed of the air passing over his wings generates sufficient lift to literally lift the airplane off the runway.

A helicopter pilot, on the other hand, must first acquire lift by judicious application of engine power and simultaneous raising of the cyclic control. The instant the helicopter leaves the ground, he must establish and maintain equilibrium between opposing forces by use of the "rudder pedals" to keep the machine from starting to spin, and then adjust the position of the rotor cone to control the direction of flight—even if that direction is not to move at all: the most difficult of all flight manuevers, the "hover."

Having accomplished all this, the helicopter is still not in a flight condition, but in an intermediate step called "transitional lift." What this means is that the helicopter is sort of floating on a cushion of air compressed between the rotor blades and the ground. When he climbs higher, or when he moves off in any direction, he "loses the cushion" and instantaneous compensatory movements of all the controls are necessary.

The easiest way to convince anyone of what a hairy bitch chopper driving is—but especially a well-qualified fixed-wing pilot—is by demonstration rather than explanation. And once the student pilot is convinced that he has a hell of a lot to learn, as he inevitably is when the chopper instantly gets away from him, he then becomes a docile and dedicated student.

Captain MacMillan's instructor pilot spent thirty minutes showing him the mechanical construction of the Bell H13. Then they climbed inside the plexiglass bubble, where he spent another fifteen minutes explaining the controls and the layout of the instrumentation. He figured he would give this guy, who seemed pretty cocky, a thirty-minute demonstration to convince him beyond any doubt, reasonable or otherwise, that he was really going to have to bust his ass before he could fly a chopper.

Following the instructor's step-by-step instructions over the intercom, MacMillan fired up the engine, and checked the instruments one by one to make sure the indicators were all within the safe operating range ("in the green") indicated by stripes of green tape on the instruments.

"Now," the IP said, "it's going to get away from you. Expect it to. Just don't overreact. Try to figure out how you're under- or over-controlling." MacMillan nodded. "Ease up, very gently, on the cyclic; and remember, you're controlling the throttle."

MacMillan nodded again and did as he was told. He picked the bird straight up. He didn't like the feeling, so he picked it up another couple of feet. He tried out the rudder pedals, to see how sensitive they were. Then he looked over, unaware that he was in a near perfect hover, just out of ground-effect.

"Now what?" he asked his instructor pilot.

"How much bootleg chopper time do you have, Mac-Millan?" the IP demanded. He did not like being made a fool of.

"None," MacMillan replied. "I've always been afraid of the goddamned things. Can I try to fly it?"

"Be my goddamned guest," the IP said. He had never until this moment believed there was such a thing as a natural he-licopter pilot. MacMillan dropped the nose, moved across the field ten feet above it, and then, increasing the pitch, soared into the air, a disgusting look of pure pleasure on his face.

(Five)

This time, Bellmon's classmate in the Office of the Assistant Chief of Staff, Personnel, was not so obliging. There was absolutely no chance of MacMillan being returned to the Far East, much less to Korea, as a chopper pilot.

"For one thing, you're a returnee. You have to spend a year in the States," the lieutenant colonel told him.

"I'll waive that," MacMillan said. "Jesus Christ, Colonel. They want to make me an IP. I couldn't take that."

The lieutenant colonel showed him the letter from SCAP in the Dai Ichi Building, addressed somewhat baroquely to "My Dear Comrade Ellsworth" (the Assistant Chief of Staff, Personnel, who was not fond of his first name and signed himself "E. James Brockman") and containing the SCAP's reluctant conclusion that Captain MacMillan's assignment to duties "which would place him in the jeopardy of the instant

situation in Korea" would not be in the overall best interests
of the army.

"As painful as it will surely be for a warrior of MacMillan's
caliber to turn a deaf ear to the sound of the battle trumpet,"
SCAP wrote, "I'm sure that, once the situation is explained to
him, he will discharge his training or administrative duties with
the same dedication he has so often demonstrated under fire."

"Bullshit," MacMillan said. "I'll quit flying before I let
them make me an IP."

"General Brockman said to give you a choice between here
and Fort Polk," and lieutenant colonel said.

"Polk? In Louisiana? What the hell's going on there?"

"It was just reactivated as a basic training center."

"Oh, Jesus Christ, Colonel!"

"Where you would be aide-de-camp to General Black."

"Black's a pretty good general," MacMillan said. "What
the hell did he do wrong to get sent to Fort *Polk?*"

"Korea's an infantry war," the lieutenant colonel explained.
"They're not going to send any armored divisions over there.
I suppose the thinking is that if the balloon goes up...in
Europe, I mean...he could activate an armored division at
Polk."

"What would I be doing here?" MacMillan said. "I'm almost
afraid to ask."

"Presidential Flight Detachment," the lieutenant colonel
said. "Flying choppers."

"I heard about that," MacMillan said. "And I heard you
needed a thousand hours, minimum, no-accident chopper
time."

"To fly the President or the VIPs you do," the lieutenant
colonel agreed.

"So what would I be doing?"

"You would be very decorative around the White House,"
the lieutenant colonel said. "Especially in a dress blue uniform
or mess kit. Wearing your medals, not your ribbons." He
paused, and then said, wryly: "You'd really be something in
a mess kit, MacMillan."

The mess kit was an ornate, formal dress uniform for evening wear. Most officers hated it.

"Did anybody bring my name up to General Black?" MacMillan asked.

"You're OK with him, if that's what you're asking. He said that after you get a little more experience, he'll even let you fly him around in your whirlybird."

VII

(One)
Schloss Greiffenberg
Marburg an der Lahn, Germany
12 September 1950

Peter-Paul Lowell, half shy and half glowering, his bunched fists pulling his mother's skirt off her hips so that it was evident she was wearing only a half slip, looked at the woman his mother was affectionately embracing.

"Got a kiss for me?" Sharon Felter asked, squatting down to his level. He buried his face in the familiar warmth of his mother's tweed skirt.

"Aunt Sharon's known you since you were a tiny baby," Ilse von Greiffenberg Lowell said. "Give her a kiss."

Peter-Paul von Greiffenberg Lowell, known as P.P., stuck his tongue out at Sharon Felter and then let go of his mother's skirt, turned and ran up the shallow stairs and into the open door of the large villa.

"A chip off the old blockhead, I see," Sandy Felter said to Ilse, and kissed her on the cheek. Felter was in civilian clothing. In civilian clothing few people suspected he was a soldier. He looked more like a lawyer, a CPA, a member of any number of sedentary professions.

Felter raised his head toward the Schloss, which was enormous, although not quite the sort of building that comes to mind with the word "castle."

"What time is the changing of the guard?" he asked.

"It's even larger than I remembered," Ilse said. "And it's even worse because most of the furniture is gone."

"What happened to it?" Sharon asked, innocently. Ilse was embarrassed. "Did I ask the wrong question?"

"I think Ilse found out that the furniture was 'liberated' by the Americans," Sandy said.

"It's not important," Ilse said. "What are we standing here for? Come on in, I'll get you something to eat and drink."

"I need the you-know-what," Sharon said. "My kidneys can't take thirty miles of cobblestone roads."

Ilse took her and the Felter kids off to the toilet. Sandy Felter was left alone in what obviously had been the library. The walls were lined with empty shelves, and in a corner, obviously awaiting a rail to roll along, a library ladder rested against the wall.

"My dear Captain Felter," a male voice cried in English, "you must forgive my manners. Have you been left all alone?"

"It's very nice to see you again, Graf von Greiffenberg," Felter said, in German.

"You are our first guests," the Graf said. "Which seems, under the circumstances, and despite the condition of the house, very appropriate."

"You're very kind to have us," Felter said.

The change in the Graf von Greiffenberg since Felter had seen him last was remarkable. On June 26—he remembered the date because it was the day the North Koreans had come across the 38th parallel—he had met the Graf at the Marburg exit of the autobahn. Less than thirty-six hours before that, the Graf had come across the East-West German border, finally released from Russian imprisonment. The Gehlen Organization kept people at the border points, and an hour after he had crossed, while he was still en route to the returned prisoner camp, Felter had been informed by telephone of his release.

The colonel had taken it upon himself to get off the train at Bad Hersfeld to see an old friend, and they'd had a hell of a time finding him, even with agents of the U.S. Army Counterintelligence Corps enlisted to locate him. The CIC had found him. They had agents waiting for him when he walked out of the bahnhof in Marburg. Felter had been notified, at Kronberg Castle, the U.S. Army VIP guest house outside Frankfurt am Main, where he had been waiting with Lt. Colonel Bob Bellmon and Craig and Ilse Lowell, and he'd gone and picked him up.

The cadaverous, musty smelling survivor of five years in Siberia—five years under an "official" death sentence, five years of not knowing if today they would take him out and garrot him, or shoot him, or run over him with a truck, or otherwise take his life in an "accident" or "while trying to escape," five years of not knowing what had happened to his family, or if he still had a family—had been reunited with his daughter at Kronberg Castle. He learned not only that she had survived the war, but that she had married and borne a son. And that his daughter's husband was a wealthy investment banker with sufficient political influence to have a French entry visa waiting, so that the colonel could be flown by chartered aircraft to Paris, where he would "be more comfortable."

The Graf von Greiffenberg was still thin, three months later, but no longer cadaverous. His eyes were no longer either sunken or bloodshot, and he smelled, Sandy thought, of expensive soap and aftershave. He was dressed in a blue, open-collared shirt, gray flannel slacks, and American loafers. But he was, Sandy thought with one corner of his mind, obviously both German and an aristocrat. Somewhat nastily, Felter thought that money could indeed work miracles—and was ashamed of himself as quickly as the thought popped into his mind.

The Graf looked around the room, and gestured at the empty shelves.

"I missed my books, most of all," he said. "In the East. And I miss them now. Furniture can be replaced. Walls can be repainted, floors refinished. But there were books in this room that simply . . ." He cut himself off, and went to a cabinet beneath the empty shelves, opened it, and came out with a large, leather-bound book and put it in Felter's hands. "The Nazis, and then Americans, and finally the democratically elected government of Land and Kreis Marburg left me this," he said. "Ironic, isn't it?"

Felter took the book and opened it to the title page.

"Russian," the Graf said. "They didn't take the Russian books."

"Reminiscences of the Crimean Campaign," Felter read. "By Major General the Grand Duke Alexander Alexandrovich, Commander of His Imperial Majesty's Kiev Guard."

"My late wife's kinsman," the Graf said. "Great, great uncle, I think." He spoke in Russian, then said what he was thinking. "Your Russian, my dear Felter, is better than mine."

"My great, great, great uncle," Felter said with a smile, "was probably a conscript in the Grand Duke's infantry."

"And do you find your command of Russian valuable in your military career, my dear Felter?"

Felter met his eyes, and paused a moment before replying. "Often of great value," he said.

"I no longer know anyone whom I might contact," the Graf said. "But I have thought, over the years, that my knowledge and experience might be of some use."

"I'm sure it would be," Felter said. "Perhaps after you get your feet on the ground, and the word gets around that you're home, something will turn up."

"Perhaps," the Graf said. "Forgive the imposition, after everything you've done for me, Felter, but I was hoping that you . . ."

"I have reason to believe that you won't have to ask for work, Colonel," Felter said.

The Graf was pleased. He nodded, and changed the subject. He had been determined to bring the subject up with Felter, who was an intelligence officer, but he was afraid that he would appear too eager, and be thought an anticommunist zealot. At the upper echelons of what he wanted to do, there was no room for zealots. He wondered what Felter knew, but he knew he should not, could not ask. He would have to let them come to him.

"Ilse heard from Craig today," the Graf said. "A letter mailed five days ago in Korea, delivered here today. The world is shrinking."

"What did he have to say?" Felter asked.

"His unit is about to be reequipped with M46 tanks," the Graf said. "The . . . what is that marvelous word you Americans use? The *pipeline*. Craig wrote that 'the *pipeline* was apparently finally in place and beginning to spew forth a cornucopia of materiel.'"

"Craig should have been born a hundred years ago," Felter said.

"Why do you say that?"

"In the days when noblemen raised their own regiments," Felter said.

"Yes," the Graf said and smiled.

"Colonel the Duke of Lowell's Squadron of Dragoons," Felter said. He chuckled. *"They* would have ridden unscathed through the Valley of Death at Balaclava."

The Graf chuckled with him.

"They call him that, you know," Felter said. "They call him 'the Duke' and he loves it."

The Graf laughed out loud. "I didn't know that, but it doesn't surprise me at all."

Sharon Felter and Ilse Lowell appeared at the door to the library, and saw the two men laughing. They looked at one another, and wordlessly agreed not to disturb them. They turned and walked back down the wide corridor. Ilse Lowell put her head into the kitchen (like the rest of the house, it showed the signs of rehabilitation: mason's and painter's and carpenter's tools and equipment put away over the weekend) and asked a plump, gray-haired woman if she would make tea, "and ask Rosa to serve it in the garden."

Then the two women went into the garden and sat down at an obviously new wrought-iron table under a striped umbrella. Ilse took a cigarette from her purse, held it up in offer to Sharon, and when Sharon shook her head, "no," put the pack back in her purse.

"Go ahead," Sharon said, "if it makes you feel good."

Ilse lit the cigarette. She told Sharon of the letter she'd had that morning from Craig. A maid, Rosa, delivered tea, which was actually a selection of cold cuts (all beef and veal, in deference to the Felters) and cheese and breads, in addition to the tea.

Sharon surreptitiously examined the bread, and found it without fault. It occurred to her that she was a long way here from the bakery on the corner of Chancellor Avenue and Aldine Street in Newark, New Jersey, where she had grown up two doors down the street from Sandy.

Sharon Lavinsky had been a year behind Sandy Felter all the way through school; she literally could not remember a time when she did not sense they belonged together. And she had known that Sandy was someone really special, smarter and stronger than anybody she had ever known.

His brains had gotten him into West Point. The congressman had gotten in trouble about passing out appointments to the service academies, and had announced that from now on he would make all appointments on the basis of competitive examinations. Sandy walked away with the exam, getting fifteen more points than the man in the second place.

Sandy's parents and Sharon's parents were of a mixed mind about Sandy taking the appointment when it was offered to him. With a brain and an academic record like his, he could really make something of himself: a doctor, a lawyer, even a judge. Even a dentist or a CPA was better than being a soldier. On the other hand, the war was on, and as long as he was at West Point, he would be safe. Sandy was the Class of 1946, and by then the war would be over and he wouldn't have to go.

What the Felters didn't know, nor the Levinskys, nor even Sharon herself, was that Sandy wanted to go to West Point because he wanted to be a soldier. He was going there to go to war, not to get out of it. His parents and hers, and Sharon herself, began to suspect this after a while, but they told each other that he would grow out of it, that he would come to his senses.

Sharon believed this. When they went up the Hudson to see him in his plebe year, he looked like a dwarf around the others, most of whom looked like football players. He didn't look as if he belonged.

And then he did something that made everybody, Sharon included, think he had lost his mind. When he came home on his Christmas leave in 1944, he told her that if she loved him, she was going to have to trust him to do what he thought was right. At first, Sharon thought he wanted them to do something together they shouldn't. She thought about it a moment, and decided that if that's what Sandy really wanted to do, all right.

But it wasn't that (Sharon and, she was sure, Sandy, too, went virginal to their wedding bed). It was a lot worse than that. Sandy, who was always reading anything he could get his hands on, had come across an army regulation which authorized the direct commissioning of linguists. He spoke Russian and German and Polish and had studied French for four years in high school, so he spoke that, too, although not as well.

They tried to talk him out of it at West Point, and actually got pretty nasty about it, he told her, before they finally gave in. But they gave in.

On 1 January 1945, while the Battle of the Bulge was still raging in Europe, Cadet Corporal Felter was discharged from the Corps of Cadets of the United States Military Academy at West Point, and immediately commissioned into the Army of the United States as Second Lieutenant, Infantry (Detail: Military Intelligence as Linguist). They swore him in at the breakfast formation, and the band played "Army Blue" ("We Say Farewell to Kay-Det Gray and Don the Army Blue") and "Dixie." Then, as the Corps of Cadets marched off to breakfast, Second Lieutenant Felter was driven to the railroad station. At four that afternoon he was over the Atlantic, en route to the 40th Armored Division, "Hells' Circus."

When Sandy came home, he insisted they get married in the chapel at West Point. If their rabbi wanted to marry them, fine; otherwise, they would be married by an army chaplain. They would have the reception in the Hotel Thayer, which was a hotel owned by the army. He told her that it would be important to her later, to be able to say that she had been married at West Point.

So they had been married at West Point, in a very nice

ceremony. A few of the members of Sandy's old class, '46, showed up. They said that as far as they were concerned, Sandy was still one of them, and they gave him a '46 class ring, and they gave Sharon a miniature of it. That made it better.

Sandy hadn't gone back to West Point, although he could have, because he had found out he could get a college degree by correspondence from the University of Chicago. Sharon went with Sandy to Fort Benning, where he went through the Parachute School, and then to Fort Bragg, where he went through the Ranger School.

"I'll probably never jump out of another airplane," Sandy told her. "And they don't want me in the Rangers. But that's part of the game, and I have to play it."

"What game?" she'd asked him.

"The army is like the boy scouts," he said. "They have a system of merit badges. The more merit badges you have, the better. I'll get jump wings from Benning, and a little strip with 'Ranger' on it at Bragg, and then I'll have as many merit badges as someone of my age and rank is supposed to have. That's the way the game is played."

So he became a paratrooper and a Ranger, and Sharon thought they would probably spend two or three years at Fort Bragg, while Sandy did what young officers were supposed to do—two years, preferably three, duty with troops.

But as the honor graduate of the Ranger School, he was given his choice of assignments, and he chose what Sharon thought was the worst one. He volunteered for duty with something called the U.S. Army Military Advisory Group, Greece (USAMAG-G). Dependents were not authorized in Greece. She would be left behind again, for a year, maybe more.

Sharon's mother cried, and said Sandy had a devil in him, and Sandy's mother was ashamed of what her son had done to Sharon. But he went. Greece was where he met Craig Lowell. Sandy wrote (often every day) and he told her about Craig. At first, to tell the truth, he hadn't liked Craig Lowell. Lowell had been sent to Greece as some kind of punishment, and Lowell didn't like the army. But as the letters kept coming, Sharon detected that Sandy was changing his mind about Lowell, and that they were becoming friends. Sharon was pleased that Sandy had found a friend. All of his life, he had really been friendless.

Sandy also wrote that he was an administrative officer, in charge of supplies. He painted a picture of himself safe behind a desk, but when he sent a roll of film home, and she got it back from the drugstore, she knew he was lying to her. Four of the pictures on the roll were of dead people. One of them showed a large, blond, good-looking young man who looked American. He was holding a Garand rifle in his hand, smiling proudly like a hunter in Africa, with his foot on the chest of a dead man with a long mustache and a bullet hole in the middle of his forehead.

The same young man was in other pictures on the roll; in one of them he was sitting with Sandy at a table, holding his fingers up in a V behind Sandy's head in a picture of six people. Sandy was carrying a gangsters' tommy gun and the young man was carrying a rifle, and Sharon knew two things: The good looking young man was Sandy's friend Craig Lowell, and what Craig Lowell and Sandy were doing was fighting a war, no matter what Sandy wrote he was doing.

Sandy wrote her that he felt sorry for Craig, that as smart and as tough as he was, he had been taken in by a girl in Germany, a girl of low morals who was making a fool of him. She hadn't written him once since he'd come to Greece, and Lowell was nearly crazy over it.

And then there had been a letter from Sandy saying that Craig had been "injured" and that he would probably be sent home, and would come to see her. He warned her not to bring up the fraulein he'd gotten into the mess with.

Three weeks later, in the Old Warsaw Bakery, glancing out the plate-glass window while she waited on customers, Sharon saw a limousine, even fancier than the Cadillac limousines the funeral homes used, turn off Chancellor Avenue. Sharon went over to the window to see if it was going to stop.

It pulled to the curb halfway down the block, and a chauffeur in a gray uniform ran around and opened the door and a young man got out. Limping a little, the young man started to walk toward the bakery, carrying the suitcase, and Sharon Lavinsky Felter went back behind the counter, so that Sandy's friend

Craig Lowell wouldn't know that she had seen him get out of a fancy limousine.

The next week was tough on Sharon. Craig, who slept on the couch in the Felters' apartment, talked about nothing but Ilse. He said he was waiting for his passport, so he could fly to Germany and marry her. Sharon was very tempted to tell Craig that Sandy—who was generally right about things like that—felt he was being made a fool of, but she couldn't bring herself to do it.

Craig flew to Germany, and came back married, and told Sharon his Ilse was pregnant. He said he didn't give a shit what anybody else thought, including Sandy. He knew Sandy thought Ilse was a kraut whore, but it was important to him that Sharon know that Ilse was a good woman.

Craig asked Sharon if she would meet Ilse when she came to New York from Germany, and see that she got on a plane to Louisville. Craig was in the Basic Armor Officer's Course at Fort Knox, near Louisville, and he didn't think the bastards would give him time off to come to New York to meet Ilse himself.

The first thing Sharon thought when she looked into Ilse Lowell's tear-filled eyes was that when Sandy was wrong, he was really wrong. This was no whore. This was an seventeen-year-old girl who was six months' pregnant and thoroughly terrified.

"Could I kiss you?" was the first thing Sharon Felter had ever said to Ilse Lowell.

In the Lavinsky Chevrolet on the way to New Jersey, Ilse said there had been "a terrible mix-up about the ticket." When she got to Rhine-Main, they had a First Class Royal Ambassador Drawing Room in the Skies ticket waiting for her.

"I asked what the difference in price was," Ilse said. "And would you believe it was two and a half times the price of a regular seat? I made them give me the difference back. We're going to need all our money for the baby." She opened her purse and displayed the money.

Sharon had decided that if Ilse didn't know Craig was rich, it was not her business to tell her. And she was pleased, too, to have the proof that Ilse hadn't gone after Craig because he was rich.

Peter-Paul Lowell was born in the U.S. Hospital at Fort Knox, Kentucky, shortly before his father graduated from the Basic Officer's Course. Sandy and Sharon saw him for the first time there, when Sandy came home from Greece and they were on their way to the Army Language School at the Presidio in San Francisco.

They later figured out that it was in the guest bedroom of Lieutenant Lowell's quarters (a converted barracks) that she and Sandy had started Little Sandy.

After the Language School, Sandy had gone to the Counterintelligence Corps (CIC) Center at Fort Holabird in Baltimore. The general's wife there had all the ladies in for a tea, and then given them a little speech saying the best way they could help their husbands' careers from now on was not to try to share it; not to ask questions; not even to think about it, just to provide a warm nest.

At first she'd liked the CIC. Sandy was assigned to the detachment in New York City. He wore civilian clothes, and they lived with his parents on Aldine Street. He went to work every morning just as if he was a businessman, even carrying a briefcase. That had lasted about five months.

Just after Craig had gotten out of the army, and he and Ilse were in Philadelphia where Craig was enrolled in the Wharton School of Business, Sandy and Sharon and Little Sandy went to Berlin.

The only question she'd asked Sandy was if he was still in the CIC and he told her no, he wasn't. She didn't like Berlin. Physically, it was all right. They had a very nice house in Zehlendorf. There was even a yard man and a driver. The yard man was never very far from his wheelbarrow, and in the wheelbarrow were a two-way radio and a submachine gun. The driver carried a gun, and Sandy carried a gun.

And then, all of a sudden, they left Berlin and went to Garmisch-Partenkirchen, in Bavaria. Sandy put his uniform back on, but he still carried a pistol all the time, under his uniform, and they lived in a compound surrounded by barbed wire. They had tried to hide the barbed wire, but it was there, and Sharon had never grown used to it.

She did not ask, or allow herself to think much, about what Sandy was doing. They were together, and he was happy, and she was happy, too.

For a while, it had looked like everything was perfect. Sandy had found out that Ilse's father wasn't dead after all, and then he had found out that he was going to be released by the Russians. He'd talked to her about that, asked her advice.

"What do I do, Sharon? Do I tell her? So that she can be here when her father comes across the border? Or do I wait until he does? In case something goes wrong?"

"Are you sure of your information?"

He thought about it a minute. "My sources are reliable."

"Then you'd better tell her," Sharon told him, and he did. And Craig and Ilse and P.P. had flown over, and were waiting for her father when he came home, after all that time in a Soviet prison camp in Siberia.

Everything was just perfect for them, and then the army had called Craig back in, and just about the next day sent him to Korea.

"At least," she had told Sandy, "if something happens to Craig, Ilse has her father."

Sandy said something funny: "Craig is not the kind that gets killed in a war, Sharon. He's the kind that thrives on it."

Sharon didn't believe that. She was nearly as worried about Craig as Ilse was, and she wondered why, whether it was for him or for Ilse. She concluded that it was because of Ilse, and when she asked herself why that was, she realized that Ilse was the first real friend she had ever had, too, the first friend she had loved, rather than just gotten along with.

"Why don't you and P.P. come and see us for a couple of weeks," Sharon asked. "Bavaria, the mountains, are just beautiful this time of the year."

"Do you have room?" Ilse asked.

"All the room we'll need."

"I'd like that," Ilse said, and Sharon was pleased for the both of them.

And she was pleased for everybody when she saw Sandy

and the colonel having such a good time together. It was a crying shame that Craig had to be so far away, in Korea.

(Two)
Pusan, Korea
12 September 1950

The harbor of Pusan was crowded with ships. There were gray warships and troop ships and supply ships of the U.S. Navy, and a motley assortment of civilian ships—cargo ships, tankers, even two passenger ships. And the white-painted hospital ship, the USS *Consolation*.

A steady stream of lighters moved between the inadequate piers and the ships, off-loading all sorts of supplies. Only when there was something aboard that could not be off-loaded into a lighter or a barge was a ship given pier space. Even the troops disembarked by climbing down rope cargo nets into small boats and Coast Guard landing barges.

Lt. Colonel Paul T. Jiggs, commanding officer of the 73rd Medium Tank Battalion (Separate), stood on the wharf of Pier One and watched as M46 medium tanks were off-loaded.

Teams of Ordnance Corps technicians, who themselves had often been in Korea only a day or two, had gone out to the transport when she was still waiting her turn to come to a pier, and had readied the tanks for instant movement. They ripped the protective coverings from the engines, charged the batteries, and fueled the tanks, then started the engines and ran them long enough to make sure they would run.

An M46 weighs forty-four tons. The ship that had carried them from San Francisco, as huge as it was, leaned toward the pier as each tank was hoisted from her holds and swung over the side. It straightened again when the tank's weight was on the pier.

Ordnance noncoms got in the tanks before the cables were taken off, and started the engines. Then, when the cables were free, being hauled up and back over the holds, they drove the M46s off the pier.

The tanks were freshly painted. They looked new. They *smelled* new, as the paint burned off their exhaust manifolds.

They were fresh from ordnance depots across the United States. But they weren't truly new tanks. They were M26s which had been rebuilt, incorporating a new turret cannon, a high-velocity 90 mm tube with a muzzle brake and a powder fume extractor; a new power train, a brand-new GM Allison combined cross drive and steering unit that made the M46 considerably easier to drive (all the driver had to do was push a "joy stick" in the direction he wanted to go, and that was it—wrestling the double levers of an M4A3 would soon be an thing of the past); and a new, more powerful Continental 12-cylinder engine.

The M26 with the new cannon and new engine and new power train were reborn as the M46, the Patton, named after the general.

Colonel Jiggs had come to Pier One to see for himself that the M46s were indeed on hand, and not the wishful figment of some G-3 planner's imagination. The reason was that the M46s being taken off the ship, and driven off the pier, were Colonel Jiggs's M46s.

He had come to Pier One from a meeting with the deputy chief of staff and the assistant chiefs of staff, G-1, G-3, and G-4 (Personnel, Plans and Training, and Supply) at the forward headquarters of the Eighth United States Army. He had learned that, as of 0001 hours that morning, the 73rd Medium Tank Battalion, (Separate) had become the 73rd Heavy Tank Battalion (Reinforced).

Instead of three line companies and a headquarters and service company, he would now command five tank companies, all M46s with that beautiful 90 mm high-velocity cannon; one cavalry troop, equipped with M24 light tanks, for reconnaissance purposes; two batteries of 105 mm howitzers, self-propelled (howitzers mounted on an M4 chassis); an ordnance ammo platoon; an ordnance maintenance platoon; a Transportation Corps truck company; a Signal Corps communications platoon; a medical team detached from the 8005th MASH; and two companies of mechanized infantry.

The ordnance types unloading the tanks before his eyes belonged to him, although they didn't know it yet.

73rd Medium Tank had become a combat command in

everything but name. Its size made it a command calling for a full colonel, possibly even a brigadier general. But they were giving it to him.

"I'm not going to sit here with my thumb up my ass wondering," he had told them. "Do I get to keep this beautiful pocket division you're giving me, or am I going to be relieved as soon as I get it organized?"

"If you can get it together and keep it together for the next month, Paul," the assistant chief of staff had told him, "it's yours."

Jiggs had nodded, deciding the assistant chief of staff would not have said that if it weren't true. He had done a damned good job with the 73rd, and they knew it. He was entitled to a chance with this pocket armored division they were setting up.

"You want to borrow some staff officers?" the assistant chief of staff said. "That's a lot of spaghetti to hold on one fork."

"No, sir," Jiggs said. "My staff is fine the way it stands."

"Anything you need, Paul," the G3 said. "Speak up. Quickly."

"Thank you, sir."

(Three)

When the last of the forty-two M46s had been off-loaded onto Pier One, Lieutenant Colonel Paul T. Jiggs drove back to the command post, slowly, knowing what he had to do, wondering if it was the right thing, wondering if he could carry it off.

When he was almost at the command post, he made a U-turn on the main supply route and drove a mile back to the MASH. He found the commanding officer, an old acquaintance, but not an old friend, in one of the wards and asked him for a few minutes of his time.

There was no problem. The MASH commander was as much an old soldier as he was a surgeon. He didn't even ask any questions. He simply nodded his head and agreed to do what Jiggs asked. It was the kindest way to do an unkind thing that had to be done for the overall good of the army.

Jiggs then drove back to his CP and went to the S-3 (Plans and Training) section. The S-3, looking somewhat haggard, was bent over thick mounds of paper on his desk, a sheet of three-quarter-inch plywood set on two-by-four sawhorses. It was a moment before the S-3 was aware that Jiggs was standing by the desk.

"Yes, sir?" he said. "Sorry, Colonel, I was pretty deep in that."

"Get your pot, Charley," Colonel Jiggs said. "I want you to take a ride with me."

Jiggs drove them out of the battalion area, down the main supply route (MSR) back toward Pusan, and then turned off onto a finger of land looking down on the ships crowding Pusan Harbor. It was a wet and miserable day, raining, and yet warm enough for the putrid stink from the rice paddies to be heavy in the air. A shitty smell, Colonel Jiggs thought, to go with a shitty job to do on a shitty day.

"Charley," he said, when he had stopped the jeep and turned sideward on the seat to face him, "how much service do you have?"

"Sixteen years, Colonel."

"I want to talk to you about you," Jiggs said.

"Yes, sir?" There was the faintest suggestion of concern, even alarm, in Major Ellis's voice.

"As of 0001 this morning," Jiggs said, "we are, in everything but name, a combat command. Our morning report strength tomorrow will be two and a half times what it was today."

"That sounds like good news, sir."

"Not for you, it isn't," Jiggs said, finally biting the bullet. Shit, get it over with. "You can't handle it."

"I'm sorry you feel that way, Colonel," Ellis said. "I've tried to do my best."

"That hasn't been good enough," Jiggs said. "We both know that Lowell's been carrying you."

"I'm afraid I can't accept that, sir," Ellis said. "Certainly,

Captain Lowell has been a great help to me, but—"

"Let me make my position clear," Jiggs interrupted him. "You are going to be relieved. That's been settled. The only question is how."

"Sir," Ellis said, "I will protest my relief."

"Are you that stupid?" Jiggs said, trying to sound more angry than he really felt. He really felt lousy, not angry.

"I resent that, sir," Ellis said.

"Resent it all you want," Jiggs said, "but get it through your head that I've got you by the balls. Don't you threaten me with an official complaint."

Ellis seemed to be forming several replies, but in the end he said nothing.

"What I really have in mind, Major, is the good of the unit. Above all else. And I know you're the same kind of a soldier— the outfit comes first."

"I like to think of myself that way, Colonel."

"Now, I can relieve you as of this moment, Ellis, and you can complain to Walton Walker himself, and you'll stay relieved. If you think that through, you'll know I'm right."

"You have that prerogative, sir."

"To do that, it would be necessary for me to write an efficiency report on you that would keep you from getting any other responsible assignment, and more than likely, would see you finishing out your twenty years with stripes on your sleeve."

Ellis looked at him, met his eyes, but said nothing for a moment. Finally, he said: "I've tried to give you my best, Colonel."

"I know you gave me your best, and I'm grateful to you for doing it; but your best simply has not been good enough."

"You're talking about Lowell, of course," Ellis said. "Colonel, he's a graduate of the Wharton School of Business. He's got a mind like a goddamned adding machine. I have to work at it, look things up. He remembers them."

"I have never for a moment believed you weren't giving me the best you had to give, Charley," Jiggs said. "But it's not good enough."

"I appreciate your breaking this to me as gently as you could, Colonel," Major Ellis said after a moment. "I won't bitch. You knew I wouldn't."

"I'm not through, Charley," Jiggs said. "I want more from you. And I'll tell you what I'll do for you in return."

"What else can you want? I've already agreed to cut my own throat."

"I want Lowell as my S-3," Jiggs said.

"The minute you relieve me, G-1 will send you a replacement. And if they've doubled the size, more than doubled the size, of the outfit, they're liable to send you a light bird. Two light birds, one to be your exec. Or, shit, you're liable to get ranked out of your job."

"I've been promised the job for thirty days. They didn't say it, but if I get through the next thirty days, I'll get an eagle. If I don't . . . up the creek."

"In any event, there's no way you can make Lowell your S-3," Ellis said.

"If my S-3 is Absent in Hospital," Jiggs said, "I can give him the job temporarily. And after thirty days, I can promote him."

"Is that what all this is about? Getting a promotion for Lowell? Christ, he's not old enough to be a captain."

"What this is all about is providing the outfit with the best S-3 I can," Jiggs said, rather coldly.

"I'm sorry," Ellis said. "I'm a little shaken. I hadn't expected any of this. Shit, what am I going to tell my wife?"

"If you want to, you can tell her you're having a little trouble with your back, which is why you're in the hospital. Give me a month in the hospital, Charley, and I'll give you a good efficiency report and have you sent home."

"That won't work," Ellis said. "They won't keep me at the MASH. They'll either send me back here, or to Japan."

"I've got that fixed," Jiggs said. "I know the MASH commander."

"You know what's funny, Colonel?" Ellis said. He didn't wait for Jiggs to reply. "Now that it's out in the open, I'm not ashamed. Goddamnit, I did my best."

"Yes, you did," Jiggs said. "This would have been a lot easier for me, Charley, if you hadn't."

(Four)

Back at the MASH, Colonel Jiggs found a sergeant and sent him to fetch the MASH commander.

"This is Major Charley Ellis, Howard," Jiggs said. "Treat him right."

"We'll start him off with a shot of medicinal bourbon," the MASH commander said. "And then a hot bath, and then we'll see what's wrong with his lower back."

Ellis reached over and shook Jiggs's hand before he got out of the jeep. Jiggs watched him walk toward the Admitting Tent. Ellis turned and looked at him. Jiggs raised his hand in a crisp salute. Ellis returned it just as crisply, and then went inside.

Jiggs turned his jeep around and drove to the CP.

He saw the sergeant major.

"Put Major Ellis's shaving gear, other personal stuff, in a bag and have someone—you, if you have the time—carry it to him at the MASH. Then ask Captain Lowell to come here."

"He's in S-3, Colonel," the sergeant major said.

"Well, then," Colonel Jiggs said, "we won't have to send for him, will we?" Then he went into S-3 and informed Captain Lowell that he was now acting S-3 of the 73rd Heavy Tank Battalion (Reinforced).

VIII

(One)
Pusan, South Korea
12 September 1950

The S-3 sergeant of the 73rd Medium Tank Battalion (Separate) was Technical Sergeant Prince T. Wallace, RA 33 107 806, of Athens, Georgia. Prince Wallace was a tall, heavy, barrel-chested man of thirty-one. He had been drafted during World War II, served in the North Africa, Normandy, and French campaigns, and had commanded the third tank in the task force under Colonel Creighton W. Abrams in the relief of Bastogne. As a master sergeant, loaded with points for long overseas service, and with decorations for valor and for having been three times wounded, he had been among the first of the troops repatriated and discharged after the war.

He enrolled under the GI Bill of Rights at the Valdosta State Teacher's College in his native Georgia, and completed a year of college training. By then he had come to the conclusion that he really didn't want to be a schoolteacher, and that the prospect of three more years in college was something he didn't want to face. He also decided that he really missed the army, so he went to Fort MacPherson, in Atlanta, and reenlisted.

Since he had been out of the army more than ninety days, he had lost the right to reenlist as a master sergeant. He reentered the army as a private first class and underwent an abbreviated basic training course at Fort Bragg. He was then assigned to the G-3 section, Headquarters V Corps at Bragg, as a clerk-draftsman. He applied for Officer Candidate School, was accepted, and was promoted to corporal before his orders to the OCS at the Ground General School at Fort Riley, Kansas, came through.

In his fourth month at OCS, it seemed quite clear to him that in the shrinking army there was going to be less and less room for officers who did not have a college degree. Looking into the future, he saw himself as a first lieutenant, possibly even a captain, who would be "nonselected" for retention on extended active duty as a reserve officer. There was no way he could qualify for a regular army commission because he did not have a college degree, and no way that he could see to get a college degree. Five or ten years down the road, he would be starting out as an enlisted man again, for the third time.

There was a third possibility for an army career, one which posed few risks. That was appointment as a warrant officer. An "officer" is correctly a "commissioned officer." That is to say, he has a commission, signed by the President of the United States, naming him an officer. Corporals and sergeants are called "noncoms," from noncommissioned. They have no commission. They issue orders under the authority of a commissioned officer. Warrant officers have warrants. They too are not officers (they cannot command), although they are entitled to a salute from enlisted men and their own juniors; and the pay of the four warrant officer grades (Warrant Officer Junior Grade, and Chief Warrant Officer Grades Two through Four) is identical to that of second lieutenant through major. Warrant Officers live in BOQs, eat at officer's messes, and are addressed as "sir" by enlisted men.

Warrant officers were traditionally expert in some military skill, from Explosive Ordnance Disposal to Enlisted Pay. Traditionally, noncommissioned officers in the top two enlisted grades were offered appointment as warrant officers, either directly, because of some skill they had, or as the result of competitive examination. Being made a warrant, and thus accorded the respect paid to an officer, was sort of the unofficial bonus paid to noncoms of long and faithful service. They spent their last few years in an officer's uniform, and were retired with the pay of a captain or a major.

Prince Wallace thought that was the way he would like to go. He would become an expert S-3 sergeant, highly skilled in the planning of military operations and the training required to carry them out, and he would, sooner or later, get his warrant. He would thus have the good life of the officer without the responsibility, and without running the risk of being busted back to the ranks.

Corporal Prince T. Wallace, having voluntarily resigned from Officer Candidate Status, was ordered to the Far East Command (FECOM) and ultimately assigned to the S-3 section of the 7th Cavalry Regiment, First Cavalry Division (Dismounted) on the island of Hokkaido, again as a clerk-draftsman. He was ordered to the First Cavalry Division's NCO Academy, and as a reward for having graduated at the top of his class, promoted sergeant. He was reassigned to First Cavalry Division (Dismounted) Headquarters, as Noncommissioned Officer in Charge (NCOIC) of the Logistics Section, Office of the Assistant Chief of Staff, Plans and Training, G-3. In the vernacular, he was now the First Cav's G-3 logistics sergeant.

A year later, he was promoted staff sergeant, and it was as a staff sergeant that he prepared to deploy to Korea when the gooks came across the border in June 1950. He made it as far as the dock, where his visibly and unashamedly furious G-3 informed him that those miserable sonsofbitches at Eighth Army (Rear) had grabbed him as cadre for some about-to-be-formed tank battalion, and how the fuck they expected the First Cav's G-3 section to function without trained people was something he didn't understand.

Staff Sergeant Prince T. Wallace made a good first impression on Lt. Colonel Paul T. Jiggs, newly appointed commander of the 73rd Medium Tank Battalion. Sergeant Wallace looked like a soldier. His hair was cropped closely to his skull, and his face was cleanly shaven. His fatigue uniform was starched and tailored to fit him like a second skin. His boots glistened.

For a couple of days, Lt. Colonel Jiggs toyed with the notion of making Wallace either the first sergeant of Headquarters and Service Company, or the sergeant major of the battalion itself. He had met both those senior noncommissioned officers and found them wanting.

But he had also met his S-3, Major Ellis, and formed the instant opinion that the man was going to need all the help he could get. Staff Sergeant Prince T. Wallace, who had been logistics sergeant for the First Cavalry Division G-3 section, was obviously the man to give him that help.

Colonel Jiggs took Staff Sergeant Wallace for a ride in his jeep and explained the situation to him. What the battalion needed was a good S-3 sergeant, even more than a sergeant major or a Headquarters and Service Company first sergeant. You could pick up sergeant majors and first sergeants anyplace; S-3 sergeants, *good* S-3 sergeants, were goddamned hard to find. Jiggs told Wallace that he recognized it was costing Wallace a couple of stripes, for the TO&E slot for an S-3 sergeant was only a technical sergeant, paygrade E6, as opposed to the paygrade E7 authorized for first sergeants and sergeants major. Staff Sergeant Wallace told Lt. Col. Jiggs that he understood the situation, and would do his best as the S-3 sergeant. Lt. Colonel Jiggs that same afternoon went to G-1 at Eighth Army and made an obnoxious prick of himself until the G-1, just to get rid of him, came through with authority to promote Staff Sergeant Wallace to technical sergeant, paygrade E6, immediately.

Jiggs's snap judgments of both Major Ellis and Sergeant Wallace were quickly vindicated. Without Wallace, Ellis would have fallen flat on his face. Ellis tried hard, but he just couldn't hack it. Jiggs tried very hard to have him replaced before the 73rd went to Korea, but there was simply nobody else around.

The first time Captain Craig W. Lowell met Technical Sergeant Wallace, he too formed a snap judgment, but not quite the "now *there's* a *noncom*" judgment of Lt. Colonel Jiggs. What Captain Lowell decided, when he became aware of Technical Sergeant Wallace's eyes surreptitiously on him, was, "Why, that big sonofabitch is as queer as a three-dollar bill."

Captain Lowell's snap judgment, like that of Lt. Colonel Jiggs, was one hundred percent on the money.

Captain Lowell had also decided that it was none of his business, that Wallace was Ellis's problem, and that unless he found out (and he would certainly make no special effort to find out) that Tech Sergeant Wallace was taking teenaged PFCs and corporals into the bunkers, he would not only say nothing but go out of his way to keep from even raising his eyebrows.

At first, Wallace was not very impressed with Captain Craig W. Lowell (except, of course, physically: Wallace thought Lowell was handsome to the point of beauty—like a fucking statue). He did not think it set a good example for an officer, particularly a company commander, to go around without his helmet, and with a Garand slung from his shoulder (two clips of ammo clipped to the strap, like a common rifleman) and a German Luger stuck in the waistband of his trousers instead of the .45 in a shoulder holster considered de rigeur for line-company tank officers. Captain Lowell, moreover, was doing a number of things either without permission or in direct contravention of regulations and the standing operating procedure (SOP).

Sergeant Wallace knew for a fact that Baker Company was drawing comfort rations (cigarettes, toilet paper, writing paper, beer, Coca-Cola, razor blades, and shaving cream) from both Eighth Army (where they were supposed to get them) and from the Korean Communications Zone depot (which supported the rear echelon troops not assigned to Eighth Army), where Captain Lowell had convinced the supply officer that his company wasn't getting anything from Eighth Army.

Wallace subsequently learned that the noncoms of Baker Company were actively engaged in the black market, almost certainly with Captain Lowell's tacit (and probably active) permission. The company's supply sergeant regularly took loads of fired brass 75 mm shell casings into Pusan, where instead of turning them in to the ordnance salvage dump, he bartered them with a Korean black marketeer. In return he would get Korean handicrafts of one form or another (most often things like cheap OD-colored cotton jackets with "I KNOW I'M GOING TO HEAVEN, BECAUSE I'VE SERVED MY TIME IN HELL—KOREA

1950" embroidered on them, or pictures of women with grotesquely outsized bosoms, painted on black velvet; but also some really rather beautifully engraved brass dishes, bowls, and ashtrays, made of course from the fired shell casings). The handicrafts themselves were then bartered. As a result, Baker Company always had ice from the Quartermaster Ice Point; it had its own movie projector and a steady supply of 16 mm films from Eighth Army Special Services; and most outrageous of all, Sergeant Wallace knew for a fact, it had its own rolling brothel, operating out of the back of an ambulance. The girls were actually delivered to the troops manning the tanks on the line, and plied their profession in the rear of the ambulance, which was equipped with a mattress, sheets, water for washing, and illuminated by a red night-light from a tank.

On the other hand, as Sergeant Wallace had to admit, Baker Company had the highest percentage of tracked vehicle availability in the battalion; the lowest incidence of heat exhaustion; an almost negligible VD rate; and most important, the highest combat efficiency. Captain Lowell lost fewer men, wounded or KIA, than any other company commander in the battalion; and Baker Company regularly killed more of the enemy than anybody else, because somehow Baker Company's tanks started when they were supposed to start, ran when everybody else's had succumbed to either overheating or old age, and fired whatever had to be fired.

However, it wasn't until Captain Lowell had started "helping out" in S-3 (when Major Ellis had been "snowed under"), that Sergeant Wallace really changed his mind about Captain Lowell. He came to respect Lowell, not only for his professional competence, but for his extraordinary tact and compassion in dealing with Major Ellis. Only he and the colonel, Sergeant Wallace was sure, were aware of what a square object in a round hole Major Ellis was. When he looked at Major Ellis, Sergeant Wallace saw himself (if he had gone through OCS and taken a commission) assigned duties he was simply not equipped to handle, which would have doubtless put him in grave risk of being knocked back to the ranks, if not thrown out of the army entirely.

Technical Sergeant Wallace had been in ths S-3 bunker

when the colonel came in and told Major Ellis to get his pot and go for a ride with him. He sensed that something unpleasant was happening, but he wasn't sure what. After Captain "Dead-eye" Lowell came in (with his M1 cradled in his arms like a hunting rifle and that German Luger stuck in his belt) and asked, "Where's the Boss?" he realized Captain Lowell didn't know either.

If anything was going to happen to Major Ellis, Sergeant Wallace knew that Captain Lowell would be among the first to know. When he told Captain Lowell the colonel had taken Major Ellis away, Captain Lowell seemed genuinely surprised. He went to one of the folding tables and asked Sergeant Wallace to get him the Wheeled Vehicle Status Report from the safe. Captain Lowell had been very careful about not asking for the combination to the safe; access to the material inside was limited to the commanding officer and the S-3 and, if the S-3 chose, to the S-3 sergeant. Company commanders, even one "helping out" as much as Captain Lowell did, were not supposed to have the combination.

Captain Lowell spent an hour with the Wheeled Vehicle Status Report, and finally came up with a list of vehicles, by serial number and date, to be turned in to the newly established Ordnance Wheeled Vehicle repair facility. The list was neatly typed; Captain Lowell typed nearly as neatly, as fast, and as accurately as Sergeant Wallace himself did.

"When the major returns, Sergeant Wallace, would you tell him those are my recommendations for the overhaul cycle?"

They both knew that Lowell's recommendations would be accepted entirely and without question. But they were playing the game. Wallace was delighted that Lowell had done the overhaul list; if Major Ellis had started on it, it would have been an all-day decision-making process. Major Ellis worried so much about making the wrong decisions and looking like a fool that he took forever to make any decision.

"Sir," Sergeant Ellis said, "may I ask the captain a somewhat personal question?"

"Shoot," Captain Lowell said.

"I've been wondering why the captain doesn't use a holster for the Luger, sir."

"Very good reason," Lowell said, with a smile. "Because it won't fit in a .45 holster. I'm aware that it offends your sense of propriety, Sergeant Wallace, but I don't know what to do about it."

"I have the most remarkable houseboy, sir, Kim Lee Song," Sergeant Wallace said. He saw Lowell's eyes tighten, and he thought: *He suspects*. But he went on. "He has connections to get things made of leather, sir. I don't mean the garbage you can buy along the side of the road. I mean quality goods."

"You think he can have a holster made for this?" Lowell said.

"I'm sure he could, sir," Wallace said.

Lowell pulled the Luger from his waist and handed it butt first to Wallace.

"There's a round in the chamber," he said. "Be careful with it." Then he reached in his pocket and passed over an oblong piece of brass. "I want that mounted on the holster somewhere," he said. Wallace looked at it, and after a moment recognized it as a German Army belt buckle. The words GOTT MIT UNS were cast into it.

"It came with the pistol," Lowell said, "and I want it on the holster."

It was, Sergeant Wallace recognized, something Lowell was not prepared to discuss.

"Yes, sir," Wallace said. "I understand."

"If Major Ellis wants me," Lowell said, "I'll be at the company."

"Yes, sir," Sergeant Wallace said.

A few moments later Colonel Jiggs entered the bunker. Sergeant Wallace called "attention," and the enlisted men jumped to their feet. Lowell continued what he was doing; his back turned to Wallace, he was tucking his shirt in his trousers.

"Rest," Jiggs said. "I was about to send for you, Lowell," he added.

"Yes, sir," Lowell said. "You caught me on my way out."

Jiggs took Lowell's arm and led him deeper into the bunker to Major Ellis's desk, and then handed him a piece of paper. Lowell's eyebrows went up as he read it. The colonel said something to him that Wallace couldn't hear, then patted Lowell on the arm, and walked out of the bunker. Lowell looked over at Wallace, and then sat down at Major Ellis's desk. He had never done that before, and Sergeant Wallace again sensed that something was up. Lowell motioned with his finger for Wallace to come over.

"Yes, sir?" Tech Sergeant Wallace asked.

"Major Ellis has been hospitalized with a lower back condition," Lowell said, his voice devoid of intonation. "I have just been named acting S-3."

"May I ask the captain how long the major will be gone?"

"At least thirty days," Lowell said.

"But it is not anticipated that a replacement for the major will be assigned?" Wallace asked.

"If anyone asks, Sergeant, we expect that the major will return tomorrow. Between you, me, and the colonel, however, the major will be gone at least thirty days."

"I'm sure the captain will be able to hold things down."

"You really think so, Wallace?" Lowell said. "Here's something else between you, me, and the colonel." He handed Wallace the small piece of paper Colonel Jiggs had handed him. It was a message form, and it had been filled out in pencil:

FROM: CG, ARMY EIGHT
TO: CO, 73RD HV TNK BN

MESSAGE: PREPARE TO MOVE REINFORCED COMPANY STRENGTH FORCE 75 MILES DIRECTION SUWON ON LINE PUSAN KOCHANG SUWON ON TWO HOURS NOTICE. EXPECT MOVEMENT ORDER WITHIN SEVEN DAYS.

WALKER
LT GEN

"We have been augmented by a bunch of troops," Lowell said. "The colonel is going to send a list over as soon as he has it copied. As soon as we have it, I want you to take a three-quarter-ton truck and go collect their company clerks."

"Sir?"

"Who knows more about a company than the company clerk?" Lowell asked. "And besides, most of them can type, and we're going to have a lot of typing to do around here in the next couple of days."

"Yes, sir," Wallace said.

"Wait a minute, Wallace," Lowell said.

"Sir?"

"I don't want anybody to know about this, or anything I do, or anything I tell you to do, but you, me, and the colonel."

"Of course, sir."

"From what I've seen of you, you're one hell of an S-3 sergeant, and I would miss you. But the minute you open your mouth, you're going to be back inside a tank. You understand me?"

"Yes, sir," Tech Sergeant Wallace said.

"I have enough trouble with the colonel as it is," Lowell said with a smile, "without having other people feed him arguments."

"I understand, sir."

"I'm glad you do, Sergeant Wallace," Lowell said. "You're a big sonofabitch, and if I can't get you to play ball with me, I'd frankly hate to have to stick the bat up your ass." He paused. "I would, of course. It would be difficult, but I would."

"I believe the captain and I understand each other, sir," Wallace said.

(Two)
Near Chinhae, South Korea
13 September 1950

Captain Philip S. Parker IV, commanding Tank Company, 24th Infantry, turned his jeep into a bowl in the terrain formed by a nearly complete circle of low hills, and stopped.

He looked up the rim of the bowl, examining the positions of his tanks. They were placed at more or less regular distances along the rim, right in with the infantry. Here and there were multiple .50 caliber machine guns, mounted on half-tracks, manned by artillerymen who had arrived in Korea expecting to sit on a hilltop someplace waiting for enemy airplanes and instead found themselves sitting between tankers and infantry-men on the front line.

Parker also looked at the dirt roads leading to his tanks and the half-tracks, as he did almost every day. He was looking for deterioration in the roads. He wanted to be sure that if they had to move the vehicles (if they had to bug out, in other words), they could.

He was an unimportant company commander, who had no idea of the big picture, but he had a gut feeling that things could not continue as they were. Either the North Koreans would get off their ass, and mount an offensive which would succeed in breaking through the Pusan perimeter, or the Americans would get off theirs and really counterattack.

There was some reason to believe the latter would be the case. There had been some replacements and some resupply. He had been astonished and pleased to see a column of brand-new M46 tanks rolling through Pusan one day. If there were M46 tanks, they could counterattack. He had experienced a moment's wild hope that he would be reequipped with M46s, but then had faced reality. The 24th Division—and his regiment—were on the Eighth Army shitlist. They were unreliable.

Eighth Army was not about to turn over new M46 tanks to the niggers. The niggers would more than likely promptly turn them over to the gooks, the way they had when they first came.

Even Tank Company of the 24th Infantry had given most of its tanks away before Parker had assumed command. That's what they would remember, not that after Parker had assumed command, Tank Company of the 24th hadn't lost one tank, or bugged out an inch without being ordered to do so.

It was known, Parker thought bitterly, as guilt by association, and there wasn't one fucking thing he could do about it.

He was a fourth-generation cavalry soldier, and he was convinced that he had fought as well, and been as good an officer, as his ancestors. But so far as Eighth Army was concerned, he was just one more nigger.

His father had warned him to expect this sort of thing. He had pointed out that the appellation "Buffalo Soldiers," applied to the 9th and 10th (Colored) Cavalry in the Plains and Indians war, had had nothing to do with the bison that roamed the plains, but had been a derogatory reference to the short, bristly, buffalo-like hair on the heads of the Negro troops.

He was surprised when an incoming artillery round detonated about seventy-five yards from where he sat in his jeep. You could usually hear them coming in. He hadn't heard this one until it went off. It was probably a single harrassing round, designed more to keep everybody nervous than for any other purpose. But you never could tell, and it never hurt to be careful. So far he had gone without so much as a scratch, even when things had been really hairy for a while. He had lost half the people he'd come to Korea with.

He reached down and flipped on the jeep's ignition switch, moving his right leg up so that he could tromp on the gas pedal at the same time. He felt something slippery.

What the fuck am I sitting in?

He looked down and saw that the seat was covered with something red, and that it was all over his pants. It was a moment before he realized what it was. He'd been hit; that red stuff was his blood.

He argued with himself: *I didn't feel a thing. How can I be hit, if I didn't feel a thing? How can I be hit if I don't feel a thing now?* But there was no goddamned question about it: that was blood.

He continued to start the engine. It didn't hurt him to move his leg. He put the jeep in gear, and drove to a battalion aid station, built against the slope of the hills, a sandbag-covered shack with a Red Cross sign leaning against it.

He blew the horn and a medic came out, and he waved him over to the jeep.

"Yes, sir?"

Parker pointed to the seat, and to his blood-covered rear end.

"What the hell happened?" the medic asked.

"I'll be goddamned if I know," Parker said.

"You got hit, Captain," the medic pronounced professionally.

"No shit," Parker said, sarcastically.

"Looks like a piece of shrapnel," the medic said. "Hurt much?"

"No," Parker said.

"It will," the medic said, matter-of-factly. "I think we better get you onto a stretcher, so's we can get you over to the MASH.

Way you're bleeding, you're going to have to go to the MASH."

It didn't hurt even to get out of the jeep, and to walk into the aid station. But almost as soon as he was face-down on a stretcher, and the medic had cut his fatigue pants away from his buttocks, it began to hurt. It began to hurt like hell.

The battalion surgeon, who had been asleep, was summoned, and he took one look at Parker's rear end and said that he wasn't in any danger. He would probably be back on duty in a month or six weeks, maybe sooner; but in the meantime, he could expect that it was going to hurt like hell.

"You better get some blood in him," the surgeon said to the medic. "And slap a compress on his ass. They can do the rest at the MASH."

Parker could cheerfully have kicked the surgeon in the balls.

Where were you wounded in the war, Daddy?

Why, Son, your heroic daddy caught one in the ass.

Shit!

(Three)
Headquarters, 73rd Heavy Tank Battalion (Reinforced)
Pusan, South Korea
14 September 1950

Surprising neither Lt. Colonel Paul T. Jiggs nor Technical Sergeant Prince C. Wallace, Captain Craig W. Lowell built Task Force Bengal, as the "reinforced company" was now known, around Company "B." Lowell was still officially the Baker Company commander, despite his "temporary" assignment as battalion S-3 ("pending the return of Major Ellis from the hospital"); and he transparently hoped to be given command of Task Force Bengal. If it was built around his company, his chances of that happening were obviously enhanced.

"You will notice, Sergeant Wallace," Lowell said, "that the word 'reinforced' in reference to the company to be reinforced has not been defined. The amount of reinforcement is being left to our judgment, that is to say, my judgment. I intend to err on the side of generosity."

Orders were drawn augmenting Company "B" by one platoon of M46s from Able Company and another from Charley

Company; and by a platoon of light M24s for "reconnaissance."

"'Reconnaissance' my ass; we'll use them to guard the fuel and ammo trucks," Lowell said. "We're going to reconnoiter by fire, with Wasps."

"'Wasps'?" Sergeant Wallace asked. He had never heard the term before.

"What you do is mount another .50 in the back of a weapons carrier," Lowell said. "And you make sort of a turret for the one in the back, and the one in the front, out of sandbags and old fuel drums. Then you barrel-ass down the road, shooting at anything that moves or that looks like it could be a machine gun or artillery emplacement. The natural tendency of people being shot at, Wallace, is to shoot back. And while they're shooting back at the Wasps, we blow them away with the M46s."

"But what about the people in the Wasps?"

"They run like hell at the first shot," Lowell said. "That makes them a lousy target, and at the same time their evasive action keeps the bad guys from thinking about the tanks, which can then, almost at their leisure, blow them away."

"Does the colonel know about the Wasps?" Wallace asked.

"Not yet," Lowell said.

"What do you think he will say when you tell him?"

"He will probably be just as enthusiastic about the Wasps as I am about the overly melodramatic name he's chosen for this little excursion of ours."

"I don't know, Captain," Wallace said, doubtfully.

"Do you understand what's really going on here?" Lowell asked.

"Maybe it would be better if you told me," Wallace replied.

"Well, take a look at the map. There is no railhead at Koch'ang. It is not a major road hub. The river is fordable at this time of year, so there's no bona fide necessity to grab the bridge. Which poses the question, why the fuck are we going to Koch'ang in the first place?"

"Forgive me, Captain. Because we're ordered to?"

"That, too, of course. But why the order?"

Wallace shrugged his admission of ignorance.

"To see what Eighth Army is facing behind the lines," Lowell said. "We're being sent out to see how far we can get before we get blown away."

"You're not suggesting that they're sacrificing us, are you?"

"They don't use that word, but don't you believe they give a shit what happens to us, just so they get the information they think they need."

"That's a brutal assessment."

"They call this war, you know," Lowell said dryly. "It's a perfectly reasonable thing for them to do. The question then becomes what do we do after we do what we are ordered to do."

"You've lost me," Wallace admitted.

"OK. We're ordered to Koch'ang. So we get to Koch'ang. Then what?" Wallace looked at him in confusion. "Look at it this way," Lowell went on. "Eighth Army is willing to spend us to find out how strong the North Koreans are between here and Koch'ang. OK, so we do that. Quicker than they think. So that leaves us in Koch'ang. So then we come back? That doesn't make any sense. To come back directly, I mean. Let's stay behind the lines and raise hell until we have to come back."

"We'd have to be supplied by air."

"Only with ammo. We can take enough fuel and rations with us. Make up a two-day ammo requirement. Triple ration for all the guns. Regular ration for small arms, except for .50 caliber. I want a lot of that."

"Yes, sir," Sergeant Wallace said. "But the colonel's not going to like this."

"Let's present him with a fait accompli and let him shoot that down."

"Yes, sir," Sergeant Wallace said. He was glad again that he hadn't taken a commission. Coming up with something like Captain Lowell had would have been impossible for him. He would never have dared to suggest, much less try to accomplish, something like Captain Lowell was doing. He wondered why he wasn't sure that Colonel Jiggs would shoot Captain Lowell down.

While Wallace prepared the lists of ammo requirements,

Lowell studied the maps. He triumphantly laid a proposed route before Wallace.

"This is what we'll do," he said. "It'll take us only the twenty-four hours, maybe less, that backtracking down our original line of advance would. We can take the airdrop either at Koch'ang, or better yet, here in this area."

"Yes, sir," Sergeant Wallace said, not wanting to argue with him, and not wanting to agree either.

"This'll turn Task Force Bengal—Jesus, what a lousy name—into a real tiger," Lowell said.

He laughed hard at his own pun, and it was contagious. Wallace joined in.

"I thought," Colonel Jiggs said, "that Task Force Bengal had a certain flair to it." They had not seen him come in.

Captain Lowell was embarrassed, Wallace saw, but he was not silenced.

"I've just been having a fascinating chat with Sergeant Wallace, sir," Lowell said. "He has come up with some very interesting ideas."

"Is that so?" the colonel asked. Wallace had no idea what Captain Lowell was talking about.

"The sergeant," Lowell said, "was pointing out on the map to me how we could turn this probing mission into a real, old-time, behind the lines cavalry raid." At that point, Colonel Jiggs realized whose ideas Lowell was advancing, but he winked at Wallace and didn't interupt Lowell.

"I've underestimated you, Sergeant Wallace," Lt. Colonel Jiggs said. "If I didn't know better, I would think that these ideas came from the fevered brain of someone who had gone to the Wharton School of Business."

"I have an idea or two of my own, Colonel," Lowell said.

"I'm sure you do," Lt. Colonel Jiggs said. "Just so that Wallace doesn't get all the glory."

"Wasps," Lowell said.

"I beg your pardon?"

"What you do is mount .50s in three-quarter-ton trucks," Lowell began.

"And you have a vision, do you, of riding in the lead, what

did you say, 'Wasp'? Leading, so to speak, this grand and glorious cavalry sweep?" Colonel Jiggs's remarks got to Lowell. He realized the colonel was mocking him, and he shut up.

Then the colonel said, "It might work. But have you got time to set something like that up?"

"Baker Company's got five ready to go, Colonel."

"You will ride in a tank," Colonel Jiggs said. "In an M46, not an M24, and you will be no closer to the point of the column than the fourth vehicle."

"May I infer from that that the colonel has decided I am to be allowed to command the column?" Lowell asked.

"Captain Lowell, where else am I to find someone who devoutly believes he is the combined reincarnation of George Armstrong Custer and George Smith Patton? Or dumb enough to try what you obviously intend to try?"

"Thank you, Colonel," Lowell said, and Sergeant Wallace saw that he said it humbly.

"Why 'Wasps'?" Colonel Jiggs asked.

"They sting," Lowell said. "You know, like a wasp."

"What an overly melodramatic nomenclature," Lt. Colonel Jiggs said dryly. "Why, that's nearly as bad as Task Force Bengal."

"My head, sir," Lowell said, "is both bloody and bowed."

"I came in here with one thing on my mind," Lt. Colonel Jiggs said. "Now I have three things. First, if you really think that you can go further and faster than anyone else does, you'd better think about what kind of supplies you'll need to have air-dropped."

"Sergeant Wallace has just about finished drawing up our requirements, sir," Lowell said.

"I can have them for you in an hour, sir," Wallace said.

"OK. That brings us to Item Two. Don't you plan on going along to the Little Big Horn, Wallace. After the Indians do in Custer here, I'm going to need you."

"I'd really prefer to go along, sir. I'm a tank comm—"

"Goddamnit, *I'd* really prefer to go along, too," Colonel Jiggs snapped. "You stay, Wallace, and that's it."

"Yes, sir," Wallace said.

"Item Three," Colonel Jiggs said, and took a message form from his pocket and handed it to Lowell. Lowell read it, and handed it to Wallace.

FROM: CG, ARMY EIGHT
TO: CO, 73RD HV TNK BN

AT 0425 HOURS 15SEP50 FOLLOWING LIFTING OF A THIRTY MINUTE ARTILLERY BARRAGE TASK FORCE BENGAL, AUGMENTED AS YOU SEE FIT FROM FORCES AVAILABLE TO YOU, WILL PASS THROUGH THE LINES AND ATTACK ON THE LINE PUSAN KOCHANG SUWON ENGAGING TARGETS OF OPPORTUNITY BUT WITH PRIMARY MISSION OF REACHING KOCHANG AS SOON AS POSSIBLE.

WALKER
LT GEN

(Four)
Pusan, South Korea
0415 Hours
15 September 1950

Task Force Bengal began to actually form only when the artillery barrage began at 0355 hours. The various components of it—a dozen tanks here; the self-propelled howitzers there; the dogfaces on their six-by-sixes; the Signal Corps radio trucks; the ammo trucks; the fuel trucks—had formed separately; and when the barrage began, they started to converge on the departure point.

Captain Lowell was already there, of course, and the first sergeant of Baker Company (who was going) and Technical Sergeant Wallace (who wasn't) stood on the road like traffic cops, making sure the vehicles were in line where they were supposed to be.

When the barrage started, the sky had been dark, and the flare of the cannon muzzles had been almost exactly like a lightning storm. But as the barrage continued, the sky grew lighter; and the artillery was less visible. It was still audible, however, a ceaseless roaring as the shells passed overhead.

Colonel Paul T. Jiggs, to his fury, had been summoned by a messenger from Eighth Army Forward. He had been afraid that Task Force Bengal was about to be scratched. But that wasn't what Victor Forward wanted him for.

He raced up to the head of column, where he found Captain Craig W. Lowell leaning on an M46. There had been changes to the M46 since Lt. Colonel Jiggs had last seen it the previous afternoon.

It was now named. ILSE had been painted on the turret. What the hell, that was his wife; he was entitled. But what pissed the colonel was the guidon flying from one of the antennae. It was the guidon of Baker Company, a small yellow flag with a V-shaped indentation on the flying end. As originally issued, it had read "B" and below that "73." Baker Company of the 73. The yellow identified it as cavalry, or armor.

Someone had carefully lettered "Task Force Lowell" on the guidon.

Jiggs controlled his temper after a moment. He knew where the change had come from. Lowell hadn't done it. His troopers had done it. They had been shoving everyone's nose in the dog shit ever since they had been picked as the nucleus of Task Force Bengal, and especially since the word had gotten out that their CO, the Duke, was to command.

Lowell stood erect and saluted as Colonel Jiggs walked up. He was as worried as Jiggs that the last-minute call had meant the operation had been either delayed or scratched.

"I like your guidon, Lowell," Colonel Jiggs said.

"That wasn't my idea, Colonel," Lowell said, embarrassed.

"Of course not," Jiggs said, sweetly, letting him sweat. He handed him a sealed manila envelope. "Signal Operating Instructions," he said.

"It goes?"

"It goes."

"Thank God! I was scared shitless when they called you to Victor Forward."

"And something else, Lowell, which explains a whole hell of a lot."

He handed him a message form.

FROM: SUPREME COMMANDER
TO: ALL US FORCES IN KOREA

AT 0200 HOURS 15SEP50 ELEMENTS OF THE FIRST U.S. MARINE DI-
VISION, AS PART OF THE X UNITED STATES CORPS, LT GEN ED-
WARD M ALMOND, USA, COMMENCED AN AMPHIBIOUS INVASION
OF THE KOREA PENINSULA AT INCHON NEAR SEOUL.

> MACARTHUR
> GENERAL OF THE ARMY

"It's about time we got off our ass," Lowell said.

"So what you are is a diversion," Jiggs said. "The more hell
you can raise, the better."

"Diversion, hell. I'll head for Seoul!"

"First try to get to Koch'ang, Captain Lowell," Colonel
Jiggs said.

Lowell looked at his watch.

"I better get cranked up, Colonel," he said.

"First get to Koch'ang, Captain," Jiggs said.

"Yes, sir."

Colonel Jiggs put out his hand.

"Try to stay alive," he said. "And remember, you are not
George Patton."

Lowell looked at him for a moment, and then he smiled.
He put his fingers in his mouth, whistled shrilly, and caught
the attention of the driver of the M46 behind his. Then he
extended his index finger, held it over his head, and made a
"wind it up" signal. A starter ground, and an 810 horsepower
engine burst into life.

"Watch it, Craig," Colonel Jiggs said, laying a hand on his
shoulder. "I want you and everybody else back alive."

Lowell was embarrassed by the emotion. He nodded his
head, and then started to climb up the bogies and onto the M46
he had just named ILSE.

The barrage stopped precisely on schedule. And precisely
on schedule, Task Force Bengal began to roll across the line
of departure.

Lowell went first. He would put his Wasps out front only
after he had gotten behind the enemy lines.

Lt. Colonel Jiggs stood where Lowell's tank had been parked, waving his hand and even sometimes returning salutes, as the task force rolled past him, vehicle after vehicle, seemingly forever.

At that moment, he hated Captain Lowell, who was taking his troops into battle, while he had to stay behind to wage war with the chair-warmers at Eighth Army.

(Five)
57th U.S. Army Field Hospital
Giessen, Germany
23 September 1950

Major T. Jennings Wilson, QMC, Chief, Winter Field Equipment, U.S. Army General Depot, Giessen, had been awake in his private room on the top floor of the hospital since daybreak, even before they brought him his breakfast.

He was horribly hung over, and it hurt him to breathe. He'd either broken some ribs when he slammed into the steering wheel, or at the very least, given himself one hell of a bruise. His knees were sore, too. They had probably slammed against the dashboard. Goddamned kraut!

Major Wilson had searched his memory. He was a little confused. Christ, anybody would be confused, but he didn't think they'd taken a blood sample, so he was probably safe from a charge that he was drunk. He didn't remember things clearly from the moment of the crash until he sort of came to in the X-ray room.

He did remember some things. He remembered getting out of the Oldsmobile, after the crash and looking at the Jaguar long enough to see that the woman driving it was dead, and that the car had kraut license plates. That was going to cause him trouble. There weren't that many krauts with enough money to drive Jaguars, and that meant it was the kind of kraut who would probably sue the shit out of him in a German court, before German judges. Did the German courts have juries? If they did, obviously there would be German jurors, who would not only find him guilty, but sock him with a million dollars' worth of damages.

Fuck it, that's what you bought insurance for. That was the insurance company's problem, not his. His problem was getting through this without seeing his career go down the toilet. The army got hysterical when you got in a wreck involving a German national. It was bad for German-American relations, and the army was going ape-shit lately about German-American relations. The bullshit they were passing out was that the U.S. Army was a "guest" of the German people.

Bullshit. The U.S. Army was here because they'd beat the Germans in War II.

He went over and over in his mind what had happened, and by the time the MPs showed up, he was reasonably sure that he was home free. Oh, there were going to be problems, of course. He was going to need a new car. The Olds was demolished; the whole fucking front end was gone. And he knew he could count on trouble with the insurance company. They were going to have to pay for this, of course, but then, sure as Christ made little apples, they were going to cancel his insurance. Or jump his premiums.

And he'd probably given Dolores fits. He remembered that the doctor who had examined him had said that his wife had been notified and told that she should wait until today to see him, that they wanted to keep him under observation for twenty-four hours. Dolores sometimes went off the deep end when something like this happened. She wouldn't understand that it was just one of those things that happens sometimes. He was sorry about the kraut woman, naturally. Nobody likes to be involved in a fatal accident. It was a goddamned shame, and he was sorry about it, but things like this happened, and it seemed to be his turn to have it happen to him.

He knew the MPs would get involved. They investigated every accident. And when it was a bad one, like this one, they sent Criminal Investigation Division, CID, agents to do the investigating. CID agents were MP sergeants who wore civilian clothes, the army equivalent of police detectives.

Major Wilson was not surprised, either, that the CID agents who came into his room were wearing officer's pinks and greens. All they wore was officer's U.S. insignia on the lapels. No insignia or rank or branch of service. Just the officer's uniform permitted to civilian employees in Civil Service Grade GS-7 or better. What the hell, pinks and greens looked good, and if he had been an MP sergeant, he'd probably have done the same thing.

"Major Wilson?" the older of the two CID agents asked.

"That's right," Major Wilson replied.

The credentials of a CID agent, a leather folder carrying a badge and a plastic-covered ID card, were flashed in his face.

"I'm Lieutenant Colonel Preston, Major Wilson," the older of the two CID agents said. "And this is Agent MacInerney."

Major Wilson wondered, fleetingly, if he really was a light colonel, or whether that was some sort of technique they used, making believe they ranked you to get you off balance. He decided it didn't matter. What was important for him was to handle these two very carefully.

"How do you do, sir?" Major T. Jennings Wilson said, politely.

"I guess you know why we're here, Major," Preston said. "To talk to you about the collision yesterday afternoon."

"I understand," Major Wilson said.

"And I'm sure you're aware of your rights under the 31st Article of War? I mean, I'm sure you know that you don't have to say anything to us that would tend to incriminate you? Or, for that matter, that you don't have to talk to us at all?"

"Yes, of course," Major Wilson said. "I'll answer any questions you have, Colonel. Any that I can."

"Thank you for your cooperation," Preston said. "I guess the best way to go about this, if you don't mind doing it this way, would be for you to just tell us what happened, in your own words. Would that be all right with you?"

"I'll do my best, sir," Major Wilson said.

"And the best place to start, of course," Preston said, "is at the beginning. I understand you were in Bad Hersfeld. Is that so?"

"Yes, sir," Major Wilson said. "I was in Hersfeld for the past two days. I was with the G-4 of the 14th Constabulary. I'm chief of the Winter Equipment Division of the Depot, and I was up there trying to get a line on the requirements of the 14th for the upcoming year."

"I see," Preston said. "And you were coming back here when this happened?"

"I almost made it," Wilson said, wryly. "Yes, sir, that's right."

"When did you leave Hersfeld?"

"After lunch," Major Wilson said.

"Have you got an approximate time?"

"Oh, say, and I really don't remember, precisely, 1400, something like that. It was really a working lunch."

"And you drove straight through? You didn't stop anyplace?"

"I drove straight through."

"Then you made pretty good time, didn't you? The collision took place at 1630, according to the German police."

That idle question worried Major Wilson. Of course he had made good time. And the only way to make good time was to speed. What were these bastards up to? Were they going to divide the miles traveled by the time it took, and then charge him with speeding? He had heard they were capable of chickenshit like that. But then he thought that through. To do that, they would need witnesses to swear that he had left at a precise time, and he didn't think anybody could truthfully swear to the time he'd left the club in Hersfeld.

"Yes, sir," he said. "I guess I did. There was hardly any traffic on the roads."

"Tell me what you remember about the accident," Preston suggested.

"Well, truthfully," Major Wilson said, "not much. It all happened so quickly."

"You remember where it happened?" Preston asked.

"Yes, of course. About four, five miles out of Giessen. There's a series of curves in the road there, S's, I guess you'd call them. You really have to take them slowly. Well, as best as I recollect, Colonel, I was in the second or third curve, when all of a sudden this kraut comes around the curve in the other direction, coming out of Giessen, I mean to say, going like the hammers of hell. A Jaguar. You know how those krauts, the ones with enough money to drive a car like a Jaguar, drive."

"Go on."

"Well, that's all there is to tell. I tried to get out of her way, but she was on my side of the road, and there was nothing I could do."

"You say the Jaguar was speeding?"

"Going like hell," Major Wilson said.

"What about you?"

"Hell, I know that road, sir. I wasn't going more than thirty-five or forty."

"Had you been drinking, Major?"

"To tell you the truth, I had a couple of drinks over lunch at the club in Hersfeld. I know, duty hours and all that, but I'd put in a tough day and a half."

"A 'couple' is two," Preston said.

"I think two is all I had, sir," Major Wilson said.

"The collision, Major Wilson, is under investigation by both the army and the German police."

"Well, I'm not surprised," Major Wilson replied.

"Why do you say that?"

"Well, the obvious reason. They get an American officer in front of a German court, an American carrying all the insurance they make us carry, and they can walk away with a bundle. You could hardly call it a trial by my peers."

"You'll be tried by your peers, Major. I think you can count on that."

"Well, that's good news," Major Wilson said. "I'll take my chances before an American court-martial any time. We know how crazy these krauts drive."

"I don't think I'm making myself clear," Preston said. "You're going to face a civil suit in the German courts. And criminal prosecution by a court-martial."

"I don't understand, sir."

"Your story doesn't wash, Major," Preston said. "For openers, we already have statements from the waiter of the officer's club in Hersfeld. You had five drinks, not two, at lunch. And then at a quarter to four, you stopped at the Gasthaus zum Golden Hirsch in Kolbe and drank two bottles of beer, to wash down two drinks of Steinhager. They remember you clearly because you were offensive when they had no American whiskey to offer."

"I deny that, of course," Major Wilson said.

"Let me go on," Preston said, icily. "The Jaguar wasn't speeding. We know that for two reasons. One, we know that the Jaguar entered the highway approximately one hundred yards from the point of impact. There is an intersection there with a back road, which leads, as you probably know, to the commissary and PX at the QM Depot. The Jag had taken that road. We have witnesses. Two, the gear shift lever of the Jag was locked into second gear by the impact. A Jag won't do more than thirty-five or forty, wide open, in second gear. And we can't prove it, of course, but we consider it unlikely that a woman with a child beside her is going to run her car flat out."

Without really thinking what he was saying, Major Wilson said: "Those krauts drive crazy, and everybody knows it."

"You're wrong about that, too, Major," Preston said. "The woman you killed when you came around that turn at between sixty-five and seventy miles per hour, on the wrong side of the road, isn't what you can really call a 'kraut.' She was a naturalized American citizen. And she was the wife of an American officer named Lowell, who's in Korea."

Major Wilson looked at Preston with horror in his eyes.

"I hope they hang your ass, Wilson," Preston said.

"Colonel . . ." the other CID agent said, trying to shut him up.

"I'd like to prosecute you myself, you shitheel," Preston said, having lost his temper beyond redemption. "They won't let me. But you better get yourself a good defense counsel, because I'm going to do whatever I can to send you to Leavenworth."

The other CID agent took Preston's arm and pushed him out of the room. Major T. Jennings Wilson looked at the closed door for a moment, and then he leaned over the side of the bed and threw up.

(Six)
Near Osan, South Korea
25 September 1950

The L-5 came out of the mountains just behind Ch'ongju,

and flew over the main supply route running through the valley, now jammed with lines of trucks and artillery. It flew around the mountains to Ch'onan. By then the build-up, as the supply line stretched, was less visible. Instead of backed-up traffic, there were small convoys of trucks, some accompanied by tanks, some quite alone. Here and there fires burned. There had been some resistance. The colonel wasn't sure how much of the smoke was from battle, or from what the North Koreans had set afire as they retreated.

Less frequently, in the crisp early morning skies, he could make out the sites of obvious battles. There were smoldering Russian T-34 tanks down there. Once they had learned how to handle them, the T-34s had stopped being invincible. After Ch'onan, the main supply route ran through the coastal valley which went all the way up to North Korea, past Inchon, where on September 15, nine days before General Ned Almond had led the X Corps ashore.

The colonel looked at his map. Twenty kilometers, about fourteen miles, to P'yongt'aek, and again that far from P'yongt'aek to Habung-ni. When he looked out the window, he saw a burning M46, but a hundred yards beyond it, not only the smoldering hulks of four T34s but the bodies of their crews. There had been a fight there, one that would never be recorded in the history books, because the war had passed it.

He had, Colonel Paul Jiggs thought, a bird's-eye view of the battlefield. He corrected himself: a Godlike view. Not here, because what had happened here was finished and done; but on other battlefields he would use an aircraft to see what was going on, while it was going on. To command troops he could see, not troops he had to pray would be where he thought they were. To literally look over that next hill and see what the enemy was up to.

He had the airplane because of Lowell, and he had frankly thought when Lowell requisitioned it that Eighth Army would tell him to piss up a rope. Tank battalions were not authorized aircraft, either for artillery spotting (tank cannon are normally used to engage targets that can be seen by the tank crew and therefore aerial fire direction is not considered necessary) or for purposes of liaison or personnel transport. More than likely he could have written a staff study, justifying the assignment of a light aircraft to the 73rd Heavy Tank (Reinforced) on the basis of its size and intended mission. But that would have taken two weeks to write and six months to be reviewed and acted upon.

Lowell had found a better way. He had found that observation aircraft were authorized to the artillery on the basis of one-half aircraft and one pilot per firing battery. He had presented a requisition on that basis to Eighth Army, and they had approved it, as they would have approved a requisition for two tons of chocolate ice cream: If you can find it, then you're welcome to it. And then Lowell had found it. The 119th Artillery (Self-Propelled) had lost two of its batteries to the 73rd Heavy Tank (Reinforced). They were in support of IX Corps, and their airplanes had gone into the IX Corps aircraft pool. An official request to IX Corps to relinquish one L-5 and two pilots for it would have been honored, of course. Say, in six months.

Lowell had driven a jeep to the IX Corps airstrip and commandeered an L-5 and two pilots on the spot. Lieutenant Taddeus Osadachy, a 235-pound Polish-American from Hazelton, Pennsylvania, known as "the Gorilla" because of certain facial features some found unattractive, was dispatched in the L-5 with one of the pilots, and Lowell brought the other one back in the jeep. The pilots didn't mind at all, but the IX Corps aviation officer and the IX Corps chief of staff were apoplectic, and had submitted an official complaint through channels.

In the meantime, 73rd Heavy Tank had the L-5, and had used it from the moment Task Force Bengal had crossed the line in order to maintain contact and to fly out the wounded. Lowell had been rampaging through the enemy rear for nine days. He was now nearly halfway up the peninsula. The radio truck had long since been blown away, and about the only reliable communication they had was with the L-5.

Colonel Jiggs picked the microphone from the side of the window, checked to see that the radio was tuned to armor frequency, and then squeezed the mike button.

"Bengal Forward, this is Bengal Six."

To his surprise, there was an almost immediate response. He hadn't expected contact on the first try.

"This is Bengal Forward. Go ahead."

"What are your coordinates, Bengal Forward?" the colonel asked.

"I don't think I'm supposed to say over the radio," the voice replied, "but the Duke said when we stopped that we were about three miles from Habung-ni."

"Let me speak to Bengal Forward Six," the Colonel said. Goddamned kids got half the message. This kid had the message that you weren't supposed to give your coordinates over the radio in case the enemy had captured a map and would be able to locate you with it. So what he did was announce their location in the clear.

"The Duke's helping them refuel," the radio operator said.

"Can you get a message to him?"

"Roger."

"Tell him to hold where he is. This is Bengal Six. You got that?"

"Yes, sir, Colonel, I got it," the radio operator said.

"Is there someplace up there we can land?" Colonel Jiggs asked.

"You could land on the road, I suppose, if the tanks weren't all over it," the radio operator said.

"Then get the tanks off the road," Colonel Jiggs replied, patiently.

"You mean right now?"

"I mean right goddamned now. We'll be there in about five minutes."

"I'll tell the Duke, Colonel," the radio operator said.

"You do that, Son," the colonel said. He hung the microphone back in its hook and bent his head to the side, leaning it against the plexiglass, so he could see further forward that way. It didn't help. The road was empty and still.

And then, a moment later, there they were.

Twenty-five, thirty (he'd started out with thirty-eight M46 tanks were pulled off on both sides of the narrow dirt road. In between the tanks were self-propelled howitzers. The tracked vehicles, tanks, and howitzers had left just enough room on the road for the ammunition and fuel trucks to pass. At the tail end of the column were the M24s, which had been put into use as guards for the fuel and ammo convoys.

Standard tactics prescribed the use of light tanks to reconnoiter ahead of the main force. Lowell was using them in exactly the opposite way, having them bring up the rear. It was a good thing Eighth Army hadn't had time to look closely at Task Force Bengal before it set out. Eighth Army would have shit a brick if they had seen Lowell's Wasps, all their gunners volunteers, the three-quarters loaded at least a half-ton over the truck's rated weight capacity with .50 caliber ammo.

Now Lowell was kind of a hero with Eighth Army. He was really fucking up the enemy's rear. They didn't know which way to run, for at any time they could encounter Lowell's tank column. Even Eighth Army had started calling it Task Force Lowell, first as a joke, and now routinely.

From the air, Jiggs thought, Task Force Lowell—he corrected himself, Task Force *Bengal*—while impressive, was not nearly as impressive as it had been when it had passed through the lines of the 24th Division. That had really been something to witness. They had come down the MSR at full bore, buttoned up, engines roaring, tracks chewing up the road, antennae whipping in the air.

Colonel Jiggs, watching it from the air now, indulged in a little self-pity, thinking that's where he should be, in the first M46, leading his troops. The temptation to assume command himself had been very strong, especially when Eighth Army had changed its mind again and again, each time adding to the Task Force's mission. They were his troops, and it was only fair that he should command them, not some kid who thought he was Patton.

But there were two inarguable facts. Lowell was a splendid commander who could think on his feet, and he continued to prove it. Besides, what was left of Task Force Bengal wasn't really much more than a company. It was amazing he had that much left, but the point was that what was left wasn't much.

And somebody, somebody with rank, had to stay behind and run the store. Somebody with a little rank had to be there to demand trucks and fuel and, as it turned out, four additional airdrops of fuel and ammo when Lowell had run faster and farther than even he thought he could. Jiggs's job was in the rear on the radio and the telephone, shaking his brand-new silver chicken in people's faces.

The colonel thought that nobody—except the troops themselves—had ever thought they'd get this far forward, this fast. Where the lead tank was stopped was the point of the advance of the Eighth Army in its breakout from the Pusan perimeter.

There was activity now on the ground. Trucks began to pull out from where they had been parked, and to head back to the M24s which would guard them on the road back to P'yongt'aek. The tanks started their engines, generating clouds of blue smoke, and pulled up close to the three-quarter-ton Wasps and the lead tank, leaving room on the road for the L-5 to land.

"Can you get in there?" Colonel Jiggs asked the L-5 pilot, the man Lowell had kidnapped, a young lieutenant fresh from civilian life in the States, a man he hardly knew.

"Yeah," he said, thoughtfully. It wasn't disrespectful. At the moment he was just making a professional pilot's judgment, unaware that he was back in the army. "I'll come in from the north. I hope to Christ the bad guys aren't dug in up there. With machine guns, I mean."

He dropped the little plane to no more than a few feet off the ground. They flashed by the trucks, the empty stretch of road, and then the tanks. Then the pilot stood the L-5 on its wing and made a 180 degree turn. They passed over the tanks so low that Colonel Jiggs was genuinely concerned that they would hit the radio antennae. Then they touched down on the dirt road and bounced for perhaps two hundred yards. The pilot stopped the plane and then raced the engine, turning the aircraft around at the same time. Then he taxied back up the road to the rear of the tank column.

The commanding officer of Task Force Bengal, of the 73rd Heavy Tank Battalion, walked, not ran, to where the L-5 had stopped and Colonel Jiggs was climbing out.

Without disturbing the M1 on his shoulder, Captain Lowell saluted. The salute was one half of one degree short of insubordination.

I know what you're thinking, you poor bastard, Jiggs thought. You think I'm here to grab your glory, to lead the column myself.

"How goes it, Lowell?" the colonel said.

"We're ready to roll again, Colonel," Lowell said. "Has something come up?"

"You've really done a bang-up job, Lowell," Colonel Jiggs said. "I know that. More important, Eighth Army knows it."

Lowell didn't even reply.

"I've got a couple of things for you, Lowell," Colonel Jiggs said.

Lowell's eyebrows rose in curiosity, but he didn't say anything. Colonel Jiggs reached in his pocket and came out with a major's gold oak leaf.

"This belongs to Charley Ellis," the colonel said. "He said to tell you you owe him a drink."

"That's nice of him," Lowell said. "I think I would have stayed pissed at me, under the circumstances."

"He's grateful to you," Jiggs said wryly. "Having him named battalion inspector general was a stroke of guardhouse lawyer genius, Lowell."

Lowell smiled, but said nothing.

"You've earned that leaf, Lowell," Colonel Jiggs said, but he did not shake hands or make a formal speech of congratulations.

"Is that all, sir?" Major Lowell said.

"I'm afraid not, Major Lowell," Colonel Jiggs said. The suspicion was instantly back in Lowell's eyes. "I had to make a decision whether to give you this before you made the join-up, or after. I decided that you should have it as soon as I could get it to you." He handed Lowell a folded sheet of teletype paper.

PRIORITY

HQ EUROPEAN COMMAND

FOLLOWING PERSONAL FROM GENERAL CLAY FOR GENERAL WALKER EIGHTH UNITED STATES ARMY KOREA.

BULLDOG, DEEPLY APPRECIATE YOUR RELAYING FOLLOWING SOONEST TO CAPTAIN CRAIG W. LOWELL, 73RD HEAVY TANK YOUR COMMAND. QUOTE I DEEPLY REGRET TO INFORM YOU THAT ILSE WAS KILLED INSTANTLY IN AUTOMOBILE CRASH NEAR GIES-

SEN SIXTEEN THIRTY EUROPEAN TIME 22 SEPTEMBER. PETER-PAUL UNHARMED AND WITH HIS GRANDFATHER. LETTER WITH DETAILS EN ROUTE AIRMAIL. SHARON AND I SHARE YOUR GRIEF. SANFORD T. FELTER CAPT UNQUOTE. BULLDOG, FURTHER PLEASE ADVISE THIS OFFICER THAT ALL FACILITIES OF EUROPEAN COMMAND ARE AT HIS DISPOSAL IN THIS PERSONAL TRAGEDY. FINALLY, BULL-DOG, ALL OFFICERS AND MEN EUROPEAN COMMAND THRILLED AT YOUR BREAKOUT. BEST PERSONAL REGARDS SIGNED LUCIUS END PERSONAL MESSAGE FROM GENERAL CLAY TO GENERAL WALKER.

SUPPLEMENTAL
FROM SUPREME COMMANDER UNITED NATIONS COMMAND
TO GENERAL WALKER EIGHTH ARMY PERSONAL
PLEASE CONVEY TO CAPTAIN LOWELL THE PERSONAL CONDO-LENCES OF MYSELF AND MRS. MACARTHUR.

> MACARTHUR
> GENERAL OF THE ARMY

"Oh, *shit!*" Major Lowell said.

The colonel handed him the cap of his flask. It held an ounce and a half of scotch.

"I'm sorry, Lowell," Colonel Jiggs said.

"Shit, even General MacArthur's sorry," Lowell said. Tears were streaming down his cheeks. He drank down the scotch, gasped, coughed. The colonel filled the flask top again, and offered it to Lowell, who shook his head in refusal. The colonel drank it himself.

"Are you all right, Major?" the colonel asked.

"Yes, sir," Lowell said. "Everything's just fucking hunky-dory."

"You want to take a few minutes?" the colonel said. "The war will wait."

Lowell didn't even reply. He saluted and started walking up the line of tanks. He had his head bent, and the colonel presumed he was crying. But as he passed each tank, he raised his hand, finger extended, over his head and moved it in a circle. One by one, the tank engines burst into life.

The colonel got back in the L-5, put the earphones on.

"All right," Lowell's voice, tear-choked, came over the radio. "Let's get this fucking show on the road."

"Say again that last transmission," someone replied.

"What I said, Sergeant Donahue," Lowell's voice came back, nearly under control, "was to have the bugler sound the fucking charge!"

The three-quarter-ton Wasps, their gunners in their home-made turrets immediately test-firing the .50s, jerked into motion. The lead tank, Lowell's, the M46 named ILSE, moved out after them. When it had gone fifty yards down the road, the second tank began to roll. Colonel Jiggs waited until they had all gone, and until the dust on the road had settled enough for the L-5 pilot to take off. Then he leaned forward and asked how much fuel there was.

"About an hour, Colonel."

"We'll wait ten minutes, and then take off. That should give us enough time to see what happens."

Thirty minutes later, in the air, when he was sure, Colonel Jiggs tuned the radio to the command frequency and picked up the microphone.

"Victor, Victor, this is Bengal Six."

"Go ahead, Bengal Six."

"Stand by to copy Operational Immediate," Colonel Jiggs ordered.

"Victor ready to copy Operational Immediate."

"To Commanding General, Army Eight," Jiggs dictated. "Operational Immediate. Personal for General Walker. Task Force Lowell, I say again, Task Force Lowell, I spell, Love Oboe Whiskey Easy Love Love, 73rd Heavy Tank, Major Craig Lowell, effected join-up with elements of X United States Corps at 0832 Hours near Osan. Recommend immediate award of Distinguished Service Cross to Major Lowell. Signature is Jiggs, Colonel, commanding 73rd Heavy Tank. You got that?"

"We got it, Colonel."

"OK," Colonel Jiggs said. Then he said to the pilot, "Now we can go home."

IX

(One)
The Farm
Fairfax County, Virginia
28 September 1950

Barbara Waterford Bellmon thought of it privately as "Belt Time." It was the time of day, between four thirty and five, when she had a little belt. The kids' problems were taken care of for the day, dinner was well underway, all her parental and wifely obligations for the day satisfied. She took a shower and did her face and her hair, and had nothing more to do but wait for her husband to come home from the Pentagon.

She then made herself a drink, generally a stiff scotch with just a little ice, so that she could taste the whiskey; and she settled herself on the couch before the fireplace, spread the newspaper out beside her, curled her feet under her, and read the newspaper at her leisure.

There was a fire in the fireplace today; it was getting chilly enough for a fire in the fireplace, and she liked that. Her man would come to the cave from a day battling dragons and dinosaurs and find his mate waiting with a fire.

Bob Bellmon came home to a drink and a meal and a smile,

rather than to a recitation of what had gone wrong in the Bell-mon household. Barbara was proud that she was able to do that much for him. He was still working sixty or more hours a week riding a desk, and she felt sorry for him.

She had a thought that somewhat shamed her. It looked as if the Korean War was about over. That meant Bob wouldn't have a chance to go there to take command of a battalion, that he would have sat out this war at a desk in the Pentagon. Was it wrong to feel sorry for him? Was it wrong to think it a shame that the war was going to be over so soon (MacArthur had been quoted as saying the "enemy was near defeat; the troops should be home by Christmas")? Was there something wrong with her, that she wanted her man to have his chance to go to war?

She flipped the pages of the *Washington Post,* scanning them quickly, reading what looked interesting. A story on the editorial page caught her eye, and she read it.

"My God!" she said, and read it again. And then she shook her head, and smiled, and looked up at the ceiling. And then she jumped off the couch and slipped her feet into loafers, and ran to the front door.

"Bobby!" she shouted. "I have to go to the store for a minute, I'll be right back!"

There was no response.

"Bobby!" she screamed.

Robert F. Bellmon III replied: "I heard you."

"When I talk to you, you answer me!"

"Yes, Mother," Bobby replied, resignedly.

God, she thought, he really is his father's son!

She went out of the house, pulling a sweater over her shoulders against the chill, and got in the Ford station wagon and drove three miles to the crossroads store. There was a stack of seven newspapers on a battered wooden table outside. She picked them all up, laid a dollar bill under the rock that had held them in place, got back in the car, and drove back to the Farm. She entered the house by the kitchen door, laid the newspapers on the kitchen table, and took a pair of scissors from a cabinet drawer.

One by one, she opened each newspaper to the editorial page, cut out the story that had caught her eye, and then neatly stacked the papers on the table, so that Bobby could bundle them up for the boy scout newspaper collection.

Then she took the seven copies of the story and carried them into the library. She took a roll of Scotch tape from the desk drawer, and began to stick the stories up all over the house. She put one on the glass in the front door and one on the glass of the kitchen door, just in case Bob came in the house that way. She stuck one to the mirror in the hall, where Bob would take off his tunic and hat. She stuck one to the mirror over the bar, one to the mirror in the downstairs bathroom, in case he would take a leak on his arrival home, another in their bathroom, and the last one to the mirror over her chest of drawers in their bedroom.

Then she went back and made herself another stiff scotch, sat down on the couch, and waited for Bob to come in.

KOREAN REPORT: The Soldiers
by John E. Morań
United Press War Correspondent

SEOUL, SOUTH KOREA (UP) (Delayed) September 26— The world has already learned that Lt. General Walton Walker's Eighth Army, so long confined to the Pusan perimeter, has linked up with Lt. General Ned Almond's X United States Corps, following the brilliant amphibious invasion at Inchon.

But it wasn't an army that made the link-up, just south of a Korean town called Osan fifty-odd miles south of Seoul; it was soldiers, and this correspondent was there when it happened.

I was with the 31st Infantry Regiment, moving south from Seoul down a two-lane macadam road, when we first heard the peculiar, familiar sound of American 90 mm tank cannon. We were surprised. There were supposed to be no Americans closer than fifty miles south of our position.

It was possible, our regimental commander believed, that what we were hearing was the firing of captured American anti-aircraft cannon. In the early days of this war we lost a lot of equipment. It was prudent to assume what the army calls a defensive posture, and we did.

And then some strange-looking vehicles appeared a thousand yards down the road. They were trucks, nearly covered with sandbags. Our men had orders not to fire without orders. They were good soldiers, and they held their fire.

The strange-looking trucks came up the road at a goodly clip, and we realized with horror that they were firing. They were firing at practically anything and everything.

"They're Americans," our colonel said, and ordered that an American flag be taken to our front lines and waved.

Now there were tanks visible behind the trucks—M46 "Patton" tanks. That should have put everyone's mind at rest, but on our right flank, one excited soldier let fly at the trucks and tanks coming up the road with a rocket launcher. He missed. Moments later, there came the crack of a high-velocity 90 mm tank cannon. He was a better shot than the man who had fired the rocket launcher.

There was a soldier in front of our lines now, holding the American flag high above his head, waving it frantically back and forth. Our colonel's radio operator was frantically repeating the "Hold Fire! Hold Fire!" order into his microphone.

His message got through, for there was no more fire from our lines and no more from the column approaching us.

The first vehicles to pass through our lines were Dodge three-quarter-ton trucks. These mounted two .50 caliber machine guns, one where it's supposed to be, on a pedestal between the seats, and a second on an improvised mount in the truck bed. They were, for all practical purposes, rolling machine-gun nests.

Next came three M46 tanks, the lead tank flying a pennant on which was lettered Task Force Lowell. The name "Ilse" had been painted on the side of its turret. There was a dirty young man in "Ilse"'s turret. He skidded his tank into a right turn and stopped. He stayed in the turret until the rest of his column had passed through the lines.

It was quite a column. There were more M46s, some M24 light tanks, fuel trucks, self-propelled 105 mm howitzers, and regular army trucks. We could tell that the dirty young man in the turret was an officer because some of the tank commanders and some of the truck drivers saluted him as they rolled past. Most of them didn't salute, however. Most of them gave the dirty young man a thumbs-up gesture, and many of them smiled, and called out, "Atta Boy, Duke!"

When the trucks passed us, we could see that "the Duke" had brought his wounded, and yes, his dead, with him. When those trucks passed, "the Duke" saluted.

When the last vehicle had passed, the dirty young man hoisted himself out of his turret, reached down and pulled a Garand from somewhere inside, and climbed down off the tank named "Ilse."

He had two days' growth of beard and nine days' road filth on him. He searched out our colonel and walked to him. When he got close, we could see a major's gold leaf on his fatigue jacket collar.

He saluted, a casual, almost insolent wave of his right hand in the vicinity of his eyes, not the snappy parade ground salute he'd given as the trucks with the wounded and dead had rolled past him.

"Major Lowell, sir," he said to our colonel. "With elements of the 73rd Heavy Tank."

We'd all heard about Lowell and his task force, how they had been ranging between the lines, raising havoc with the retreating North Korean Army for nine days. I think we all expected someone older, someone more grizzled and battered than the dirty young man who stood before us.

At that moment our colonel got the word that the young soldier who had ignored his orders to hold fire and two others near him had been killed when one of Lowell's tanks had returned his fire. The death of any soldier upsets an officer, and it upset our colonel.

"If you had been where you were supposed to be, Major," our colonel said, "that wouldn't have happened!"

Young Major "Duke" Lowell looked at the colonel for a moment, and then he said, "What would you have us do, Colonel, go back?"

There shortly came a radio message for Major Duke Lowell, and he left his task force in Osan. He had been ordered to Tokyo, where General of the Army Douglas MacArthur was to personally pin the Distinguished Service Cross to his breast.

Barbara Bellmon heard Bob's Buick on the stones of the driveway. She pretended to be fascinated with the newspaper spread out on the couch beside her. She heard his footsteps before the front door, and knew that he was reading the newspaper story.

She heard him come in the house. He said nothing to her, and she wouldn't have looked at him if her life depended on it. She heard him go to the bar, where another newspaper clipping hung where he couldn't miss it. She heard him pour himself a drink. He said nothing.

"Oh, for God's sake, Bob," she said, finally. "Don't be such a lousy sport. You were wrong about Craig. Admit it!"

"Lowell didn't go to Japan to get the DSC," Bob Bellmon said. "He went there to go on compassionate leave."

"He doesn't get the medal? What do you mean, compassionate leave?"

"He got the DSC," Bellmon said. "But I don't think he cares one way or the other."

"What are you talking about? What's this about compassionate leave?"

"On September 22," Bob Bellmon said to his wife, "while Ilse was driving home from the commissary at the Giessen Quartermaster Depot, a major, who was drunk, ran head on into her."

"Oh, my God!" Barbara said, faintly, almost a wail.

"Killing her instantly," Bellmon went on.

"P.P.?" Barbara asked, in a hushed voice, her hands in front of her mouth.

"He was thrown clear, and bruised somewhat, but he's alive."

"Oh, my good God!" Barbara repeated. "What can we do?"

"Not a hell of a lot," Bellmon said. "I spoke with the count on the telephone, and Felter sent flowers to the funeral in our name."

"What can we do for Craig?"

"Craig is probably already in Germany," Bellmon said.

(Two)
Fort Polk, Louisiana
18 April 1951

Major General Ezakiah Black was a good soldier. When he was given an order, he said, "Yes, sir," and without bitching performed that duty to the best of his ability. He had been ordered to assume command of the U.S. Army Replacement Training Center, at Fort Polk, and immediately devoted his best effort and most of his thought to taking a steady stream of enlistees and draftees and recalled reservists and turning them into soldiers.

Fort Polk, a hastily built World War II training camp, had been on "standby" status (for all practical purposes, closed) since the end of War II, when it had been last used as a separation center. The Louisiana National Guard had used a small portion of Polk for summer camp, and there was a small caretaker detachment stationed there. But the post looked like a ghost town when General Black arrived. The parade ground was grown up in weeds, the wooden buildings all needed paint, and the macadam roads had simply deteriorated.

There were problems with sewerage, with electricity, with the telephones, with dry rot in barracks and office buildings, with fuel storage tanks. Anything subject to deterioration from disuse or the elements had deteriorated. The Corps of Engineers let millions of dollars' worth of contracts to bring things up to at least minimal standards, but the post was really not ready when the first trainload of draftees arrived.

Getting it ready, getting the operation running smoothly, was for a month a bona fide challenge to General Black's managerial skills. But after that, the job was a great goddamned bore.

There was a basic nine-week cycle. Recruits arrived, spent a week getting their shots and their uniforms, getting tested, given orientation lectures. Then they started on the eight week, Phase I, of their basic training.

There were six hundred men in each cycle. When the pipeline was full, that meant 4,800 men in one week or another of Phase I. About half of each graduating class remained at Polk for Phase II training as infantrymen. The others were sent to Phase II training in other branches, artillerymen to Sill, tankers to Knox, Signal Corps to Monmouth, and so on. When the first group was in the third week of training, Black was informed his weekly input would be doubled. and that was followed by another burst of frenzied activity to double the number of barracks, and to have their stopped-up toilets fixed, their leaking roofs repaired, and their smashed windows replaced.

But that was it. Things calmed down, and there really wasn't a hell of a lot for a major general to do except follow the course of the war in Korea and keep an eye on Germany, which was where the Russians would strike if they came in.

General Black began to divide his day in two. In the morning he dealt with what he thought of as the current situation. In the afternoons he planned for the future. If the Russians came in, he would be expected to form and train an armored division. He planned, quite unofficially, to do just that. He went over the assets of the post and determined where he would house an armored division, where he would have firing ranges, fuel dumps, beer halls, and garbage dumps.

He went further than that. He started looking around for the equipment an armored division would need. He visited, officially and unofficially, the quartermaster depots and the ordnance depots and the general depots. He looked around the on-post warehouses at Knox and Sill and Benning, to see what they had stored away.

One of the things he had inherited when he got the basic training camp was an army aviator. All he knew about Captain

Rudolph G. MacMillan, when McMillan was proposed to him as an aide-de-camp, was that he had the Medal, that he'd picked up a Silver Star Medal (his third) in the opening days of the Korean War, and that Jesus H. Christ MacArthur himself had written the Deputy Chief of Staff, Personnel (DCS-P) to keep him out of the war. That was enough for Black. Another soldier they didn't want for this war needed a home, and he had a home to give him.

They sent him an airplane pilot, but didn't give him an airplane to go with him. No aircraft, his G-4 had been informed, were available at the moment. They would be sent to Fort Polk when they were available. He didn't think MacMillan stood a chance in hell of getting airplanes or helicopters, but he gave him permission to scrounge for one.

MacMillan disappeared. When General Black asked the G-4 if he had sent him someplace, the G-4's reaction had been one of righteous outrage.

"The general is not aware that Captain MacMillan is in the Panama Canal Zone?"

"No, I'm not," Black said, and stopped himself just in time before he finished aloud the question in his mind: "The Panama Canal? What the *hell* is he doing in Panama?"

"Captain MacMillan informed me, General," the G-4 said, "that he was traveling to Panama VOCG." (Verbal Order, Commanding General.)

"I wasn't aware that he had left," General Black replied, wondering why he had impulsively covered for MacMillan. Because he was entitled to special consideration because of the Medal? Or because the S-1 was such a fucking sissy?

MacMillan returned from Panama with three Hiller H23/CE helicopters. General Black knew so little about helicopters that it wasn't until later that he learned they were not supposed to be flown over such great distances. They were supposed to be disassembled and shipped. MacMillan, with two borrowed Panama Canal Zone aviators, had flown them up, in 150 and 200 mile jumps, via Nicaragua, Costa Rica, Honduras, and Mexico.

It was the first excitement General Black had had recently, and it amused him. MacMillan had learned that the H23/CEs, specially modified versions of the H23 for use in mapping operations by the Corps of Engineers (hence, the CE designation), were in Panama, and not being used, because their pilots and the mapping crews had been sent to Korea.

He had gone down there and talked Panama into turning the machines over to him on the basis that while they were doing Panama no good at all, they could be put to "temporary" use as aerial ambulances at Fort Polk. MacMillan then found two helicopter mechanics who could be transferred and arranged for the medical evacuation helicopters and the mechanics to be assigned to the post hospital, where they would be unlikely to be discovered and even less likely to be taken away if they were.

Next, he arranged for the Medical Corps to assign two helicopter pilots to fly the "med-evacs" and turned one of the H23/CEs—now properly adorned with Red Crosses—over to them. The other two machines he kept, hinting that since there was a parts supply problem, he was going to use one of them for cannibalization. That is, it would furnish parts to the other helicopters, the one at the post hospital and the one which now permitted General Black to travel anywhere on the enormous Polk reservation in comfort and in a matter of minutes, rather than after an hour-long ride down bumpy roads that wouldn't take a staff car.

MacMillan next turned up (in Alaska) a five-passenger Cessna LC-126, an airplane designed for operation in the "bush" of Alaska and Canada. With the first money to fight the Korean War, the army had come up with a new airplane it thought it wanted, another "bush" airplane, a DeHavilland of Canada "Beaver." It was being "user tested" in Alaska, and doing splendidly; and Alaska hoped that by giving one of their old LC-126s to Fort Polk, they would thus be able to plead that they should be allowed to keep a "Beaver" after the user test.

While nothing had been said to General Black about his frequent trips to other posts and the supply depots, he had been a little uneasy. While he had the authority to order himself anywhere he wanted to, it being presumed that he knew what was official business and what was not, copies of the orders he issued to himself for travel to Forts Knox and Benning and the supply depots at Atlanta and Anniston and Lexington were routinely sent to Fourth Army Headquarters at Fort Sam Houston. Eventually, somebody was going to ask him about it, and tell him, either officially or unofficially, that when it was time for him to start gathering the logistics for an armored division, he would be told; and until then, he should not be making a nuisance of himself.

The LC-126 MacMillan had brought back from Alaska and which no one seemed to know about (officially or unofficially) was an ideal means to make his "visits," and traveling in it could be performed without putting himself on orders.

So General Black came to spend a good deal of time in MacMillan's company, visiting the widespread activities of the basic training operation in the H23/CE and traveling to other posts and the supply depots in the LC-126. He learned a good deal about MacMillan that he hadn't known before. General Black, as a colonel and then as a brigadier general, had commanded Combat Command B of the late Major General Peterson K. Waterford's "Hell's Circus" in Europe. He knew about Waterford's son-in-law, Bob Bellmon, being a prisoner. MacMillan had been in the *stalag* with Bellmon; and at the time Porky Waterford had bought the farm (he had dropped dead playing polo, which everybody who knew him thought was the way Porky would have wanted to go out), MacMillan had been his aide-de-camp.

In General Black's opinion, MacMillan was not overendowed with brains, but he knew how to keep his mouth shut, and there was no question about his scrounging ability. They became, if not quite friends, then a good deal more like pals than a general and his dog robber normally are.

MacArthur sent Ned Almond in with X Corps at Inchon, as brilliant a maneuver as General Black had ever seen. Walker had finally broken out from the Pusan perimeter, and in the first maneuver of General Walker's that met General Black's approval, had sent a flying column, a battalion-sized M46 force, racing around behind the enemy lines. It was a classic cavalry sweep, destroying the enemy's lines of communication, keeping him off balance, and then finally linking up with X Corps.

Almond and X Corps had been on the Yalu when the chinks came in. Black and MacMillan had been at the Lexington Signal Depot.

Almond had pulled X Corps, with all its equipment, all of its wounded, and even its dead, off the beach at Hamhung on Christmas Eve, 1950, after the chinks had chewed up Eighth Army again. Black and MacMillan had spent Christmas Eve in the Prattville, Alabama, Holiday Inn, forced to land there by weather on the way home from a "visit" to the Anniston Ordnance Depot.

Truman relieved MacArthur. General Black was really of two minds about that. MacArthur was right, of course. There is no substitute for victory. But Truman was right, too. Soldiers take orders, and they stay out of politics.

In March 1951, General Black learned that MacMillan had not been using the third H23/CE as a source of "unobtainable" parts to keep the other two flying. When he thought about it, he realized that he should have known that if MacMillan could scrounge entire helicopters, he would have no trouble scrounging parts to keep them flying.

On a Saturday afternoon, drinking a beer on the back porch of the general's quarters after a basic training graduation parade (the general always felt bad watching the trainees march proudly past; in a month, a lot of those handsome, tanned, toughened young men would be dead), MacMillan said if the general didn't have anything important to do on Sunday morning, say about 0900, he had something he wanted to show him.

The general had absolutely nothing to do on Sunday morning.

At exactly 0900, MacMillan fluttered down in the third H23/CE into the general's backyard. There was something hooked up to the skids, and when the chopper was on the ground, the general saw that there was an air-cooled .30 caliber machine gun on the right skid, and four tied-together 3.5 inch rocket launchers on the left.

"What the hell is all this, Mac?" General Black asked, but he got in the helicopter.

"The cavalry rides again, General," MacMillan said. "C Troop of the 7th Cavalry, Second Lieutenant George Armstrong Custer—that's you—has just been ordered to check out a story that Sitting Bull is moving an armored column around the Little Big Horn River. You and your first sergeant, that's me, 1st Sgt. John Wayne, ride out together."

"You're starkers, MacMillan," General Black said, but he was smiling.

MacMillan picked up the H23/CE, not far, not more than fifty feet off the ground, and flying no more than ten feet over the top of the pine trees that covered the Polk reservation, flew out to the Distance Estimation Course.

While located in the range area, the DEC was not a firing range. What it was was a field 1,000 yards long and 400 yards wide on which worn-out trucks and jeeps and even two ancient M3 tanks from War II had been scattered among pill boxes, foxholes, and trenches. Basic trainees were required to estimate how far away the various battlefield targets were from their positions.

"Geronimo, Geronimo," MacMillan's voice came over the intercom. "This is Geronimo Forward. Enemy force consisting of three jeeps, three trucks, and two M3 tanks spotted 1,000 yards from Little Big Horn. Engaging."

"You're in your in your second childhood, MacMillan. You know that?" General Black said.

"Watch this," MacMillan said. He zoomed low over the DEC, and came to a hover 200 yards from the M3 tank hulks. There was a sudden, frightening whoosh two feet below General Black's feet, followed by an orange flash. A 3.5 inch rocket flashed away, and passed fifty feet over the M3.

"Maggie's Drawers, MacMillan," the general said, making reference to the red flag waved on firing ranges to indicate a complete miss.

"I haven't had very much practice," MacMillan said. "I had one hell of a time stealing these rockets from ordnance."

There was a second roar and a second burst of smoke.

The 3.5 inch rocket hit the M3 hulk's chassis. The hulk seemed to lift, just barely, off the ground, and then settle again. In the split second he had to look before MacMillan moved the helicopter, almost violently, to engage the second M3, General Black saw a cratered hole in the M3, right in front of the driver's hatch. MacMillan hit the second M3 with both of his two remaining 3.5 inch rockets. Then he moved the helicopter 150 yards from the remains of an ancient GMC six-by-six truck.

The .30 caliber machine gun on the other skid began to chatter. There was surprisingly little noise, but General Black felt the entire helicopter vibrate, alarmingly, from the recoil. He was frightened for a moment, but then fascinated as he watched MacMillan move the tracer stream (every fifth round in a normal belt of machine gun ammo was a tracer; from the steady stream of tracers here, Black realized that MacMillan was firing all tracers) across the ground and into the old truck.

Finally, the ammunition all gone, MacMillan zoomed off from the truck, and flew back to the nearest M3 hulk, where he put the H23/CE gently on the ground, and turned to look at General Black.

"I'm not the brightest guy in the world, General," MacMillan said. "How come I had to figure this out?"

General Black didn't reply. He got out of the H23/CE and examined the crater hole in the M3's hull. And then, impulsively, he hoisted himself onto the tank, and then onto the turret, and lowered himself inside. He'd fought, briefly, in M3s in North Africa as a technical liaison officer with the British, teaching them the M3. The older models, this one, had had riveted hulls. When they were hit, the hulls came apart, and the rivets rattled around the interior of the hull, killing the crews. Later models were welded. The British had called it the "Priest," because the side-mounted cannon made it look something like a pulpit in a church.

The M3s had been replaced by the M4s, and that's what he'd commanded in Europe. And now they were gone. The task force that Walker had sent north from Pusan had had M46s. And now Bulldog Walker was gone. Bulldog bought the farm, in a jeep accident, on Christmas Eve in Korea. And here he sat at Fort Goddamned Polk, Louisiana, giving basic training and dreaming of an armored division he knew goddamned well wasn't coming.

The interior of the M3 didn't stink as bad as he thought it would. There was evidence of animal life, squirrels probably; he didn't think there would be rats.

He squeezed himself into where the driver's seat had been. That 3.5 rocket had blown a neat hole right through the hull. If this had been an operational tank, it would be a dead tank now.

He heaved upward, and with effort got the driver's hatch to open on its rusty hinges. He saw a jeep coming hell bent for election across the field. He ducked back into the hull. Let them think it was MacMillan, alone. Let Mac get rid of them, and they could fly home, and he could consider the ramifications of rocket-armed choppers.

MacMillan certainly was not the first one to think of arming choppers, he thought. But, under that goddamned Key West Agreement of 1948, the army was forbidden armed aircraft. In 1948, when the Defense Department had been formed, and the Air Corps, previously a part of the army, had become a separate service, they'd held a meeting at Key West and defined the roles of the army, the navy (which included the Marine Corps), and the new air force. The air force, logically enough, had been given responsibility for things that flew. They had promised to support the army with air power as needed. It was, on the surface, a logical arrangement, except that it was the air force that decided what the army needed in aerial support, not the army. And the air force was far more interested in spending its budget on intercontinental bombers and rockets than on supporting the dogfaced soldier. Arming aircraft was the air force's—and only the air force's—privilege. The air force was not about to waste money developing armed helicopters when they had the capability of atomizing the enemy. It was General Black's solemn opinion that the Key West Agreement was goddamned stupid.

He thought that it was likely that MacMillan was the first one to actually try rockets and machine guns on choppers. The other people who had thought about it were also smart enough to know about the Key West Agreement and afraid to violate it.

There was the sound of angry voices outside. What the hell was that all about?

General Black stuck his head out of the commander's hatch. A tall, thin light bird, whose name he could not recall, but whom he remembered was the range officer, was giving MacMillan hell. Unauthorized use of the ranges, firing on a range that wasn't supposed to be fired on at all, was absolutely, unquestionably, against regulations.

"Colonel," General Black called out. The skinny light bird, his face still contorted with rage, snapped his head in the direction of the general's voice. For a moment, until he recognized the general (who had left his fatigue cap in the H23/CE), he glowered at the partner in crime of the idiot who had befouled his range.

Then he saluted, literally struck dumb. The last person in the world he expected to see crawling out of a derelict M3 was the post commander.

"I thought you might be interested to see what Captain MacMillan's rocket did to the interior of this," General Black said, conversationally. He hoisted himself out of the hatch, and made room for the skinny light bird to climb in. Then he jumped to the ground.

"I've seen enough, Mac," he said. "Let's go home."

(Three)
Fort Polk, Louisiana
1 May 1951
HQ DEPT OF THE ARMY WASH DC
CG FT POLK LA (ATTN: MAJ GEN E.Z. BLACK)

INFO: CG USARMYFOUR FT SAM HOUSTON TEX
      CCG USARMYEIGHT KOREA

1. TELECON BETWEEN VICE CHIEF OF STAFF, USA: DC/S-PERSONNEL HQ DEPT OF THE ARMY AND MAJ GEN E. Z. BLACK, CG US ARMY REPLACEMENT TRAINING CENTER AND FORT POLK LA 2030

HOURS WASH TIME 30 APR 1951 CONFIRMED AND MADE A MATTER OF RECORD.

2. MAJ GEN E. Z. BLACK (LT GEN DESIGNATE) IS RELIEVED OF COMMAND US ARMY REPLACEMENT TRAINING CENTER AND FT POLK LA EFFECTIVE 0001 HOURS 2 MAY 1951, AND WILL PROCEED BY FIRST AVAILABLE AIR TRANSPORTATION TO HQ FAR EAST COMMAND TOKYO JAPAN FOR FURTHER ASSIGNMENT WITH USARMY-EIGHT AS COMMANDING GENERAL XIX US CORPS (GROUP). GEN BLACK IS AUTH A PERSONAL STAFF OF FOUR.

FOR THE CHIEF OF STAFF
RALPH G. LEMES
BRIG GEN, USA
DEPUTY THE ADJ GEN

(Four)
Kwandae-Ri, North Korea
8 May 1951

Master Sergeant Tourtillott, a heavyset man in his forties, with a full head of curly silver hair, a Thompson submachine gun resting against his hip, and presenting a picture of a dog-like devotion to General Black's protection that he didn't intend (although his devotion to General Black was in fact, doglike; he had been with him since Africa), stood by the rear door of the XIX Corps Conference Room and waited for the general to appear.

He did. He wore fatigues, tanker's boots, and a .45 automatic in a shoulder holster.

"Gentlemen," Master Sergeant Tourtillott called out, "the Commanding General. Atten-hut!"

Fifty officers rose to their feet.

General Black, wearing three stars on each of his collar points, walked into the room, trailed by Technical Sergeant Carmine Scott, his clerk.

"Be at ease, gentlemen," he said.

There were three armchairs in the center of the front row of chairs. One was occupied by the deputy corps commander, a major general, and the other by the corps artillery officer, a brigadier general. The center chair was obviously intended for General Black. Black walked to the chair, and smiled at Sergeant Scott.

"General," he said to the brigadier general, "would you mind giving Scotty your chair? He takes notes for me, and he has to be next to me."

"Somebody get the sergeant a chair," the corps artillery officer called out, moving his own chair to make room.

"General, you're going to have to listen carefully to what I say," General Black said. "I didn't say, 'Get Sergeant Scott a chair.' I asked you to give him yours."

Flushing with mingled anger and humiliation, the corps artillery officer signaled for a colonel to give up his chair. Sergeant Scott sat down next to the general and took out a stenographer's notebook and three pencils. He held the two spares in the same hand as the notebook, and poised the third over a blank page.

"Get on with it," General Black said.

The deputy corps commander went to the stagelike platform.

"On behalf of the officers and men of XIX Corps, General, welcome."

"Thank you," Black said.

The briefing, designed to inform the new corps commander of every possible fact concerning his new command, went on for an hour and a half.

General Black leaned his head toward Sergeant Scott every few moments and spoke softly to him. Sergeant Scott, his head moving almost constantly to signal his understanding of what was being said, scribbled steadily in his stenographer's notebook.

Presentations were made by the General Staff, G-1 (Personnel), G-2 (Intelligence), G-3 (Operations), and G-4 (Supply). They were followed by the Special Staff (the medical officer; the provost marshal; the ordnance officer; the signal officer; the transportation officer; the aviation officer; the civil affairs and military government officer; the finance officer; the chemical officer; and the special services officer).

When it was all over, General Black got to his feet and

turned and faced the roomful of officers.

"Gentlemen," he said, "I am a simple soldier. When I was a cadet at Norwich, I was told, and I believed, and my subsequent career has proven true, that the essence of command is to make sure the troops have confidence in what they are doing. Troops must have faith in their officers Officers build and maintain that faith in a very simple manner: They never lie to their troops; they never ask them to do something they cannot do themselves, or are unwilling to do themselves; and they never partake of creature comforts until the last private in the rear rank has that creature comfort. If you'll keep that in mind, I'm sure that we'll get along."

And then he walked out of the room, with Master Sergeant Tourtillott and Technical Sergeant Scott trailing along after him.

One by one, the General Staff officers presented themselves in his office. Prompted by Technical Sergeant Scott, working from his notes, General Black asked each of them specific questions and issued specific orders. He asked each of them if they had questions. None of them did, until he got to the adjutant general.

"We seem to have a problem, sir, with Captain MacMillan," the adjutant general said.

"Already? For Christ's sake, he hasn't been here seventy-two hours."

The adjutant general handed General Black a TWX.

HQ DEPT OF THE ARMY
CG XIX US CORPS KOREA

REF: PARAGRAPH 6, SPECIAL ORDER 87, HQ USA REPL TNG CNTR & FT POLK LA DTD 1 MAY 51.

(1) CAPT RUDOLPH G. MACMILLAN, 0-367734, INF, HAVING BEEN RETURNED TO THE ZI AFTER COMBAT SERVICE IN THE KOREAN CONFLICT, IS NOT ELIGIBLE FOR FURTHER SERVICE WITHIN EUSAK UP OF POLICY LETTER 285-50, OFFICE OF THE ASSISTANT CHIEF OF STAFF, PERSONNEL.

(2) IN VIEW OF CAPT MACMILLAN'S PREVIOUS DISTINGUISHED RECORD, AND THE UNDESIRABILITY TO EXPOSE HIM TO THE HAZ-

ARDS OF COMBAT AGAIN, NO REQUEST FOR WAIVER IS DESIRED.

(3) THIS MSG WILL SERVE AS AUTHORITY TO ISSUE ORDERS REASSIGNING CAPT MACMILLAN TO HQ MIL DISTRICT OF WASHINGTON FOR DY WITH PRESIDENTIAL FLIGHT DETACHMENT.

> FOR THE ASSISTANT CHIEF OF STAFF, PERSONNEL
> RICHMOND HULL
> LIEUT COL AGC
> ASSISTANT ADJUTANT GENERAL

"Tourtillott," General Black called out, "get MacMillan in here."

"He's down at the airstrip, General," M/Sgt. Tourtillott replied.

"Get in a jeep and go get him," Black ordered.

When he handed MacMillan the TWX, and took a look at his face, General Black's carefully rehearsed speech vanished from his mind.

"Tourtillott, get back in your jeep and go get the aviation officer," General Black said.

"You're not going to pay any attention to this thing, are you, General?" MacMillan asked.

"Just keep your mouth shut, Mac, for once," General Black said.

The aviation officer, a full colonel, appeared ten minutes later in a crisp fatigue uniform.

"What took you so long, Colonel?" Black asked.

"Sir, I was in a really rotten flight suit," the aviation officer said.

"Try to remember for the future, Colonel," Black said, "that when I send for you, it's very likely that I have something on my mind more important than the cleanliness of your uniform."

"Yes, sir."

"Do you know Captain MacMillan?" Black asked.

"Yes, sir. I just met him. He was explaining the general's rotary-wing requirements, sir."

"Colonel, have you got any flying missions that don't get any closer than, say, five miles to the MLR?" General Black asked.

"I don't think I quite understand the question, sir."

"Think about it," General Black said, nastily.

"Yes, sir," the aviation officer said; and then, having thought about it, said, "Yes, sir," again. "We operate TWA, sir. Teeny-Weenie Airlines. We supply radio relay stations, and weather stations, and an outfit on the East Coast at Socho-Ri that supports a South Korean intelligence outfit."

"The aircraft involved do not get closer to the line than five miles. Is that a correct statement?"

"Yes, sir."

"Tell me about the outfit supporting the South Korean intelligence outfit," General Black said. "How far are they from the line?"

"About ten miles south of it, sir."

"And is there any reason MacMillan couldn't stay with them?"

"No, sir. They're right in with a radio relay station. One of ours, I mean."

"OK, Mac," General Black said. "Here it is. You quarter yourself with the Americans over on the coast. You occupy your time flying back and forth between here and there, never getting any closer to the line than five miles, thereby freeing one of the colonel's pilots and permitting me to assure those who are worried about your health that you are in no danger whatever."

"General, what about my aerial cavalry?" MacMillan protested.

"Take it or leave it, Mac," General Black said. "You either fly these supply missions for the colonel here, or you pass out hors d'oeuvres in the White House."

"I'll stay here, sir," MacMillan said.

"I'll have your ass if I find you've flown anything, anywhere, that the colonel hasn't told you to fly, and I'll have the colonel's ass if you do and he doesn't tell me. Have I made myself quite clear, gentlemen?"

"Yes, sir," MacMillan and the aviation officer said in unison.

"Colonel," Black said to the adjutant general, "send the following TWX to the Deputy Chief of Staff for Personnel, Headquarters, Department of the Army: 'Captain Rudolph G. MacMillan has been assigned essential noncombatant duties.'"

"Sir, you can't do that," the adjutant general said.

"I beg your pardon?" General Black said, as if he didn't believe that he had heard correctly.

"The regulation . . . I read it before I brought this to your attention, General . . . is quite clear. MacMillan's remaining here would be in clear violation of the regulation."

"Let me tell you something, Colonel," Black said. His normally ruddy face had turned white with anger, but he had control of his voice. "I don't know how you got to be a colonel without learning this, but since you apparently have, I'll try to embed it in your memory: Regulations and policy are for the *guidance* of a commander. Nothing more. Don't you *ever* tell me again that I can't do something because it's against regulations. I *command* this Corps, which is a horse of an entirely different hue than *administering* it to the satisfaction of some pencil-pusher in the Pentagon. Now, is that clear enough for you, or will it be necessary for me to have to make you write it a hundred times on that goddamned blackboard of yours?"

"It's perfectly clear, sir," the adjutant general said, faintly.

"You are dismissed, gentlemen," the XIX U.S. Corps commander said.

X

It took Mac MacMillan about three days to figure out what was going on at Socho-Ri. It was a low-level intelligence outfit. It was attached for rations and quarters to XIX Corps (Group), but it wasn't assigned to Eighth Army, or to the nearly autonomous X Corps. It was assigned to Supreme Headquarters, United Nations Command.

That explained the willingness of the XIX Corps (Group) aviation officer to assign a Beaver solely to supply the needs of the 8045th Signal Detachment. It was easier to simply turn a Beaver over, and thus insure their satisfaction with the quality of the support they were receiving from XIX Corps (Group), than to have Supreme Headquarters, United Nations Command breathing over their shoulders.

The XIX Corps (Group) aviation officer must be similarly pleased with the assignment, MacMillan realized. That freed one of his pilots for other duties.

MacMillan would have preferred to have been given command of a company of parachute infantry (the 187th Regimental

Combat Team was in Korea). Failing that, any infantry company. Failing that, he would liked to have flown artillery spotting missions in an L-5 or the new L-19 Cessna they were supposed to be getting. And failing that, he would have preferred to be General Black's personal chopper jockey.

All of those things were obviously out of the question, which caused him to examine the 8045th Signal Detachment with great care. The commanding officer was a captain of the Signal Corps, but Mac outranked him, if it got down to that. There were three other officers, and a flock of sergeants, but only a very few lower-ranking enlisted men.

What they were doing was maintaining communications with intelligence agents—mostly Korean, though with a rare American involved—in North Korea. Most of the communications were by radio. But there were some messages that had to be carried by hand. And sometimes there was film that also had to be hand-carried out. In addition, the agents themselves had to be taken in—in other words, landed secretly on the beaches of North Korea—and when the time came, picked up from the beaches and taken home.

In that process, MacMillan saw his opportunity to make a greater contribution to the war effort than flying a Beaver back and forth between Socho-Ri and the XIX Corps (Group) airstrip.

There was an exhilaration he had almost forgotten when he thought about being behind enemy lines. He'd done that six times, five jumps into enemy-held terrain, and one odyssey across Poland when he'd left the POW camp. He was just about as good at that as he was at anything else.

There was no reason he could see why he couldn't go with the people planting and extracting agents, and while they were doing what they did, he would blow up railroad bridges, tunnels, and generally make a nuisance of himself.

But there were going to be some problems.

If General Black heard about it, he would find himself on the next plane to the White House Army Aviation Detachment. And he had given Black his word as an officer and a gentleman that he wouldn't fly within five miles of the front, so he couldn't use an airplane. But the important word there was "fly." He hadn't given his word about walking or riding or going on a boat.

The second problem was the detachment commander. He was under the impression that Mac had been assigned to him as an airplane driver, period. He judged army aviators the way most people in the army did, including MacMillan; he thought of them as commissioned aerial jeep drivers. So Mac began to cultivate the Signal Corps captain, to let him know that he was not your run-of-the-mill asshole aviator.

And then, an omen literally out of the fucking blue, that problem solved itself. A Navion landed unannounced on the dirt strip running parallel to the beach at Socho-Ri. The strip wasn't on charts, and it wasn't supposed to be used, but a Navion made one pass over the village and then touched down.

MacMillan and the Signal Corps captain went down to run whoever it was the hell off. And then the canopy opened.

"Well, look what the fucking cat drug in!" MacMillan called.

"Jesus Christ, the world's ugliest Scotchman," Lt. Colonel Red Hanrahan, the Navion's sole passenger, said. He jumped off the wing root and embraced MacMillan.

Lt. Colonel Hanrahan was the officer in charge of the operation, back in Tokyo. Mac had known him for years. As a second lieutenant, when MacMillan had been a corporal, Hanrahan had been MacMillan's platoon leader when what was later to become the 82nd Airborne Division was two provisional companies of volunteers jumping out of small airplanes with civilian parachutes.

Hanrahan had left the 82nd Airborne under mysterious circumstances. MacMillan had learned he'd been in the OSS, in Greece during the German occupation, and that he'd later been in Greece after the war when Lowell had been there.

"What the hell are you doing here?"

"General Black sent me over to make sure your people got treated right, Red," MacMillan lied, and purposefully used Hanrahan's nickname, rather than his rank, in the correct belief that Hanrahan would not correct him, and that this would awe the shit out of the Signal Corps captain.

Right on both counts.

The next time the Signal Corps captain planted an agent, MacMillan went along for the ride. The captain was not about to tell the colonel's asshole buddy he couldn't.

What this outfit needed, MacMillan decided, was some better equipment than the Korean junks they were using. What they needed was something fast, maybe a junk powered by a diesel. Maybe double diesels. Maybe even a PT boat. He had heard there were some PT boats at the U.S. Navy Yard in Yokohama. He'd have to come up with some excuse to get to Japan, and look into that. He knew where there were a couple of Marine diesels. Just to try his feathers, he flew to XIX Corps, and submitted a requisition through the XIX Corps G-2, saying it was from the outfit—the Supreme Headquarters, United Nations Command's outfit—in Socho-Ri.

Eleven days later, a GI tractor trailer delivered two marine diesels to Socho-Ri. There was a Korean shipyard further down the coast. MacMillan acquired a junk they didn't have much use for, for a truckload of gasoline in five-gallon jerry cans. XIX Corps (Group) gave him whatever fuel he asked for and asked no questions. For an additional 1,000 gallons of gas, the Koreans installed the diesel engines and reinforced the junk in several places, so that MacMillan could mount .50 caliber machine guns.

He ran into General Black one time at the XIX Corps (Group) airstrip.

"You staying out of trouble, Mac?"

"Yes, sir."

"You been flying any closer to the front than you should be, to get to specifics?"

"To be specific, sir, I never fly closer than ten miles to the front."

That same night, he blew up the first of what was to be more than seventy North Korean railroad bridges.

(Two)
Ch'orwon, North Korea
20 May 1951

Headquarters, IX U.S. Army Corps, Eighth U.S. Army,

had established itself in a ravine off the main supply route about six air miles (fourteen by road) from the main line of resistance. The commanding general and his staff had been put up in quonset huts, and the General Staff and the Technical Services (including the four messes, field-grade officers, company-grade officers, first three graders, and enlisted men) in tropical buildings, that is to say, sheet steel buildings on poured concrete slabs.

Four huge diesel generators provided electricity. There was a water purification plant, a laundry, and two shower points, one for enlisted men and company-grade officers, and a second for field-grade and senior officers. The general officers (three of them, the commanding general, the chief of staff, and the artillery commander) had their own mess and shower.

There was an airstrip, serving both C-47 aircraft and the light aircraft: Stinson L-5s, Cessna L-19s, Navion L-17s, DeHavilland L-20 Beavers, and Hiller H23 helicopters organic to IX Corps and its subordinate commands. There was the 8404th Military Police Company to provide security and the 8319th Transportation Car Company to provide jeeps and light truck transportation. The 8003rd Army Band played twice a day, at the reveille formation and at retreat, and also provided popular music at the IX Corps recreation center to which troops on a roster basis were brought from the front lines for a day's recreation, including hamburgers and ice cream sodas.

It was, in other words, what Colonel Thomas C. Minor felt was a *proper* headquarters, one in keeping with the requirements of a senior command, one from which he, as assistant chief of staff, G-1 (Personnel), could bring order from administrative chaos. The smooth functioning of the army (not only here, in the field but the army worldwide) depended on adherence to regulations.

Personnel-wise, the major problem was twofold. In the confusion which had been rampant since the police action started, commanders had seen fit to ignore army regulations under the authority granted them (an error, in Colonel Minor's judgment) to do whatever they considered necessary for the discharge of their mission in combat. They had been particularly blind to regulations regarding both enlisted and officer promotions, and in the assignment of officers without regard to suitability and qualification and even date of rank.

Enlisted men had gotten off the ships as privates and privates first class and five *months* later, as the result of a *series* of highly irregular and often blatantly illegal promotion policies, had become master sergeants and first sergeants. One of the first things Colonel Minor had done upon taking over as assistant chief of staff, G-1, three weeks before was to stop that. There would be no promotions above staff sergeant below division level and no promotions to the first two enlisted grades without Corps, that is, *his* permission. God alone knew what havoc had already been wrought on the Enlisted Personnel Picture worldwide by promoting draftees to master sergeant. The Enlisted Personnel Picture was sort of the colonel's own ball of wax. Before coming to Korea, he had been Deputy to the Chief, Enlisted Personnel Division, Manpower Section, Office of the Assistant Chief of Staff for Personnel, Headquarters, Department of the Army in the Pentagon. He knew, probably better than anyone else in the army, what was going to happen to carefully thought-out Enlisted Promotion Programs (promotion from private to master sergeant should, it had been decided, take a minimum of twelve years active service) if every other soldier who went to Korea as a PFC came home as a technical sergeant or higher. That had had to be stopped, and Colonel Minor had stopped it.

The officer personnel situation was even worse. The subordinate commands of IX Corps were riddled with officers who held down table of organization and equipment positions for which they were totally unqualified, or who had been promoted with little or no consideration being given to qualification or time in grade, or both.

On the other hand, the careers of many officers who had previously been quite good, and even outstanding, to judge by their service records, had been ruined by the whim of combat commanders, who had relieved them on the spot without so much as a moment's warning and sent them packing. Officers were entitled by regulation to counseling before any action— much less relief—which might be considered detrimental to their careers could be taken.

Colonel Minor, during a visit to the 73rd Heavy Tank Battalion (Reinforced), had seen something even worse, insofar as good order and discipline were concerned: Apparently with the approval and certainly with the knowledge of the battalion commander, there was an obscenity painted on the turrets of the tanks. It was even worse than obscenity, even though it was certainly that. It was clearly prejudicial to good conduct and order. The army functioned on cooperation between separate commands. There was simply no justification for the philosophy of the 73rd Heavy Tank Battalion (Reinforced) which was painted on the turrets: YOU PLAY BALL WITH THE 73RD, OR WE'LL STICK THE BAT UP YOUR ASS.

The general had agreed with him about *that*. Just as soon as he had returned to the IX Corps CP and briefed the general on what he'd seen, the general had authorized him to send a TWX absolutely forbidding the painting of any obscene or vulgar word or term or drawing on army property.

Colonel Jiggs's response to that order had been right on the edge of insubordination. Colonel Minor had decided he wouldn't carry *that* tale to the general. He would wait until the general visited the 73rd Heavy Tank Battalion (Reinforced), and saw for himself that the only thing Colonel Jiggs had done was paint over one word.

There was still outrageously emblazoned over the turrets of the 73rd's M46 tanks the legend, "YOU PLAY BALL WITH THE 73RD OR WE'LL STICK THE BAT UP YOUR XXX." There was no mistaking what the painted-over word was.

The second thing Colonel Minor had seen at the 73rd Heavy Tank Battalion that he never thought he would see in this man's army was the S-3. For one thing, he was barely old enough to vote. For another, he was a National Guardsman. For another, not only had he not attended the Command and General Staff College, a normal prerequisite for staff duty, he hadn't even attended the Advanced Armor Officer's Course. When Colonel Minor was as old as Major Craig Lowell, he had been looking forward to his promotion to *first* lieutenant.

Another proof that Colonel Jiggs was a fool was his blunt statement that his Boy Wonder was the best S-3 he had ever known as well as a superb combat commander. It was the sort of thing one could expect from an officer who had relieved fifteen officers without so much as counseling any *one* of them, just *ruined* their careers. He had actually led the breakout from the Pusan perimeter with lieutenants commanding companies and sergeants commanding platoons, and the whole task force under the actual command of his Boy Major.

The Boy Major had been awarded the Distinguished Service Cross for his part in the breakout. Immediately, in the emotion of the moment—rather than after calm, deliberate collection and evaluation of the facts, the way it was supposed to be done.

So far as Colonel Minor was concerned, that was ample reason to relieve Colonel Jiggs as summarily as he had relieved the others "for lack of judgment in a combat situation."

But Jiggs had been lucky. His breakout, thanks to the co-operation of the enemy, had been successful. And so had his withdrawal from the Yalu when the Chinese came in. The 73rd Tank had come out of *that* smelling like a rose. Just luck. If General Almond had been as impressed with the 73rd Heavy Tank Battalion as they would have you believe, he would never have given it up to IX Corps. He had been very glad to get rid of it probably, if the truth were known. Let somebody else clean up the mess they had made for themselves.

Jiggs was a sonofabitch; there was no mistake about that. When Colonel Minor had sent a fully qualified major to be the 73rd Heavy Tank's S-3, instead of being grateful to Minor, he had called Minor to protest; and when Minor had told him that he was simply complying with regulations and policy, as well as the general's personal directive to him to make sure that the IX Corps officer corps was brought up to snuff, Colonel Jiggs had announced that he was going to personally protest to the commanding general.

At first Minor had thought that was just an idle threat, but his friend, the assistant to the Secretary of the General Staff, a fine young lieutenant, had telephoned him the night before to say that Colonel Jiggs had requested and been granted a personal interview with the general.

Colonel Jiggs was up there in the White House now with the general, and God only knows what allegations and outright untruths he was making.

One could not permit oneself to dwell on things like that. One was far better off simply putting them out of one's mind and going on with one's duty.

He was still thinking about how the administration of the army could really be fouled up unless there was someone in charge who knew precisely what he was doing, when his General Staff telephone buzzed. The general had a special telephone circuit, giving him instant communication with his General Staff. When he dialed 1, the G-1's (Colonel Minor's) telephone rang.

"Minor, sir," Colonel Minor said, catching it before it had a chance to ring again.

"Come up, will you?" the general said, and hung up.

Colonel Minor strapped on his web belt and .45 and then stepped in front of the mirror to make sure that his face was clean, that his camouflage parachute scarf was properly folded around his neck, and that the sandbag cover on his helmet was still drawn tautly. And then he walked quickly up the hill to the White House.

(Three)

Colonel Jiggs was with the general when Colonel Minor reported, saluting crisply and remaining at attention until told to stand at ease. He was pleased to see that Jiggs was wearing his pearl-handled, gussied-up, chrome-plated .45 in a civilian shoulder holster. The general wasn't going to like that. He would have thought that Jiggs would have had more sense than to wear it.

"You know Colonel Jiggs, of course, Colonel," the general said.

Jiggs, who was sprawled in a most unmilitary fashion in one of the general's folding canvas chairs, made no move to get up or shake Minor's hand, and when Minor started toward him, he *waved* at him.

"I've had the pleasure," he said, sarcastically.

"Colonel Jiggs is a bit upset about his S-3," the general said. "Let's hear your side of it."

A bit upset, Colonel Jiggs thought, was the fucking understatement of the year. What he would like to do is ram a shovel up the ass of this paper-pushing sonofabitch, and then spin it around and jerk his chickenshit guts out with it.

"I can't imagine why there is any cause for concern, sir. I've managed to acquire for Colonel Jiggs a fully qualified major, who was second in his class at Leavenworth. He has four years in grade as a major, and this assignment is right for him at this point in his career and right for the 73rd Tank, who obviously needs a fully qualified officer."

"And did Colonel Jiggs tell you that he was perfectly satisfied with his present S-3?" the general asked.

"I believe the colonel mentioned something along those lines."

"I told you, Colonel," Jiggs said, "that Lowell is the best S-3 I've ever known, that I couldn't do without him, and that if you persisted in this business, I would take it up with the general," Jiggs said. "Don't tell me you've forgotten our little discussion so soon, Colonel."

Jiggs got a dirty look from the general, and reminded himself again that he would gain nothing by losing his temper.

"He is not really qualified, Colonel, no matter how well he's been able to fill in the breach," Colonel Minor said, reasonably.

"Sir," Jiggs interrupted, "Major Lowell did so well that we gave him the DSC."

"I consider that award, given under those circumstances, somewhat questionable," Colonel Minor said.

"Fortunately for the major, then," Jiggs said icily, "we'll just have to go with the decision of General Walker. General Walker gave Major Lowell his DSC."

"Be that as it may—" Minor began.

"I have just told the general," Jiggs interrupted him again, "that in addition to the DSC, I got him the DSM for the way he pulled us out of North Korea when the chinks came in."

He had not told the general that the last man in the world he expected to see on the Yalu was Major Craig W. Lowell. He would have bet his last dime, right after the link-up, that he, as well as the U.S. Army, had seen the last of Major Craig W. Lowell.

He had started getting what the army called "senatorial inquiries" about Lowell right after Lowell had been flown out of Seoul and put on compassionate leave. He'd gotten four or five of them a day. Lowell had a lot of friends in very high places, and those friends were not at all concerned that the army was in a war. They wanted Lowell instantly returned to the United States on the first available air transport, and they wanted his application for release from active duty, on compassionate grounds, approved yesterday.

At first Jiggs had been a little pissed. The army took care of its own. The wheels to get an officer whose wife had been killed home to his child had already been in high gear when Lowell arrived in Osan. He had been in Germany five days later.

But then he realized that under the same circumstances, if he had the clout, he would have done exactly the same thing.

And then, not quite a month later, Major Lowell had walked into his tent in North Korea.

"You should let a fellow know where you've moved," he said.

"What the fuck are you doing back here?"

"I'm here for duty, Colonel, if you'll have me," Lowell said, and there had been something in his eyes that had kept Jiggs from asking any further questions.

It wasn't until later, until just before the chinks came in, that he got an answer. They had an hour or so alone and a bottle of scotch, and Jiggs had asked him if he was hearing from Germany.

"I get a letter a week," Lowell said. "Teutonic efficiency."

"Is your boy getting adequate care?" Jiggs asked.

"He's surrounded by relatives," Lowell said. "He lives in a castle. In the castle in which his mother is buried. And her mother. And his side of the family going back five hundred years."

It had poured out of him then, and Jiggs had sat and listened.

His mother was in and out of mental hospitals. His father was dead. His only blood relative was a banker he couldn't stand. The only home life, as Colonel Paul T. Jiggs understood the term, had been with the German girl he had married.

"So there I sat, Colonel," Lowell had told him, "in a crypt. Like a goddamned Boris Karloff movie. With a bottle of scotch. Looking at a piece of marble on which somebody had chiseled Ilse Elizabeth Lowell, Gräfin von Greiffenberg, 1929–1950, Requiescat in Pace. My wife was behind that fucking piece of marble, and I was thinking that I was never, really never, going to see her again. And then, as drunk as I was, I had a clear thought: I didn't belong in that goddamned crypt. And neither did I belong in the States, which everyone from my fucking cousin to my father-in-law was telling me was best thing for me, under the circumstances. I suddenly realized where I belonged."

"You don't mean here?" Jiggs asked.

"Yeah, ain't that a bitch? That's just what I thought."

"You're going to stay in the army?"

"Don't laugh. It's the only home I've ever really had. The only friends I have are soldiers."

"There are worse ways to spend your life," Jiggs said.

"Investment banking being high on that list. What do you think my chances are for a regular commission?"

"You should be a shoo-in," Jiggs had told him. "They don't pass out that many DSCs. And not many people get to be majors at twenty-four."

"You think I can keep the majority?"

"I think so," Jiggs had said. He had vowed then to do what he could, and he had, and now this paper-shuffling asshole was trying to shove another asshole into Lowell's job.

"As far as I'm concerned, Colonel," Colonel Jiggs said, relatively calmly, "an officer who had demonstrated his skills in a mess like the bug-out from the Yalu is a hell of a lot more qualified than the number two man at C&GS."

Colonel Minor's silence, as he well knew, eloquently said, "So what?"

"And where is it your intention to assign this outstanding young major?" the general said.

"That did pose a problem, sir," Colonel Minor said. "As you point out, Major Lowell is very young. As a general personnel policy, it is ill-advised to put an officer in a position where he is younger than his subordinates."

"What do you plan to do with him, Minor?" Jiggs said.

"I thought I would bring him here, sir," Colonel Minor said. "And give him some staff experience at this level of command."

"Where?" Jiggs pursued. The general gave him a pained look.

"In civil affairs and military government, actually," Colonel Minor said.

"That's going to look great on his service record," Jiggs said, sarcastically. "From S-3 of a combat command to civil affairs."

You're a fine one talk about careers, Colonel Minor thought. The way you *ruined* careers of regular officers by summary relief. He said: "He's a National Guardsman, he really doesn't have a career."

"He's applied for the regular army, and I have heartily endorsed his application," Jiggs said.

"If he is accepted into the regular army, it will be as a first lieutenant, possibly even a second lieutenant, considering his age . . ." Minor said.

"In which case, I have recommended that he be retained on active duty in his reserve grade," Jiggs said. "I don't want that boy's career ruined by a tour as a civil affairs officer."

"I would hardly say ruined," Minor said.

"I don't really much care what you would hardly say, Colonel," Jiggs snapped.

"Take it easy, Jiggs," the general said.

"I beg your pardon, sir," Jiggs said.

"How much time has he got to do in Korea?" the general asked.

"About four months, sir," Jiggs said. "He's been here ten months, maybe eleven."

The general suddenly stood up and walked to a connecting door.

"John, can you come in here a minute?" he said. A very small major general in a starch-stiff set of fatigues walked into the room. Jiggs jumped to attention.

"John, we have a problem officer," the general said. "According to Colonel Minor, he's wholly unqualified to be what Colonel Jiggs says he is, the best S-3 he's ever known."

The little general looked amused.

"Do I have to take sides, sir?" he asked.

"He's also the young buck who ran that cavalry sweep through South Korea during the breakout. So he's only got about four months to go in Korea," the general said. "Jiggs is afraid that a tour in civil affairs, which is what Minor recommends, would look lousy on his service record."

"Jiggs is right," the little general said.

"You need an aide," the corps commander went on. "Presuming the chemistry is all right, would you be interested in him?"

"What do you think, Jiggs?" the little major general asked.

"I think Major Lowell would make the general a very fine aide-de-camp, sir."

"OK," the corps commander said. "I've just done my Solomon act for today. You two may go."

"How soon do I get him?" the small major general asked.

"Today, sir, if you like," Jiggs said. "Colonel Minor has been very efficient in sending me his replacement."

"One more thing," the small major general said. "Knowing you, Jiggs, I just have to ask. Is he housebroken?"

"Not only that, sir, but he can read and write. He wrote, for example, our battalion motto."

The little general laughed. "If that's going to go in the history books, you're going to have to have it translated into Latin. The general and I were talking about that last night. It belongs at C&GS, of course, as a morale booster. But how are you going to put it in the manual?"

"Cooperation with the 73rd Tank Battalion is expected and anticipated," Colonel Jiggs said. "Our disappointment will be manifested by the violent insertion of a sports implement into the anal orifice."

"Good to see you, Jiggs," the little general said, chuckling. "Come on up and have dinner sometime." He looked at the corps commander and got silent approval to leave.

Jiggs came to attention.

"Thank you, general," he said.

"OK, Jiggs," the corps commander said, "I hope you're satisfied."

"Yes, sir. Thank you very much," Jiggs said, and saluted and walked out of the general's office.

Well, you win some and you lose some. That was about a tie, Colonel Minor thought.

XI

(One)
Kwandae-Ri, North Korea
18 August 1951

"E.Z., I hate to speak to you like a battalion commander to an overzealous shavetail," the Supreme Commander, United Nations Command said to the commanding general of the United States XIX Corps (Group). "But you are obviously in need of guidance."

"With all due respect, sir, has the Supreme Commander ever heard of the phrase, 'the blind guiding the blind'?" Lieutenant General. E. Z. Black replied.

"When the last Supreme Commander gave the faintest hint that something would please him. . . ."

"With all due and profound respect, sir, you ain't the last Supreme Commander."

"His subordinate commanders fell all over themselves," the Supreme Commander went on, "in the eagerness to make him happy. This is known in some circles as 'cheerful and willing obedience to the lawful orders of a superior officer.'"

"Will you settle for 'senior' officer?" the XIX Corps (Group) commander asked, innocently.

237

"If you understand that that's an order, I will," the Supreme Commander said.

They were sitting alone at the fieldstone bar of the general officer's mess of XIX Corps (Group), a room known as the Jade Room after the XIX Corps' radio code name, Jade. They were drinking, neat, 24-year-old Ambassador scotch, brought to Korea by the Supreme Commander, United Nations Command.

"I've only been here a couple of months, Matt," Lieutenant General E. Z. Black said. "It's not time for me to take an R&R."

"A couple is two," the UN Commander said. "You've been here four. During which time you have put in eighteen-hour days, seven days a week. And you're not, although you sometimes act like one, a twenty-three-year-old cavalry lieutenant any more."

"Woman works from sun to sun, but a gen'rul's work is never done," General Black said.

"I don't know why the hell I'm arguing with you," the Supreme Commander said. "Now, whether you want to accept it as your due for breaking your ass straightening out XIX Corps in half the time I thought it would take you—and I mean that, E. Z., you've done a hell of a job—or the concern of an old friend who doesn't want you dropping dead of a heart attack brought on by overwork, you *will* take seven days rest and recuperation leave in connection with TDY to Tokyo. This is an order."

General Black sipped at his scotch, then raised his glass to the Supreme Commander, giving in.

"The troops call it 'I&I,'" he said. "For 'Intercourse and Intoxication.' I'm a little old for that."

"As Georgie Patton once said, 'A soldier who won't fuck, won't fight,'" the Supreme Commander said.

"That wasn't Georgie, that was Phil Sheridan," the XIX Corps commander said.

"You have reservations at the Imperial Hotel for seven days, starting next Friday."

"Why then?"

"Because that's the soonest Marilyn could get over here," the UN Commander said.

"Marilyn's coming over?" General Black asked. Marilyn was Mrs. Black.

"I called her up. And told her I felt duty bound to report that word had reached me you were carousing with Oriental ladies."

"You're capable of that, you bastard," the XIX Corps commander said.

"And since Marilyn is flying halfway around the world to save her marriage, the least you can do is show up at the Imperial, sober, shaven, and wearing a smile."

"It'll cost a fortune to fly her way out here," E. Z. Black said.

"You cheap sonofabitch," the Supreme Commander said. "You've got more money than Carter has liver pills."

"I don't know how well this is going to sit with the troops," E. Z. Black said. "They don't get their wives to come out here."

"They're not lieutenant generals, either. For Christ's sake, E. Z., they like that sort of thing. *Their* general is supposed to be somebody special, to do special things. About the only way you can tell a general officer from a PFC these days is because the general is usually older and fatter."

"It smacks of special privilege," E. Z. Black insisted. "It *is* special privilege."

"Let me worry about that," the UN Commander said, and his voice showed impatience. "If you weren't rich, E. Z., you wouldn't think twice about it. You lean so far over backward, you're always falling on your ass."

"OK, OK," General Black said. "You win."

"Your Supreme Commander may not always be right, but he's always your Supreme Commander," the UN Commander said. He looked at his watch. "Time, isn't it?"

"Yes, sir," Lieutenant General E. Z. Black said. The intimate conversation between friends was over. It was the responsibility of the XIX Corps (Group) commander to insure that the schedule of the visiting United Nations Commander was followed. He didn't even finish the inch of 24-year-old scotch in his glass.

"Finley!" he called, and in a moment a full bird colonel wearing the insignia of an aide-ce-camp to a three-star general stuck his head into the Jade Room.

"Anytime, General," Colonel Finley said.

The two general officers put on their headgear—a helmet with a taut sandbag cover in the case of the XIX Corps commander, a stiffly starched fatigue cap for the UN Commander—checked to see that their buttons were buttoned and that the gold buckles of their special general officer's leather pistol belts were properly centered on the bellies, then walked out of the Jade Room.

A platoon from each battalion of the units assigned to XIX Corps (Group) were lined up on one side of the small parade ground between the rows of prefabricated tropical buildings. Each platoon had the national colors, and there was a sea of divisional and regimental flags and company guidons. Before the assembled troops was a three-cannon battery of 105 mm howitzers.

The moment the two general officers appeared before the headquarters's quonset huts, the band began to play. First "ruffles and flourishes" and then "The Star Spangled Banner." When that was over, the cannons fired, fifteen rounds, the prescribed tribute to a four-star general officer.

Then both general officers climbed into a glistening jeep, which bore a four-star plate on both bumpers. Steel railings permitted both of them to stand up. The jeep started off, followed by a half dozen other jeeps containing lesser officers. As they reached the assembled troops, an order was shouted, and all the flags except for the national emblem dipped in respect. Both general officers saluted, holding the salute as the jeeps slowly passed before the troops and dipped colors.

At the end of the line, they completed their salute, and then sat down and drove across the oiled dirt road to the XIX Corps (Group) airstrip where an Air Force C-47 sat waiting.

The aircraft had already been loaded with the baggage of the visiting party. All that remained now was for them to board the plane. The last to board was the UN Commander. He returned the salute of the XIX Corps commander, made a final personal remark ("Marge'll want to have you and Marilyn to dinner, of course"), and then got on the airplane. The door closed, and the engine starters began to whine.

The XIX Corps commander's jeep driver looked at General Black for instructions.

"We'll wait until they get off the ground," the XIX Corps commander said, as he lowered himself into the front seat.

The C-47 got its engines going and taxied down to the far end of the runway.

The XIX Corps commander suddenly had a crisp and clear image of his wife. He could almost smell her, could almost feel the softness of her breasts against him, see her still shapely legs flashing under her skirt, see her (it still excited him, after all these years) rubbing her breasts when she took off her brassiere.

The C-47's engines roared, and it came racing down the runway toward them.

It had been General E. Z. Black's intention to stand in the jeep and render a final hand salute as the C-47 passed over them. That was now quite impossible. If the XIX Corps commander stood up, it would be immediately obvious to the two dozen or more senior officers and enlisted men standing near him that their commander had a hard-on.

Sitting down, the XIX Corps commander waved an informal farewell to the United Nations Commander.

(Two)
Tokyo, Japan
24 August 1951

The 1941 Cadillac limousine (which had been MacArthur's) picked up Lieutenant General E. Z. Black at the Imperial Hotel a few minutes after the UN Commander's personal car, a Buick, had picked up Mrs. Black to deliver her to the UN Commander's quarters for cocktails with the headquarters ladies.

It drove him to the Dai Ichi Building, where an MP who must have been six feet six opened the door for him. A bird colonel, one of the UNC's aides, saluted and smiled and escorted him into the building, through the lobby, and into an elevator.

They rode to the third floor, and then walked down a corridor to a conference room. There were chairs at the enormous table for thirty people, but there were only a handful in the room. Someone called "attention" when E. Z. Black walked in the room, which told him that the UNC wasn't here yet.

"Rest," E. Z. Black said. He identified, as well as he could, the people in the room. The only two he recognized were the UNC's G-2 and a colonel, whose name for the life of him he could not recall, but whom he recognized as a spook, an army officer on sort of permanent TDY to the CIA.

Then he remembered the name: Hanrahan. He had met Hanrahan at a party at Jim Van Fleet's quarters in Washington. He had been introduced as a civilian, but Van Fleet had quietly informed Black that Hanrahan had been one of his people in Greece and was one of the officers the army had sent over to the CIA. A good man, Van Fleet had told him. For Jim Van Fleet, that was a compliment of the highest order.

Black walked over to him.

"Hello, Red," he said. "Nice to see you again."

"I'm flattered the general remembers me," Hanrahan said.

"I see you've reenlisted," Black said. He wanted Hanrahan to know that he knew.

There was also a captain, a little Jew, who wore a CIB and parachutist's wings and the crossed rifles of infantry.

"Why don't you sit down, General?" the aide-de-camp said. "I'm sure the general will be along in a moment."

An interior door opened, and the UN Commander walked in. Everyone came to attention without formal order.

"Sit down, gentlemen," the UNC said, and took a seat at the head of the table. "Howard, get us some coffee, and then secure the place," he ordered.

A master sergeant, who had apparently been waiting outside, rolled in a tray with a silver coffee service, and then left the room, closing the door behind him.

"Do we all know each other? Hanrahan, have you met General Black?"

"I know Colonel Hanrahan, General," Black said.

"And do you know Captain Feldman?" the UN Commander asked.

"It's Felter, sir," the captain said. "How do you do, General?"

Captain Felter was wearing a ring. General Black took a good look at it when Felter crossed the room to shake his hand. I'll be goddamned, he's a ring-knocker, E. Z. Black thought. Will wonders never cease?

"Before I turn this over to Colonel Hanrahan," the UN Commander said, "I want to officially announce this meeting is classifed Top Secret/Mulberry. Everyone present is so cleared."

What the hell is "Mulberry"? General Black wondered.

Hanrahan got to his feet. "To get right to the heart of the matter, General Black, I'm afraid we're going to take one of your assets away from you."

"What asset is that?"

"The 8045th Signal Detachment," Hanrahan said.

General Black had to think a moment before he could identify the 8045th Signal Detachment. His troop list, the list of units assigned to XIX Corps (group), filled three single-spaced typewritten pages, everything from the "40 US Inf Division" through the 8807th Ordnance Ammo Bn" to the "8656th Signal Pigeon Platoon." He was finally able to sort out the 8045th Signal Detachment as the outfit where he had cached Mac MacMillan. They were the people over on the East Coast at Socho-Ri, the radio relay outfit also charged with supporting a South Korean intelligence operation of some sort.

After he had been over there about a month, flying an L-20 "Beaver" back and forth between the Jade CP and the East Coast, MacMillan had asked that he be assigned to them rather than to headquarters. They needed an old soldier assigned to them, Mac had said, one who knew how to deal (the General had read "scrounge") with Eighth Army and Korean Communications Zone (KCZ) supply depots on their behalf. They were doing a hell of a lot, MacMillan had said, with very little; and with adequate supplies, they could really earn their pay.

He had given in. There had been repercussions to his "Captain MacMillan has been assigned essential noncombatant duties" TWX, and it would be better if he were able to honestly say that MacMillan was assigned to some unimportant rear area Signal Corps unit, rather than to XIX Corps (Group) Headquarters.

He had smiled on learning from the XIX Corps (Group) aviation officer that the first thing MacMillan had scrounged on behalf of the 8045th Signal Detachment was an H23 helicopter to go with the Beaver.

"Otherwise known as 'MacMillan's Floating Circus,'" Colonel Hanrahan said.

"You know Mac, don't you, Colonel?" General Black said, smiling. "I didn't have the heart to send him home. So I sent him over there."

"I found it very interesting, General Black," the UNC said, dryly, "that I knew virtually nothing about the little operation of yours until Colonel Hanrahan brought it to my attention."

"It was hardly worth bringing to the general's attention," General Black said. "A couple of officers, a handful of men, who when they were not otherwise occupied with a radio relay mission, were helping, I guess, now that I see him here, Colonel Hanrahan."

"'Helping Hanrahan,' as you put it, E. Z.," the UNC said, "is not all they've been up to."

"I'm afraid you've lost me, sir," Black confessed.

"You mean you don't know about the blowing up of railroad tunnels, the knocking down of bridges?"

"No, sir," Black said. Goddamn that MacMillan! He should have known that MacMillan's silence was proof that he had not quietly accepted an assignment that put him on ice.

"What about the PT boat, E. Z.?" the UNC asked, obviously enjoying his discomfiture. "Did you know about that?"

"I knew he got a boat from the navy," Black said, somewhat lamely. Before he had asked for a transfer, MacMillan had asked for permission to scrounge a boat from the navy, to "make it easier to get around."

Hanrahan was smiling broadly.

"I didn't know it was a PT boat," General Black went on. "I thought maybe an LCI, or an admiral's barge, or something."

"But you did know about Task Force Able, didn't you, E. Z.?" the UNC asked.

"Yes, sir. That was explained to me as a logistic convenience. If the Signal Detachment and the Koreans were under a joint command, they'd have an easier time getting logistic support."

"Persuasive chap, this Major MacMillan, isn't he?" the UNC said, dryly.

"I didn't hear about that, either," General Black confessed. "The last I heard he was Captain MacMillan."

"That just came through, General," Hanrahan said. "Mac doesn't know about that yet, either."

"I plead guilty and throw myself on the mercy of the court," General Black said. He sensed that he was in over his head here, and wondered what the hell it was all about; what MacMillan had done to get all this attention.

"General," Black said, deciding to get it all out in the open, "I have probably indulged MacMillan more than I should have."

"Indeed?" the UNC said, with a strange smile.

"Yes, sir. Hell, what he is is an old-time regular army sergeant. He's a good officer, but I suspect that he would really be happier to be first sergeant at Scofield Barracks. Sending him home to be a hero on display at the White House would kill him. What the hell, he was in a kraut prisoner cage with Porky Waterford's son-in-law. He won the Medal going in, that and a commission, and he won the DSC breaking out. He got another Silver Star, his third, the day this war started. If I've given him special consideration, I plead guilty. But I'd probably do it again for him tomorrow. What I don't understand is how this got all the way back to you."

"What about the Chinese junks, E. Z.?" the UNC asked. "Do you know about those, too?"

"I know about one of them," Black said. "Until just now, I thought it was a supply vessel for the Koreans."

"He has two, Colonel Hanrahan informs me," the UN Commander said. "And has a third under construction. He has paid for them with gasoline. Do you have any idea where MacMillan could lay his hands on enough gasoline to buy three ocean-going, very fast, multiple-engined, diesel-powered junks?"

"No, sir, I don't."

"I am really impressed, General," the UNC said, "with this demonstration of your firm hand on the logistics pipeline."

"As General Black is aware," Colonel Hanrahan said, "the Koreans are running an intelligence operation out of Socho-Ri. The point is, that the intelligence operation is really a diversion for another intelligence operation."

"I don't understand that at all," General Black said.

"Under cover of infiltrating low-level operatives, General, we have been inserting, and withdrawing, more important people."

"I still don't understand," Black admitted.

Hanrahan thought it over before replying.

"I don't think there is any harm in telling you that we're dealing with the Chinese, via their forces in North Korea," Hanrahan said. "I really can't go any further than that, General."

"OK," Black said. "I get the picture."

"So MacMillan was one of those things that sometimes happens," Hanrahan said. "When I found him over there, the first thing I thought was to get him out of there as quick as I could. I've known Mac a long time, General. I knew there was no way he was going to sit there and fly rations back and forth for long."

"No, that's not exactly his style, is it?" General Black said.

"And then it occurred to me to let him run a little wild," Hanrahan said. "The more trouble he caused, the more activity there was, the greater chance that our people could be concealed in the general confusion. You follow me, sir?"

"Yes," General Black and the UNC said together. Black was not sure to whom Hanrahan had addressed his remark.

"So I'm responsible for a good deal of MacMillan's success," Hanrahan said. "I got him the PT boat, for example."

"I see," the UNC said.

"What has happened now," Hanrahan said, "is that things are getting a little out of hand." He was obviously choosing each word with care. "At a time when our operation is in a critical place." He paused, and then went on: "We sent a submarine offshore to pick up one of our agents. They sent a team in rubber boats. They had just about reached shore when MacMillan blew up a railroad tunnel about a hundred yards away."

"And your people got hurt?" General Black asked.

"No, they weren't hurt," Colonel Hanrahan said. "The agent we were picking up had enough sense to go back in the bushes when the tunnel went up. And there was, of course, an alternative pickup plan. But when the sub went back, they weren't sure if they were going to have to fight off the North Koreans or what the sub commander referred to as 'pirates.'"

"OK," General Black said, "I get the picture. Colonel, you can take my word for it that as soon as I can get to a radio, MacMillan's private army will be disbanded, and Captain . . . *Major* . . . MacMillan will be on the next plane to the States."

"That isn't what we have in mind, General," Colonel Hanrahan said.

"Oh?"

"There has been a good deal of resistance from State, the State Department, about our using submarines. World opinion is apparently against submarines. They seem to be afraid that the other side can stage a sinking which would make us look bad."

"Go on," General Black said.

"After the incident where the submarine extraction party arrived precisely at the moment MacMillan was blowing up a tunnel, State managed to convince the . . . State has been successful in having us forbidden the use of submarines in any further operations of this nature."

"I see," General Black said.

"Which leaves us with MacMillan, and his junks, as our only asset," Colonel Hanrahan said.

"So you're going to take over MacMillan, and his junks, and presumably whatever else you need?" the UNC asked.

"We're going to take over direction of the MacMillan operation, General," Colonel Hanrahan said. "The operation will continue, much as it has, but under our supervision. He will go on doing very much what he has been doing, with this major change in priority. Inserting and withdrawing our people takes priority. It's as simple as that."

"I understand," General Black said.

"Now that I've been faced with the fact that submarines are no longer available to us," Hanrahan said, "I think maybe State is right. MacMillan can, for example, go in with twenty people, and come out with nineteen, leaving an agent on the shore— or pick one man up at the same time he's blowing a bridge— with a much lesser risk of being discovered, or even suspected, than if we use a sub. The Chinese are clever. They know you don't use subs unless what you're doing is very, very important."

"You think MacMillan is capable of handling this for you?" General Black asked.

"That's where Captain Felter comes in," Hanrahan said.

General Black had been wondering about the role of the little Jew with the West Point ring.

"We've got a radio crew coming in from the States with some really fancy radioteletype cryptographic equipment," Hanrahan went on. "We'll have a direct link between Washington and Captain Felter, and Felter can give the word to MacMillan."

"I have a rude question to ask," General Black said. "And there's nothing personal in this, Captain, believe me. But if this operation is as important as you tell me it is, isn't Captain Felter a little junior for all that responsibility?"

"Washington wants one of their own men on the scene, General," Colonel Hanrahan said.

"What's he doing in an army uniform if he's one of yours?" General Black said.

"Captain Felter thinks of himself as a soldier, General," Colonel Hanrahan said, somewhat tartly. "Like myself, he has declined an offer of civilian employment with the agency to which we are attached. I had Captain Felter sent from Germany. I can think of no other officer as well qualified to handle this operation. Captain Felter was with me in Greece."

"E. Z.," the UNC said, cutting off the exchange, "the real purpose of this meeting, my presence here, is to impress on you the importance of Hanrahan's mission. And to tell you that the word I got, when Colonel Hanrahan was 'attached' here, was that what Hanrahan wants, Hanrahan gets."

"Yes, sir," General Black said. "I understand, sir." He turned to Felter. "Anything we've got you can have, Captain," he said. "And if you run into any trouble with MacMillan, as you're liable to, you come to see me."

"I can handle Major MacMillan, sir," Captain Felter said, matter-of-factly.

(Three)
Kwandae-Ri, North Korea
30 August 1951

Captain Sanford T. Felter, wearing the crossed flags of the Signal Corps (and without his Combat Infantry Badge, his parachute wings, and his West Point Class of 1946 ring) went to Korea with Lt. General E. Z. Black at the conclusion of the general's R&R leave. General Black's L-17 Navion met them at K16 in Seoul and flew them to the XIX Corps (Group) airstrip.

General Black's aides-de-camp met the Navion. General Black's junior aide was instructed to have Captain Felter equipped with field uniforms and to have him standing by the General's office no later than 1600. General Black's senior aide was told to contact Major MacMillan at the 8045th Signal Detachment and have him at the general's office no later than 1530.

Then General Black went to his quarters and changed into his fatigue uniform. He had—wondering if it made him some sort of a pervert—stolen a handkerchief from his wife. He sniffed its perfume and then carefully wrapped it in plastic and slipped it into his breast pocket. He wondered how long the perfume would last.

He then underwent a two-hour briefing by his G-3 on what had happened in his absence. When it was finished, MacMillan was waiting for him. When they walked through the outer office of General Black's personal office, Captain Felter was already there, dressed in mussed fatigues, brand-new combat boots, and looking, General Black thought, like the Israeli version of Sad Sack.

"You miserable sonofabitch," General Black said to MacMillan, "not only did you make a three-star horse's ass out of me in front of the Supreme Commander, and in front of a professional spook named Hanrahan, but you broke your word to me. You gave me your word you wouldn't go within five miles of the MLR."

Very lamely, MacMillan explained: "I said I wouldn't *fly* within five miles of the line."

"You're a goddamned guardhouse lawyer, that's what you are. That's a bullshit excuse and you know it is. I meant, and you know I meant, that you were not to stick your ass in the line of fire."

"Goddamnit, General," MacMillan said, now shamed that he had been caught, "I'm paid to be a soldier. Take the fucking Medal back and let me go to a line outfit."

General Black was wholly unaccustomed to having that sort of language directed to him by a very junior major, who didn't even know he was a major. His face whitened, but in the end he concluded that not only was there something wrong with a personnel system that ordered an officer out of combat solely because he had performed superbly in combat previously, but that, under identical circumstances, he would have done exactly what MacMillan had done. Probably not as well, General Black decided. But he would have tried.

"At least you could have told me about the goddamned submarine, Mac," General Black said, taking a bottle of the 24-year-old Ambassador scotch from his desk drawer and pouring two drinks. He looked up at MacMillan. "Why didn't you?"

"Well, I figured the general had enough on his mind," MacMillan said.

"Your escapades have come to the attention of the highest authorities," General Black said. He and MacMillan upended the shot glasses, swirling the scotch around in their mouths, then swallowing it, together, as if it had been rehearsed. "God, that's good whiskey."

"I'm really sorry if I got you in trouble, General," MacMillan said. "I really am. I never thought anybody would find out."

"Congratulations," General Black said, pouring more 24-year-old scotch into their glasses.

MacMillan looked at him in confusion.

"You are now a field-grade officer, Mac," Black said.

"No shit?" MacMillan asked, pleased and surprised.

"The UNC is going to give us a parade," Black said. "You get the gold leaf pinned on your shirt, and I will be awarded the Horse's Ass Medal with crossed swords and diamonds for letting a dumb shit pull what you pulled on me."

"We're not in trouble," MacMillan said, relaxed and smiling.

"You know Colonel Red Hanrahan?" the General asked.

"Yes, sir."

"Hanrahan is so impressed with your little operation that he's taking it over."

"Where does that leave me?"

"Did you happen to notice that captain sitting outside? The one who looks like Sad Sack?"

"His name is Felter," MacMillan said. "I've never met him, but I know who he is. He's in thick with Red Hanrahan. And Bob Bellmon, too. What's he got to do with this?"

"You're now working for him, effective immediately," General Black said.

"He's CIA? Since when is the CIA getting involved in blowing up bridges?" MacMillan asked.

"Who said CIA? I didn't use that word."

MacMillan shrugged. "Hanrahan's CIA."

"They're going to use your operation as a cover for them," General Black said. "Putting their people in and getting them out."

"That's all?"

"They have priority of mission," General Black said. "You take your orders from Captain Felter."

"I can handle that. I was afraid you were going to put me behind a desk."

"I should," General Black said. "If you get yourself knocked off running around like John Wayne, Mac, my ass will be in a crack."

"I have no intention of getting myself killed," MacMillan said.

"Watch yourself, is all I'm saying. I mean it, Mac. I don't want to find myself in a position explaining why I allowed a Medal of Honor winner to get himself shot."

"Yes, sir. Is that all you've got for me?"

"Not quite," the General said. He gave MacMillan the rest of the bottle of the 24-year-old Ambassador scotch.

MacMillan put the whiskey in a musette bag and walked out to pick up Captain Felter.

"I thought I knew who you were," he said, putting out his hand. "But I wasn't sure if I should admit it."

"It's nice to meet you, Major," Felter said, shaking his hand.

"You heard about that, too, huh?"

"I heard. Congratulations."

"Yeah, well. You keep your mouth shut, and your nose clean, and you can't help but get promoted," MacMillan said.

"I saw Colonel Bellmon, Colonel and Mrs. Bellmon, in Washington. They asked to be remembered to you, if I saw you. I said I didn't think I would see you."

"Yeah, I'll bet she sent her best regards," MacMillan said. "And speaking of asshole buddies, I saw an old friend of yours the other day. Lowell. Would you believe that pissant is a major?"

"I heard he was."

"He just got himself named aide-de-camp to the chief of staff at IX Corps."

"You heard what happened to Ilse?" Felter asked.

"Who? Oh, you mean that kraut he married. I never could remember her name. Yeah, I heard. Tough."

"Yeah," Felter said. "Tough."

"I've got a Beaver at the airstrip," MacMillan said. "Whenever you want to go."

"I'm ready anytime you are," Sandy Felter said.

"I want to stop by the PX and buy some major's leaves,"

MacMillan said. "But that's all I have to do. You got the time, we could run over to IX Corps and see Lowell. Take us about an hour."

"I'd like to see him, of course," Felter said, "but I don't think we're going to be able to find time for that. Or that it would be a good idea, even if we could find the time."

Macmillan recognized the rebuke.

"Hey," he said, "I got the word. I mean *I got the word*. But put your mind to rest. There aren't half a dozen people aside from my people who know what we're doing. The word is that we're a radio relay outfit. My guys tell that story when they get to the IX Corps for the PX and a steak and whatever. What I'm saying is that I don't let anything get in the way of my mission, either."

"Sorry," Felter said, after a moment. "You tend to get paranoid in my line of work."

(Four)
Socho-Ri, South Korea
30 August 1951

An hour later, as darkness fell, MacMillan dropped Task Force Able's L-20 DeHavilland Beaver out of overcast skies and landed on a dirt road fifty yards from the Sea of Japan, near the village of Socho-Ri.

The inhabitants of the village had been evacuated. The thatch-roofed, stone-walled houses had been fumigated and taken over as living quarters. The three American officers, twenty-seven American enlisted men, and seven Korean officers occupied the seven best houses, one of which served as a mess hall, bar, and transient quarters. These houses were surrounded with concertina barbed wire and were known as the compound.

The senior Korean officer, Major Kim Lee Dong, had been a lieutenant in the Imperial Japanese Army, with long service in China. Among other duties, he had been charged with housekeeping. He had been levied upon the women's section of the Republic of Korea for mess personnel, selecting from the more than two hundred eager volunteers for special duty forty women who understood that members of an elite unit expected more of their mess support personnel than cooking, washing, and tending the furnaces of the hootches. Presuming the performance of their duty was satisfactory, they could expect not only a triple ration to do with what they wanted, but supplemental pay as well.

MacMillan, once he had assumed command of Task Force Able, had arranged for the Korean military personnel, officer and enlisted, to be placed on the American ration return. Inasmuch as Task Force Able was considered to be combat unit on the line (MacMillan had arranged for that determination, too), each individual on the ration list was authorized a ration and a half, plus a comfort ration of cigarettes, toilet paper, candy bars, and even writing paper and envelopes. There was a special ration of two cans of beer per day.

While the appetites of the Americans were phenomenal by Korean standards (the breakfast menu of Task Force Able, for example, was fruit juice, coffee, reconstituted milk, cereal, eggs to order, bacon, ham, biscuits, toast, butter, jam and marmalade, and fresh fruit), there was invariably enough food left over (indeed, uncooked) to provide mess personnel with an additional source of income via the black market, even after augmenting the Korean ration.

A jeep and a three-quarter-ton truck met the DeHavilland L-20. The American driver of the truck, the mess sergeant, supervised the off-loading of that day's ration of fresh fruit and fresh meat (picked up while MacMillan was at XIX Corps) so that the fucking slopes wouldn't make half of it disappear before it got to the fucking kitchen, while the Korean driver of the jeep drove MacMillan and Felter to the club in the compound.

The club was crowded with American enlisted men, most of them sergeants, and all of them somewhat older than the teenagers who constituted the bulk of enlisted men in Korea. They were at the bar. A captain and a warrant officer were sitting before a table reserved for officers, drinking beer and bourbon.

"Gentlemen," MacMillan said, "this is Captain Felter, who has been attached to us as an advisor. And I am, in case you are all blind, Major MacMillan, your new field-grade commanding officer."

He said it loud enough for everybody in the building to hear, and they all came over to congratulate him.

"I suppose I'm stuck to buy all you thirsty bastards a drink," MacMillan said. "Just make sure you beer drinkers don't get a sudden scotch urge."

"Welcome, Captain," the captain who had been sitting at the table said, once the commotion died down a little. "Welcome to MacMillan's Floating Circus."

Felter was experiencing a strange emotional experience. He took a moment to analyze it, to try to explain it, as he shook the captain's and the warrant officer's hands. Then he knew what it was. He didn't feel at all like a stranger here. It was Ioannina, the 24th Royal Hellenic Mountain Division, the U.S. Military Advisory Group, Greece, all over again. It was as if, instead of having come to an obscure village in the middle of nowhere, he had come home.

"I'm going to move Felter in with me," MacMillan said. "Which means you'll have to move out, Paul." The captain's face registered surprise. "The 'advice' Felter is going to give us is advice we're going to follow," MacMillan added. "Get the message?"

"I don't want to move the captain out of his quarters," Felter said.

"My pleasure, Captain," the captain said. "Besides, MacMillan snores."

Without asking, a Korean girl in army fatigues delivered a liter bottle of Asahi beer and a glass and set it before MacMillan.

Felter spoke to the girl in Korean. She was visibly surprised, and giggled, and covered her mouth with her fingers. Then she scurried away and returned in a moment with a bottle of white wine. Felter thanked her in Korean.

"I'm impressed, Felter," MacMillan said. "There aren't many people who speak Korean."

"I get by," Felter said, shyly.

The sliding door opened and a heavyset Signal Corps captain, followed by a slight warrant officer stepped inside the room.

"Who the hell are they?" the captain who had lost his room to Felter asked. There were few visitors to Socho-Ri, and no welcome ones.

The newcomers looked around the room, saw the officers at their table, and walked over to them.

"What can I do for you, Captain?" MacMillan asked, not very friendly.

"Hello, Captain," the newcomer warrant officer said, putting out his hand to Felter. "Nice to see you again."

Felter got to his feet and shook the warrant officer's hand and said it was nice to see him, too. It was evident to MacMillan that Felter hadn't the foggiest idea who the warrant was.

"We're looking for Captain Felter," the captain said. "I see we found him."

"Can I help you?" Felter asked.

"I got two commo vans for you," the captain said.

"Oh, yes," Felter said. "I didn't expect you so quickly."

"I've got orders to get the net in by 2000," the captain said. "You want to tell me where to put it?"

"I really don't know," Felter said, looking at MacMillan.

"Mr. Davies is my commo officer," MacMillan said. "Maybe he can help."

"I need a place to rig some ninety-foot antennae," the captain said.

"Go show him where, Davies," MacMillan said. Davies got to his feet and so did Felter. They left the room. The newly arrived warrant officer sat down in Davies's chair.

"I'm crypto," he said. "I don't know diddly shit about antennae, fortunately. Hey, honey, get me a beer, will you?"

"I gather you're going to be with us?" MacMillan asked, almost sarcastically.

"It looks that way, Major," the cryptographic warrant officer said.

"Mac," the captain said, "just who the fuck *is* that little Jew?"

"I told you," MacMillan said, "he's here as an advisor. From above."

"But who the fuck is he?"

"I'll tell you who he is, Captain," the cryptographic warrant officer said. "That's Mouse Felter."

"Is that supposed to mean something?" MacMillan asked.

"He's one mean little son of a bitch, for one thing. I wouldn't recommend letting him hear you call him a little Jew, Captain."

"Why do you say he's mean?"

"I was with him in Greece. I don't think he remembers me. I was an EM then. But I remember him."

"What did he do mean in Greece that so impressed you?" MacMillan asked.

"I'm not sure I should talk about it," the warrant officer said.

"Goddamnit, you started it, now finish it," MacMillan said sharply. He was more than a little curious to know what the warrant knew about Felter.

"Well, we had a captain who didn't want to relieve some Greeks stuck on a hill," the warrant officer said. "They was dropping mortars on the road. And the Mouse figured he should at least try. There was some kid American lieutenant on the hill with the Greeks."

"The kid's name was Lowell, right?" MacMillan said.

"Yeah, you know about it, huh?"

"Doesn't everybody who's been in the army more than two weeks?" Mac replied. Guessing it was Lowell was a wild shot. It had hit the fucking bull's-eye.

"I have nine years, six months, and four days, Major, sir," the captain said. "And I don't know about it."

"Tell him," MacMillan said, grateful that he would now hear the rest of the story himself.

"When this captain lost his nerve, and not only wouldn't go up the hill, but told the Mouse he couldn't go either, the Mouse blew him away with a Thompson," the warrant officer said. "Just like that." He made the stuttering sound of a Thompson.

"No shit?" the captain said.

"No shit," the warrant officer said. "Don't fuck around with him, he's meaner than shit."

Unknowingly, Captain Sanford T. Felter had jut been raised 95 Brownie points in the opinion of Major Mac MacMillan.

(Five)

It took just over three hours to erect the antennae required. Felter stayed on the site until the network was in, and then saw to it that the enlisted men were fed and given places to sleep. Then he went to the club and asked if he could have an egg sandwich or something. When he'd eaten that, and drunk a Coke, he said that he was going to turn in, that it had been a long day, and would someone please show him where to go.

MacMillan summoned the waitress who had served them before, with whom Felter had spoken in Korean. He signaled for her to go with Felter.

Felter followed the girl to the thatch-roofed house. She showed him where the latrine was and the heated shower. He thanked her and went to the latrine, and then took a shower. Then he sat down at the folding wooden desk and took out his pen to write Sharon a letter.

There was movement behind him. For some reason, he was startled. He pushed himself sideward off the chair, rolled on the floor, and when he came up, he had his Colt .45 automatic, cocked, in his hand.

It was the Korean girl. She was no longer wearing the army fatigues. She was dressed in a flimsy nylon robe, so short that he could see her nylon panties and the tuft of black hair beneath.

He had frightened her; she yelped, almost screamed.

"You frightened me," he said, laying the pistol on the desk. "I'm sorry."

"I'm sorry," the Korean girl said. "I did not mean to displease you."

"You didn't displease me," he said. "Is there something I can do for you?"

"You don't like me?"

"Oh," Felter said, finally understanding. "I have a wife."

"Here?"

"No, in America."

"But here you need a woman."

"I don't need a woman," he said.

"You want, maybe, a boy?" she asked. "I go ask . . ." She had switched to English.

"You can speak Korean with me," Felter said.

"If you don't want me, the major will send me away," the girl said.

"Well, you go tell Major MacMillan that I said I want you to take care of me," Felter said. "You tell him I said that."

"You are a great gentleman," she said. "I will take very good care of you." She made a deep curtsy, and then backed out of the room.

Felter sat back down at the table, and began to write.

Dearest Sharon,

Well, here I am in Korea. I have been put in charge of a small radio station on the Sea of Japan. It's far from the front lines, so I am in no danger at all. As a matter of fact, the only bad thing about this place is that there's no indoor plumbing. There's a shower, but when you have to go, you have to use a place in the backyard.

It is a small detachment of men, to operate the radio station, and to provide transportation of people and supplies along the coast. They have two Chinese junks, just like the ones you see on postcards, and I hope to get a ride in one tomorrow or the day after.

I will write more tomorrow, when I've had a chance to look around. I'll close now, because it's been a long day, and I'm very tired.

I love and miss you and our child very much. Many kisses and hugs to you both. Your adoring,

Sandy.

PS: There is a major here named MacMillan, who knows Craig. He told me that Craig is now an aide-de-camp to the chief of staff of IX Corps. I'd like to see Craig, but it's a long way from here, and I don't see how I'll be able to make the trip anytime soon. I was glad to hear that he won't be in combat anymore.

XII

Major General John J. Harrier, Chief of Staff, IX Corps, pulled the sheet of paper from his sergeant major's typewriter, gave what he had written a quick glance, took a pen from a pocket sewn to the sleeve of his stiffly starched fatigue jacket, and wrote, "I Love You, Johnny," on the bottom of the page. He put an envelope into the typewriter and addressed it to his wife, then folded the letter in thirds and put it in the envelope. He tossed the letter in the MAIL drawer, the upper of four stacked open boxes on the sergeant major's desk, and stood up.

He picked up a can of Schlitz beer, drained it, and then put the empty can in the sergeant major's wastebasket. He looked at his watch. It was nearly eleven. He had hoped that the beer would make him sleepy. It had not.

Maybe, he told himself, if he took a little walk it might help him sleep. The corps commander and the chief of staff took turns making middle-of-the-night visits to the IX Corps Operations Room. Tonight was Harrier's turn to sleep through.

It made no sense to be off-duty, so to speak, and wake up two or three times in the middle of the night.

General Harrier picked up his soft leather pistol belt and Colt .32 ACP automatic pistol and strapped it around his middle. He went into the outer office. The duty officer stood up.

"Sit," General Harrier said. "I'm going to take a little walk before turning in. I should be in my quarters by midnight."

"Yes, sir," the duty officer said. "Good night, General."

General Harrier walked down the hill from the White House on the path that led past Colonel's Row. Colonel's Row was actually two rows of one-man tents, twenty in all, in which the fourteen full colonels of Headquarters IX Corps and the six aides-de-camp for the Corps' three general officers were housed, the latter for the convenience of the generals, not as a special privilege for the aides-de-camp.

As General Harrier walked past Colonel's Row, he was surprised to hear the staccato sound of a typewriter. He located the tent from which the sound came from faint cracks of light around the door of one of them; the others were dark, their occupants either on duty or off in one of the messes. It was coming from the tent of his junior aide, Major Craig W. Lowell.

So far as aides-de-camp went, Major Lowell was a mixed blessing. Harrier had suspected that would be the case from the moment he had first laid eyes on him. First of all, he had not reported for duty immediately, as Colonel Paul Jiggs had implied he would. It had been six days after the session in the corps commander's office, between Jiggs (a fine officer, in Harrier's opinion) and Minor (a fine paper-pusher; necessary, of course, but not really what General Harrier thought of as a fellow soldier), over Minor's purely chickenshit intention to assign Lowell to civil affairs.

"I expected you some days ago, Major," Harrier had said to Lowell when he finally showed up.

"Sir, it took me some time to brief my replacement."

The implication was that training an S-3 of a tank battalion on the line was more important than being a dog robber. That was true, but most officers would have rushed to duty with a general.

Lowell, moreover, had arrived somewhat out of uniform.

Because of the heat around tanks, made nearly unbearable in the heat of the Korean summer, Jiggs's battalion (it was more like a combat command) had special, unofficial permission to wear their fatigue jackets outside of the trousers and to roll up the sleeves. Not only had Lowell reported for duty so dressed (unofficial protocol in the army would have seen him showing up in the uniform prescribed for his new organization), but wearing, instead of either a web pistol belt and a .45 or an issue shoulder holster (prescribed only for tank crews, but worn by most tank officers), a German Luger in a nonissue shoulder holster. On the holster was a shiny brass medallion reading GOTT MIT UNS.

Before he had suggested that Lowell take the rest of the day off to get himself settled and into uniform, Harrier had given him Speech Three, in which he traced the role of aides-de-camp in the military from the days when they were general officer's messengers on horseback to the present, when the assignment of aides to general officers had a dual purpose: to relieve the general officers of bothersome details, and to give the aides an intimate glimpse of the duties and responsibilities of general officers.

The next day, Lowell, in proper uniform, had served briefly as Harrier's senior aide. That same day, Lieutenant Colonel Edmund Peebles had arrived from duties as executive officer of the 35th Infantry Regiment to become General Harrier's senior aide-de-camp. As General Harrier in his bones knew there would be, there was an instant personality clash between the two men.

Colonel Peebles was infantry, West Point, and thirty-eight years old. He had not been given command of an infantry battalion, and he suspected, correctly, that service as a regimental exec was not going to be worth as many Brownie points at promotion time as command of a battalion would have been. His performance as senior aide to General Harrier was about his last chance to make bird colonel. Peebles knew he was never going to command a regiment, but he was perfectly willing to settle for a silver eagle as a staff officer.

He knew the way to convince the general of his talents in a staff position was to function in a staff position, and the obvious way to do that was to make sure the junior aide was fully occupied with household chores, so that he wouldn't have the chance to function as a staff officer.

Unfortunately, but unavoidably, Major Lowell looked at Lieutenant Colonel Edmund Peebles, his immediate superior, through the eyes of a commander and saw in him the same things Peebles's other commanders had seen, the things that had kept him from command. Peebles was a good officer, providing someone told him what to do. He was incapable of making important decisions quickly, and often not at all.

Moreover, Lowell was generously endowed with self-confidence. He was, after all, a twenty-four-year-old major. He saw his role as aide-de-camp to General Harrier as Part Two of the functions of an aide: to see how upper echelon command worked, as training for the day when he would wear stars. Arranging the general's itinerary or composing rosters of people who would be invited to dinner in the IX Corps general officer's mess or seeing that the general's jeep was polished were not what he was there to do. Whenever Peebles assigned him such duties, Lowell delegated them to lieutenants and sergeants.

Major Craig W. Lowell was, in his own mind, a commander en route from a junior command (and Task Force Lowell, which had earned him the nation's second highest award for gallantry, the Distinguished Service Cross, was by any standard a more important command than an infantry battalion) to a larger one. Lowell had quickly seen that Colonel Peebles was en route from one desk to another.

Paul Jiggs had accepted General Harrier's vague invitation to "come to dinner" by showing up the day after the session in the corps commander's office and had used the opportunity to tell Harrier what a splendid young officer he was getting for his aide: that rare combination of logistician and combat commander. Jiggs was not given to undeserved praise, and there had been other evidence of Lowell's popularity as a commander. There had been a steady stream of officers and noncoms who, having completed their tours, had scrounged a jeep and driven to IX Corps to say so long to Lowell, their former commander, before going home.

They had come singly and in twos and threes as they'd

gotten their orders, and it had been impossible not to hear their often drunken and sometimes quite emotional reminiscences.

"I'll never forget the day this chickenshit baby face took over the company. Goddamn, did he shake us up!"

"So, finally, after running all up and down the goddamned peninsula for nine days, we finally make it to Osan, and we're almost there, and some dumb fucking infantryman can't tell the difference between an M46 and a T34, and lets fly with a bazooka at us. Well, shit, one of the tanks blows him away, and we finally make the link-up. So there's this full bull infantry colonel, and *he's* pissed, believe it not, because this dumb fucker of his has taken a shot at us and gotten himself blown away, and he jumps on the Duke's ass, and he says, 'Major, if you had been where you were supposed to be, this wouldn't have happened.' So the Duke looks him right in the eye, and says, 'Colonel, what would you have us do, go back?'"

"So we're making the bug-out from the Yalu, and we just barely get our ass off the beach at Hamhung, and there we are on this goddamned troop ship, assault ship, whatever the fuck they called it. It was Christmas Eve, and for the first time in a month, six weeks, we're warm and we get a bath and something besides fucking 10-in-1 rations, and the Duke comes down in the hold with a couple of the officers carrying a couple of cases of 90 mm HEAT, and this Swabbie officer flips his lid, and says, 'The Major should know that he can't bring live ammo into a personnel compartment.' The Duke tells him not to worry, it ain't ammo, it's booze. Goddamn, that made him even madder. I don't know how the Duke handled it, but the 73rd Heavy Tank had a drink on Christmas Eve, the night we come off the beach with all our equipment and our wounded and even our KIAs, and fuck the navy and its regulations."

Harrier especially remembered the warrant officer, a great big bull of a man. Lowell had told him later he'd been his S-3 sergeant, and he'd gotten him the warrant. Mean-looking son of bitch, looked like he could chew spikes and spit out tacks. He stood there with the tears running down his cheeks as he said good-bye, and finally ended up hugging Lowell. For a moment, it had looked to General Harrier like he was going to kiss Lowell.

General Harrier suspected that Lt. Colonel Peebles was one of those officers who based their philosophy of command on the belief that all an officer can expect from his subordinates is obedience and that most good commanders are hated and feared by their troops (a commonly held belief, inspired by George Patton, and one with which Harrier disagreed). Harrier was also aware that Peebles deeply resented Lowell's troops, especially the officers, taking the trouble to come by and say "so long."

It had been necessary to get Major Lowell out from under Colonel Peebles before there could be trouble. Harrier had arranged for Lowell to work with the Secretary of the General Staff and for his sergeant major to handle the dog-robbing tasks for him. Lowell was shortly to go home, anyway, and Harrier decided he was entitled to go home without having an official run-in with Peebles.

Idly curious to see what Lowell was up to, pushing a typewriter at midnight in his tent, General Harrier turned off the pebble path, walked to Lowell's tent, and pushed open the door.

Wearing nothing but his drawers, Lowell was sitting before a typewriter, his fingers flying over the keys, and for a moment General Harrier thought he was writing a letter. Then he realized that was wrong. Lowell was retyping something. There were sheets of carbon in the typewriter, and all sorts of official-looking documents strewn on the folding table and on Lowell's cot, which he had dragged beside the typewriter.

General Harrier watched him for a moment, and then he said, softly: "We have typists, you know, to do that sort of thing."

Lowell instantly stood up.

"Sorry, sir, I didn't know it was you. I thought it was Colonel Peebles."

"What the hell are you doing, anyway?" Harrier asked, and walked to look at what was in the typewriter.

"This is the staff study for the organic air section, sir," Lowell said.

"I'm touched at your dedication," the general said, dryly.

"You said as soon as possible, sir," Lowell said.

"What I meant to suggest was that you apply the whip to the typing pool," the general said, "not do it yourself."

"Well, sir," Lowell said, "the truth of the matter is, I've made several changes in your study. While the typists are typing yours, I'm typing mine. It was my intention to present both of them to the general for his consideration, sir."

"You have *improved* what I gave you, Lowell?" the general asked. "Is that what I hear you suggesting?"

"There were several areas I thought perhaps the general had overlooked," Lowell said.

"Why don't you tell me about them now?" the general said, dryly sarcastic. "You might save yourself a lot of typing."

The air section had simply evolved. According to the tables of organization and equipment, aircraft—either airplanes or helicopters—were provided only to tactical organizations. L-5s and L-19s were assigned to the Corps for messenger service as aerial jeeps; to the Corps of Engineers for aerial survey; and to the Medical Corps for use as ambulances.

As far back as World War II, it had been obvious to some officers that there were other uses for light aircraft. Patton had ferried an entire infantry battalion across the Rhine River, one man at a time, in the back seat of two-man L-5s taken from tactical units and pooled for that specific purpose.

Once the Korean War had started, the need for more and more aircraft within the army had become immediately evident. The commander of the X Corps at Inchon, General Ned Almond, had had to borrow a helicopter from the Marines to make his way around Korea.

So far the solution to the problem had been unofficial. There were far more aircraft and pilots than the tables of organization and equipment (TO&E) provided. They were just carred as "excess."

The "excess" aircraft and pilots had been pooled at division and corps to provide aerial support to the headquarters and to units which were not provided with aircraft. The aircraft and their pilots, however, remained assigned to the units which were authorized on the TO&E. When a division was shifted from one corps to another, or relieved, their aircraft and pilots left with them.

For some time General Harrier had wanted to make the assignment, the authorization, official, but had put off doing anything about it until he had Lowell dumped in his lap. The boy came with a reputation as an S-3. OK. Let him do it. He told the Secretary of the General Staff to get it done and had not been at all surprised when the SGS had given it to Lowell to do. Working from General Harrier's detailed draft, Lowell was supposed to prepare the final version of the staff study, the basic army document for a change in policy, which Harrier would sign and send off on its lengthy bureaucratic journey to the Pentagon.

Given Major Lowell's seldom hidden belief that the army (with a few exceptions such as himself) was equipped with staff officers who were less than fully competent, General Harrier was not surprised that Lowell had made changes in his arguments and his proposals. Harrier was also aware that there were few majors who didn't believe they had better solutions to a given problem than the one proposed by a general. So it came as no surprise to General Harrier that Lowell would try to "improve" on the work of a man literally old enough to be his father and who had been an officer when he was born.

What surprised General Harrier was that when he read Lowell's version of the staff study he had to admit there *had* been improvements to his original proposals and the arguments in favor of them. There was no mistaking it; it was excellent staff work, and Harrier recognized it as such.

There were some places where Lowell was dead wrong, too, and Harrier pointed them out to him.

"We'll go with your version," Harrier finally said. "As changed. Have it typed up."

"Yes, sir."

"To tell you the truth, Lowell—and I'm aware I'm running the risk that your head will swell even larger—that was pretty clear thinking. Perhaps you're not quite as incompetent as Colonel Minor suggests."

"Thank you, sir."

"I meant that, Lowell, just the way I said it. *Have* it typed up. All work and no play makes Lowell a dull boy. Go down to the club and get yourself a drink."

"One of the reasons I did this, General," Lowell said, simply, "was to keep myself out of the club."

"Oh?"

"It's a good thing I'm not rich," Lowell quipped. "I could very easily become a drunk."

Harrier was concerned. Jiggs had told him about Lowell's wife. The day he'd earned himself a footnote in the history books with Task Force Lowell, the day he had become a twenty-four-year-old major, there had been a TWX telling him he was a widower. Maybe he was into the sauce and worrying about it.

"But you *are* rich," General Harrier said. "I just got the report of your Top Secret background invesigation. Fascinating reading."

Lowell didn't reply.

"Getting yourself a reputation as a teetotal, a drudge," General Harrier said, "could do your career as much harm as being rich. A lot of business is transacted at an officer's club bar. You can tell a man, at the bar, that he's as full of shit as a Christmas turkey, and get away with it. You can't do that in an office."

"Yes, sir," Lowell said.

"Your trouble, Lowell, if you do stay in the army, is not going to be doing your duty," Harrier said. "It's going to be concealing your opinion that most people are horse's asses."

Lowell didn't reply.

"Most of them are, Lowell," General Harrier said. "But you can't let them know." He smiled at the young officr. "Good night, Lowell."

"Good night, General."

(Two)

When General Harrier left Lowell's tent he started to walk back up the hill toward the White House and the general officer's quarters. Then he changed his mind about going to bed. He wasn't sleepy. He walked to the sandbagged G-3 operations bunker. The MP guard on duty outside was standing more or less erect with his Thompson submachine gun in the proper sling-arm position rather than sitting down on the sandbags with the Thompson on his lap, so Harrier knew that someone senior was inside.

"Good evening, sir," the MP said, giving him a crisp hand salute.

"Good evening, Sergeant," Harrier said, and walked inside. Inside, there was the sound of the smaller, separate diesel generator that provided power for the Ops Center, and the clatter of a teletype machine. The G-2 and G-3 were in the Ops Center, and so was the general.

"Insomnia," Harrier explained his presence. "Tomorrow night, I won't be able to keep my eyes open."

He walked to the enormous situation map, and one of the G-2 sergeants told him what was going on. Not much. With the exception of some harassing and intermittent artillery fire on the positions of the 45th Division, and a couple of platoon-sized probing patrols against the 187th Regimental Combat Team, the front was quiet.

The bureaucrats were at work, however, General Harrier thought. The teletype machine was still clattering. He turned to look at it. The general was watching it, and possibly something was up, for the general waited until the lengthy message had been completely transmitted and then tore it from the machine himself. He carried it to one of the two upholstered chairs facing the situation map, sat down, and started reading the three-and-a-half-foot length of yellow teleprinter paper.

General Harrier went and sat in the other upholstered chair and waited patiently for the general to finish reading the TWX. The general snorted, swore, and made unbelieving faces as he read the document, and Harrier knew that whatever it was, the general didn't like it. Finally, he handed the yellow sheet of paper across the small table between the chairs to Harrier.

"When I was a G-3," the general said, "I moved an entire infantry division from North Africa to Sicily with a shorter Ops Order."

Harrier glanced at the heading of the TWX in his hands.

FINAL ITINERARY: THE WAYNE BAXLEY AND HIS ORCHESTRA USO TROUPE.

Harrier began to skim over the TWX. In infinite detail, it

listed the members of the USO troupe, by age, sex, and as-similated rank, ranging from the lowest stagehand, who would be accorded the privileges of a lieutenant while in Korea, to Mr. Wayne Baxley and Miss Georgia Paige, the movie star, who would be treated as VIPs, that is, provided with quarters and transportation normally reserved for major generals. Then, in fifteen-minute segments, it traced where the troupe would be from the moment it landed at K1 Airfield outside Pusan until it boarded the transport planes which would fly it back to Tokyo from K16 (Kimpo) outside Seoul thirteen days later.

But the general was not finished: "Furthermore," he said, "I entertain very serious doubts that these troupes really do anyone any good."

"Sir?" General Harrier asked, to be polite. The general wanted an audience.

"The alleged purpose of these USO things is to raise troop morale," the general said.

"I thought it was to remind the troops of the girls they left behind," General Harrier replied. "For whom, along with Mom's apple pie, they are allegedly fighting."

"It reminds them of girls, all right," the general said. "And, if you get right down to it, that's pretty damned cruel, maybe even perverse."

Harrier was surprised to realize that the general was quite serious.

"They bring these girls over here, and get them to prance around the stage wearing just enough clothes to keep them from getting arrested, and that reminds these healthy, horny young troopers of girls all right. And then we tell them they can look, but they can't touch. Now, that's cruel *and* perverse."

"I really hadn't thought of it that way," Harrier said.

"In terms of efficiency," the general said, "it would be cheaper to do what the French do."

"From what I've heard," General Harrier said, chuckling, "that solution occurred to Paul Jiggs, too."

The reference was to the French custom of providing broth-els to troops on the line, and to the rumor that the ambulances of the 8222nd Ambulance Platoon attached to the 73rd Heavy Tank Battalion (Reinforced) had carried warm female bodies to the MLR as often as they had carried wounded bodies away from it.

"Shame on you, General," the general said. "Those were volunteer native nurses, bringing what comfort they could to the troops."

There was general chuckling, involving the sergeants as well as the colonels and the generals. The general took notice of it.

"It's a good thing I know you guys don't talk about what you hear in here at the NCO mess," he said. "It always breaks my heart to send a good G-2 or G-3 sergeant down to walk around a QM dump with an M1 on his shoulder."

The sergeants laughed.

"Well, what about it?" the general asked one of the G-3 sergeants. "Do the troops get any good out of these USO shows?"

"Even if all I can do is look, General," the sergeant replied, "that's better than nothing."

"OK, so I'm wrong," the general said.

"General," the G-2 sergeant said. He was a thin man in his early thirties. "You know what pisses the troops off? The way the women wind up with the officers. I mean, in the messes."

"Well, damn it, that's not my fault. They tell us where to feed them," the general said. He pointed to the TWX. "Hell, they even tell us who we have to assign as escort officers. Did you see that, Harrier? Paragraph 23. Or somewhere along in there."

General Harrier found Paragraph 23 on the long sheet of teleprinter paper.

23. In order to facilitate the movement of the Troupe through its itinerary, each Corps (and the XIX Corps, Group) will assign one officer, preferably an aide-de-camp, in the grade of major or above as escort officer for the Troupe while it is within the respective Corps area. (Or the area of the XIX Corps, Group). Such officer will report to the Wayne Baxley Troupe Escort Officer (Col. Thomas B. Dannelly, or his designate) two (2)

days before the Troupe is scheduled to arrive at the respective Corps (or at the XIX Corps, Group) and will
remain attached to the Troupe until it departs the respective Corps (or the XIX Corps, Group).

"What do you think about that?" the general asked. Harrier
handed the TWX to the G-3, who, it occurred to him, had been
too polite either to ask for it, or to read it over Harrier's shoulder.

"Sorry, Charley," General Harrier said, and then responded
to the general's question. "I presume, General," he said, "that
the press of urgent military duties has, regrettably, made our
aides unavailable for anything else, no matter how worthy an
enterprise."

"What do you propose?" the general asked.

"Let the special service officer handle it," Harrier said. "Let
him go himself, if it comes to that."

"No," the general said. "Do you know that they actually run
an after-operations critique on these things? And if we didn't
give up one of the aides, there would be a paragraph in there
saying we had failed to comply with paragraph such and such,
and some chair-warming sonofabitch with nothing better to do
would have us replying by indorsement stating our reasons. It
will be less trouble to send them an aide."

"Yes, sir," Harrier said.

"Just keep those people away from me, Harrier, while
they're here," the general said.

"Away from you, sir?"

"Another paragraph in there 'strongly recommends' that the
commanding generals entertain them at dinner. As of right
now, General, entertaining visiting movie stars and band leaders is the responsibility of the chief of staff."

"Yes, sir," Harrier said.

"Just get them in here, and out of here, with no waves,"
the general said.

"Yes, sir," Harrier said. "Sir, the chief of staff has always
believed it is his duty to bring to the corps commander's attention facts of which the corps commander may not be aware."

"Such as?"

"Does the same Georgia Paige register with the general, sir?"

"That the one who goes around without a brassiere?" the general asked.

"Yes, sir."

"What about her?"

"Does the corps commander really wish to forego the opportunity to reconnoiter that anatomical terrain personally?"

The general laughed.

"The chief of staff is herewith advised," he said, "that in his heart of hearts, the corps commander is like any nineteen-year-old trooper in the Corps. If he can't have it, he doesn't want to have it waved in his face."

"Does the chief of staff have the corps commander's permission to look, sir?"

"You ought to be ashamed of yourself, Harrier," the general said, and laughed again. "Just keep those boobs away from me."

"Yes, sir," Harrier said.

General Harrier took a pencil from his pocket and bent over the sheet of teletype paper.

"Action: SGS," he wrote. "Maj Lowell. Harrier." He held the teletype in the air, and the commo sergeant came and took it from his hands. Major Lowell was the junior field-grade officer among the six aides-de-camp. Junior officers get the dirty jobs.

Christ, knowing Lowell, General Harrier thought, he was liable to wind up getting his hands on the magnificent boobs of Miss Georgia Paige. She really had a gorgeous set. General Harrier had seen her picture on the posters announcing the coming of Wayne Baxley and his Orchestra. He wasn't that old.

It had been a flip, irreverent thought. And then he had a somewhat sobering thought: Maybe a woman was what Lowell needed. Lowell had never taken an R&R. He'd been in Korea since he'd returned from the compassionate leave he'd taken right after his wife had been killed. Was it "devotion to duty," an unwillingness to leave his duties? Harrier didn't think so. It was probably that he was afraid he was going to lose control. He was holding it all in. He couldn't do that forever. Maybe he could get himself laid.

Bullshit. These people didn't come over here to fuck the troops. They come to entertain them, and to get their names in the papers.

The odds against Major Craig Lowell, or any soldier, getting into the pants of Georgia Paige, or any of the other women in the Wayne Baxley Troupe, were probably precisely the same as they would be if they paid a ticket to see them in the Paramount Theater in New York. On the order of two million-to-one.

(Three)
Kwandae-Ri, North Korea
30 August 1951

When Lieutenant General E. Z. Black walked out of his office into the office of the Secretary of the General Staff of the United States XIX Corps (Group), he found that officer, a thirty-five-year-old major, having words with another officer who looked just about old enough to be a lieutenant, despite the gold major's leaf on his fatigue jacket collar.

That aroused General Black's curiosity, as did the fact that the young major wore a nonstandard holster with a German Luger in it. And then, when the SGS saw General Black and shut off the conversation and got to his feet, and the young major came to attention, he saw that he was wearing some very interesting insignia, the two-starred aide-de-camp's insignia on the other collar point, and the triangular armored force insignia with the numerals 73 where the armored division number was supposed to go.

"Go on," General Black said, "I can wait. Take care of the major."

"Sir," the SGS said, "I just informed the major that we have no Major MacMillan here."

"And?" General Black said.

"And I asked the major if he was inquiring on behalf of General Harrier, and he tells me he's inquiring personally."

"What do you want with MacMillan, Major?" General Black asked.

"He's an old friend, sir," Lowell said. "I was under the impression he was your aide, sir."

"He was," General Black said. "But I'm afraid he's not available. I can get word to him, if you'd like, that you were here to see him."

"Thank you, sir," Lowell said. "It's not important. I just happened to be here and thought I'd take a chance and try to look him up."

"Is General Harrier coming here?" General Black said.

"No, sir. Not that I know."

"You just came to see Mac, is that it?"

"No, sir. I'm here about the USO troupe."

The young major was obviously less than thrilled about being baby-sitter to the movie stars. Understandable. He was a tank officer.

"How long were you with the 73rd Heavy Tank?" General Black said.

"About eleven months," the young major said.

"Then you were in on Task Force Lowell?"

"Yes, sir," the young major said, with a funny kind of a smile.

"Well, when you go home," General Black said, "you can remember that, and forget the USO baby-sitting."

"Yes, sir."

"You have the advantage of me," General Black said. "You know my name, but I don't know yours." He put out his hand.

"Lowell, sir," he said.

"You're Lowell?" General Black said. "That Lowell?"

"Yes, sir. I had the task force, if that's what you mean."

"What are you doing as a dog robber?" General Black asked.

"I've got a couple of months to go before I rotate, sir. And when they sent in a qualified S-3, Colonel Jiggs found a home for me."

"And now you're baby-sitting the USO? Jesus Christ!"

Lowell didn't say anything.

"I gather you're not tied up with them now?" General Black asked.

"No, sir. I've got a transportation truck company due here by 1800, to move the troupe baggage. The air force is going to pick up the movie stars at 0745 tomorrow."

"In that case, you've got time for a cup of coffee?" General Black said. "I read that after-action report. You gave a lot of people fits using M24s as supply guards, and armored trucks to take the point."

"I hope I didn't give you a fit, sir."

"Hell, no," Black said. "The way to use armor is to hit as hard as you can with the most you've got, not telegraph your punches."

He threw a stack of papers to the SGS.

"See if you can keep people from bothering me for the next forty-five minutes or so," he said to the SGS, and then he motioned Major Lowell into his office ahead of him.

General Black was bored. If they wouldn't give him an armored force to command, and since he was too old, anyhow, to command a tank force in a classic cavalry maneuver, the next best thing was to do it vicariously. He wanted to talk to this young officer, full of piss and vinegar, who had proved pretty goddamned clearly that there was still a place for cavalry and a balls-to-the-leather attitude in the age of nuclear warfare.

"You can either have coffee, Major," Lt. General Black said, "or a belt of this." He held up his last bottle of 24-year-old Ambassador scotch.

"I think the booze, sir," Major Lowell said.

"I was afraid you'd say that," General Black said. "The most dangerous place in the world to be is between a bottle of booze and a thirsty cavalryman."

He poured Lowell three inches in a glass.

"Christ," he said, "from what I read in the after-action report, I'd have really liked to have been along on that operation. Tell me, Major, where did those armored trucks—what did you call them, 'Wasps'?—come from?"

Lowell sat down without being asked to, sipped on the

general's splendid scotch, and told him about the Wasps and
Task Force Lowell.

(Four)

When Miss Georgia Paige saw the blond young major enter
the XIX Corps (Group) general officer's mess with the corps
commander himself, it confirmed the feeling she had had in
their first, ninety-second encounter: This was somebody special.

He had reported to Colonel Dannelly, the troupe escort
officer, during lunch. He had looked at her long enough, Georgia thought, to be disappointed to see that she wasn't bras-
siereless under her khaki shirt. That was the first thing they all
checked to see. That no-bra business had been a stroke of pure
genius on the part of Tony Ricco, her press agent. It had even
gotten her on the cover of *Life* long before her career had
reached the point where *Life* would have paid any attention to
her at all, much less put her on the cover.

It had been a little embarrassing when Tony had called to
her in front of all those people in the studio to blow on the
nipples so they'd stand up, but that had been what really made
that photograph take off when they handed it out to the press,
and then used it in the advertising. The *New York Times* and
the *Chicago Tribune* wouldn't use the picture without airbrush-
ing the nipples sticking up under the shirt, but Tony had gotten
press mileage out of that, too.

Georgia was aware that her nipples were the first thing men
thought of when they saw her. The good-looking young major
had been no different from the others about that, but there was
something different about him. Maybe because after he'd
looked and saw that she was wearing a bra, he had just stopped
paying attention to her.

He even refused Colonel Dannelly's invitation to sit down
and have some lunch. He said that he had a friend he wanted
to look up, if he could. She had been disappointed, and that
had surprised her. What the hell difference did it make? Christ,
there were enough good-looking young men in her life, some

of whom actually liked women. What was one soldier, more or less?

She had been curious to meet this general. Her father had told her that he was one of the legendary generals from World War II, one of the tank generals under somebody named Waterford (whom she had never heard of) and Patton, whom everybody had heard of. And this general, unlike the other ones, seemed to have gone out of his way to avoid meeting with the troupe. That had made Wayne mad. Wayne Baxley was very conscious of being a star, leader of what he really believed was "America's Favorite Orchestra," and he considered it his right and due to be fawned over by the brass. She wondered if this general had really been as busy as his flunkies said, or if he just didn't want to be around Wayne Baxley and the other "stars." There had even been some question as to whether he was going to show up on this last night.

But here he was, and the young major was with him, and it was obvious to Georgia that Colonel Dannelly couldn't figure that out.

"It's a pleasure to meet you, Mr. Baxley," the general said. "We're happy to have you with us."

Wayne Baxley, oozing charm, replied that he always tried to do whatever he could for the boys in uniform. He told the general that Bob Hope had told him he was Number Two in terms of miles traveled to entertain the boys in uniform. Georgia thought that was so much crap, and wondered if the general believed him. For one thing, she didn't think that Bob Hope would be seen in public with Wayne Baxley, and if they had actually met, she was sure Baxley had called him "Mr. Hope" and hovered around him the way the brass here was hovering around this general. Finally, Wayne got around to introducing her.

"And every GI's dream girl, General, Georgia Paige," Wayne said. Georgia was surprised he hadn't called for a round of applause.

"How do you do, Miss Paige?" the general said. He had not looked to see if she was wearing a brassiere.

Then the general said: "I suppose, Lowell, you've met our guests?"

"Yes, sir," the good-looking young major said.

He looked at her, and then away, as if embarrassed to be caught looking. Georgia flashed him one of her warmest smiles, but it was too late. He was examining the stones in the fireplace of the general's mess.

A sergeant walked up to them with a tray full of drinks.

The general took a drink, and then he leaned over and spoke softly into the sergeant's ear. Georgia shamelessly eavesdropped: "Put Major Lowell beside me," he said. The sergeant nodded.

For a moment, Georgia wondered if the general had something going with the young major. He was pretty enough. And then she discarded that notion, reminding herself this was the army, not show business, and the army was funny about faggots. Wayne had given a speech to the fairies, telling them that if anyone started fooling around with the soldiers, he would have to answer to him.

The way they were seated at dinner was with Georgia between two generals, the one, Black, her father had told her about, and the other a major general (two stars), one rank lower than Black. The young major was on the other side of General Black, and Wayne Baxley on the side of the other general. Where he was just about completely ignored by both generals, even when he went into his drunken Italian harmonica player routine.

The general spent dinner talking about tanks, and some task force, and the other general listened in to that conversation. And the young major had trouble keeping his eyes on the general, and off of her, which made her both feel better and worry a little. Could he tell she was interested, or was he finally aware that she was a movie star?

After dinner, of course, Dannelly moved in as quickly as he could when they were standing around the bar with brandy and coffee. She stayed with the general, because it was obvious that Major Lowell was wanted there. She was surprised how much: When Colonel Dannelly "suggested" that Lowell might like to watch them take the stage down after the last show, so that he could see what was involved, the general had shot that idea down.

"I'm sure he didn't get to be a major at his age without knowing how to load a trailer truck," General Black said. "And if you can spare him, we haven't finished our conversation."

"Certainly, sir," Dannelly said. "I'm sorry, sir."

"How old are you, Major?" Georgia heard herself asking. "You look a little young to be a major."

"Twenty-four," he said.

"Christ," General Black said, "I knew you were young, but not that young." Then he looked at Georgia. "George Armstrong Custer was a brigadier general when he was twenty-one, Miss Paige," he said. "But that was during the Civil War. You see very few twenty-four-year-old majors these days. As a matter of face, you see practically *no* twenty-four-year-old majors." The subject seemed to fascinate him. He turned back to Lowell. "Jiggs get you the leaf after Task Force Lowell?" he said.

"Actually about two hours before we linked up," Lowell said.

"Oh, you were with Task Force Lowell, were you, Major?" Colonel Dannelly asked.

"That's why they called it Task Force Lowell, Colonel," General Black said, sarcastically.

"What's a Task Force Lowell?" Georgia asked.

"This young man took thirty-eight M46 tanks, Miss Paige," General Black said, "and some self-propelled artillery, and using them as an armored force is supposed to be used—which hasn't often happened in this war, unfortunately—ran them around the enemy's rear, disrupting his lines of communication, blowing up his dumps and his bridges, for nine days. Phil Sheridan couldn't have done any better."

Georgia had no idea who Phil Sheridan was. But it was obvious that the general, for different reasons, was as favorably impressed with this blond young man as she was.

The young major sensed Georgia's eyes on him, looked at her, and blushed.

All of a sudden, it occurred to Georgia Paige that when these people talked about George Armstrong Custer, they weren't thinking of Errol Flynn playing a role, but a real person. General Black, who was obviously impressed with the young major, had *really* known and fought with General Patton. The young man who blushed when he looked at her, had actually done whatever the general had said he had done, "disrupting lines of communication, blowing up dumps and bridges."

Confirmation came when they were walking from the general's mess to the outdoor theater where they would give the final performance in the XIX Corps (Group) area.

"Well, that explains what he's doing as an aide," Colonel Dannelly said.

"The blond kid, you mean?" Wayne Baxley asked. "I didn't get to hear much of that conversation."

"What were you saying, Colonel?" Georgia asked.

"Every once in a while, a really outstanding young officer turns up," Dannelly said. "One that they know is going to be a general. So they give him assignments to train him. Working as a general's aide is one of them."

"You mean, they could look at that kid and tell he's going to be a general?" Wayne asked, disbelievingly.

"He's halfway there already," Colonel Dannelly said. "I feel a little foolish. I should have known who he was. He's wearing the 73rd Tank patch."

Midway through her act (which consisted of a couple of minutes of repartee with Wayne Baxley, most of his "humor" a mixture of innuendo and wide-eyed staring at her boobs, followed by three vocals, during which she had the chance to slink around the stage in a dress cut incredibly low in the back to remind everybody that she was the one who went braless), she looked into the wings and saw Lowell standing there in a shadow.

She sang the rest of the song to him, looking over the microphone right at him, wondering (the thought somewhat shocking her) if he screwed as well as he fought. She normally didn't have thoughts like that, and even if she was attracted physically to some man, she didn't think words like "screwing." She was a little bit afraid of him, she realized. Now that she thought of it, she didn't believe he was twenty-four. They had been pulling Dannelly's leg. She was twenty-three. He had to be older; otherwise, how could he make her feel like a foolish girl?

He was gone from backstage when she finished her act, and she didn't see him again that night, although she hung around the general's mess until it was late, hoping he would show up.

He wasn't at breakfast either, and when she asked Dannelly where he was, Dannelly said he'd flown ahead to IX Corps to make sure the trucks with the troupe's portable stage and all the props had arrived safely.

When the C-47 landed at the IX Corps airstrip, she looked out the window for him. He was sitting on the hood of a jeep. When the door of the airplane opened, and the photographer's flashbulbs started going off, he was standing to one side. Their eyes met. Georgia smiled. She had a funny feeling in the pit of her stomach. Down there.

He knows, she thought. And I should be embarrassed, but I'm not.

At lunch, when they had a rare moment alone, Georgia realized she had to get him away from the others. She had an idea.

"I've never been close to a tank," Georgia said, winsomely.

"They're all on the line," he said. "You're not permitted up there."

"Please," she said. For some damned reason it was important.

"I'll see if I can get one down here for you to see," he said.

"Thank you," Georgia said.

She touched him then for the first time, letting her hand rest for a moment on his lower arm. He was warm and muscular.

He was also (although perhaps with the exception of Captain Sanford T. Felter, who was his best friend, no one would believe it) very inexperienced with women. Certainly none of the men in the 73rd Heavy Tank would believe that the Duke had known only two women sexually in his life. There had been an afternoon session in a sailboat just before he had been expelled from Harvard College. He got so excited finally getting her white shorts off, finally seeing what one really looked like, that his loss of virginity occurred on the second stroke.

When he had been sent to Germany, where women were quite literally available for a half-box of Hershey bars, or a box of Lux from the PX, he had remained chaste, less from a sense of morality than a sense of horror of what would happen to him, down there, if he caught something. The army had prepared a technicolor training film with a lot of footage taken in Walter Reed Army Medical Center, in the ward where patients suffering from the third stage of syphilis were treated. There was a lot of footage of suppurating open ulcers on the genital organs. Eighteen-year-old Private Craig W. Lowell had been convinced. He took his sexual gratification through masturbation, thinking of the girl at college, and what it had looked like, felt like, in the thirty seconds it had been all his.

And then there had been Ilse. He hadn't been able to get it up with her the first time he tried it with her. But it had finally worked, and he had fallen in love, and if you are nineteen and in love, you don't cheat on your beloved. Not even if you are an officer serving with the 24th Royal Hellenic Mountain Division, and women are provided to take care of the officers.

And certainly not if you are an officer and a gentleman and an Episcopalian off in a war. As a happily married husband and father, you are aware of sexual drives, certainly, and what a strain abstinence is. You might possibly arrange for a group of Korean women to be examined by the battalion physician, but you don't have anything to do with them. What you do, if you're an officer and a gentleman and a faithful husband and father, is jerk off in a Kleenex feeling just a little ashamed that the imagery is that of your wife.

And when some drunken fucking quartermaster major in an Oldsmobile comes racing down a cobblestone road on a rainy afternoon, and wipes out your wife, then you just don't have any urges. The only thing it's now good for is to piss. It will probably never work again. It's better that way. What the hell, they had better than three years together. He had known it was too good to last. But he had thought that he would be the one to get blown away over here, not that some fucking QM asshole would wipe her out.

He didn't even think of women. He thought he would never think of women again.

And then, when Georgia Paige had leaned over to pick up something from a table, thirty seconds after he met her, and he saw the white of her brassiere down her open collar, it all came back. The photographs of her with her nipples standing up against the material of her shirt. Knowing that they were there, six feet away, right under that white brassiere.

And what was under her underpants, the outline of which he could see through her tight khaki pants.

And part of his brain telling himself he was a fucking fool. For one thing, she was a famous movie star, and what the hell would she want with him, especially after she found out how old he was. Maybe, if she'd thought he was thirty, he could have succeeded in making a pass at her. But if she did fuck him, then that meant she would fuck anybody, that the only difference between her and the Koreans in the ambulance was that she was white and didn't smell of kimchee.

"I tried to find a tank," he told her. "There aren't any in reserve that I could get."

"You mean there's no extras at all?"

"I mean there's only so many hours on their clocks, and I wasn't going to order one down here that they may need to-night."

That just slipped out. For Christ's sake, what was the matter with him? She wasn't some goddamned sergeant he could tell off like that.

"I'm sorry," he said.

"I shouldn't have asked," she said. "I'm sorry."

"All it is is a big tractor with sides," he said. "Nothing but a big steel casting one tracks. You're not missing anything."

"I want to see what you do," she said. His heart beat very heavily, once, twice, three times.

"I'm sorry," he said.

"Take me up there," she said.

"Out of the goddamned question," he said.

She braided her hair and pinned it on top of her head. In the jeep, there were two steel helmets and two ponchos. She drove. The MPs didn't look at jeep drivers, he said.

They got to the helmet line, and he folded the top of the jeep down and laid the windshield flat on the hood, and showed her how to drape the poncho over the steering wheel. The rain on the helmet sounded like rain on a tin roof.

They went up the side of a mountain at four miles an hour, the transmission in low-low. There were fireworks overhead, beautiful orange streaks that seemed to float through the sky. He told her they were harassing and intermittent .50s, and that for every orange tracer she saw, there were four bullets she couldn't see.

A soldier with a submachine gun pointing out at them from under a poncho stepped in front of them.

"Who the fuck are you?" he asked, and then he saluted. "Jesus Christ, Major, we didn't expect to see you back up here."

"You didn't," he said. "OK?"

"You got it," the soldier said.

"Where's Baker Company?"

"Right here," the soldier said. "You're right in the middle of it."

There was a sound like a freight train right over their heads.

"That's that motherfucking 8 incher," the soldier said. "Cocksuckers try to see how close they can come."

The soldier looked at her, idly curious, in the dim red glow of a shielded flashlight.

"Jesus Christ, I don't believe it," he said.

"That's why you didn't see me, OK?"

"Hey, Miss Paige," the soldier said, "I'm sorry about the language, but this is the last fucking place... Sorry."

"It's all right," she said.

"She wants to see a tank," Lowell said. "Where's Blue-balls?"

"Second down the line," the soldier said. "You going to take her in the CP?"

"If you guys can keep your mouth shut," Lowell said.

"Hell, Major, you know we can."

"Don't leave your post," Lowell said. "I'll have somebody relieve you."

They gave her coffee and doughnuts in the CP, and apologized for not having any milk. Somebody had a box of flash-bulbs, so they crowded everybody they could together in the pictures, until the bulbs were used up.

And when everybody in Baker Company, 73rd Heavy Tank, had either shaken the hand of, or gotten the autograph of, or been kissed by Miss Georgia Paige, Lowell took her back out in the rain and showed her Blueballs. That's what she thought he had said, and there it was, painted on the turret in yellow: BLUEBALLS.

"That's quite a name," she said.

"It used to be called something else," he said. "But then the colonel said we had to use names with a B."

"What was it called before?"

"I forget," he said. And then he said, "Ilse."

"Who's Ilse?" Georgia asked, jumping on that. "Your girl?"

"I used to be married to a girl named Ilse," he said.

"I'm sorry," she said.

"She's dead," he said. "She was killed in a car crash."

"While you were here?" She knew that, somehow.

"Yes," he said.

"Oh, honey," she said, "I'm so sorry." She put her hand on his arm.

The crew climbed out of Blueballs, and then helped her climb up on it.

Lowell went in first, then put his hands on her hips and lowered her inside. It was white inside, dirty, and smelled of burned powder and burned electrical wiring and oil. There were 90 mm cannon shells in racks, and boxes of machine-gun ammunition, and leather helmets.

"This was yours?" she asked.

"Yes. From Pusan to the Yalu," he said. There was deep pride in his voice.

"Blueballs?" she asked.

He blushed again.

"For the reason I think?" she asked.

He didn't reply. She put her hand out and touched his cheek.

"We better get out of here," he said. "They'll be looking for us."

He put his hands on her hips again and hoisted her half out of the turret. She could feel his hands trembling.

"Wait a minute," she said, and found a footing on something, then pulled furiously at her khaki shirt and jerked the brassiere out of the way. Then she lowered herself back down inside the tank, until her breasts were at the level of his face, and he could suckle at her famous nipples.

XIII

(One)
Ch'orwon, North Korea
5 September 1951

Miss Georgia Paige's good intentions to keep her personal life and her professional life separate vanished as she stood in the door of the C-47 which would take her, and the other members of the Wayne Baxley troupe, from the IX U.S. Corps airstrip to K16 at Seoul and eventually, via Tokyo, home.

Dressed in a khaki shirt (fetchingly unbuttoned almost to her navel) and khaki trousers, with a fatigue cap perched on top of her head, she smiled and waved for the photographers, and actually turned to duck her head and enter the aircraft. But then she jumped off the airplane and ran weeping into the arms of an impeccably dressed young major, clinging tightly to him, her face first buried against his chest, and then raised to kiss him.

The hundred or more troops gathered to watch the troupe make its departure applauded, whistled, and cheered. Wayne Baxley finally had to get off the C-47 to get her, wearing a broad "Ain't that touching" smile on his face for the benefit of the photographers, but actually furious in the knowledge that photographs of her smooching that goddamned Lowell kid were the ones that would make the papers, not those taken of himself.

In the door, finally, tears streaming down her face, Georgia Paige threw Major Lowell a kiss and mouthed the words, "I love you."

And then Wayne Baxley pulled her inside, and the door was closed. The C-47's left engine kicked into life with a cloud of blue smoke and the plane taxied to the end of the pierced-steel planking landing strip and took off.

It was the first time an oral expression of love had passed between the young officer and the young actress. They had, however, frequently expressed their affection physically following Georgia's uncontrollable urge to offer Lowell her breasts in the turret of Blueballs. They had spent that night making love on Lowell's narrow cot in his tent on Colonel's Row, getting no more than an hour's sleep at a time, one or the other of them waking to lightly stroke and awaken the other, and then to join their bodies and fall asleep entwined together.

At 0400 Georgia had "sneaked" back into the VIP quonset hut on the hill, past one of the guards who had an enormous knowing grin on his face. If she was going to fuck some officer, the enlisted men were generally agreed, Major Lowell was the deserving one. The Duke had class.

At 0530, Major Lowell had carried a tray with toast and coffee and jelly from the general's mess to the VIP quonset in case one of the VIPs had wakened early and wanted toast and coffee. Only one of the VIPs was awake, and she was not interested in toast and coffee. She was fresh from her shower, and at 0535 she and Major Lowell were making the beast with two backs in the somewhat wider and more comfortable bed with which the VIP quarters were equipped.

At 0615, when the corps commander entered his mess after his ritual first-thing-in-the-morning check of the situation map, he found Major Lowell and Miss Paige, heads close together, having breakfast, and saw what looked very much like the imprint of human teeth marks on Major Lowell's lower neck.

The Wayne Baxley troupe gave a 1030 performance near the 8077th MASH for MASH, ordnance, engineer and chemical units in the immediate area. A second performance on the same stage was given at 1430 for personnel of the 223rd and 224th Infantry Regiments of the 40th U.S. Infantry Division, and their immediate supporting units, the 555th Artillery Group and the 73rd Heavy Tank Battalion (Reinforced). The 73rd lived up to their reputation, as reported to Colonel Minor by the captain he had dispatched to "keep an eye on things."

Many of them were drinking, the captain reported, and long after the performance was over, four military policemen were found tied up and less their trousers. They had made the mistake of remonstrating with the tankers over the beer and whiskey.

The 73rd had sent a tank to the performance, God only knows why, and the obscenity painted on the turret ("Blueballs") was certainly going to appear in press photographs, for Miss Paige had obligingly agreed to pose for photographs with the men of the 73rd and their tank. What was worse, they had appeared with a hand-lettered sign three feet tall and twenty feet long, with the legend, "Georgia Paige Can Play With Our Bats Anytime."

Colonel Minor realistically concluded it could have been worse. With Colonel Jiggs having gone home, and Major Lowell now at Corps Headquarters—the two of them replaced by a colonel and an S-3 who understood the necessity of strict discipline—things were a lot better than they had been, even considering the beer and whiskey drinking and the vulgar sign. While there was obviously a good deal yet to be done, the 73rd Tank Battalion was considerably less a uniformed group of thugs and madmen than it had been.

Neither Miss Paige nor Major Lowell appeared for dinner that night in the general's mess, but they turned up in the general's six-by-six van, loaded for use as the star's dressing room, when the troupe showed up at the new location for the performance for troops of the 24th Infantry Division that night.

On the final day in the IX Corps area, after the daytime performances intended to entertain troops who for one reason or another could not attend the earlier ones, there was no evening performance. It was believed that now that the troops had received their creature comforts, it was all right for the brass to be entertained. The troupe entertained in the field-grade officer's mess. Those who had hoped to meet Miss Paige personally were to be disappointed, however. She disappeared immediately after performing, claiming to have a headache.

A rumor circulated that the chief of staff's aide, that boy-faced major, was fucking the ass off her, but this was generally discounted. General Harrier, not to mention the general, wouldn't stand for something like that, and anyway, why would someone like Georgia Paige want to fuck a lowly major?

The general, entering the chief of staff's office three hours after the C-47 had carried the Wayne Baxley troupe away, smiled warmly at the chief of staff's junior aide-de-camp, and politely observed that he looked a little peaked. "You getting enough sleep, Lowell?"

Twenty-two times. Twenty-two times for sure. Maybe twenty-three or twenty-four. Sometimes, it was twice in a row. He had lost count, although he tried very hard to remember each time. Jesus, he had never believed you could really fuck that often. But all she had to do was touch it, and it popped up like a spring, ready to go.

At 1500 on the day the troupe departed, General Harrier told Major Lowell that he had obviously been working around the clock, and why didn't he just knock off for the rest of the day and come in in the morning with his eyes open.

Lowell lay on his cot, half dozing, half dreaming of Georgia, but he didn't sleep. And by 2000, he came back to earth. He got dressed and went up to the White House and went to work. It was amazing how goddamned much paper could accumulate in five days.

By midnight Lowell had cleaned up the work that had accumulated while he had been off baby-sitting the USO troupe and falling in love. He went to his tent and got undressed. He realized he wasn't sleepy, and that if he didn't want to toss and turn for an hour, if he wanted to get some sleep, he would need a drink. Booze always made him sleepy. But there was no booze in the tent. He would have to go get a drink. He put on a fresh, stiffly starched fatigue uniform and started for the general's mess.

He realized he didn't want to go there. For one thing, General Harrier was liable to be there, and Harrier had told him to get some sleep. Or the general would be there, and the general's innocent crack about whether he had been getting enough sleep hadn't been innocent at all. He didn't want to see the general, or any of the other aides, especially Peebles. That left the field-grade mess.

But he didn't want to go there, either. At this hour of the night, the only people in the field-grade mess were going to be field-grade drunks, the majors and lieutenant colonels who really had nothing to do the next day they couldn't do hung over. And they could be counted on to make a pitch to the chief of staff's aide-de-camp, either for some specific, invariably idiotic personal project, or just on general principles, so they would have a friend in high places.

To hell with that, too. He kept walking, and headed for the company-grade mess, where his drinking companions would be lieutenants and captains and a few majors who preferred that company to the more prestigious company they could find in the field-grade mess.

There was an enormous black man sitting alone at the bar, hunched over a drink.

Lowell walked up behind him, deepened his voice, and said: "I really hate to drink with ugly niggers."

Captain Philip Sheridan Parker IV, after a moment's absolutely rigid hesitation, turned slowly on his stool to the right, cold fury on his face. As he turned to the right, Lowell moved out of his line of sight. Parker suddenly swung around the other way.

"Jesus Christ, look at you!" Phil Parker cried out. He grabbed Lowell by the ears and kissed him wetly in the middle of the forehead. "Oh, my God, a major! How the hell did you do that?"

"I cheated," Lowell said.

"What the hell are you doing here?" Parker asked, as Lowell slid onto the stool beside him.

"Slumming, actually," Lowell said. "How the hell goes it, King Kong?"

"How's Ilse? And P.P.?"

"Ilse's dead, Phil," Lowell said.

He was shamed to realize that he hadn't thought of Ilse, or P.P., at all in the last ninety-six hours.

"Oh, my God!" Parker said, in anguish. "How the hell did that happen?"

"Automobile accident, in Germany," Lowell said. "In September. Just about a year ago."

"For Christ's sake, you should have written," Parker said, angrily. "Goddamn, that's awful."

"That's the way things go," Lowell said.

"So you came back in the army?"

"I was here when it happened," Lowell said. "Some quartermaster asshole in Germany got drunk and ran head on into her."

"My God, Craig, you know how sorry I am!"

"Yeah, thanks," Lowell said.

"A year ago?" Parker asked. "You were here a year ago?"

"Yeah. I'm about ready to rotate." He thought: And now I have a reason to go home. I have someone to go home to.

"Seventy-third Heavy Tank?" Parker asked softly.

"Yeah."

"I should have known that was you," Parker said. "But I asked around and they said the task force commander had been a major, and in my innocence, I decided there was no way you could have been a major."

Lowell didn't want to talk about that, and he didn't want any more of Parker's sympathy about Ilse. It made him very uncomfortable.

"How long have you been here?" he asked.

"From the beginning," Parker said. "I had the first M4A3s in Korea."

"Company commander?"

"Tank Company, 24th Infantry," Parker said. "And I was so proud of myself for making captain. I should have known you'd one-up me."

"Just a natural recognition of my genius."

"But you went home, when . . . it happened, I mean?"

"I went to Germany," Lowell said. "It turned out that Ilse's father really is a colonel and a count. P.P. is with him."

Phil Parker was naturally curious about that. It was a long time before Lowell could change the subject again.

"You haven't told me what you're doing here. If my tour is just about over, you should have been sent home a long time ago."

"They're having a general court-martial," Parker said.

"And you're on it?" Lowell said. "Great, it will give us some time together. I'm dog robber for the chief of staff."

"I'm not on it," Parker said. "I'm the accused."

"What the hell did you do?"

"I am charged with violation of the 92nd Article of War," Parker said.

Lowell searched his memory for what that meant.

"Article 92 is murder-rape," he said, after a moment. "What happened, Phil? Some nurse change her mind?"

"I'm charged with murder," Parker said.

"If this is some kind of joke, Phil, I miss the point."

"No joke, Craig."

"You want to tell me about it?"

"Not particularly."

Lowell grabbed the bottle from the bar.

"I'm taking this with me, Sergeant," he said to the bartender. "Put it on my bill."

"Major, you can't do that," the bartender said.

"Sergeant, I'm not supposed to do it. There's a difference between 'not supposed to' and 'can't.'" He took Phil Parker's arm. "Let's go, King Kong," he said.

"Where are we going?"

"Colonel's Row," Lowell said. "Try to behave."

They didn't go directly to Colonel's Row. They stopped by the company-grade officer's tents, where Parker shared a squad tent with three other officers. Parker took a large manila envelope from beneath his air mattress, and when they were in Lowell's tent handed him a thick report, bound together with a metal fastener.

"Once they have decided to go through with the court-martial," he said, "they have to let you know what they have against you."

He gave the document to Lowell.

SECRET

HEADQUARTERS

EIGHTH UNITED STATES ARMY

OFFICE OF THE PROVOST MARSHAL

17 August 1951

SUBJECT: Report of Investigation into Allegations Concerning Captain Philip S. Parker IV, 0-230471
TO: Judge Advocate General
Eighth United States Army

1. Attached hereto are interviews conducted with various personnel by agents of the Criminal Investigation Division, OPM, Eighth Army, in connection with certain allegations concerning the conduct of subject officer.

2. These interviews are summarized as follows:

a. CPL Francis F. YOUNG, RA 32777002, formerly assigned to Company "I," 24th Infantry Regiment, 24th Division, was interviewed at the Tokyo Army Hospital where he is undergoing treatment for wounds. YOUNG stated that on or about 14 July 1950 near Sangju, Republic of Korea, during retrograde movement, he saw a "tank officer" shoot to death with a "six-shooter" LT Ralph J. ROPER, Commanding Officer of "I" Company. ROPER was then making his way to the rear. Troops then accompanying ROPER were returned to the line. It has been established that CAPTAIN PARKER (then 1LT) was in the vicinity at the time, and that he carries, as a personal weapon, a revolver believed to be a 1917 Model Colt .45 ACP. YOUNG, however, on being shown a photograph of PARKER, was not able, or was unwilling, to positively identify PARKER as the officer who shot ROPER to death.

b. LT ROPER was initially carried on the rolls as Missing in Action and Presumed Dead. Attempts to locate his remains by Quartermaster Graves Registration Service following the breakout were only recently successful.

c. 1LT Charles D. STEVENS, 0498666, Tank Company, 24th Infantry Regiment, was interviewed at Tokyo General Hospital, where he is undergoing treatment both for burn injuries received in combat and in the neuropsychiatric division, related the following: On 16 September 1950, shortly after he joined Tank Company, 24th Infantry Regiment, in the vicinity of Tonghae, Republic of Korea, he was serving as a crew member of an M4A3 tank. This was apparently part of an on-the-job training program instituted by PARKER in contravention of regulations. STEVENS was serving as a loader on a tank commanded by 1SGT Amos T. WOODROW, RA 36901989.

Tank Company, 24th Infantry, PARKER commanding, had participated in an unsuccessful attack by the 24th Infantry against the enemy near Tonghae. After an initial penetration of enemy lines, heavy enemy mortar and artillery fire made it impossible for 2nd Battalion, 24th Infantry, to cross a rice paddy and take up positions in support of Tank Company, then commanded by PARKER.

PARKER was in radio communication with 2nd Battalion, and the interchange between them was audible to STEVENS over the tank intercom system. PARKER informed 2nd Battalion that he was in control of former enemy positions and would hold until such time as 2nd Battalion could make their way to him. STEVENS described PARKER'S judgment of the security of his position as unsound, stating that they were under severe artillery and mortar fire, and that it would be only a matter of time until all the tanks involved were destroyed. 2nd Battalion advised PARKER by radio to withdraw, stating that another attempt would be made following an artillery barrage.

At this point, a tank commanded by SFC Richard M. OGLEBY (ASN unknown) was struck by enemy artillery fire which destroyed its right track and severed its radio antennae. The tank, however, remained operable, if immobile, and continued to engage the enemy. The damage to SFC OGLEBY'S tank was reported by WOODROW to PARKER by radio. PARKER then ordered WOODROW to leave his tank, make his way to the disabled tank, and order its crew to abandon the

damaged vehicle. WOODROW complied with this order and
STEVENS assumed command of that tank. In making his way
to the damaged tank, WOODROW was struck and killed by
mortar fire.

STEVENS reported that WOODROW had been killed
by radio to PARKER. PARKER then ordered STEVENS to
move his tank, and to recover WOODROW'S body, and then
to proceed to the damaged tank to evacuate its crew.

STEVENS reported that, in his judgment, PARKER'S
order was suicidal, and he requested reconsideration. PARKER
repeated the order. At this time STEVENS overheard a radio
message to PARKER ordering him to withdraw to the departure
line. Presuming this order superseded PARKER'S order, STE-
VENS ordered the driver to back out of the position, and to
withdraw as ordered. (The driver was SGT Quincy T. AR-
RANS, JR., RA 14375502, a newly assigned replacement.)

STEVENS states that PARKER, observing this movement, went on the radio and said, "Hold in place, you yellow
sonofabitch, or I'll blow you away," or words to that effect.
STEVENS attempted to relay this order to ARRANS, but,
probably because of a defective intercom, ARRANS did not
hear the order, and continued to move the tank.

At this point, STEVENS'S tank was struck by what he
believes to be a HEAT round fired by PARKER. It struck the
right rear track, and fragments penetrated the engine compartment, severing fuel lines and setting the tank on fire. ARRANS
successfully exited the burning tank, but was killed a few minutes later by mortar fire. STEVENS, in exiting the tank, suffered second and third degree burns over 25 percent of his
body. He extinguished the flames on his clothing, and sought
shelter in a ditch.

At approximately this point, enemy artillery and mortar
fire decreased to such a level that the Commanding Officer of
2nd Battalion chose to mount a second assault, which was
successful. STEVENS was located by medics of the 2nd BAT-
TALION and evacuated, in a semiconscious condition, to the
8048th MASH.

d. SGT Lowell G. DABNEY, RA 35189632, Tank
Company, 24th Infantry Regiment, was interviewed at Tokyo

General Hospital where he is undergoing treatment for wounds suffered in the same engagement. DABNEY was the gunner of the WOODROW-STEVENS tank. He had joined Tank Company as a Private after his unit, "I" Company, 224th, had been involved in the incident described in the YOUNG interview.

(1) He stated that he heard PARKER order WOODROW to send STEVENS from the tank over to the disabled tank, and that STEVENS refused to comply with WOODROW'S order, whereupon WOODROW left the tank, leaving DABNEY in charge.

(2) When WOODROW was hit, DABNEY state he left the tank to offer what aid he could.

(3) That the moment he left the tank, it began to withdraw, and was a moment later struck by an enemy mortar in the engine compartment, which set it ablaze.

e. Records of the 8112th Ordnance Company indicate the tank, which was recovered after this action, was struck with a HEAT round, probably of American manufacture.

f. Attempt to garner further information from other personnel of the Tank Company, 24th Infantry Regiment, by agents of the CID have been generally unsuccessful. Apparently no other personnel heard the radio traffic referred to, or if they have knowledge of such traffic are unwilling to relate it. CAPTAIN PARKER has declined to answer questions of any sort, claiming the protection of the 31st Article of War.

LaRoyce J. Wilson
Colonel, Corps of Military Police
Provost Marshal

1st Ind
HQ EIGHT US ARMY 23 Aug 51
201-PARKER, Philip S (Capt) 0-230471
TO: Commanding General, IX US Corps

For appropriate action and reply by endorsement hereto.

FOR THE COMMANDING GENERAL
Steven G. Galloway
Colonel, Judge Advocate General's Corps
The Judge Advocate General.

2nd Ind

HQ IX US CORPS 1 Sep 51
201-PARKER, Philip S (Capt) 0-230471
TO: Commanding General, Eight US Army

1. In consideration of subject officer's performance in Korea, which included a battlefield promotion to the grade of Captain, and the award of the Silver Star and Purple Heart Medals, he was offered the opportunity to resign from the service for the good of the service under the provisions of AR 615-365.

2. Subject officer has declined to submit his resignation.

3. A board of officers convened under the provisions of the 31st Article of War has considered the allegations made against subject officer, and has recommended that he be tried by General Court-Martial for murder and attempted murder.

4. This headquarters will try subject officer before a General Court-Martial and your headquarters will be advised of their decision.

> FOR THE COMMANDING GENERAL
> Thomas C. Minor
> Colonel, Adjutant General's Corps
> G-1

"Pure chickenshit," Lowell said. "Why the hell didn't you resign?"

"I'm a soldier, Craig," Philip Sheridan Parker IV said.

"And you're innocent, right?"

"They have their facts straight," Parker said. "Or almost."

"And you're going to just walk in there and lay down, right?"

"I'm going to do whatever happens."

"Why don't you resign, if you're not going to fight it?"

"Because I would rather be cashiered for doing what I did, than have people think I resigned because they found out I was a thief, or queer . . . or any of the other reasons they let people resign for the good of the service."

"You're liable to wind up in Leavenworth, you realize that?"

"I've considered that."

"Well, we can't have that," Lowell. "We'll just have to beat this court-martial."

" 'We'll' have to beat it?" Parker asked, chuckling.

"Shit, if they throw you in Leavenworth, then it would be just me against the system," Lowell said. "I don't want to be all alone."

"And you've already figured out a way to beat the court-martial, right?"

"No," Lowell said, "but I just figured out who to ask." He looked at Parker, and their eyes met, and they both were embarrassed by the emotion.

"Christ," Lowell said, after a moment, "that's the trouble with you junior officers. Take our eyes off you for thirty seconds, and you've stuck your dick in the fan."

(Two)
Beverly Hills, California
9 September 1951

The moment the Pan American DC-6 rolled up before the terminal building at Los Angeles International, and Wayne Baxley looked out the window and saw the reporters, print and television, rushing out to the plane, he realized bitterly that the scene the big-teated cunt had staged at the IX Corps airstrip just before they left would grab her all the press.

There was no chance the press was there to meet him. Standing in the middle of the assembled press corps was the cunt's wop press agent, holding a copy of the *Los Angeles Times* over his head in both hands. The *Times* was carrying the same photo he had seen in the *Honolulu Reporter-Gazette* when they had refueled there, a three-column photograph of Miss Georgia Paige, tears running down her cheeks, in the embrace of a soldier.

Wayne Baxter had no trouble reading the headline: GEORGIA SAYS GOOD-BYE TO HER GI. *"Georgia,"* for Christ's sake, as if everybody knew her by her first name. He wasn't a GI, either, goddamn it, he was a goddamned officer. The story in the Honolulu paper had made it even worse:

SOMEWHERE IN NORTH KOREA Sept 7 (AP)— He was just one of the more than a hundred combat-weary GIs who slipped out of the trenches and sandbag bunkers of this battle-torn land to say good-bye to Georgia Paige as she left for home after entertaining the troops. Then the actress whose pictures adorn every fox-hole here became just another American girl as she ran weeping into the arms of her GI, who was going to have to stay here and fight while she went off to what the GI's call the "land of the big PX."

There were cheers and applause and more than a few teary eyes in battle-weary faces as the girl all the GIs dream of clung desperately to one of their own. Wayne Baxter, whose band was part of the Paige USO Troupe, finally had to separate the young lovers and put her on the plane. Georgia turned in the door of the Air Force transport for a final look at her GI, and then the door closed, and the GI vanished in the crowd before anyone could learn his name.

It wasn't a goddamned band, for God's sake. It was the Wayne Baxter Orchestra. And it wasn't the cunt's USO troupe, it was the Wayne Baxter Orchestra Troupe. She was just fucking excess baggage.

Wayne Baxter had a hard time smiling as he made his way through the reporters and photographers. He declined to be interviewed, asking the boys for their understanding. It was a long way home from Korea, and he and the orchestra were tired.

He knew himself well enough to know that if he said anything to the press, he was liable to tell them just what he thought of that big-boobed publicity stealing cunt.

In the studio-sent limousine on the way to Beverly Hills, Mr. Tony Ricco, Miss Georgia Paige's press representative, leaned over and kissed Miss Paige on the cheek.

"I'm proud of you, baby," he said. "How the hell did you manage the tears."

"Fuck you, Tony," Miss Paige said, angrily,

"What the hell's the matter with you?" Mr. Ricco inquired. "Don't tell me you've got the hots for this guy?"

"I've got the hots for him," she said. "OK?"

Mr. Ricco put his hands up in front of himself, as if to ward off an attack.

"How long does it take to get a roll of film developed?" Miss Paige inquired.

"Couple of days," he said. "What kind of film?"

"You can do better than a couple of days," Georgia Paige said. "Like today, Tony." She handed him a roll of 35 mm film.

"What the hell is this anyway?" Tony asked. "A picture of Mr. Lucky?"

"Yeah, and they're personal, Tony. Just get them souped and printed and give them to me. Craig's going to be mad enough about that story in the papers."

"Why should he be mad?" Tony asked, in honest bewilderment.

"You wouldn't understand," she said.

"Try me," he replied.

"He's not just a GI," Georgia said. "He's an officer."

"I'm glad that wasn't in the papers," Tony said. "It's better that Mr. Lucky's an enlisted man."

"What I want you to do," Georgia said, "is count the people in the pictures, and get them to make me up two 8 x 10s for each one. I promised the kid who took them I'd do that."

"Whatever you say, baby," Tony said.

"And get it done today," Georgia said. "With what I spend on publicity photos, they can do that for me right away."

"I'll take care of it," Tony said.

When the first print came off the drum dryer, Tony saw that he had something special. For one thing, dumb luck probably, the pictures were perfectly exposed and focused. For another thing, they were taken right up on the line. There was a sign: YOU ARE UNDER ENEMY OBSERVATION FROM THIS POINT FORWARD. And the GIs looked like combat soldiers. They looked like combat soldiers who couldn't quite believe that Georgia Paige was right there with them.

"Marty," Tony called out, "make me another set. One of each, 11 x 14s."

Then he picked up the telephone and called the Time-Life LA Bureau.

"Bob," he said, "how would you like, exclusively, some first-class color shots of Georgia actually on the front line?"

(Three)
Socho-Ri, North Korea
10 September 1951

It wasn't that Major Craig Lowell said that he was on the official business of Major General Harrier. It was simply that it was presumed that he was, when he showed up at the airstrip and announced he had to go find a major over in the XIX Corps area, and that he'd better go in a chopper, in case there would be no landing strip for an L-19.

Half a dozen aviation section pilots were sitting around operations on homemade couches. The only difference between them, Lowell thought (as he often did), and the half dozen GIs who sat around the office in the motor pool was that the clowns who flew the puddle jumpers and whirlybirds had benefitted from an aberration in the system which decreed that people who flew little two-seater $15,000 airplanes and $75,000 choppers had to be officers. M46 tanks, which cost $138,000 and had a crew of four, were commanded by staff sergeants.

Major Lowell had once been heard to say that army aviators had to back up to the pay table. It had not endeared him to the army aviators, but there wasn't much they could do about it. He was both a major and the aide-de-camp to General Harrier.

"Fortin," the operations officer called to one of the pilots, "take Major Lowell where he wants to go."

Finding MacMillan wasn't all that difficult. He was an aviator, and they all knew each other. When they touched down at the XIX Corps airstrip, Lowell sent the chopper jockey inside to ask where MacMillan was. He was back out in two minutes.

"He's at a strip on the East Coast, Major," he said. "But you're supposed to have special permission to land there."

"You got it," Lowell said. "Let's go."

Thirty minutes later, the H23 fluttered down at Socho-Ri. A competent-looking technical sergeant carrying a 12-gauge trench shotgun drove up to the chopper in a jeep and politely informed them that this was a restricted area. If they were broken down, he added, he would relay any messages they had, but they couldn't leave the airstrip.

"I'm here to see Major MacMillan," Lowell said.

The sergeant, with a perfectly straight face, said that there was nobody named MacMillan around Socho-Ri.

"I don't have time for any of your cloak-and-dagger bullshit, Sergeant," Lowell said. "I know MacMillan is here. And what happens now is that we're going to get in that jeep and you're going to take me to see him."

The sergeant examined Lowell closely and thoughtfully for a long moment before he made up his mind, and gestured with the shotgun toward the jeep.

The sergeant drove them to a small village, now surrounded by a double row of concertina barbed wire. There were guards, armed with Thompson submachine guns and the trench shotguns, but they didn't stop the jeep when it passed through the gate in the barbed wire.

They stopped before the largest of the thatched-roofed, stone-walled houses.

"This is where you want to go, Major," the sergeant said.

Lowell entered the building. There were several enlisted men and a warrant officer inside, and a table with nonstandard communications radios.

"Major," the warrant officer said, "I don't think you're supposed to be in here."

"Where's the commanding officer?" Lowell demanded. The warrant officer indicated a closed door. Lowell walked to the door, knocked on it, and then pushed it open without waiting for an invitation.

"I'll be damned," he said.

"Well, hello, Craig," Captain Sanford T. Felter said, moving his hand away from the .45 Colt automatic that lay on the desk beside a manila folder imprinted with the words TOP SE-

CRET in three-inch-high red letters.

The two men looked at each other without saying anything else for a moment.

"You're not supposed to be here," Felter said. "But I guess you know that."

"If I had known you were here, I would have been here sooner," Lowell said.

"Yes," Felter chuckled, "I know you would have. That's why I didn't let you know that I was."

"I never got a chance to really thank you," Lowell said, "for what you did when Ilse...."

"No thanks are necessary, Craig," Felter said. "You know that."

"I owe you," Lowell said. "Don't forget that."

"How are you doing, Craig?"

"All right," Lowell said. "Actually, how I'm doing is that I'm in love with a movie star named Georgia Paige. But I don't think now is the time to tell you about that."

"Craig," Felter said, "you really shouldn't be here. You shouldn't even know about this place."

"Funny," Lowell said, "I thought we were on the same side of this war."

"You don't understand," Felter said.

"I understand you're a spy," Lowell said. "But don't worry. I have a Top Secret clearance myself."

"It would be better if I came to see you," Felter said.

"I'm here to see MacMillan," Lowell said. "You're an unexpected bonus."

"What do you want with him?" Felter asked, rather coldly.

"A friend of mine is up before a general court-martial," Lowell said.

"And you think that MacMillan will be able to come up with some clever little trick to get him off?" Felter asked, sarcastically, almost angrily.

"Yeah. That's what I hope," Lowell said. "MacMillan is the best guardhouse lawyer in the army." He was growing annoyed with Felter.

"I know what you're going to think, and say, before I say

this, Craig," Felter said, "but you're going to have to do without MacMillan."

"You want to tell me why?"

"Because what we're doing here is more important than your friend in trouble," Felter said. "And you know me well enough to know I wouldn't say that unless I had to."

"If I wasn't desperate, I wouldn't be here."

"I'm sorry, Craig," Felter said. "It's a matter of priority."

"What my friend is accused of is shooting an officer who refused to fight. You know how that happens sometimes." The look in Felter's eyes was frightening. They locked eyes for a long time.

"You can talk to MacMillan," Felter said, finally; and it was, Lowell realized, the voice of command, a decision beyond argument. "But you are not to involve him. I don't want any attention directed to us through him. You understand that?"

Felter called in one of the sergeants and told him to take Lowell to MacMillan. MacMillan was aboard one of the junks Lowell had seen as the H23 prepared to land. From the air, it looked like any other junk. Up close, he saw what it really was. There were mounts for .50 caliber machine guns bolted to the deck, foreward and aft. There were radio antennae mounted to the masts, and through an open hatch, Lowell saw large diesel engines.

MacMillan himself was sitting on the deck of the aft cabin with three Koreans, all of them carefully inspecting belts for .50 caliber machine guns. MacMillan seemed neither pleased nor surprised to see Lowell, although he got to his feet when he saw Lowell and broke out a bottle of 12-year-old scotch. And he said, after a moment, what he was thinking: "Jesus Christ, what are you, twenty-three?"

"Twenty-four," Lowell said. "Me being a major bothers the shit out of you, doesn't it, Mac?"

"Yeah, I guess it does," MacMillan said. "You're a long way from the golf course at Bad Nauheim, aren't you, PFC Lowell?"

"I would never have guessed that you, Captain MacMillan, sir," Lowell said, a little annoyed, "would end up as a pirate."

"I don't think this is really auld lang syne time," MacMillan said. "What do you want, Lowell?" But before Lowell could start to reply, MacMillan said something else. "Felter told me what happened to your wife. Sorry about that, Lowell. What did you do with the kid?"

"He's in Germany. His grandfather came home from Russia."

"I wrote Roxy and told her, and she wrote back and said I should send her your address. I never got around to it, but what Roxy wants to do is offer to help. You need anything?"

"Not for the boy," Lowell said. "But a friend of mine is in trouble. You remember the big guy I ran around with at Knox?"

"Man Mountain Coon, you mean?"

"They're going to put him before a general court-martial," Lowell said.

"Charged with what?"

"In the early days over here, he blew away an infantry officer when he wouldn't fight."

MacMillan sipped deeply at his drink before replying. "I heard of that happening," he said, "to people you wouldn't believe."

"I need some help," Lowell said.

"For openers," MacMillan said, "You start by saying, he *is accused* of blowing this guy away. You don't admit it if he did it on the White House lawn with the President watching."

"The first thing I thought about," Lowell said, "was getting on the telephone and having a criminal lawyer sent over from the States. But then I thought that might make him look guilty. And then I thought of you."

"You don't need a high-priced lawyer for the trial," MacMillan said. "That pisses the court off. Later, on appeal, is when you need the real shysters."

"You sound pretty sure they'll find him guilty."

"Is he?"

"He did what they say he did."

"That doesn't necessarily mean he'll get convicted of it," MacMillan said. "But the thing you have to keep in mind is that general courts generally know what the convening authority wants done. If the general who convened the court wants your friend hung, he'll probably be found guilty."

"Shit!" Lowell said.

"Well, it's no big deal," MacMillan said. "Even if they sock him with a death sentence, it won't be carried out; aside from rapists and criminal types, the army has executed only one man since the Civil War. What will probably happen, the worst that will happen, is that the court-martial will find him guilty, sentence him to death, or life, to make the point that you aren't supposed to go around shooting people, and the general, on review, will commute death to life, or life to twenty years, and he would be out, with good behavior, in maybe five, six years."

"How do we keep him out of jail at all?" Lowell asked. "I don't care what it costs, Mac."

"Money won't do you any good here," MacMillan said. "Maybe later. The best thing you can do is check around and find some reserve judge advocate officer, who's really pissed about being called back in the service and doesn't give a shit for his army career or efficiency report. Get him to defend your friend. He may be lucky. But even if he's not, a good civilian lawyer can generally get anybody off on appeal. Somebody is bound to fuck up something in the paperwork."

Sandy Felter showed up on the junk as they were killing the last of the 12-year-old scotch. Lowell wondered if he had really come to drive him back to the airstrip, now that he was finished, or if he had come to let him know his time was up. But on the way to the airstrip, Felter said, obviously sincere: "Hey, I'm sorry about the reception."

"Forget it."

"What we're doing here is important," Felter said. "It comes first."

"In other words, nice to see you, but don't come back?"

"Yeah."

"I won't."

"I hope your friend comes out all right," Felter said.

"But you really don't give a damn one way or the other, do you?" Lowell asked.

"No, I guess I don't, when you get right down to it."

"What if it were me?" Lowell asked.

"I don't know," Felter said, honestly.

"If you had to do it again, Sandy, would you blow away Captain Whatsisname?"

Felter gave him another incredibly cold look, one almost of hate, and certainly of contempt.

"You don't understand, do you?" he said. "I didn't do what I did to save your neck. I did it because that officer was interfering with the mission."

"No, Sandy, I guess I don't," Lowell said. He put out his hand, and they shook hands, and they smiled at each other, but it was as if it was between strangers.

XIV

(One)
Ch'orwon, North Korea
15 September 1951

Major Craig W. Lowell was aware that he was not only on the shit list of Major General John J. Harrier, but that he was about to become the ne plus ultra persona non grata of the IX Corps chief of staff.

The trouble he was in, in other words, was not one half the trouble he was going to be in.

He wasn't sure if he had gone slightly crazy, or if the reverse was true, that he had finally come to his senses, but the bottom line, in that quaint vernacular of Wall Street, was that he really didn't give a damn.

At the moment, it seemed to him that the army, which was having a shit fit about what had happened when Georgia had been in the Corps, was acting quite childishly. Morality and propriety had been offended, and he was the guilty party. It reminded him somewhat of the time his school had been in New Jersey playing tennis against Peddie and had been entertained by the students and faculty of Miss Beard's School in Orange, where he had put Ex-Lax on the candy plates. It had given seven or eight fifteen-year-old girls diarrhea, and sent the head into a frenzy.

The only difference seemed to be that the head at St. Mark's hadn't known who had put the Ex-Lax on the candy plates, and the head here knew who the sinner was.

There had been a lightning bolt from the Pentagon. A heavy manila envelope, sealed and stamped BY OFFICER COURIER, had been sent from the Pentagon in the hands of a replacement lieutenant colonel, brought from the Dai Ichi Building in Tokyo to Eighth Army Headquarters by the warrant officer courier carrying the week's cryptographic codes, and from Eighth Army to IX Corps by the Eighth Army commander's junior aide-de-camp, who personally put it in the hands of the corps commander.

The corps commander had then opened it and summoned the chief of staff, and both of them had then solemnly contemplated a short, square piece of notepaper, the letterhead of which was a representation of a full general's four-star flag, flying in the breeze.

The message was brief: "The Chief of Staff desires your comments on the article on pages 73-78 of *Life* magazine, enclosed."

Life had somehow come into possession of the roll of film Georgia had taken at the 73rd Heavy Tank Battalion and then carried with her back to the States. *Life* had run a full-page photo showing Georgia, wearing body armor, standing with a group of tankers. There were eight tankers, six enlisted men and two officers, including Major Craig W. Lowell. Behind them was Blueballs.

They were good photographs, and the name "Blueballs" was clearly legible. So was what the troops of Baker Company— in mockery of the air force practice of painting kills on the side of the aircraft fuselages—had painted on the turret: eight silhouettes of Russian-built T34 tanks, with an X drawn through them, signifying the eight confirmed kills made by Blueballs (five of them when it had been "Ilse" on the way up the peninsula, and three by later commanders). There were also, for a laugh, silhouettes of ox carts, Korean papa-sans, and people in wheelchairs, with X's indicating they had been wiped out, too.

There was a large line of type superimposed on the picture: GEORGIA PAIGE VISITS THE FRONT LINES.

The caption beneath the picture read: "Her world-famous bosom hidden beneath a bulletproof vest, her long locks in braids, Hollywood's hottest new star slipped away from the USO troupe entertaining troops in the rear areas to visit this tank battalion on the front line 'somewhere in North Korea.'"

The other five pages showed Miss Paige while an unshaved GI poured bourbon in her canteen cup; autographing a copy of the famous erect-nipples photograph stapled to a company situation map; kissing one soldier while a line formed behind him; and being helped down from Blueballs by two eager soldiers. Her shirt was improperly buttoned, as if she had had it off. Lowell was in most of the pictures, sometimes looking at Miss Paige as if she gave milk, and wearing his German Luger in the shoulder holster with the GOTT MIT UNS belt buckle gleaming.

Lowell had been called in by General Harrier to answer for his sins. There had been a recitation of them.

"There seems to be absolutely no question, Major Lowell, that, in direct violation of regulations, and showing less common sense than that expected of a corporal, you actually took that woman up to the front."

"No, sir," he said. "I mean, yes, sir. I took her up there."

"What were you thinking?"

He could hardly have told the general what he was really thinking.

"I regret any embarrassment I have caused, sir."

"That's not good enough, Lowell. I can't remember ever having been so humiliated by the actions of one of my officers."

"With all respect, sir, I fail to see how my actions could humiliate you."

I am, after all, a fucking major, and I don't think they

expect major generals to go around holding majors by the hand.

"There you are, for all the world to see, wearing an unauthorized weapon, in an unauthorized shoulder holster, with a Nazi motto on it."

"God is with us" is a Nazi motto? Does he really believe that?

"And standing in front of a tank with an obscenity painted on it."

"I repeat, sir, my regret for any embarrassment I may have caused you."

"And I repeat, Major, that's not good enough!"

"Yes, sir. What would the general have me do, sir, to make amends?"

"Just close your damned mouth," General Harrier had said. "When I want a reply, I will ask for one."

There followed a long pause.

"What I really would like to do to you, Lowell," General Harrier finally said, "is stand you before a court-martial for conduct unbecoming an officer and a gentleman!"

I wonder where it says in Amy Vanderbilt that what I've done is ungentlemanly.

"With the press around here, however, that would only result in even greater embarrassment to the army."

You're goddamned right it would. The army would really look silly if you tried to throw a court-martial at me.

"You stand relieved as my aide," General Harrier said. "Your behavior will be reflected in your efficiency report. Until your orders are issued, you will remain in your tent except for meals. You will come here to empty your desk between the hours of 2000 and 2030 tonight. Aside from that, I don't want to see you around this headquarters again. You are dismissed."

"Yes, sir," Lowell said. He saluted and about-faced, then walked down to Colonel's Row.

When he went back that night to clean out his desk, he saw how the general had replied to the Chief of Staff. The letter had been typed and then placed on the aide's desk, so that he could give it to the general for his signature first thing in the morning.

Hq IX Corps
APO 708
San Francisco, Cal.
16 Sept 51

Dear General Malloy:

The Corps Commander has asked me to reply to your note regarding the article in *Life* magazine. My junior aide-de-camp, Major Craig W. Lowell, was the IX Corps Escort Officer for the Baxley USO Troupe while they were in the IX Corps area.

Major Lowell, who, you may recall, commanded Task Force Lowell during the breakout from the Pusan perimeter and the link-up with X U.S. Corps, is a responsible combat commander who would not, obviously, endanger the life of Miss Paige by taking her (or any other civilian) into a position where there would be any danger of enemy action.

When the Baxley Troupe performed for troops including the 73rd Heavy Tank Battalion (Reinforced) near the 8077th MASH, some troops of "B" Company, 73rd Heavy Tank, Major Lowell's former command, and without specific permission to do so, brought one of the "B" Company tanks from the line to the 8077th MASH area. I can only presume that they hoped their former company commander would be able to get them special consideration to pose with Miss Paige in photographs; in any event, this obviously transpired. Enclosed are photographs of Miss Paige, the tank Bluebell, and troops of Baker Company taken at the time, and which were not published in *Life*.

Both this unauthorized movement, and the very questionable "humor" of the lettering and symbols on the tank in question were brought to my attention by the IX Corps G-1, Colonel Thomas C. Minor. I am attaching a copy of his report, including photographs of the tank in question, together with the copy of my letter to the CO, 73rd Heavy Tank Battalion, directing him to immediately correct the spelling of the name of Bluebell, and to obliterate all symbols except those of the eight T34s Bluebell has been officially credited with killing.

We have, obviously, as you are well aware, no control over what *Life* magazine, or any other publication, chooses to say. However, what responsibility there is for this unfortunate incident is clearly mine. I have counseled Major Lowell, informing him that his special consideration for troops of his former command was ill-advised and unseeming.

I stand ready, of course, to answer any other questions you might have.

Sincerely,
John J. Harrier
Major General

Lowell checked his uniform. His aide-de-camp's insignia were gone, and the crossed sabers of cavalry superimposed on an M46 tank were back. The Luger and the shoulder holster were locked in his footlocker, as were his tanker's boots and his tanker's shoulder holster. He had gone to supply and drawn a standard web belt and holster. He was, he decided, in the perfect uniform prescribed for a field-grade officer "awaiting assignment" at IX U.S. Corps.

Then he walked up the hill to the White House, and entered the office of the Secretary of the General Staff.

"I thought that you were told to stay in your quarters until you got your orders," the SGS, a normally pleasant, just promoted to full bull colonel, said.

"Yes, sir."

"I sent you orders sending you home an hour ago," the colonel said.

"Sir, I am in doubt as to which orders I should obey," Lowell said. "And am coming to you for clarification." Then he laid a letter on the Secretary of the General Staff's desk. It was signed by First Lieutenant Bennington T. Morefield, Judge Advocate General's Corps, and informed him that he was to hold himself available to appear as a witness for the defense in the case of *The United States of America* v. *Captain Philip S. Parker IV*.

(Two)
Ch'orwon, North Korea
16 September 1951

Major General John T. Harrier went into the office of the corps commander, and closed the door.

"Major Lowell has not left the Corps, sir," he said. "He has been summoned as a witness in Captain Parker's court-martial."

The general thought that over a moment, and then he asked: "As a witness for the defense?"

"Yes, sir."

The general thought that over a moment, too; then he said: "I think that it would be a very good idea, John, if you attended the trial. I want to avoid, of course, any suggestion of command influence on the outcome. But I think it's entirely appropriate that everyone concerned be aware that this case is of special interest. I would hate to have the trial disrupted by the irrational behavior of anyone."

"Yes, sir."

"What the hell has Lowell got to do with that trial, anyway? I wasn't even aware they were acquainted."

"I don't know, sir."

"Keep me advised," the general said.

Despite what he had said about wanting to avoid "any suggestion of command influence," there was no doubt in Harrier's mind that the General wanted Parker hung. He wondered why. Some personal feeling that Parker deserved punishment? Racial prejudice? There was *something*, otherwise they could have sent any other officer in the headquarters to "keep him advised."

When the general's chief of staff walked into the courtroom, the court would draw the obvious conclusion, that having decided to court-martial Parker, the general wanted a report on anyone who appeared to be trying to frustrate that desire.

Harrier walked down the hill from the White House and entered the tropical building with the sign SILENCE: COURT IN

SESSION outside. There were two MPs outside the building, who saluted him, and two more inside the building, who pulled the door to the courtroom open for him.

He walked in and tried to make himself as inconspicuous as possible in the rear of the small room. It was like trying to hide an elephant, he thought, under a tulip.

He was surprised at the initial steps of the trial. He had been a defense counsel in his younger days, and he would not have stricken from the court, on preemptory challenge, the two officers Lieutenant Bennington T. Morefield struck from it. They were a bird colonel and a lieutenant colonel, both wearing the Combat Infantry Badge. He would have kept them, as probably being sympathetic to another combat officer.

And he was surprised at Lieutenant Bennington T. Morefield's behavior during the prosecution testimony. He had expected objection to practically everything the CID agents said, as well as the quoting of arcane legal principles which would be beyond the understanding of the court-martial officers.

He did nothing of the kind. He didn't challenge the facts at all. The court could have no question in their minds that Captain Parker did in fact shoot the officer of the 24th Infantry who couldn't find it in himself to stand and fight. The facts concerning who shot up the tank, the second charge, were even more clear, and General Harrier was surprised that Morefield didn't even try to muddy those waters, to try to form a reasonable doubt, as much as he could, as Harrier would have done had he been in his place.

But this JAG lieutenant didn't. He as much as admitted that Parker had indeed blown the other tank away.

The only thing he did, Harrier realized, was impress upon the court that the enlisted witnesses against Captain Parker testified against him with great reluctance and thought rather highly of him.

He asked each of them the same question: "Now, I realize that no one wants to go into combat, but if circumstances made it necessary for you to go back into combat, under the circumstances in which these events allegedly occurred, would you be in any way reluctant to serve under Captain Parker?"

And the answer was always the same: "No, sir."

"Even if the allegations against Captain Parker are true?"

"No, sir. Or yes, sir. I mean, Captain Parker is a good officer."

"You would have no fear that Captain Parker would go berserk and turn any weapons under his control on you, instead of the enemy?"

"No, sir."

When the defense's turn came, Morefield introduced classified after-action reports, which painted a clear picture of confusion, chaos, and cowardice on the battlefield, and which in three instances mentioned that Tank Company, 24th Infantry, had held its positions when the rest of the regiment had "withdrawn without orders."

Score one for the defense, Harrier thought.

The next round, Harrier concluded, was lost. Colonel Howley, the regimental commander, who should have gone to bat for Parker, didn't. Howley hadn't brought the charges against him. The goddamn provost marshal had. Either Howley hadn't known, at the time, what Parker had done—which was damned unlikely—or he had known and lent his tacit approval as something made necessary by the situation. If that was the case, he had a moral obligation to help Parker now. But Colonel Howley apparently lost his nerve once he got on the witness stand. If it had been his intention to do Parker any good, he failed. All he testified was that Parker was a good tank company commander.

On cross-examination, he discounted the chaos, confusion, and cowardice. He probably thinks it was a reflection on him, Harrier decided. Colonel Howley stated that he could conceive of no situation in which he, or any other combat commander, would have to resort to shooting an officer on the field of battle.

(Three years later, sitting on a secret Selection Board for Brigadier Generals, General Harrier would cast a nay vote regarding Colonel Howley. A single "nay" vote is sufficient to deny an officer the star of a general officer.)

"The defense calls Major Craig Lowell," Lieutenant Bennington T. Morefield said, softly.

It occurred to Harrier for the first time that the officers on the court just might interpret Lowell's appearance the wrong way; they might decide he was appearing with the blessing of himself and the command structure. Harrier felt the eyes of the members of the court flicker over to him, wondering if this was indeed a message from on high.

Lowell's salute to the court-martial would have done credit to a cadet at West Point. His uniform was crisply starched and his boots glistened. The Combat Infantry Badge with Star (Second Award) glistened on his chest.

"Major Lowell," Lieutenant Morefield said, "you have been called as a character witness in this case. You know the accused? And if so, will you point him out?"

Lowell pointed to Parker.

"Let the record show that Major Lowell pointed out the accused Captain Parker," Morefield said. Then he turned to Lowell. "Major, you don't know what happened on the dates in question, do you?"

"No, sir."

"You don't know any more about what really happened than I do, than the officers of the court know, than my learned opponent, the prosecutor, excuse me, the trial judge advocate, knows, do you?"

"No, sir."

"What we're all trying to do here today, Major, is to reach the facts in this case. And once we have the facts, to weigh them, to decide whether or not Captain Parker's actions were detrimental to good military order and discipline."

"Objection!" the trial judge advocate said, jumping to his feet. "What we are trying to determine here is whether or not the accused is guilty of violation of the 92nd Article of War, murder."

The president of the court looked thoughtful.

"I'll sustain that objection," he said. "The court will ignore in its deliberations Lieutenant Morefield's last comment."

"With all respect, sir, I invite the court's attention to the 92nd Article of War, which states that murder, and also rape, are offenses in that they are detrimental to good military order and discipline. Shall I read the Article, sir?"

"We can read it ourselves, thank you," the president said,

icily, and when he read it, said: "I don't quite understand your point, Lieutenant."

"Sir," Morefield said, slowly, carefully, "the Congress in its wisdom has decided that the federal statutes which govern behavior of the civilian populace are not applicable to the military. Hence, the 1928 *Manual for Courts-Martial* and its precedent Articles of War. The difference, sir, is that under federal law, and the laws of the several states, murder, to use that as an example, is considered to be an offense against—a commonly used phrase—'the peace and tranquility' of the community. Military offenses, on the other hand, as the Congress has carefully spelled out, are those actions which are 'detrimental to good military order and discipline.'"

"I think that's nonsense," the trial judge advocate said. "Murder is murder."

"Are you trying to tell me, Lieutenant," the president of the court asked, "that murder is sometimes justified in order to preserve good military order and discipline?"

"What I am saying, sir, is that an action necessary to preserve good military order and discipline cannot be an offense."

"That's absolute nonsense, and you know it!" the trial judge advocate said furiously. "I've never heard such absurd reasoning!"

"The objection has been sustained," the president said.

"Sir, with all respect, the defense enters an objection for the record, and in order that the appellate authorities might have all the facts clearly before them, should there be a conviction at this level, the defense respectfully requests that the court reporter read back from his notes what my statement was, the objection to it, my counterargument, and the court's final decision."

The court reporter read the whole thing back.

Clever as hell, Harrier thought. Morefield is giving them another chance to think over what he said. And there's that threat of review.

General Harrier had been curious when Captain Philip S. Parker IV, on being advised that a Board of Inquiry had recommended his trial before a general court-martial and that the general had approved the recommendation, had requested that Lieutenant Bennington T. Morefield, Judge Advocate General's Corps, 45th Division, be assigned as his defense counsel.

Whatever he was, Parker wasn't stupid, and there had to be some reason he had asked for the services of a specific lieutenant, when he would have been able to pick any of the majors and lieutenant colonels of the IX Corps JAG office to defend him.

General Harrier had made discreet inquiries about Lieutenant Morefield, and learned that he was regarded as a smart-ass Harvard Law School type. He had been a deputy U.S. attorney in New York before being called into the service, where he had promptly earned a reputation at Fort Polk, Louisiana, for getting his accused off. Lieutenant Morefield had been sent to Korea with a subtle recommendation that his background and experience suited him for duty as a prosecutor.

Harrier said nothing to anyone about what he had learned about Parker's defense counsel. For one thing, if the IX Corps JAG had been doing his job, Morefield would be assigned here as a prosecutor, where he could have been sent down to the divisions as necessary to prosecute the serious cases. That the JAG would be facing a smart-ass Harvard lawyer was the JAG's own fault.

Furthermore, General Harrier believed that the accused was indeed entitled to the best possible defense. He privately hoped that Parker would beat the charge, although he realized that his chances were slim to do so. For one thing, he was obviously guilty as charged, and for another, the officers picked for the court were well aware the general believed he should be found guilty, *pour encourager les autres.*

"I thank you for your indulgence, sir," Morefield said.

"Get on with it, Lieutenant," the president said impatiently.

"Major Lowell," Morefield said, "I notice that you are wearing the Expert Combat Infantry Badge with a star, signifying that it has been awarded to you twice."

"Yes, sir,"

"You earned both awards as an officer?"

"Yes, sir."

"Which means then, that on two different occasions, you have commanded troops in combat?"

"Yes, sir."

"Where?"

"Here and in Greece," Lowell said.

"Have you ever been a tank company commander?"

"Yes, sir."

"You were in fact, the commanding officer of Task Force Lowell, which effected link-up with the X Corps when Eighth Army broke out of the Pusan perimeter?"

"Yes, sir."

"For which, I understand, you were given the Distinguished Service Cross?"

"Yes, sir."

"I also understand that you have been decorated with the Distinguished Service Medal for your performance of duty as S-3 of the 73rd Heavy Tank Battalion during retrograde movement from the Yalu River in December 1950?"

"Yes, sir."

"You have, then, experience in combat in the attack *and* the retreat?"

"Yes, sir."

"I also understand that you were awarded the second highest medal for valor bestowed by the Greek government, the Order of St. George and St. Andrew, for your behavior above and beyond the call of duty in Greece. Is that, also, true?"

"Yes, sir."

"Were you a tank commander, a commander of armored forces, in Greece?"

"No, sir."

"What did you command in Greece?"

"I was an advisor to a Greek regiment."

"But you were decorated for your performance as an infantry company commander, were you not?"

"Yes, sir."

"How did that come to be, Major?"

"I assumed command when the Greek officer was killed, sir."

"And you led troops who were not even legally subject to your orders? So well that their King decorated you?"

"They gave me a medal," Lowell said, obviously embarrassed.

"You could fairly be described, then, as a young officer whose experience of command in combat, as well as whose personal valor, has seen him promoted to a rank unusually high for someone of his age. Would that be a fair statement?"

"Objection!" the trial judge advocate said. "For what it's worth, the prosecution will stipulate that Major Lowell is an outstanding, valorous young officer. But I don't see what that has to do with this case."

"Thank you," Morefield said smoothly. "Major, I want to ask you a hypothetical question. On the field of battle, in the midst of 'chaos, confusion, and cowardice,' to use the phrase from the after-action reports, can you imagine a situation where the maintenance of good military order and discipline would require a summary execution?"

"Objection!" the trial judge advocate said.

"Yes, sir, I can," Lowell replied.

"Objection sustained," the president of the court said. "The court will not consider defense counsel's last question, or the response to it, in its deliberations."

"I have no further questions," Morefield said softly. "Your witness."

The trial judge advocate was surprised at having the witness turned over to him. He had expected Morefield to keep pursuing the notion that combat demanded extraordinary measures. But he stood up and walked over to Lowell.

"We know each other, Major, don't we?" he asked.

"Yes, sir."

"I'm a little confused, Major," the trial judge advocate said. "I was under the impression you were aide-de-camp to General Harrier."

"Not any longer, sir."

"Oh?"

Lowell said nothing.

"Why aren't you aide-de-camp to General Harrier any longer, Major?"

"I believe that I was found wanting," Lowell said.

Harrier decided that line of questioning had backfired on the trial judge advocate. He saw quickly stifled smiles on the faces of several members of the court. The word was out: Lowell was in trouble for fucking the movie star. That was a sin, of course, but it was the sort of sin that paled in comparison with the recitation of Lowell's military virtues that Morefield had brought to the court's attention.

" 'A soldier that won't fuck won't fight!': General Philip Sheridan," thought Major General John Harrier.

"In other words, despite the picture Lieutenant Morefield has painted of you as a truly extraordinary officer, Major, you were relieved of your duties as aide-de-camp to the general because you were unable to perform them satisfactorily?"

"I don't believe the general was concerned with the performance of my duties, sir," Lowell said, dryly.

One of the officers on the court guffawed. There were chuckles. The trial judge advocate finally realized he was marching in the wrong direction, and changed the subject.

"I would like to ask you this, Major," he said. "Would you have this court believe that you, personally, would summarily execute an officer, or a soldier, simply because you felt he had not measured up to your standards on the battlefield?"

"That's not what I said, Captain," Lowell said. "We weren't talking about my standards."

"What exactly, then, did you say?"

"Please have the reporter read back my question, and Major Lowell's response, from the record," Morefield said, getting to his feet.

That was done.

"Now, to get back to my question, Major," the trial judge advocate said. "Would you, or would you not, personally shoot someone, officer or enlisted man, out of hand?"

"I would do so reluctantly, sir," Lowell said. "But to answer your question: If someone's cowardice threatened my mission, or was threatening the lives of my men, yes, I would."

"I put it to you, Major, that anyone who feels he may take the law into his own hands is unfit to wear the uniform of an officer of the United States Army."

"Objection!" Morefield said.

"Sustained," the president said. "That wasn't a question, Colonel, that was a statement."

"I have no further questions for this...*officer,*" the trial judge advocate said. He made *officer* sound like an obscenity.

"A couple of question on redirect," Morefield said. "Major Lowell, you seem to have no question in your mind that you would, as the prosecution puts it, summarily execute someone under the circumstances described. Is this a philosophical position you have taken, or is it based on experience?"

"It's based on experience, sir," Lowell said.

"Go on."

"I was once in a situation where I was the beneficiary of such a decision," Lowell said. "An officer had been ordered to relieve my unit. He elected not to. His second in command was forced to shoot him and assume command."

"Forced to shoot him?"

"Yes, sir. If he hadn't, we would have been overrun and wiped out. More important, two missions would have failed. Ours on the hill, his to support us. He had to do it."

"And what happened to the officer who was forced to take this action?"

"Nothing," Lowell said. "He is presently serving."

"Mr. President," the trial judge advocate said.

"Just a minute," the president of the court said. "I can't permit you to make an unsupported statement like tha., of that magnitude..."

"Mr. President, Major Lowell is under oath," Morefield said.

"Major Lowell, you have made a charge against the entire disciplinary structure of the army," the president said. "I am now going to ask you for the name of the officer who has taken the law into his own hands and ask you if he is available to this court. Is he in Korea?"

"Sir," Lowell said, "he's in Korea. But I won't give you his name."

"What did you say?"

"I am unable to give you his name," Lowell said.

"Unable or unwilling?"

"I respectfully decline to do so, sir," Lowell said. "His action saved my life. I can hardly repay that by subjecting him to the same sort of difficulty Captain Parker is in."

"Sir," the trial judge advocate said angrily, "I respectfully request that the witness be ordered and directed to reply to the question."

The president of the court looked at Lowell for a long time, and then up and down the table at the faces of the court.

"The court," he said finally, and with finality, "will not consider in its deliberations anything Major Lowell has said regarding his personal experience with a combat situation in which an officer allegedly shot another officer."

That did it, General Harrier decided. Parker will beat it. Parker and Lowell have come across as good commanders who had the balls to do something unpleasant that had to be done. The trial judge advocate looks to them like some noncombatant who is digging up something that should have been left buried.

The general, he thought, is really going to be pissed.

Screw him. Of all the officers under whom John Harrier had served in his military career, the general was the one who had given him the most difficulty in being a loyal subordinate. He was one of those who had managed to rise to high rank by delegating embarrassment and failure, and assuming responsibilities for other men's successes.

Once that thought had come forward in his mind, General Harrier grew really angry. Chickenshit sonofabitch hadn't even had the balls to call Lowell in and eat his ass out. "Get him out of the Corps, John," he said. "Quietly. And since he's yours, you reply to the Chief of Staff."

He was going to sacrifice that kid's career over a couple of photographs in a goddamned magazine.

(Three)

A victory party was held in Major Lowell's tent on Colonel's Row. Lieutenant Bennington T. Morefield finally took enough of the Haig and Haig Pinch to say what was on his mind.

"I hope that the two of you realize you're both through in the army," he said. "Unless you want to pass the time until you're retired in one idiot job after another."

"You think it's that bad?" Parker asked, surprised.

"May I speak freely?" Morefield said, with infinite sarcasm, and then went on immediately. "So far as you're concerned, Captain, you have ceased being a safe and responsible token nigger. From this day forward, you're going to be the nigger captain who beat a general court for murder with a smart-ass civilian lawyer."

"I've never thought I was anything *but* a nigger captain," Parker said. "I can live with that. My father spent thirty years as a nigger officer. I have no illusions."

"Oh yes you do, you dumb shit," Morefield said. "You think that by trying just a little harder than anybody else, you can make it. You think that since your father did that and got to be a colonel, you can do it, and because 'times have changed' you can probably even make general."

"I was found innocent, wasn't I?"

"You were acquitted. There's a difference. Lowell and I got you off. That's not being found innocent. No one thinks you didn't blow those people away. You won't ever be given another command, and neither will Lowell."

"You don't seem to understand," Parker said. "We have both proved ourselves as company commanders."

"You proved nothing," Morefield said. "Can't you *see* that? The fact that I managed to convince those guys that you should not be locked up for doing something they could see themselves doing, doesn't mean that they're patting you on the back. They felt sorry for you, that's all. And when the time comes to pick somebody to command a battalion, they're going to pick anybody but the nigger who blew the people away when he had a company, and almost got locked up for it. Can't you see that?"

Neither Phil Parker nor Craig Lowell replied. Morefield went on.

"And you, *Major*, do you *really* think the army is going to give a command to an officer who stood up in a general court-martial and announced that he can find nothing wrong with shooting people who get in his way?"

And still there was no reply.

"I'm not getting through to either one of you, am I?" Lieutenant Bennington T. Morefield said. "OK, fuck it. Forget I said anything."

"I don't think we got through to you, Morefield," Parker said.

"Try again," Morefield said, sarcastically.

"I'm not sure if I can," Parker said. "It sounds so simple that it's hard to comprehend. We're soldiers, the Duke and I. *Soldiers*. What do we do for a living is lead people in combat. We do it well. And leading people in combat is what the army is all about."

"Get it through your head that what you might be able to do isn't going to count," Morefield said. "They're not going to give you the chance."

"I happen to have a little more faith in the army than that," Parker said.

Morefield didn't reply. He just swung his head back and forth. There was nothing more he could say. And then he thought of something to say.

"Look at it this way," he said. "You're a danger to the army, the both of you, exactly as the guys who got in your way were a danger to the army. The difference is that they're not going to have to shoot you to get rid of you. They're going to stick you away in some bullshit job, and do it with pleasure. But they're going to keep you from posing any further danger to the army. You better believe that."

Goddamn him, Craig Lowell thought. He's right. He sees the army much clearer than Phil does. The sad thing is that I see it, now, like he does. It's time for me to go home and grow up.

He realized sadly that that was really the last thing in the world he wanted to do, even if Georgia Paige was waiting for him in Los Angeles.

XV

The People's Democratic Republic of Korea
0205 Hours
16 November 1951

The junk lay dead in the water, a mile offshore a deserted stretch of the North Korean coast. Despite a weather report to the contrary, the night was cloudless, and the light from a half-moon was far brighter than expected.

Captain S. T. Felter, dressed in a black rubber wet suit, watched silently as two eight-man aviation life rafts were inflated. Their yellow color had been designed to provide the greatest visibility under all conditions of light, and their designers and manufacturers had done their job well. All attempts to paint over the yellow had failed; the paint either immediately flaked off, or, in the case of one initially promising experiment, promptly ate through the rubberized fabric.

Shrouds had been sewn by female members of the Korean Army, sort of slipcovers made of black cotton. They were draped over the curved sides of the rafts and laced in place with the grommets and rope designed to permit downed aviators to climb aboard.

Once the rafts had been inflated, and the shrouds laced in place, the rafts were carefully lowered over the side of the junk. Two Korean Marines slid down ropes and climbed into the rafts. Next, strapped to a four-foot square of plywood to provide stability, two three-quarter-ton-truck batteries were lowered by rope, and the plywood carefully put in position so that the flexing of the inflated boat would not chafe through the rubberized canvas.

Finally, the electric motors, which operated almost silently, were lowered from the junk and fixed in place on the bouncing rafts. A third Korean Marine in a wet suit, his face blackened with what was actually lipstick, manufactured with a black rather than red pigment, slid down the rope into one of the converted life rafts.

"You better put some more of that crap around your mouth," Rudolph G. MacMillan said to Captain Sanford T. Felter, who was known as "the Mouse," though only behind his back. "You look like Al Jolson."

The Mouse vigorously spread the black lipstick around his mouth with his fingers.

"Better?"

"Yeah," Macmillan said.

The Mouse stepped to the rail of the boat and carefully lowered two walkie-talkies into the rafts, and then the weapons—two fully automatic carbines, their stocks cut off at the pistol grip, a Thompson .45 caliber submachine gun, without the butt stock, and a Winchester Model 1897 trench gun. Each item was wrapped in heavy plastic.

Felter turned and looked at MacMillan. Then he shrugged. There really wasn't anything to say. He grabbed the rope and slid down it into one of the rafts. Over the sound of the water lapping at the junk's hull came the sound of a click; then, faintly, the hum of an electric motor. Water churned under the end of the rafts.

By the time they passed around the bow of the junk, the four men in them were lying flat on their stomachs, so that nothing above the sides of the rafts could be seen.

MacMillan walked to the high stern of the junk and followed the boats as long as he could through night glasses. He could see them far longer than he wanted to. He was half sure he could see the phosphorescence of the waves breaking on shore. He had a gut feeling that something was going to go wrong.

He stepped into the cabin, closed the door, and lit a cigarette. He took two puffs, nervously, and then crushed it out and went back outside. He looked through the night glasses again, and wondered if he could really still make out the two rafts, or whether it was simply his imagination.

Fifty yards offshore, just as they could detect the action of the breaking waves, there was another click, and the hum of the electric motors stopped. Two of the Korean Marines, chosen for their height, quietly slipped into the water, trying to find the bottom with their feet. One of them raised his arm straight above his head and pushed himself to the bottom. Only his hand remained above the water.

Felter slipped into the water and whispered in Korean, "A little further in should do it."

They pushed the rubber rafts another ten yards toward shore. The Korean Marine could now stand on the bottom, his head out of the water. Felter was still in over his head. He swam a few strokes, tried it again, and then swam another few strokes. He could now make his way to the beach, walking in the trough of the waves, letting the crests lift him off his feet. He looked over his shoulder. The Korean Marine who was to accompany him was to his left, a few feet behind him.

As they came closer to the beach, he bent his legs further and further, so that only his head was out of the water. Toward the end, he was nearly in a squatting position.

He took a look up the beach, and down it, and then signaled to the Korean Marine. He came smoothly, but not quickly, out of the water, and then, without taking his foot completely out of the water, so there would be no splashing sound to be heard above the crash of the waves, walked out of the water and onto the beach. He ran across the sand into a small valley between dunes. There was only about fifteen feet of hard-packed sand, and then the dunes. The dunes were more rock than sand, the granite mountains of Korea meeting the Sea of Japan.

He took up a position behind a rock and unwrapped the Winchester trench gun. He pulled the exposed hammer back with his thumb. There was already a round in the chamber, and silence was important. He heard the click-clack as the Korean Marine opened the action of the carbine, just far enough to check to make sure there was a round in his chamber.

He pulled up the elastic cuff of his wet suit sleeve and stole a quick look at the luminous face of his watch. They were fifteen minutes early. As much as it terrified him to spend so much time ashore early, he had learned that unless he was at the rendezvous point when the agent to be picked up arrived, the pickups had a habit of taking off to try again another day.

It was better to be early. The risk to the whole operation was less that way. This operation was important. They were bringing out a Red Chinese colonel who was chief of staff to a Red Chinese lieutenant general. The Red Chinese lieutenant general, who had been educated at Southern Methodist, had come to the painful decision that Mao Tse-tung was not China's savior, and that his Stalinist policy of exterminating the middle class was as wrong, as sinful, as impractical, as Stalin's had been.

It was believed the lieutenant general would be useful.

He heard the sound of a jeep engine.

A jeep?

He crawled around the rock, far enough out onto the narrow strip of sand to look both ways.

A jeep's blackout lights were coming down the beach.

The Mouse crawled backward behind the rock.

With the light from that damned moon, he realized, they had decided they could patrol the beach by vehicle using blackout lights only, without running the risk of being seen from offshore and fired upon.

And, Felter realized, there was enough light for them to see that the smooth sands had been disturbed, if not the actual footprints.

The jeep was close enough now so that he was aware of the peculiar whining noise of the transmission in four-wheel drive.

Then they saw where the sand had been disturbed. The jeep stopped. The brakes squealed; the jeep needed a brake job.

"In there," a Korean voice said.

"I will call the lieutenant," another voice said.

Shit, a radio.

"Now!" Felter said, in a whisper.

He and the Korean Marine fired almost at once. The blast from the muzzle of the short-barreled riot gun was painfully yellow. Felter fired twice, to make sure. One of the Koreans screamed, a painful wail. Felter fired a third time, and the scream stopped abruptly.

The Mouse stepped toward the jeep, to make sure everyone was dead. He was falling. He had no control over his left leg. He fell against the rear of the jeep, then fell to the ground. His shotgun fell onto the sand, and he thought, now I'll be up all night cleaning the damn thing.

All of a sudden, he was aware that his leg was asleep. He put his hand down the leg. His fingers felt something wet and warm. He put his fingers in front of his face. It was blood.

The Korean Marine bent over him.

"What's the matter with you?" he asked.

"I've been shot," Felter said.

If he had been shot, then he had been shot by the Korean Marine. A stockless carbine, fired full automatic, had a life of its own.

"Are we going to go?" the Korean Marine asked. It was really a question. It was not a request.

"If the pickup was anywhere around here," Felter said, "he heard that shooting. He won't be coming."

The Korean Marine nodded.

Felter pulled himself to his feet by clinging to the jeep. His face passed the left rear bumper. 1CAV. Half the vehicles in the North Korean Army had been captured from the 1st Cavalry. They called them the "Chinese Quartermaster." God *damn* the 1st Cavalry, Felter swore mentally. Erect now, he took a step toward the water. And then another, and then he crashed heavily onto the sand.

There was a shocking pain in his knee now, and he screamed in pain. The Korean Marine came back to him. There was a question on his face. The orders were clear. The wounded were to be shot, rather than have them fall into North Korean hands. Torture cannot force answers from dead men.

"Help me into the water," Felter said. "Maybe I can swim."

He was a little ashamed of himself. He had issued the eliminate-the-wounded order. Now that it applied to him, he was unwilling to live up to it.

The Korean Marine straddled him, grabbed him under the armpits, and ran awkwardly with him to the water's edge. Felter scurried into the shallow water like a crab, until he was deep enough to feel the water start to buoy him up.

He remembered he had left MacMillan's shotgun on the beach.

Without thinking, he kicked both his legs. He screamed and got a mouthful of water and choked. He got into a somewhat erect position, his head out of the water, and threw up. And then he pushed himself back into the water, out toward the rafts. He bit his lip to keep from screaming again. The undulation of the water moved his knee—he knew now that he had taken a carbine bullet in the knee—so that the broken bones grated against one another.

He saw, momentarily, the Korean Marine swimming strongly away from him. He isn't supposed to do that, Felter thought, angrily. He is supposed to kill me before he leaves me.

He felt nauseous, and wanted desperately to throw up, but forced the urge down by sheer power of will. He swam using his arms only, trying at the same time to press his legs together in the hope that that would keep the wounded knee from flexing.

At least he could get into deep water, so that when he passed out, he would drown.

The damned trouble was that when he was reported missing, Sharon would keep hoping. If that damned Korean Marine had done what he was supposed to have done, then she would know.

The pain, as incredible as it was, was getting worse. He screamed and water filled his mouth, and he felt himself losing consciousness. And then something jerked his head, grabbed him by the hair. He wondered if it was a shark. There were sharks in these waters, and sharks were attracted by blood, and when you were bitten by a shark, you weren't supposed to feel it.

Something pulled at his knee. It *must* be a shark, he thought. They take successive bites at people. He wondered how long it would take him to die.

He felt himself slowly, but inexorably, losing consciousness.

He was throwing up. He was throwing up everything he had ever eaten. That meant he wasn't dead. He smelled the peculiar smell of the rubber of a raft. He was in a raft, his face pressed against the curved sides, his face smeared with his vomitus.

He rolled over on his back. He screamed again when the knee twisted.

And then there were fireworks in the sky, a brilliant white light.

Oh, shit. Illuminating rounds. Now they'll get the junk, too.

There was the crump of mortars now, the whistles of the descending rounds, a flash of light and a somewhat muffled roar as they exploded.

Oh, Jesus, I hope the junk is getting out of range.

He could hear its diesels, roaring, the mufflers cut out. There was no sense in running quietly now. The thing to do was get away.

The sound grew louder and louder. He turned again, in the direction of the sound, and he screamed again when the knee was twisted, and this time he didn't swim up from the blackness. He settled into it, felt its comforting blackness close in over him.

(Two)

The first thing MacMillan thought when he saw the illuminating flare was that it was American. He'd seen enough of the sonsofbitches to recognize an American flare when he saw one. Then he realized that while they might have been manufactured in the United States for the United States Army, they had not been fired by United States troops.

"Sonofabitch," he said. He put his binoculars to his eyes and searched the shoreline. Just as the first mortar round whistled out of the sky and landed, exploding on the surface of the water seventy-five yards away, he picked out the little rubber raft.

He stepped to the controls, jerked the lever which cut out the mufflers, and with the other hand shoved the throttles forward. The diesels roared.

"Get those fucking sails down!" MacMillan shouted.

The sails would slow the junk down, acting as air brakes, rather than the opposite, when he got the junk up to speed.

If he ran into a sandbank, he thought, that would be all that anybody would write. But it never entered his mind not to try to get Felter and the Korean Marine off the beach.

A second and third mortar round landed. The first landed in the spot where the junk had been thirty seconds before. The second landed in his wake, now a double cocks's tail of water churned up by the powerful diesels.

He spun the wheel to the left, and then to the right, and then straightened the junk up.

The Koreans were having trouble with the rigging.

"Cut the goddamned ropes!" MacMillan shouted, at the moment the forward sail fluttered down the mast. The second followed a moment later.

Now, he thought, he could get some goddamned speed.

"I take? I take?" the Korean Marine who was nominally the junk's skipper asked.

"Yeah," MacMillan said. "We pick up. You understand?"

The Korean looked at him out of his dark, expressionless eyes. He nodded his head.

MacMillan stepped away from the wheel and the throttles. He went to a .50 caliber machine-gun ammo box, to which a hasp for a padlock had been welded. He unlocked the padlock with a key hanging from his dog chain, opened the ammo box, and took from it a manila envelope. He tore it open. Inside was a cover sheet stamped TOP SECRET. Below that, the Signal Operating Instructions in case of emergency. This was clearly an emergency.

He found what he was looking for. He went to the radio, switched in the channel assigned, and picked up the microphone.

"Mulberry, Mulberry," he called. "This is Balaclava, Bala-clava."

He was surprised when Mulberry came right back.

"This is Mulberry, go ahead."

"Condition Yellow," MacMillan said. "Condition Yellow."

The pitch of the diesels stopped. They slowed to idle. What the fuck was going on?

And then their pitch increased again, and he felt the junk slow. The Korean Marine had slowed the engine to shift into reverse, and was now racing them to stop the junk in the water. They were obviously about to try to pull Felter and the Korean Marine out of the water.

But even over the roar of the diesels, he could hear the incoming mortars. He ducked involuntarily as he heard the whistle of one that he knew was going to be close.

It landed on the port side. If that's where the rubber boat was, that was the end of them.

Two other mortar rounds landed in the water. MacMillan heard the whistle of their shrapnel overhead.

What the fuck was taking them so long to get Felter and the Marine back aboard?

He saw the body basket he had scrounged from the navy being lowered over the side. One of them, *at least* one of them, had been hit.

There came the whistle of mortars again.

The first two missed. The third landed on the high forward deck and blew away the .50 caliber mount and the Korean Marines who had been manning it.

"Balaclava, Mulberry," the radio said. They had apparently gotten the message, "Condition Yellow," which meant the mission had been detected. "Do you require assistance, over?"

Shit, what a dumb fucking question.

"Mulberry, Mulberry. This is Balaclava," MacMillan said to the radio. "Condition Orange. I say again, Condition Orange." "Condition Orange" meant "Under attack, require assistance."

The navy body basket came over the side. MacMillan ran to see who it was. Three more mortar rounds came in, landing where they had been. The North Korean on the mortars simply had never seen a junk that could move like this one. Otherwise they would have been blown out of the water long before this.

The body basket held Felter, who was unconscious and bleeding badly from a wound in his knee. He'd thrown up and pissed and shit his pants, and he stank; and he almost made MacMillan sick to his stomach.

They were headed out to sea now, the diesels roaring, the junk crashing into the waves. In a little while, they would be safe from the mortars. But that didn't mean safe. The North Koreans would probably come after them with patrol boats, or planes, and they would shell them when they were within range of shore batteries.

MacMillan put a tourniquet on Felter's leg, put a Korean Marine beside him to hold it, and ran back to the controls.

"Right out to goddamned sea!" he ordered, gesturing toward the open sea.

The Korean skipper didn't like that. He would have preferred to run along the coast, away from the North Korean patrol boats. But he did as he was told, and he didn't have much time to consider whether Major MacMillan was wrong.

Another three mortar rounds bracketed the fleeing junk. One of them landed amidships, and a piece of shrapnel struck the skipper in the stomach and passed out his back, severing his spinal column. He flopped around on the deck for fifteen seconds before he lay still.

MacMillan caught pieces of the same round. One sliced a chunk out of his left thigh, and the other opened a neat gash in his forehead. He had to wipe the blood out of his eyes to find the microphone.

"Mulberry, Mulberry," he said to the microphone. "This is Balaclava, Balaclava. Condition Red. I say again, Condition Red."

Condition Red was the code phrase for "Vessel damaged, in immediate danger of sinking."

Then MacMillan hobbled over to the controls. Slapping a compress on the hole in his thigh, he steered the junk straight out into the Sea of Japan.

(Three)
USS Charles Dewey, *DD404*
Latitude 41 Degrees 17 Minutes
Longitude 129 Degrees 21 Minutes
0235 Hours
16 November 1951

"Ambrose," the radio said. "This is Hammerhead."

Ambrose was today's radio call sign for the USS *Charles Dewey*, DD404, a destroyer attached to Destroyer Squadron K-06, radio code Hammerhead.

"Go ahead, Hammerhead," the radio operator reported.

"Ambrose, stand by to copy Operational Immediate."

"Hammerhead, Ambrose ready to copy Operational Immediate." The radio operator got half out of his swivel chair and pushed a switch. "Skipper..." he began, and then the radio spoke again. The operator put his fingers on the typewriter keys.

"Ambrose, Operational Immediate follows: Execute Balaclava. End message. Acknowledge."

"Ambrose copies Operational Immediate, Execute Balaclava."

"Roger, Ambrose. Hammerhead, clear."

"Ambrose, clear."

"You get that, Skipper?" the radio operator asked.

"I got it," the skipper's voice came over the intercom. "Stand by."

It was half past two in the morning. The skipper was dressed in his skivvies, and had been asleep. He went to his bulkhead safe, and worked the combination. It took him three tries. He took out a vinyl zippered pouch, not unlike a bank deposit pouch. There were a half dozen sealed envelopes in it. He went through them until he came on one marked BALACLAVA. He tore it open. There was a cover sheet, a dashed red line surrounding the edge of the sheet reading TOP SECRET. He lifted the cover sheet. He stepped to the intercom.

"Sparks?"

"Yes, sir."

"Get on 225.35 megacycles. Identify yourself as Florence

Nightingale. Establish contact with United Parcel. Get their position."

"Two twenty-five, thirty-five, got it, Skipper," the radio operator said. He spoke to the microphone: "United Parcel, United Parcel, this is Florence Nightingale."

There was no response, so he made the call again. This time there was a reply.

"Florence Nightingale, this is United Parcel. Go ahead," MacMillan said.

"United Parcel, Florence Nightingale," the radio operator said. "What is your position? I say again, what is your position?"

"Florence Nightingale, Fox Item Item George Fox Able. I say again, Fox Item Item George Fox Able."

"Understand Fox Item Item George Fox Able," the radio operator said. "Stand by."

The skipper, still in his skivvies, rushed from his cabin to the bridge. He jammed the heel of his hand against a palm-sized brass knob by the passageway door. A bell immediately began to clang.

The speaker, who had been leaning against the starboard compass, stood erect and pressed his microphone switch.

"General Quarters, General Quarters," he said. "This is no drill. This is no drill."

The skipper looked at his chart table. The officer of the watch indicated their position with the points of his dividers.

"Steer one three zero," the skipper ordered.

"One three zero it is, sir," the helmsman replied, spinning the wheel to port.

"Have the engineer give us emergency military power," the skipper said. The engine room telegraph clanged, and the officer of the deck picked up the telephone to the engine room. "Emergency military power," he said.

The destroyer heeled sharply. The skipper almost lost his balance. He regained it and went to the intercom.

"Sparks, advise United Parcel Florence Nightingale is en route at flank speed. Estimate one hour and five minutes."

"Aye, aye, sir. Skipper, they advise they are on fire and about to lose power."

"OK, Sparks, thank you," the skipper said.

"Somebody in trouble, Skipper?" the officer on the deck asked.

"You heard it," the skipper said. "I'm going to get my pants on."

"Seas are smooth, Skipper," the officer of the deck said. "They can take to the boats."

"I don't think 'a wooden sailing vessel bearing the appearance of a junk' is able to have any small boats," the skipper said. "I hope they can all swim."

(Four)
Kwandae-Ri, North Korea
0240 Hours
16 November 1951

One of the sixteen radio teletype machines in the XIX Corps (Group) Communications Center rang a bell and immediately began to type out a gibberish series of five character words both on the roll of yellow teletype machine paper and on a strip of perforated tape which spilled out the side of the machine. One of the operators on duty waited until there was about two feet of perforated tape dangling from the machine.

Then he carefully ripped it off and walked across the room to another machine. He inserted the tape in a hole, pushed a switch, and watched as the machine began to swallow the tape. A moment later, the keys of the machine clattered into life.

OPERATIONAL IMMEDIATE
TOP SECRET MULBERRY
FOR JADE SIX PERSONAL
BALACLAVA REPORTS CONDITION ORANGE. PREPARE TO RENDER
ASSISTANCE WHEN REQUESTED.

"Captain," the operator said. The communication officer on duty, who had been reading the *Stars and Stripes* at his desk, laid it down and walked to the cryptographic machine. The operator went to the clattering radio teletype machine and ripped off another length of perforated tape and inserted it in the cryptographic machine. It began to clatter again.

OPERATIONAL IMMEDIATE
MULBERRY BUSH NUMBER 2
BALACLAVA REPORTS CONDITION ORANGE.

The communications officer picked up a telephone and dialed a number.

"Black," a voice answered on the second ring. Jesus, the Old Man himself. The communications officer wondered if he had dialed the wrong number.

"General, I was trying to get Colonel Newburgh," he said. "This is the comm center, Captain Tailler."

"What is it, Captain?"

"I've got a Mulberry Operational Immediate coming in, sir. Colonel Newburgh requested that he be informed whenever that happens."

"OK, Captain," Lt. General E. Z. Black said. "Thank you very much. I'll be right down. Try the G-3 Operations Room for Colonel Newburgh."

General Black entered the comm center. A moment later, Colonel Newburgh—who, the troops said, because of his silver brush mustache and curly hair, looked like a model in a booze ad in *Esquire*—walked in. The commo officer handed the two Operational Immediates to General Black, who read them and handed them to Colonel Newburgh.

The machine began to clatter again. In foot-long lengths, the operator tore the perforated tape from the teletype machine and fed it to the crypotgraphic machine.

OPERATIONAL IMMEDIATE
MULBERRY BUSH NUMBER 3
BALACLAVA SIX WOUNDED LEG AND HEAD BALACLAVA FIVE
WOUNDED LEG AND FACE.

"Six is Felter, right?" General Black said.

"Yes, sir," Colonel Newburgh said. "MacMillan is five."

"Goddamn him!" General Black said.

OPERATIONAL IMMEDIATE
MULBERRY BUSH NUMBER 4
EXECUTING OPERATION BALACLAVA. USS DEWEY DD404 EN ROUTE
POINT CHARLES. ETA ONE HOUR FIVE MINS

"Get in touch with that destroyer," General Black said softly. "See if they have a medic aboard. Send it in the clear. Encrypting takes too long."

One of the commo sergeants sat down at a radioteletype keyboard and rapidly typed out:

FROM JADE

TO HAMMERHEAD

QUERY: DOES BALACLAVA HAVE MEDIC ABOARD? SIGNED BLACK LT GEN.

"If they have a doctor aboard," General Black said, "what about other facilities? Get the aviation officer up here, Carson."

Colonel Newburgh picked up the telephone and dialed a number from memory. There was no answer. He broke the connection and dialed another number.

"This is Colonel Newburgh," he said. "Where is Colonel Young?" There was a reply, and then Newburgh said, "Please wake him up and ask him to join me in the comm center immediately." He hung up the telephone.

OPERATIONAL IMMEDIATE

MULBERRY BUSH NUMBER 5

BALACLAVA SIX SUFFERED SEVERE LOSS OF BLOOD TYPE AO.

"Carson, take care of that," General Black said.

Colonel Newburgh picked up a telephone and dialed 1. An operator came on the line.

"Get me Massachusetts Six," he said.

HAMMERHEAD TO JADE SIX

USS DEWEY CARRIES MEDICAL OFFICER ABOARD. NO INFORMATION AVAILABLE RE STOCKS OF BLOOD. SUGGEST TRANSFUSION POSSIBLE.

"This is Carson Newburgh, Doctor. I want you to put enough Type A and AO blood to treat two seriously wounded men in a jeep and get it to the Jade airstrip right now. You had better send a surgeon, too, if you have one available," Colonel Newburgh said to the commanding officer of the MASH serving the nearest division to XIX Corps (Group). Colonel Daniel Young, the XIX Corps (Group) aviation officer, out of breath, ran into the comm center. He walked up to Colonel Newburgh.

"Yes, sir."

"Young," General Black called from across the room, "what time is daybreak?"

"It's 0442, sir," Young said. General Black looked at his watch.

"Sir," Colonel Young said, "I only need daylight to land. I can take off anytime."

"Carson, show Young where he will have to go," General Black said.

"Yes, sir."

(Five)
Point Charles
0405 Hours
16 November 1951

"Skipper," the officer of the deck said, and the skipper went and lowered his head into the black eyepiece of the radar.

"Bring us around to one twenty-five," the skipper ordered.

"One twenty-five it is, sir."

"I see a hell of a lot of smoke, Skipper," the officer of the deck said.

"And we're five miles away," the skipper said.

"Captain?" the loudspeaker said.

"Go ahead."

"Operational Immediate from Jade, sir. Helicopter en route with blood and surgeon aboard. Estimated time of arrival thirty minutes."

"Acknowledge the message, Sparks, and tell the doctor."

"Aye, aye, sir."

(Six)

The destroyer seemed to settle on her stern as her engines went to full reverse.

"I'll be a sonofabitch," MacMillan said. "Here comes the goddamned cavalry."

He was sitting on the deck, beside Felter. The stern of the junk was on fire. There weren't many visible flames, just a hell of a lot of dense greasy smoke from the burning diesel fuel. For some reason it just sat there and burned rather than exploding or even spreading, and MacMillan idly wondered why.

There were only six people left alive. He and Felter had been wounded, Felter pretty badly, himself lightly, and the others were unhurt, unless you counted a burned hand as a wound.

The junk was dead in the water, and seemed to be slowly sinking, although it was hard to tell.

MacMillan gently shoved Felter's shoulder. He wanted to tell him that a destroyer was now inching its way through the ocean toward them. Felter woke up, as if he had been asleep, and moved, and then screamed.

MacMillan, who had the hypo ready, jabbed it into his arm. It worked quickly. He threw the empty syringe over the side, and then, after a moment, the three full ones he had in his hand. It had been his intention, if the fire reached them, to give Felter several of the hypos. Enough so that he wouldn't feel the flames.

The destroyer loomed over them, so close that MacMillan was genuinely concerned they would be overturned, and drowned at the last goddamned moment.

And then people were coming down knotted ropes. They wore those silly-looking navy steel pots and life preservers. One of them was an officer, getting tar or whatever it was on the ropes all over his clean, starched khakis.

"Over here," MacMillan said.

"I'm from the *Dewey*," the navy officer said.

"You got a doctor aboard?"

"Yes, we do."

"You better take care of him," MacMillan said, indicating Felter in the body basket. "He's in pretty bad shape."

"You don't look so hot yourself, sir," the navy officer said.

"I'm all right," MacMillan said and got to his feet and passed out.

He woke up in a bed. From the way the destroyer was rolling, he knew they weren't moving. His trousers had been cut off him, and there was a bandage on his leg, although he was still dirty.

Temporary dressing, he decided, while they work on Felter. He felt his forehead, and found another bandage.

He sat up in the bed, and saw that he could see out an open door. The junk, still burning, was three hundred yards away. He swung his feet out of the bed, and made it to the door just in time to meet a doctor, an army doctor, coming in.

"What the hell's the matter with you?" the doctor said. "Get your ass back in bed."

"Why aren't we moving?"

"They just got orders to destroy the junk," the doctor said.

MacMillan was pleased that it took five rounds from the destroyer's 5-inch cannon before the junk finally rolled over and sank beneath the surface of the Sea of Japan.

Only then did he permit the surgeon to have a look at his leg and face.

"You haven't mentioned Felter," he said, as the surgeon cleaned the wound in his leg. "Does that mean he didn't make it?"

"He's got a pretty badly torn-up leg," the doctor said. "But he'll make it."

"Where are we going now?"

"Pusan," the doctor said. "To the hospital ship *Consolation*."

"Am I that bad hurt?"

"No. Not at all. You'll be sore. You lost a chunk of meat, but it was mostly fat. No muscles, I mean. You were lucky."

"Then why do I have to go to a hospital ship?"

"Because General Black said that I was to permit nothing whatever to interfere in any way with your recovery to the point where he can put you on a plane to the United States at the earliest possible moment," the doctor said.

MacMillan laughed, deep in his belly, loudly.

(Seven)
Pusan, South Korea
0900 Hours
17 November 1951

The U.S. Navy hospital ship *Consolation*, her sides and superstructure a brilliant white, a Red Cross thirty feet square painted on each of her sides, floated sedately in Pusan Harbor.

Captain Rudolph G. MacMillan, dressed in hospital pajamas and a bathrobe, watched as a powerboat, known as the Captain's Barge, glistening brass and spotless white paint and polished mahogany, put out from Pier One in Pusan and made its way to the *Consolation*'s landing ladder. Two sailors in spotless white uniforms and a lieutenant junior grade stood on the landing platform. The sailors secured the boat to the landing platform, and the lieutenant held out his hand for the passenger of the barge. The passenger jumped onto the platform at the bottom of the landing stair without help. The lieutenant saluted.

"Welcome to the *Consolation*, General," he said. "The captain's waiting for you." He gestured up the stairs.

Lt. General E. Z. Black walked briskly up the stairs, trailed by an aide-de-camp.

When he reached the top of the stairs, six sailors blew on long, narrow brass whistles.

Lieutenant General E. Z. Black smiled and saluted.

A navy captain in a white dress uniform, complete with sword, and a navy captain in dress whites without a sword took two steps forward and saluted.

"Permission to come aboard, sir?" General Black asked.

"Permission granted," the captain with the sword said. General Black threw a crisp salute to the national colors flying on the flagstaff aft. Then he saluted the two captains again. He spotted MacMillan, and smiled, which relieved MacMillan.

"Don't think I came to see you, you disobedient sonofabitch," General Black said. All was right with MacMillan's world. If the general were really mad, he would have been icily formal.

"Welcome aboard, General," the captain with the sword said, a little confused by the interchange between the general and the major. "It isn't often we're honored by the presence aboard of a senior army officer."

"Thank you very much," General Black said. "You know why I'm here?" he asked but didn't wait for a reply before going on. "I want to make sure that nothing gets in the way of Major MacMillan's prompt return to the ZI. And I want to check on Captain Felter."

"Felter's got problems, General," MacMillan said solemnly.

"What kind of problems?" General Black asked. He directed the question to the captain without a sword.

"There's not much left of his knee, sir. After consultation, we have concluded that amputation of the leg is indicated."

"I'm sorry to hear that," General Black said.

"Felter doesn't want it cut off, General," Mac said.

"What do you mean, he doesn't want it cut off?" Black asked sharply.

"He says he'll take his chances, and he won't let them cut it off," MacMillan explained. "He made me promise I'd tell you."

"What the hell does he expect me to do about it?" Black asked, very uncomfortably.

"There's a psychiatric problem involved with the loss of a limb, sir," the hospital ship commander said.

"I suppose there would be a problem," General Black said. "But is 'psychiatric' the right word?"

"I don't know what other word to use," the navy physician said. "By definition, Captain Felter is, at the moment, deranged."

"Because he doesn't want his leg cut off, he's crazy? Is that what you're saying?"

"Not that we believe him, of course, General," the hospital ship commander replied. "Or that it would affect our decision if we did, but he has threatened me personally, and any other medical officer involved, with physical violence if we proceed with the procedure."

"If Captain Felter threatened your life, Doctor," General Black said, "I would take it very seriously."

"I had hoped, sir, that you might have a word with him."

"Is their no way his leg could be saved?"

"Not here, sir. Possibly at San Diego Naval Hospital. Just possibly. The damage is severe."

"But there's a chance it could be saved at San Diego?"

"I don't think anyone could restore that knee, General. At best, his leg would be stiff for the rest of his life."

"I think I would rather have a stiff leg than no leg at all," Black said. "Why don't we send him to San Diego?"

"It's against policy, sir."

"What do you mean, against policy?"

"We are fully equipped here to render general hospital treatment. We provide such treatment."

"But you just told me they could save his leg at San Diego," General Black said.

"I said they might be able to, sir," the captain said. "If he were there. But he's not there. He's here and it's against policy to transfer patients between facilities of equal capability."

"I have never, in twenty-nine years of military service," General Black said, "heard such unmitigated bullshit." His aide winced. MacMillan smiled. Both had been treated before to an E. Z. Black rage.

"General, there is no cause for..."

"Shut your mouth, Captain," E. Z. Black said. "If I want any more bullshit out of you, I'll squeeze your head like a pimple." He turned to the aide-de-camp.

"Give your pistol to MacMillan," he said. The aide did as he was ordered.

"If any of these butchers get within fifteen feet of Felter, Mac, shoot them," Black ordered. He turned to the aide. "You get back in this jackass's Pirates of Penzance rowboat," he said, "and go ashore, and get on the telephone to United Nations Command, and you tell them I have two officers aboard this floating abattoir that I want transferred immediately by air to the U.S. Army General Hospital in Hawaii. You got that?"

"Yes, sir."

"And then you come back out here, and you make personally sure, at pistol point if necessary, that they put Felter and MacMillan on the plane."

"Yes, sir."

"I intend to make a formal report of this encounter, General Black," the captain without a sword said.

"So do I," Black said. "And when I'm through with you, you pasty-faced sonofabitch, you won't be allowed to put a Band-Aid on a soldier's pimple. You'll be back in the VD ward of Charity Hospital in Havana, treating syphilitic whores. Where, goddamnit, you obviously belong."

He turned to MacMillan.

"I presume you know where I can find Felter, Mac?"

"Yes, sir."

"Take me there."

"I'll be happy to escort the general," the hospital ship commander said. He had regained control of his temper after remembering that that morning's *Stars & Stripes* had reported that the President had recommended Black for his fourth star.

"You keep out of my sight!" General Black snarled. "Lead the way, Mac."

"Right this way, General," Major MacMillan said.

XVI

(One)
Los Angeles, California
2 January 1952

The bellman at the Beverly Wilshire Hotel set the two Valv-Paks immediately inside the revolving door, where they would be out of the way and convenient to carry back outside. It was the bellman's professional judgment that the man in the somewhat rumpled clothing would not be staying. He admitted to not having a reservation.

On the other hand, the desk would try to fit him in. Whenever possible, the hotel tried to do what it could for servicemen. The bellman knew the tall, rather good-looking man was a serviceman, because the Valv-Paks were stenciled in black with his name and rank.

He could see where "CAPT" had been obliterated with black paint, and "MAJ" added. MAJ XXXX C W Lowell 0-495302.

"May I have the pleasure of serving you, sir?" the desk clerk asked. He thought that the young man before him was rather interesting. His clothing, a tweed jacket and gray flannel trousers, was mussed, as if he had slept in it, or it had been stored or something, but it wasn't cheap clothing. And the man himself looked a bit *worn*, as if he had been drinking, or gone without sleep. But he was beautiful.

"Can you put me up?"

"You don't have a reservation?" It was more a statement of fact than a question.

"No," he said. "I'd like a suite. For a day at least. Possibly longer."

"I'm afraid there's very little available, without a reservation, Mr. . . ."

"Lowell," he said. "C. W. Lowell. Major C. W. Lowell."

"Yes, of course. *Major*. Forgive me." He didn't look old enough to be a major. But he probably looked marvelous in a uniform. "Let me see what I can do for you," the desk clerk said, with a warm smile. He checked his file. "I do have a cancellation. A nice room on the fourth floor, front."

"If that's the best you can do," Lowell said. Good God, did they have a union rule? That you had to be a faggot, have a phony English accent, and smell like a flower shop to get a job as a desk clerk?

"Front!" the desk clerk called, and told the bellman to take Major Lowell to 407. Then he checked the registration card to see where Major Lowell was from. It told him hardly anything at all.

"C. W. Lowell, Maj USAR, c/o The Adj Gen, The Pentagon, Wash DC," it said, and his purpose for being in Los Angeles was "personal."

The bellman was pleasantly surprised with the newest guest of the Beverly Wilshire Hotel. He had expected two dollars, a dollar a bag. He got instead, a twenty dollar bill, from a thick wad of twenties (the bellman had been in the service and guessed, correctly, that Major Lowell had just been paid; the army paid in twenty dollar bills).

"I've got a lot to do," Major Lowell said to him. "And not much time to do it in. First order of business is to get me a bottle of scotch, either Johnny Walker Black, or Ambassador, something like that, and some soda. Will twenty take care of you and that?"

"That'll take care of it fine, sir," the bellman said, snatching the twenty.

"I've got to commune with nature," Lowell said, pointing

to the bathroom. "If I'm still in there when you bring the scotch, stick around. I've got more for you to do."

When he came out of the bathroom, the bellman had not yet returned. He emptied his trouser and jacket pockets, and then took off his clothing, down to his underwear, sat on the bed, and reached for the telephone. The bellman came in.

"Open that up and make me a light one," Lowell said. To the telephone he said, "Please get me Mr. Porter Craig at Craig, Powell, Kenyon and Dawes at 22 Wall Street in New York City. I'll hold."

The bellman opened the bottle of Ambassador 12-Year-Old and made the maior a drink and handed it to him. The major reached for the stack of twenty dollar bills tossed casually on the bed and came up with two more.

"Take that jacket and pants and have them pressed," he ordered. "It's worth ten bucks to me to have that done immediately. How you split that with the valet is up to you. The rest of it is to get me a box of good cigars, Upmann Amatistas, if the tobacconist has them. If not, any good, large Cuban cigar. If they have them, get Ring Size 47. If not, the larger the better."

"Upmann Amatistas," the bellman said. "The larger the better. Yes, sir."

Lowell turned his attention to the telephone. The number was ringing.

"Craig, Powell, Kenyon and Dawes, good afternoon."

"Long distance is calling Mr. Porter Craig."

"I'll connect you with his office."

"Mr. Craig's office, good afternoon."

"Long distance is calling Mr. Porter Craig."

"I'm sorry, Mr. Craig isn't in at the moment."

"Find out where he is," Craig Lowell said.

"May I ask who is calling?"

"Craig Lowell."

"Sir, if you wish to speak to the party on the line, I'm required to charge you for the call."

"OK. OK. Where is Mr. Craig?"

"I'm sorry, sir. Mr. Craig is in conference and cannot be disturbed."

"Tell him I'm on the phone," Craig Lowell said.

"I'm sorry, I can't disturb him, sir. He left specific word."

"Goddamn it, woman, you tell him I'm on the line!"

"One moment, sir."

"This is Mr. Lucas. I'm Mr. Porter Craig's administrative assistant. With whom am I speaking?"

"Craig Lowell. Get him on the line."

"One moment, please, Mr. Lowell."

There was a pause, and then a voice with the somewhat nasal, somewhat clipped intonations of a Wall Street investment banker out of St. Mark's School, Harvard College, and the Harvard School of Business Administration.

"Craig! How are you, boy?"

"Christ, you're harder to get on the phone than God."

"The girl in the office is new, Craig. She didn't know who you were. You really didn't have to swear at her."

"Porter, I've had enough bullshit in the last twelve hours to last me a lifetime. I don't need any more from you."

"Where are you, Craig?"

"Los Angeles. In a six-by-six-foot cubicle in the Beverly Wilshire."

"You're home then. Welcome home, boy!"

"I need some influence out here, Porter. Who do we have out here?"

"What kind of influence?"

"I need a movie star's unlisted telephone number for one thing," Craig said.

"That can be arranged, I'm sure. Any movie star in particular? Have you been partaking of the cheering cup, Cousin?"

"Not yet. I asked you who we have out here."

"I never know with you. Are you serious about the movie star's telephone number?"

"Dead serious."

"Then Ted Osgood is your man. He's keeping an eye on our participation in *The Fall of Carthage* at Magnum."

"How large is our participation?"

"If you had been reading the tons of paper I've been sending to you, you would know."

"I've had other things to do."

"Two point five million; thirty-seven point five percent."

"That's the guy I want."

"Well, he's right there in the Beverly Wilshire with you. Call him and tell him who you are, and I'm sure he'll get any telephone number for you that you might want."

"He probably wouldn't answer his phone, either," Lowell said. "You call him, and you tell him who I am. Tell him to speak to the management and get me out of this closet, and then tell him to arrange a car for me, and then to meet me. I'll either be in my room, the bar, or the barbershop."

"I'll call him as soon as you get off the line. Anything else? When are you coming East?"

"When you opened our safety deposit box, did you find my passport?"

"Yes. I remember seeing it."

"Well, get it out, and check it to see if it's still valid. If it's not, get it brought up to date."

"Craig, I think you have to do that yourself."

"Porter, arrange it. Call that goddamned senator of yours."

"It'll take a couple of days, I'm sure," Porter Craig said. "I gather you're going to Germany?"

"Of course, I am."

"Then what, may I ask, are you doing in Los Angeles?"

"You may not ask," Lowell said. "Porter, I really would like to see this Mr. Osgood within the hour."

"I'll do my best," Porter Craig said. "You'll stay with us, of course, when you're in New York."

"I'll let you know when I get my feet on the ground."

"Do you need any money?" Porter Craig asked.

"I probably will," Lowell said. "I'm presuming your man Osgood can get a check cashed for me."

"Of course."

"So long, Porter."

(Two)

Mr. J. Theodore Osgood, Senior Vice President, Entertainment & Recreation Division, Craig, Powell, Kenyon and Dawes, Inc., drove up to the Bevery Wilshire Hotel in a limousine arranged for him by his financial courterpart at Magnum

Studios immediately after Mr. Porter Craig's telephone call.
Mr. Osgood was not anxious that it get back to Mr. Craig that
the car he had rented for his business use while in California
was a red Chrysler LeBaron convertible.

He spoke first with Mr. Hernando Courtwright, the hotelier,
and told him that it was very important that one of his guests,
a Major Craig Lowell, be immediately provided with at least
a suite, and preferably one of the better ones. He confided to
Mr. Courtwright that Major Lowell, like Porter Craig, was a
grandson of the founder of Craig, Powell, Kenyon and Dawes,
whose estate had been equally divided between them.

Mr. Courtwright went with Mr. Osgood to the barber shop,
where they waited patiently for Major Lowell to emerge from
under a hot towel, and then introduced themselves. Mr. Courtwright apologized for the mix-up at the desk—they sometimes
made monumental errors of judgment—and informed Major
Lowell that his luggage had already been transferred to Pent-
house Three.

Mr. Osgood said that an automobile was on its way to the
Beverly Wilshire Hotel, and that since Mr. Craig had relayed
no preference, he had taken the liberty of ordering a Jaguar
coupe.

That earned Mr. Osgood a very pained look, confirming
Mr. Craig's announcement that, frankly, Craig Lowell was
sometimes a very difficult sonofabitch, and had to be handled
with the finest of kid gloves. He was sure for a moment that
the Jaguar was going to be unsatisfactory. But, finally, Lowell
had nodded his head and said, "Thank you."

"I understand you may be running a little short of cash,"
Osgood said next. "Now, while I'm sure the hotel will take
your check..."

"Our privilege," Mr. Courtwright said.

"No numbers were mentioned, so if you like," Mr. Osgood
went on, "I'll call our correspondent bank...actually, as you
know, it's more of a subsidiary...and tell them you may be
stopping by."

"I'll just need some walking around money, thank you."

"And then, I understand, there was the matter of an unlisted
telephone number."

"Georgia Paige," Lowell said. He felt like a goddamned fool about that. He'd simply presumed her number would be in the book, and when he'd gotten off the airplane from Tokyo, he'd tried to call her, to tell her he was home. There was a number, but it was unlisted, and the operator would not give it. So he'd sent a telegram to the house in Beverly Hills, telling her he was home, and asking her to telephone him, any hour of the day or night, at the transient field-grade officer's BOQ at Fort Lewis. He included the number. There had been no call.

So he decided the next thing he would do would be to arrive in LA unannounced and simply take a cab to her house. She had already written, in some detail, what kind of a welcome home present he could expect when they were together again. He flew from Seattle to LA wallowing in that scenario. What she would we wearing. How quickly he would take it off of her, and where. And what they would do when he had her clothes off.

When he got to the house in Beverly Hills, there was no one there but a Mexican couple, about equal in size at 300 pounds, neither of whom spoke English. They were absolutely unable to comprehend his gestures that Georgia was his beloved and he wanted to speak to her on the telephone. He had already paid the cab off, so he had to walk away, carrying both goddamned bags. After about a mile, some cops came along, and after more or less politely insisting that he prove he was indeed a field-grade officer of the U.S. Army and not a burglar with two Valv-Paks full of somebody else's silver and jewelry, they found a cab for him.

"All you would have had to do is ask," Mr. Courtwright said, picking up the telephone and asking to be connected with his secretary.

"And, if Osgood here hadn't shown up," Major Lowell said, "you would have politely told me to go piss up a rope."

"Major Lowell is just home from Korea," Mr. J. Theodore Osgood offered in extenuation.

Courtwright smiled and wrote Georgia Paige's unlisted number on his business card.

"She's not home, Major Lowell," J. Theodore Osgood said.

"They're shooting *Unanswered Prayer*. I passed the sound stage on my way off the lot."

"Can you get me into wherever she is?" Lowell asked, as the barber finished his shave and began to rub something oily onto his face.

"Yes, of course," Osgood said. "I'll call ahead if you like and have a pass ready for you at the gate."

Osgood didn't use the telephone in the barbershop. He used a house phone in the lobby and he telephoned his counterpart at Magnum Studios and told him that Craig Lowell, who was likely to be hard to handle, was coming to the studio to see Miss Georgia Paige. He had no idea why.

When Lowell saw the car provided for him, he wasn't surprised. The goddamn Jaguar was identical to Ilse's. He had impulsively shipped it to Marburg an der Lahn because she so loved that car. She had been driving it when the drunken quartermaster asshole had slammed into her.

As he drove to Magnum Studios, he had a clear mental image of Ilse sitting on the passenger seat with P.P. in her arms, and with her legs innocently arranged so that he could see her pants. Sex and motherhood.

"Major Lowell," the man waiting for him at the gate said, "I haven't had the opportunity to meet you before, and I'm happy to now. I'm John Sanderland, and I'm Magnum's Vice President, Finance."

"I see you spent some time in Philly, Mr. Sanderland," Lowell said. Sanderland was wearing the insignia of alumni of the Wharton School of Business at the University of Pennsylvania.

"Doesn't everybody?" Sanderland said.

"'49," Lowell said.

"Hail fellow, well met," Sanderland said delightedly. "'40." Perhaps, he thought, Major Craig W. Lowell wouldn't be as difficult as Osgood suggested.

They drove onto the lot. It was Lowell's first visit to a motion picture studio. He was somewhat disappointed to see that it looked more like a factory than anything else. Then he realized that it was a factory, the word actually being a shorter form of "manufactory," a place where things are made by hand.

There was a red light flashing over the door of one of the warehouse-like buildings, and what looked like a retired cop, in a private policeman's uniform, standing in front of it with his arms folded. Lowell had seen enough movies about Hollywood to know the flashing red light meant that they were "shooting" inside.

The private cop did not step out of the way, however, as Lowell expected him to, when the red light went off.

"Closed set," he announced. "You got to have a pass."

"I'm a vice president of this corporation," Sanderland said.

"I don't doubt that for a minute, Mister," the guard said. "But you still got to have a pass. The set is closed."

"Oh, for Christ's sake!" Sanderland said, but they had to get back in Lowell's car and go to the Administration Building for passes. When they returned to the sound stage, the red light was flashing again, and they had to wait ten minutes in the hot sunshine for it to go off again.

"They weren't shooting that long," Sanderland said, angrily, as he hauled back on the heavy, soundproof door. "They just didn't want to be interrupted."

"What the *fuck* is this?" a man screamed in a high-pitched voice, as they entered the sound stage.

Lowell, who had been looking for Georgia and had just seen her across the wide, cluttered room, was startled. Then he became aware that the screaming man was pointing at him.

The excited pansy recognized Sanderland. "What the *fuck* do *you* want?" he demanded of him. "And *who* the *fuck* is *he*?"

Lowell looked across at Georgia. She seemed to be running away. No wonder, with this sewer-mouthed pansy screaming his head off.

"You say 'fuck' one more time, Slats," Lowell said, "and I'll wash your filthy fucking mouth out with fucking soap."

"*Who*ever this cocksucker *is*, Sanderland," the skinny man said, "get him off *my* fucking set!"

Without much apparent effort, Lowell spun the skinny man around, marched him to a red fire bucket mounted on the wall, and ducked his head in it.

A man in a business suit who had been rushing toward the door when the incident started, now gestured to two burly laborers. They restrained the skinny man when Lowell turned him loose.

"What the hell is going on around here?" he demanded of Sanderland.

"Major Lowell," Sanderland said, "this is Mr. Berman, the producer of this film. Mr. Berman, Major Lowell is from Craig, Powell, Kenyon and Dawes, and he seems to object to your director's characterization of him as a cocksucker."

"I'm walking, Sanderland," the skinny pansy screamed. "I'm walking. That's it. I'm finished." The laborers let him go, and he stormed, dripping, across the set.

"I'm not saying that wasn't a good idea, Major," Mr. Berman said. "I just hope you realize what that gesture cost us."

"I have no idea," Lowell said. "But whatever it was, I'll be happy to pay it."

"I don't think so," Mr. Berman said. "It will be two days before our director will feel the muse has returned sufficiently for him to resume the practice of his art. We're budgeted at thirty-nine five a day. Are you really willing to pay nearly eighty thousand dollars for the privilege of washing out that mouth, even considering how foul it is?"

"Hell, I'm sorry," Lowell said, feeling like a fool.

"May I ever so politely inquire what we can do for you on this closed set?" Berman asked, sarcastically.

"I came to see Georgia Paige," Lowell said.

"Indeed? Might I inquire why?"

"We're friends," Lowell said.

"Well, in *that* case," Berman said, sarcastically, "why don't you go over to her dressing room? She has nothing else to do at the moment but entertain friends. Not now. And probably not tomorrow. And probably not on the day after tomorrow, either. That should give you plenty of time for a friendly visit." Berman gestured to a small house trailer on the far side of the building.

Aware that eyes were on him, Lowell started to walk toward it. He heard Berman ask Sanderland who he really was, and part of Sanderland's reply. Then there was an explosion immediately behind him, and by reflex action, he threw himself on the floor. He couldn't control it. He hit the dirt even as one part of his mind told him that the explosion was a bursting light bulb, maybe a big one, but a light bulb only, dropped from somewhere up above.

Shamed and furious, he got to his knees and looked upward. A burly man was sliding down a ladder, a look of concern on his face. He reached Lowell just as Lowell stood up.

"Hey, I'm sorry," he said.

"About as sorry as I am for dunking the other wise-ass in the fire bucket," Lowell said.

"No," the man said. "Hey, I mean it. I dropped the bulb to say 'hurray for you.' I didn't know you jump the way people like you and me jump when you think a sudden noise is incoming."

"You got me, you bastard," Lowell said, smiling. "You really got me."

"You looked as shocked as our director," the man said, "when you ducked his head in the fire bucket."

He looked over the man's shoulder. Georgia was standing there, looking at him unbelievingly.

"My God," she said, "Is that *you?*"

She came and he hugged her. She raised her face to his and he kissed her. Her lips were warm, but not as hungry as they had been on the IX Corps airstrip. He remembered that he had felt her heart beating then. She hadn't pressed herself close enough against him now for him to feel her heart beating, and neither were her arms holding him the way they had on the airstrip.

It wasn't the homecoming embrace he had held in his mind.

Sanderland came up to them.

"You should have told me you knew Major Lowell, Georgia," he said. "I would have treated you differently."

"How so?" she asked, somewhat confused that Lowell knew Sanderland.

"I would have treated you with greater respect and offered you less money."

"What the hell are you talking about?"

"You've often told me you'd like to meet one of the money men from New York," Sanderland said. "To tell him off. So here's your chance."

"Is he putting me on?" Georgia asked, looking at Lowell. Then she thought it over. "I get the feeling he's telling me the truth."

"Does it matter?" Lowell asked.

"He must be telling the truth," she said. "Otherwise you couldn't have gotten on the set. Why didn't you tell me you were coming?"

"I tried. I got out two days before I was supposed to."

She dismissed him for something more important.

"Where's Derek?" she asked.

"He went home," Sanderland said.

"What do you mean, 'he went home'?" she snapped. "We're not finished."

"Your friend gave him a shampoo," Sanderland said. "In a fire bucket."

"I don't believe any of this conversation," Georgia said, smiling, showing her red gums and perfect teeth. "What the *hell* are you talking about?"

"Derek talked dirty in front of your friend, and your friend washed his mouth out by dunking his head in a fire bucket," Sanderland said.

Georgia Paige immediately decided this was the truth.

"Great!" she exploded. "Great! Thanks a lot!"

She glowered at Lowell for a moment, and then walked quickly across the building toward the trailer Berman had pointed out to him.

"Now we're even," Sanderland said. "*That* cost you."

"Go fuck yourself," Lowell said to him, and walked across the floor to the trailer. He knocked, but there was no reply. He pushed open the door and went inside. Georgia was lying on a chaise longue, legs spread, her head resting on her hands. Lowell walked up to her and looked down.

"I'm sorry," he said.

"You don't understand," she said. "I have been working myself up all day for this shot. And then I don't get to make it."

"I'm really very sorry," Lowell said.

She looked up at him and smiled and held her arms out to him. She held him against her, but when he tried to touch her breast, she pushed him gently but firmly away.

"Not here," she said. "Let's get the hell out of here."

He didn't even get a chance to watch her change clothes. A gray-haired woman came into the trailer without knocking, gave Lowell a dirty look, and jerked her thumb toward the door. It took her fifteen minutes to change clothes, during which a steady stream of people entered and left the trailer, while he stood around outside.

He had to follow her to the house in Beverly Hills, trailing a studio Cadillac limousine in the Jaguar. Her house, he decided, was probably entitled to the term mansion. The banker in the recesses of his brain suddenly came to life. She hadn't been successful that long. He had read in a fan magazine that her father was in the insurance business in Ohio, and that she'd gotten her start in the movie business while acting in plays at the University of Ohio. Her rise, the fan magazine had said, had been "meteoric." That meant that it was only recently that she had been making a lot of money, and that meant the house was hers only technically. The money for the house had probably come from the First Federal Savings and Loan of Beverly Hills.

They'd driven past that. The houses in Beverly Hills, Lowell thought, deserved much larger lots than they had been given. He had a quick mental image of the gate at Broadlawns, and the drive inside the gate. He came to the conclusion (which he shamefully acknowledged to be snobbish) that Beverly Hills, generally speaking, was a high-priced housing development, Levittown for the affluent.

When they finally got inside her house, there were half a dozen people there, including a man she introduced as her press agent, and whom Lowell disliked on sight. It was a very long time before they were rid of them, and the press agent lingered longest.

And then Georgia said she was hungry, and that Consuela, presumably the 300-pound Mexican, wasn't there. So they went to the Villa Friscati on Sunset Boulevard. A steady stream of people stopped at their table, all of them ignoring him after finding out that he was a soldier.

They finally made love about nine thirty, but it wasn't what it had been in Korea, and she threw him out, saying that despite what he'd done, Derek might want to shoot the next day. That meant she would have to get up at half past four and needed her sleep.

"When are you going to be finished with this movie?"

She told him. Six weeks, maybe seven. When she saw the look on his face, she asked if something was wrong.

"I was hoping you would go to Germany with me in a couple of days."

"Germany? Why do you want to go to Germany?" And then she remembered. "Oh, yeah. Your little boy is there. I forgot about him."

They put a good face on it. They discussed it calmly and logically. He would go to Germany and do what he had to do about the little boy. And by that time, the picture would be nearly done, or maybe, if nobody else ducked Derek's head in a fire bucket, finished. And then they would have some time to be together and really talk things over.

But they both knew when he walked out of her door at a quarter past ten on his first night home that they had both been kidding themselves.

(Three)
Walter Reed U.S. Army General Hospital
Washington, D.C.
16 February 1952

Sharon and Sandy had been expecting Craig ever since the flowers had arrived. The flowers were fifty dollars' worth of carnations, stuck into a five-foot chicken-wire horseshoe, and with the gilt letters spelling out GRAND OPENING glued to a purple six-inch-wide sash. It took up a whole corner of Sandy's private room.

He arrived the following Saturday, about four o'clock in the afternoon, in a pink-and-green uniform, complete with all his decorations. Sandy was surprised to see that. Lowell normally wore only his Expert Combat Infantry Badge. He was struck again with the realization that Lowell looked the way an officer was supposed to look.

"You little bastard," Lowell greeted him, "I thought I had taught you how to duck. What happened to you, anyway?"

"I thought the man said 'stand up,'" Felter said. "So I stood up. And here I am."

The men shook hands. Sharon stood beside Lowell, and very naturally, Lowell put his arm around her shoulders. Sharon leaned against him.

"I didn't know," Lowell said. "I ran into MacMillan at Knox. He told me."

Felter nodded.

"So how are you doing?" Lowell asked, awkwardly.

"I'm in what they call physical therapy," Felter said. "Once in the morning, and once in the afternoon, they give me a bath, and then they torture me."

Sharon suddenly shook loose from Lowell and went to the bedside table. Sandy was embarrassed.

"Look," she said. She handed him a lidded leather box six inches by three. Lowell opened it, looked down at the Distinguished Service Cross, and then unfolded the copy of the citation.

HEADQUARTERS

DEPARTMENT OF THE ARMY

WASHINGTON, D.C.

AWARD OF THE DISTINGUISHED SERVICE CROSS

4 January 1952

By Direction of the President of the United States, the Distinguished Service Cross is awarded to MAJOR SANFORD THADDEUS FELTER, 0-357861, Infantry, U.S. Army.

CITATION: During the period 30 August–16 November 1951, MAJOR FELTER (then Captain), while engaged in military operations of the highest importance, repeatedly, without regard to his own possible loss of life, demonstrated valor above and beyond the call of duty. His actions reflect great credit upon himself and the United States Army. Entered the Military Service from New Jersey.

Lowell folded the citation and put it back in the case, and then snapped the case shut.

"Well," Lowell said, "at least they gave you the leaf. You can spend that."

"That's a terrible thing to say," Sharon flared. "That makes you sound as if you're jealous, Craig!"

"Why should he be jealous?" Felter said. "Look close, honey. He's got one of his own."

"I don't care if he does or not," Sharon said. "You shouldn't make fun of a decoration."

"Oh, I'm proud of him," Lowell said. "MacMillan told me all about it."

"You're kidding," Felter said.

Lowell, beaming at him, shook his head, "No."

"Damn him!" Felter said. "He knows better than that."

"He has this odd notion, Sandy, that we're on the same side."

"That has nothing to do with it," Felter said, and threw both hands in the air.

"Well, I guess you could write him a letter of reprimand," Lowell said.

"You know what he did, Craig?" Sharon asked.

"Certainly, I do," he said. "I'm a major in the U.S. Army. They tell me everything."

"Then you tell me," she said. "Sandy won't. All I know is that he wrote and told me he was running a radio station, and the next thing I know, Colonel Hanrahan came to the house and told me he was here."

"Well, Sharon—" Lowell said.

"Goddamn it, Craig!" Felter interrupted.

"First of all, Sharon," Lowell said, "he did a fine job of cutting the VD rate among the troops."

Sharon blushed. "Oh, Craig!" she said.

"And then he got everyone in the unit to make a contribution to the Red Cross. The army is really interested in a hundred percent contribution rate to the Red Cross."

"So tell me about you," Sandy said.

"How's P.P.?" Sharon asked.

"With his grandfather," Lowell said. "I spent thirty days in Marburg."

"How is he?"

"Surrounded by kraut aristocrats," Lowell said, "who will probably, in time, be able to forgive him for being half-American."

Sharon looked disturbed, and Lowell saw it.

"There's a whole family there, aunts and uncles, cousins, second cousins twice removed. Most important, women. How the hell could I care for him?"

"Sandy and I talked about that," Sharon said. "If you could see your way clear to letting us have him. You know we love him, Craig."

"Jesus, you know what that means to me," Lowell said, emotionally. "But I think the thing to do with him is what's being done. You've got your own kids, and I don't know what the hell I'm going to be doing. And they are his family. They're making sure that he doesn't forget how to speak English. I guess what I'm saying is that they're taking good care of him."

"I understand," Sharon said. "Maybe, when you get re-married . . ."

"You seem pretty sure about that," Lowell said, making a joke of it.

"You're even younger than Sandy," Sharon said. "You'll get married again."

"I put you on warning, lady, that if you start matchmaking . . ."

"I'm not impressed," Sharon said. "You should get married again."

"I don't think so," Lowell said, surprisingly firmly. Sharon let it drop after saying, "I'd love to see him again. Have you got a new picture?"

While she was looking at P.P. in the arms of his father, Sandy said: "I asked before, what are you doing?"

"You will be delighted to hear, Major, that I am on my very good behavior—you will note the medals—and trying very hard to make the right impression on my peers and superiors."

"What are you doing?"

"Killing time until I get out," Lowell said, "at the Advanced Officer's Course."

"I thought you put in for regular army?" Sandy asked. "What did you do, change your mind?"

"It was changed for me," Lowell said. "The application hasn't come back yet. They are probably trying to find the right words to reject it."

"Why would they reject it?"

Lowell said, obviously quoting verbatim, "'While this officer has demonstrated outstanding ability at command at the company level, it is obvious that he sometimes acts impulsively and without adequate consideration of all factors concerned. It is to be hoped that as he matures, he will acquire the stability of personality necessary for command at the battalion level. In the meantime, however, the undersigned cannot in good conscience unreservedly recommend him for such command.'"

"Who did that to you?" Felter asked, disturbed.

"That's the efficiency report I got from His Excellency, the IX Corps commander."

"What did you do? Did it have something to do with your friend's court-martial?"

"You don't want to talk about this," Lowell said.

"What did you do?" Felter pursued.

"I got up in a general court-martial and testified that I could indeed see circumstances in which an officer is justified taking another officer out of a situation," Lowell said. "The corps commander had decided that he wanted to put my friend in jail. He was piqued when the court let him go, and blamed it on me."

"I heard he was acquitted," Felter said. "But no details. What happened to him?"

"He's at Knox with me," Lowell said. "Captains and lieutenants who have heard very few guns go bang in anger are teaching us how to command tank companies by the book."

"That's obviously a waste of your time," Felter said. "But I don't suppose there's anything you can do about it."

"Not that I can think of," Lowell said dryly.

"So you withdrew your application for the RA? Is that what

you meant when you said you were killing time until you can get out?"

"No. I figured I'd let them squirm trying to turn me down. I meet every single criterion, and then some. I'm not even giving them a chance to say that I've been a wise-ass in class. I'm getting 4.0's, which is more difficult than I would have believed."

"You never had any trouble with school," Felter said.

"We had an interesting class problem last week," Lowell said. "A brand-new one. It seems that when the Eighth Army in Korea broke out of the perimeter, a reinforced tank company was sent as a task force to disrupt the enemy's lines of communication and eventually to effect link-up with X Corps. It was rather a challenge to offer constructive criticism, to improve the operation. I thought it was done right the first time."

"You're kidding," Sharon said.

"Oh, no," Lowell said. "But, just to prove how cooperative I am, I came up with a long list of improvements to the way it was done. If I had done any of them, I would still be tied-down fifty miles from Pusan, attempting to coordinate liaison with supporting arms and services." He paused, and chuckled, adding, "Especially if I had waited for confirmed intelligence to give me the strength of assaulted units."

"It's something out of Franz Kafka," Sandy said sympathetically. "Well, what *are* you going to do?"

"I can only answer that negatively," Lowell said. "I'm not going to go back to the bank. Aside from that, I really don't have plan one."

"When do you get out?"

"In five months," Lowell said. "Now, what happens to you?"

"I've been selected for the War College," Sandy said.

"I thought you had to go to Command and General Staff first," Lowell said.

"Sandy made that on the five percent list, too," Sharon said, proudly. "Major and the War College on the five percent list."

"I took C&GS by correspondence," Sandy said. "In Korea. It was either C&GS or a course in how to upholster your own furniture."

"And then what?"

"Here," Sandy said. "We bought a house in Alexandria. A hundred dollars down and a hundred dollars a month for the rest of our natural lives."

"What are you going to be doing here?"

"The same sort of thing I've been doing," Sandy said, uncomfortably.

There came a light in Lowell's eyes, and Sandy Felter was sure he knew what it was. Lowell was going to apply for Intelligence.

They let the subject drop, talked of other things.

Two months later, shortly before he was to be released from the hospital on limited duty, an agent of the Counterintelligence Corps showed up at Walter Reed, flashed a badge, and said he was conducting an investigation into the character of one Major Craig Lowell, who had given Major Felter as a reference.

"Could you, without reservation, recommend him for a position of great trust and authority?"

"I could, and do," Felter said. "But I think I know what this investigation is really all about, and the answer to the real question, 'Would Craig Lowell be any good as an intelligence officer?' is 'No, he would not.'"

"That's pretty strong, Major," the CIC agent said. "What do you base that on?"

"The one thing an intelligence officer cannot be is impulsive," Felter said. As the words came out of his mouth, he felt like a hypocrite. He had several times acted impulsively. Who was he to criticize Lowell?

"Rephrase," he said. "An intelligence officer must know how to restrain his impulsive urges. Major Lowell does not have that characteristic."

"That sort of thing would be decided by the people who evaluate his application, Major," the CIC agent said. "They'll want to know what you think of him as an officer. They'll determine if he's liable to make a good intelligence officer."

"I'm one of the guys who sits on those boards," Felter said. He rolled over on his hospital bed, and opened his shaving kit, and took out a well-worn leather folder. He opened it and showed it to the CIC agent.

"I didn't know that about you, Major," the CIC agent said.

"There's no reason you should," Felter said. "When you make up your Report of Interview, make sure it includes the information that I revealed my duty assignment to you, and my statement that recommending that Major Lowell not be considered for an intelligence assignment was personally difficult for me. He's my best friend."

The CIC agent nodded his head.

"And the next time you find yourself wishing that you were through with backgrounds, and 'really doing something in intelligence,'" Felter said, "remember this interview. That isn't the only decision I've had to make that makes me a little ashamed of myself."

(Four)
Fort Knox, Kentucky
17 May 1952

When Major Craig Lowell was informed by the adjutant of Student Officer Company, the Armor School (SOC-TAS), that his application for integration into the regular army had been approved, and that, presuming he could pass a precommissioning physical examination, he would be integrated into the regular army as a first lieutenant, with adjusted date of rank 24 July 1950, and that he would be permitted to continue on active duty as a reserve officer in the grade of major, he simply nodded his head.

He had toyed with the notion of endorsing the correspondence "insert your RA commission violently upward into your anal orifice."

But when the commission was actually tendered, even though he told himself that he knew better, he thought perhaps he was at least partially vindicated, that if they were really out to hang his ass, they would have thought of some excuse not to offer the RA commission.

His application for intelligence was still in. Certainly Sandy would have said a number of good words about him, and he had the Greece experience, and that would certainly be a hell of a lot better than going back to the bank.

His application for assignment to intelligence duties came back with an endorsement saying that "no vacancies exist at the present time for an officer with your qualifications nor are any anticipated in the foreseeable future, and therefore reapplication is not encouraged."

He swallowed that.

Captain Philip Sheridan Parker IV was honor graduate of Advanced Officer's Course 52-16. He was given a replica of a Civil War cavalry saber and a one year's free membership in the Armor Association. He was assigned to Fort Devens, Massachusetts, as assistant dependent housing officer.

Major Craig Lowell, who was .05 grade points behind Captain Parker (3.93 and 3.88, respectively, out of a possible 4.0), received permanent change of station orders to proceed to the Bordentown Military Academy, Bordentown, New Jersey, as deputy to the army advisor to the Junior ROTC Detachment at the private military high school for boys.

XVII

(One)
New York City, N.Y.
16 October 1952

When Porter Craig, president and acting chairmen of the board of Craig, Powell, Kenyon and Dawes, returned to his office from the Luncheon Club on the 38th floor of the Morgan Guaranty Trust Building, where he had lunched with his cousin, Major Craig W. Lowell, he sat down at his desk and swiveled the high-backed leather chair so that he could look out the huge plate-glass window at lower Manhattan Island and the Hudson River. He put his feet up on the marble window sill, and sat with the balls of his fingers touching, as if praying.

Then he suddenly spun the chair around, pushed the concealed button on his desk which activated a microphone concealed in the cigar humidor, and told his secretary to get the senator on the telephone just as quickly as she could.

"Porter Craig, Senator. Thank you for taking my call. I know what a busy man you are."

The senator replied that it was always a pleasure to speak with his good friend, and asked how he might be of service to his favorite man on Wall Street.

"I've just had lunch with my cousin, Craig Lowell," Porter Craig said. "And let me make clear to you this telephone call is my idea, not his. I'm quite sure that he would be furious if he even suspected I would pass what he told me any further. Or in any way interfere in his affairs."

"I remember the name," the senator said. "He was in the army in Greece, as I recall, five or six years ago? Was wounded, and something of a hero, wasn't he?"

"That's the man."

"Your grandfather asked me to find out what I could about his condition. I was, of course, happy to be of assistance. Now, what about him?"

"He's about to resign from the army," Porter Craig said. "And while I would, of course, be delighted to have him here with me in the firm . . . he's a Wharton graduate, and smart as a whip, and I can't really see why he stayed in the army at all, frankly."

"But apparently, he did," the senator said. He was beginning to sense the reason behind the call.

"And did rather well, I must say. He's a major, which I understand is truly extraordinary for someone his age."

"He was just a boy, I recall, when he was in Greece."

"He's hardly more than a boy now," Porter Craig said. "Twenty-five."

"Extraordinary," the senator said.

"He's just back from Korea," Porter Craig went on. "Looking like a young Patton. He has the Distinguished Service Medal and the Silver Star, and God knows what else. There's barely room for his ribbons on his uniform."

"Indeed," the senator said. He wished Porter Craig would make his point.

"I suppose that's what makes me angry enough to bring this to your attention," Porter Craig said. "It seems to me that he's entitled to more from the army, because of what he's done for the army, than is apparently the case."

"Go on," the senator said.

"He told me that he's about to resign."

"Did he say why? It would appear to me that with a record like that, he should have a brilliant career ahead of him."

"I suspect that he may have risen a bit too fast," Porter Craig said. "I suspect there may be some jealousy involved."

"I'd be surprised if there were not," the senator said. "But surely, he can rise above that?"

"The reason he gives for resigning from the army is that he thinks he has been removed from consideration for meaningful advancement."

"Why does he think that?"

"Because of the assignment they've given him."

"Which is?"

Porter Craig was not about to be brought to the point until he was ready to make it.

"And it's not only Craig who has been, in my judgment, rather shoddily treated. He just graduated, with honors, from the Army School at Fort Knox, second in his class. The honor graduate, Senator, if you can believe this, has been assigned as a dependent housing officer in Massachusetts. Craig, who was second in his class, has been assigned to Bordentown Military Academy, where he says he is in the charge of the sergeant who is teaching the little boys how to march."

"That doesn't seem to be a very satisfactory assignment for a bright young major, does it?" the senator asked. "Nor a very wise expenditure of the taxpayer's dollar?"

"I didn't think so," Porter Craig said. "That's why I called you. I would not ask for special treatment, and he certainly wouldn't ask for it himself. But I don't think I am asking for special treatment when I bring what I consider an outrageous waste of the taxpayer's dollar to your attention."

And just incidentally, the senator thought, keep Cousin Craig from coming home again and claiming his half of Craig, Powell, Kenyon and Dawes, Inc.

"You don't happen to know the number of the course he attended at Fort Knox, do you?" the Senator asked.

"No, I'm afraid I don't."

"Well, I can find out," the senator said. "I'll get back to you, Porter. I understand the situation. Sometimes, you have to call the military to attention."

"As I say, I'm not seeking any special treatment for my cousin," Porter Craig said. The senator was annoyed.

"But if it could be arranged to keep him in the army, fine, is that it?"

There was a long pause.

"That would seem to sum it up rather aptly, Senator," Porter Craig said finally.

"I'll see what small influence I have on the Pentagon can do for you, Porter," the senator said. "In the meantime, try to talk him out of submitting his resignation."

(Two)
Washington, D.C.
19 October 1952

The senator met the Vice Chief of Staff of the United States Army at a cocktail party and dinner given in honor of the junior senator from Iowa at the Occidental Restaurant by the American Farm Machinery Foundation.

"Tell me, General," the senator said, laying a fraternal arm around the Vice Chief of Staff's shoulders, "how is your new personnel system working out? Is it getting round pegs in round holes, or are you still trying to make bakers out of candlestick makers and vice versa?"

The Vice Chief of Staff of the U.S. Army knew the question was not idle.

"So far as I know, Senator," he said, "it's working out very well."

"The right officer in the right assignment, right?"

"We try to do our best, Senator," the Vice Chief of Staff said.

"And how often does that work?"

"How about ninety-nine times out of a hundred?"

"You don't mean to say?"

"Have you something specific in mind, Senator?" the Vice Chief of Staff asked.

"I was wondering about the school system, as a matter of fact," the senator said.

"What, sir, were you wondering?"

"Whether it's really worth all the money it costs the poor taxpayer."

"Well, if a man can't drive a truck when we get him, and we need truck drivers, we have to teach him how to drive one. It's as simple as that."

"I was thinking more of the officer-level schools."

"What level?"

"The Advanced Officer's Courses. Are they really necessary?"

"Absolutely."

"And you can put their graduates to work, doing what they're trained to do?"

"We can, and we do."

"You don't mean to say!"

"Yes, sir."

"And after they're trained, right into that little round hole, right? Presuming it's a little round officer?"

"To the best of my knowledge, Senator," the Vice Chief of Staff said. He wondered what the hell the senator was leading up to.

"If we were playing poker, General," the senator said, "would you bet on that hand? Or would you want to see if you could draw some better cards?"

"I've got all the cards I need, thank you, Senator," the Vice Chief of Staff said.

"I'll call," the senator said. "Get out your little notebook, Son," he said to the silver-haired, full bird colonel aide-de-camp of the Vice Chief of Staff.

"I didn't hear the bet," the Vice Chief of Staff said with a broad smile that showed just faint signs of strain.

"You're telling me you're assigning officers so that their service, in terms of their records and the expensive education the taxpayer has bought for them, will give the taxpayer the best possible return on his investment," the senator said. "I'm betting you're not."

"But what's the bet?"

"Just a fun game, between friends," the senator said. "Now, just for the hell of it, let's find out—picking something out of the air, you understand—how you assigned the two officers at the top of their class at the last Advanced Officer's Class at Fort Knox. The last class, I believe, was Number 52-16.

You write that down, Son, so we all remember. I would be very interested to know who they are, what kind of records they have, what their assignments are, and why they were made."

"You get that, Dick?" the Vice Chief of Staff said to his aide.

"Yes, sir."

"Put it in writing, General," the senator said. "You're a silver-tongued devil, you are, always making me think you said something you didn't say."

(Three)
Fort Devens, Massachusetts
25 October 1952

In addition to his other duties, the assistant dependent housing officer at Fort Devens, Massachusetts, had been assigned as assistant club officer. The club officer himself, a major of the Transportation Corps, set a fine table, as they say, but he wasn't much with the books. Taking care of the books was just the job for a jigaboo captain who had been the honor graduate of the Advanced Course at Knox.

When four telephone calls, spaced at precise forty-five-minute intervals, failed to raise Captain Philip Sheridan Parker IV at his bachelor officer's quarters number, his caller, somewhat embarrassed that he hadn't thought of this before, told the long distance operator to try to locate Captain Parker at the officer's club.

There was the sound of a barroom.

"Officer's open mess, main bar room, Sergeant Feeney, sir."

"Long distance is calling Captain P. S. Parker," the operator intoned.

"I'm not sure if he's here," the sergeant said.

"Look for him," the caller said, flatly.

"I beg your pardon?" the sergeant-bartender said.

"I said, look for him," the caller repeated.

"May I ask who's calling, please, sir?"

"This is Colonel Philip Sheridan Parker," the caller said.

There was a long wait, and then the click of an extension telephone being lifted.

"Captain Parker, sir."

"You may get off the line, Sergeant," Colonel Parker said. The background sound of the barroom vanished.

"Hey, Dad, how are you? Is anything wrong?" Phil Parker asked, concern in his voice.

"Nothing is wrong. Is this telephone relatively secure?"

"Nobody else is on it, if that's what you mean. You sound upset, Dad. Is something wrong?"

"Have you been considering resignation?"

Phil Parker hesitated a moment before replying. "The thought has run through my mind," he said. "I haven't done anything about it."

"I'm glad to hear that," Colonel Parker said.

Phil didn't reply.

"Have you been drinking?" Colonel Parker asked.

"No, but that's one thought that really has been going through my mind." And then he understood the reason for the question. "Oh," he said. "In addition to my other duties, I am assistant club officer. I've been going over the books. That's why I'm here."

"I would like to suggest that you put off any action with regard to resignation for a while," Colonel Parker said.

"Dad, I have no intention of spending my life fighting with dependent wives about grease spots on kitchen walls, or counting bottles of whiskey and A-1 sauce in officer's clubs. A classmate of mine is in the shipping business in Boston. He's offering me a hell of a lot of money, and the chance to live for a couple of years in Africa."

"You're a soldier," his father said.

"I'm beginning to have serious doubts about that," Phil Parker replied.

"I had a telephone call late this afternoon from an officer with whom I served in Europe. I am not at liberty to provide his name."

"And?"

"This officer is also a soldier," Colonel Parker said. "He leads me to believe that your situation is not quite as hopeless as you might think."

"Club officers are in short supply," Parker said.

"Two things are about to happen," Colonel Parker said. "You are about to be transferred, within the next couple of weeks, from Fort Devens."

"No kidding? Where am I going?"

"He didn't say," Colonel Parker said. "But he said that you are also going to be offered an opportunity which will provide a chance for you to get your career back on the tracks."

Phil Parker didn't reply.

"I will not bore you with maudlin tales of unpleasant assignments I had," Colonel Parker said. "You're a man. You'll have to make your own decisions. I would suggest, however, that whatever you're thinking of doing can wait for three months."

"You're not going to tell me who called?"

"Nothing more than to tell you he is a general officer for whom I have a good deal of respect. And affection, too, if that seems germane to you."

"I don't understand how he knew I was thinking of resigning," Phil Parker said. "I haven't mentioned that to anybody."

"We go back a long time together, Phil," Colonel Parker said. "He once dissuaded me from resigning."

"OK, Dad. I'll wait a while."

"Your mother said to tell you the young lady in the photograph is quite handsome."

"And what do you think?"

"I have been wondering if there is something significant in your having sent her photograph at all."

"She's really something special," Phil Parker said. "I met her at the Pops."

"The orchestra? Is that what you mean?"

"Yes," Phil said.

"Who introduced you?" his father asked.

"You really want to know?" Phil said, and chuckled. "Well, what I did, Dad, was walk up and hand her my card. I said

I'd call her. Her date didn't like that at all. But he wasn't large enough to react violently."

"*L'audace, l'audace, toujours l'audace,*" Colonel Parker said, a faint chuckle in his voice.

"She's a pathologist," Phil said. "What do you think about that?"

"A medical doctor?"

"At Harvard Medical School," Phil said. His father heard a touch of pride in his son's voice.

"I'm impressed," Colonel Parker said. Then, bluntly, "What kind of an officer's wife do you think she'd make?"

"Because she's a doctor, you mean?"

"Because she's a Negro," his father replied.

"They say 'black' now, Dad."

"You've thought about that, however?"

"Oh, yeah," Phil Parker said. "Her parents don't think much of soldiers."

"Few people do," Colonel Parker said.

"I've got to throw that into the equation, too, Dad."

"Contemplation of marriage is the one exception to the rule that any action is better than none," Colonel Parker said.

"I'll let you know what happens," Phil Parker said.

"Don't act hastily, Philip," his father said. "Whatever you do."

(Four)
Bordentown, N.J.
23 October 1952

The Bordentown Military Academy took pride in the medical care, routine and emergency, it provided for the Corps of Cadets. The medical staff included a full-time physician, given the brevet rank of major, and four registered nurses, one brevet captain and three brevet first lieutenants.

Since no member of the Corps of Cadets happened to be confined in dispensary with any of the illnesses which strike boys in either their immediate postpuberty or teenage years, Evelyn Wood, R.N., was not required to remain in the eight-bed dispensary, but was instead required only to be in white uniform, to remain on the campus, and to keep the school switchboard operators and the duty officer aware of her location.

Her crisp white uniform was carefully laid on top of her red-lined nurse's cape, and her underthings were laid on top of the uniform, all of it on one of the two small upholstered chairs provided for each of the bedrooms in staff quarters number two.

Evelyn Wood herself, when the telephone rang, was lying naked on her stomach between the legs of Major Craig W. Lowell, who was the duty officer and similarly obliged to remain on campus in a location where the telephone operator could immediately locate him.

At the first ring, he reached down and gently but firmly disengaged Nurse Wood's mouth, and then turned on his side and reached for the telephone.

"Duty officer," he said. "Major Lowell."

She understood his concern, but she really would have taken great pains not to bite it off. Slightly piqued, she thought that at least he could have said, "Excuse me."

Evelyn Wood had seen Major Craig Lowell the day he reported for duty, a week late, for the fall semester. She wasn't exactly proud of how far she'd had to go to get them where they were, but on the other hand, there weren't that many good-looking single men who drove red Lincoln Continental convertibles around Bordentown, and desperate measures had been necessary.

He simply hadn't been interested in her at first. She had hoped that she would have a chance to meet him, more or less alone, somewhere on the campus, at the movies, someplace like that, but the only times she saw him were in staff quarters, and then he had looked right through her.

He spent his weekends off campus, leaving just as soon as he could on Friday afternoons and returning very late on Sunday.

What she'd had to do was lie in wait for him in the dispensary, when he was the duty officer and required to check on the dispensary twice during his tour of duty. She'd told him that since he had to be up anyway, he should come by her quarters after she finished her tour at midnight, and she would give him a cup of coffee.

He hadn't come. Instead, he had telephoned her quarters and told her to come to his, unless what she really had in mind was coffee.

That had been really humiliating, going down the corridor in her dressing gown, a shameless admission that what they both had in mind was s-x, instead of making a friendship that might result in courtship, and only then, possibly, s-x. She had really been tempted to turn around and tell him to go to hell.

But she had gone to his quarters and ten minutes after she walked in the door, she had been in his bed, and God, he was good there. Once they'd started, it was really actually better than it would have been the other way. There was something very exciting about not putting up any phony modesty and pretense. When she got turned on, *anything* went, and anything she wanted to do was fine with him.

She found out that he was a widower with a little boy, and the idea of an instant family finally had given her cause for concern, until she realized, feeling something like a fool, that he hadn't come within a hundred miles of suggesting anything like making anything of their relationship.

He too her out sometimes during the week, on her two nights off, to Trenton, and once to Philadelphia. He took her to really nice places, as if money didn't mean a thing to him. It would have been nicer if she had more seniority and got weekends off, but she didn't, and she hadn't really expected him to hang around the campus. He still went to New York or someplace every weekend.

All she could hope for, Evelyn Wood told herself, was that their relationship would gradually ripen. She knew he liked her.

"Is that you, Craig?" a woman's voice asked. It was familiar, but he couldn't place it.

"Who's this?"

"I'm crushed that you don't remember," she said. "This is Barbara Bellmon."

"Well, I'll be goddamned," he said.

"Probably," she said. "What are you doing? Can you talk?"

"Sure. What's on your mind?"

"Actually," she said, "Bob wants to talk to you." He heard her say, "Craig is on the line, honey."

"How are you, Lowell?" Bob Bellmon said a moment later. It wasn't at all hard to detect that he wasn't thrilled with the prospect of talking to him.

"Why I'm fine, Colonel," Lowell said. "May I offer my congratulations? I saw in the *Army-Navy Journal* that they've finally given you your silver chicken."

"Thank you," Bellmon said, stiffly. "Very kind of you."

"How may I be of service, Colonel?" Lowell asked lightly, enjoying Bellmon's discomfiture.

"In point of fact," Bellmon said. "Your name came up at lunch today."

"My ears haven't been burning," Lowell said. "What was said about me?"

"In the opinion of the officer with whom I had lunch..."

"Who was that, Colonel?"

"I'm not at liberty to say," Bellmon said. "A senior officer, who somehow knew that I know you."

"And what did this anonymous senior officer have to say about me?"

"He holds the opinion that there was something of an overreaction to that business with you and the movie star."

"You're talking about my efficiency report?"

"Yes, of course I am."

"That efficiency report was a result of my testifying for Phil Parker in his court-martial."

"That's not the story I get."

"Well, Bob, that's the story."

"Your case, as you are probably well aware, has been brought to the attention of a very senior officer by one of your politician friends."

"Now, I really don't know what you're talking about."

"You're denying it?"

"Yes, I'm denying it. I've been thinking about having a word with my senator—my cousin's got one in his vest pocket—about getting me permission to resign, but so far I haven't talked to him."

At that point, he thought of Porter Craig.

"My cousin may have done something like that," he said. "But, believe me, Bob, I didn't."

There was a pause before Bellmon went on.

"In any event, your case was brought before a senior officer by a senator."

"The one you had lunch with, no doubt?"

"I had lunch with his aide-de-camp," Bellmon said.

"And?"

"As I said, he feels there has been an overreaction to what happened to you in Korea."

"I wish you would get to the point," Lowell said.

"You'll shortly receive orders to Sill," Bellmon said. "To an assignment more in keeping with your experience and abilities."

Now Lowell paused before replying.

"What about Phil Parker?" he asked.

"Phil's going to Sill, too."

"Virtue, I gather," Lowell said, "is its own reward. Thanks for calling me. I appreciate it."

"I can't accept credit for something like that," Bellmon said. "It was pointedly suggested to me that since we were such old friends, that I make the call."

"What do I have to do, Bob," Lowell flared, "to get in your good graces? Win the goddamned Medal? There's two sides to the Korean story, believe it or not!"

"Both of you stop it," Barbara Bellmon said angrily, apparently on an extension. "Craig, he told me again and again he thought you got a raw deal in Korea."

"I apologize, Lowell," Bellmon said.

"You apologize, *'Craig,'*" Barbara Bellmon said firmly to her husband.

"I apologize, Craig," Bellmon said dutifully.

"Now I'm embarrassed," Lowell said. "You don't owe me an apology, Bob. I know I grate on your nerves. I can't help it."

"Daddy grated on his nerves, too, Craig," Barbara said. "You're in good company."

"That's right, that's right," Bob Bellmon said righteously. "You and Porky Waterford are two of a kind, Lowell."

"'Craig,'" Barbara corrected him again.

"I'm a full colonel," Bellmon said. "He's a lousy major. I can call him anything I want to call him."

It was a joke, and they all laughed. And they talked of P.P., and Lowell promised to come by the Farm on his way to Sill, when he got his orders. Finally, he hung up.

He rolled over onto his back.

"What was that all about?" Evelyn Wood asked, smiling at him, stroking him.

"I'm about to be sprung from durance vile," Lowell reported.

"I don't know what that means," Evelyn said. "You're going somewhere?"

"Right."

"Where?"

"Fort Sill, Oklahoma," he said. He smiled happily. "Now where were we?"

Damn, she thought, as he took him in her mouth again. She should have known it would turn out like this.

XVIII

The United States Air Force traces its heritage to the aviation section of the Signal Corps in the days before World War II. Army aviation traces its heritage back to the Civil War, when Thaddeus Lowe provided the army with balloons, from which Union Army artillery fire was directed against the Confederate Army of Northern Virginia attacking Washington.

The vast bulk of army aircraft (as opposed to *Army Air Corps* aircraft) in World War II, almost all of them Piper Cub L-2s or Stinson L-5s, were assigned to the artillery for the same purpose, aerial direction of artillery fire.

It was natural, therefore, that artillery took over the role of pilot training. Artillery observers were trained at the same time as the gunners were trained, on the huge Fort Sill reservation.

In both separate batteries, and as part of armored formations, a large portion of U.S. Army artillery is self-propelled; that is, the cannon are mounted on tracked tank chassis.

Major Craig Lowell thought there was nothing really unusual about his assignment to the Office of the G-3 (Plans and Training) of the Army Artillery Center, Fort Sill. It was the sort of assignment to which he was entitled. He was an armor officer with S-3 experience. He knew tracks, and how to teach people to operate and maintain them.

Neither was it surprising, only a pleasant coincidence, that Phil Parker should have been called from passing out dependent housing at Fort Devens for assignment to Sill, following what Lowell thought of as "the conditional pardon." It was a logical place for him to be assigned, too. Parker was made motor officer, tracked vehicles, in the Self-propelled Artillery Department of the Artillery School. His job was to make sure that sufficient self-propelled tracks were available to carry out the training missions prescribed by the G-3.

They weren't in armor, but it was the next best thing. The BOQs were ghastly, perched so that the sand of Sill was blown into everything by the never-ending wind. Regulations did not permit bachelor officers to live off post, that privilege being reserved for officers with dependents, for whom no housing was available on the post.

It was a question of semantics. They were not confined to the post, but they would not be paid a housing allowance since BOQs were available to them.

Lowell, on his third day at Fort Sill, after investigating the available hotel accommodations and rental housing nearby, and finding them just about as bad as the BOQs, had thrilled a salesman at Lawton Realty by making a five-thousand-dollar down payment on the demonstration model of the Holly Crest Split-Level ($26,500) in the Lawton Heights subdivision, sufficient to get quick approval of the mortage at the First National Bank of Lawton. He then gave him another check for the furnishings, which were on sort-of-a-loan from Oklahoma Home Furnishings.

All that was required to move in was a visit to the department store for sheets, towels, and that sort of thing, and to the grocery store.

It did cause some raised eyebrows from the neighbors, first when the wives came bearing gifts for the wife, and learned

there was no wife, and next when an enormous black captain
also moved in.

They didn't look like fairies, but you couldn't tell anymore,
these days.

There was some talk like that until the next Friday, when
a tall and elegantly dressed black woman got out of a taxi and
smiled at the horseshoe of flowers propped against the door
with a ribbon reading, "WELCOME TO THE WILD WEST, ANTOI-
NETTE." She had been mailed a key, since Phil couldn't get off
during the day to meet her at the plane.

Antoinette, despite her parents' protests that doctors of
medicine or not, nice girls don't fly thousands of miles to spend
weekends with a soldier, was a frequent guest at 2340 Bubbling
Creek Lane, and she was there when the telephone call came
on New Year's afternoon. So was Harriet Albright, the assistant
vice president at the First National Bank of Lawton. Harriet,
a redheaded divorcée, had been thrilled at the prospect of
"burning some steaks" at Major Lowell's house, after having
been informed by the Morgan Guaranty Trust—of whom she
had made the necessary inquiries relative to granting a mort-
age—that there was no question whatever regarding his credit
rating, and even after he had carefully pointed out to her that
his roommate was colored, and that they had, as their house
guest, his roommate's fiancée, who was also colored.

Harriet had never been personally prejudiced herself, and
there weren't that many bachelors around whom a vice president of the Morgan Guaranty Trust would describe as "very
rich."

Craig was in the kitchen with Antoinette, having just tasted
Antoinette's Pommes Frites d'Alsace, when the pale yellow
telephone matching the wallpaper went off in his ear.

He was on his fourth martini, and feeling better than he had
felt in a long time.

"Hello," he said to the telephone.

"Major Lowell, please," an obviously military voice said.

"What number are you calling, please?" Lowell said. He
had no intention of running out to the post to do something
that damned well could wait until Monday morning.

"The number I got from information," the caller said. "Is that you, Lowell?"

"Yes, sir."

"My name is Roberts. We have a mutual acquaintance, Bob Bellmon."

"Oh, yes, sir."

"I've been looking for you, and for Captain Parker, since Thursday," Roberts said. "I presume he's there with you?"

"Yes, sir."

"My wife and I would like to call on you, Major," Roberts said, and it was clear from the tone of his voice that whatever this was about, it was not social. "Would in an hour be convenient?"

"Could you give me some idea what this is all about . . . is it Colonel?"

"Lieutenant Colonel," Roberts said. "I'm the deputy post aviation officer."

"Colonel, we're in the middle . . . we're about to have dinner."

"I'll give you an hour and a half then," Colonel Roberts said. "2340 Bubbling Creek Lane, isn't it?"

"It's the house with the 'Sold' sign nailed to the 'Furnished Model' sign on the lawn," Lowell said.

Antoinette laughed at him.

"Why don't you take that down?" she asked.

"It beats a street number all to death, doesn't it?"

Antoinette laughed, and then she said: "Every time I have my girlish dreams of getting you two out of the army, and into respectability, I have this nightmare: I see that 'For Sale/Sold' sign, and I remember you're not really housebroken, socially speaking. It's probably better my parents haven't met either one of you."

"I'll have you know," Lowell replied, "you beskirted chancre mechanic, that Congress has decreed that Phil and I are gentlemen."

He patted her on the bottom, and then he went in to where Phil was mixing another pitcher of martinis and told him what was about to happen.

An hour and fifteen minutes after his telephone call, Lt.

Colonel and Mrs. William Roberts got out of their Mercury coupe and walked up to the door of 2340 Bubbling Creek Lane. Colonel Roberts pushed the doorbell, and he and his wife could hear the first eight notes of "Be It Ever So Humble." Mrs. Roberts giggled.

Lowell opened the door. He was dressed in a polo shirt and slacks.

"Colonel Roberts, I presume," he said.

"I *love* your doorbell," Mrs. Roberts said, with a wide smile.

"Wait till you see the wallpaper in the downstairs lavatory," Lowell said. "It's an artistic rendition of that famous statue in Belgium of the little boy doing you know what."

"Fantastic!" she said, and she and Craig Lowell smiled at each other.

"Please come in," Lowell said. Roberts shook his hand, but didn't say a word.

Captain Philip Sheridan Parker IV, who had been on the couch with Dr. Antoinette Ferguson, got up.

"'I just can't get over,' as they say," Mrs. Roberts said, "'how big Sweet Little Philip has grown!'"

"I beg your pardon?" Parker said.

"I have been brought along on Bill's recruiting expedition as proof that at least he's married to someone friendly," she said. "I knew you at Riley before the war. My folks and yours still exchange Christmas cards. I'm . . . I was . . . Jeanne Whitman."

"Oh, sure!" Parker said, his face widening with a smile. "How's your father?"

"Fine. And yours? My parents are out in Carmel."

"Mine are still outside the gate at Riley," Phil said. He turned to Antoinette. "Mrs. Roberts, may I present Dr. Antoinette Ferguson? And this is Mrs. Albright."

"Doctor of medicine?" Colonel Roberts asked. "Or of philosophy?"

"I'm a pathologist," Antoinette said.

"And Harriet is a banker," Lowell said. "Make sure you mention that when you write his mother."

"Our neighbors refer to this place as Respectability Hall," Parker offered.

"I'll bet they do," Colonel Roberts said. "Well, now the small talk is out of the way, why don't you regale the ladies, Jeanne, with stories of the Old Army while I talk to these two?"

"I'm really sorry to break into your party this way," Jeanne Whitman Roberts said, "but there's no stopping Bill when he gets this way."

"Is there somewhere we can go?" Roberts asked.

"Can I fix you a drink?" Lowell asked.

"I'm a little afraid you've had too many already," Roberts said bluntly.

"And I intend to have at least one more, Colonel," Lowell said coldly. "Phil and I have fixed up the third bedroom as sort of an office. We can go up there." He picked up the martini pitcher, poured a drink and held it out to Roberts. Roberts paused, and finally gave in and took it. Lowell offered another martini to Phil Parker, who shook his head, "no." Then Lowell poured one for himself and waved Roberts up the stairs.

"OK, Colonel," he said, when Roberts had helped himself to the only upholstered chair in the room, "what's this all about?"

"I've got a couple of questions to ask you," Roberts said. "And do me the courtesy of giving me straight answers." Both Phil and Craig nodded.

"What do you think, by and large, of army aviators?" Colonel Roberts asked.

Phil Parker shrugged his massive shoulders. "Not much," he said. "I mean, I never thought of them much, period. But now that I am thinking of them, per se, I don't think much of them, either. Is that straight enough for you, Colonel?"

"Lowell?" Roberts asked, without replying.

"I have always wondered why the army feels it can turn a half-million-dollar tank and command of a four- or five-man crew over to a sergeant, and on the other hand has to have a lieutenant or a captain—or even a major—flying a two-seater, fifteen-thousand-dollar airplane."

"In other words, you don't think much of army aviators, or, for that matter, of army aviation?"

"You want it straight?" Lowell asked. "OK. There's obviously a place for airplanes in the army. God knows, there's nothing better for column control. I've used them myself. I've even wondered why the hell we can't put rockets on some of those little planes. Maybe even on choppers. They'd be good tank killers. But that's not what's happening. Army aviators are a collection of commissioned aerial jeep drivers playing air force."

"You don't think much of the typical army aviator, is that what you're saying?"

"No offense intended, Colonel. But you asked for it. And there it is. I'm like Phil. I don't think much of them, period, except to wonder why the hell they should be officers."

"A good many aviators leave a good deal to be desired," Roberts said. "A number of them, in fact, are officers who got into some scrape in their basic arm, saw the handwriting on the wall, and came to aviation because it was either into army aviation or out of the army."

"Tell me, Colonel, have our reputations preceded us?" Lowell asked.

"I know a good deal about the both of you," Roberts said. "Including the bad."

"And since we are such certified fuck-ups, you're here to recruit us for army aviation?" Lowell challenged. "I don't think I'm quite that fucked up, Colonel, thank you just the same."

"Shut up, Craig," Phil Parker said, sharply. "The colonel is a guest in our quarters. We didn't expect visitors, Colonel. We've been drinking."

"It doesn't seem to make you forget that you're supposed to be an officer and a gentleman," Roberts said. He glowered at Lowell as if waiting for an apology. He didn't get one.

"Flight classes at the aviation section of the Artillery School consist of thirty-two officers," Roberts said, after a long, tense pause. "In the event that, during the first two weeks of flight training, something causes an officer to drop out of flight school, Fort Sill is authorized to replace those officers from qualified officers already present at Fort Sill. The training schedule, as you can understand, Major Lowell, will have to go on regardless of the number of officers present to take the training."

"And you just happen to have lost two of your students, is that it?" Phil Parker asked.

"Well, I'm sorry this has been a wild-goose chase for you,

Colonel," Lowell said. "But before I would become an aerial taxi driver, I would resign."

"There are nineteen officers at Fort Sill at the moment on the waiting list," Roberts said, undaunted. "Ready and willing to take flight training."

"Then why do you want us?" Phil Parker asked.

"Because, in your case, Captain Parker, you have been identified to me as a solid and stable officer, from a long line of soldiers, who was given a raw deal in Korea."

Parker didn't reply. Roberts looked at Lowell.

"And you, Lowell, I want you because of what's written in your Counterintelligence Corps dossier."

"I don't understand," Lowell replied.

"You have political influence at the highest levels," Colonel Roberts said, "and you will continue to have it, no matter which party holds temporary power, because you are, through inheritance, not because you did anything at all to earn it, obscenely rich."

"I have never attempted to use my financial position," Lowell said, slowly and distinctly, so that Parker, recognizing this as a sign of fury, looked at him with concern, "in any way whatsoever to seek special privilege in the army."

"You were relieved of your duties at the Bordentown Military Academy, Major, by the Vice Chief of Staff, at the request of the senior senator from New York."

"I was presented that as a *fait accompli*," Lowell said. "My cousin arranged that. He doesn't want me in New York."

"I believe that," Roberts said. "But nobody else will. And I notice you didn't complain that you were receiving special treatment."

"Oh, *shit!*" Lowell said. "I should have known something like this would pop up."

"It's not the end of the world," Roberts said.

"If you know about it, Colonel," Lowell said, "it will be all over the fucking army."

"Your political influence is one thing that makes you attractive to me," Roberts said. "I was not overly impressed with that grandstanding ride you took out of Pusan. You're lucky you didn't get the whole task force wiped out."

"Colonel," Lowell said, "don't talk to me about Task Force Lowell. I was there, and you weren't, and that was the proper use of tanks in that situation."

"You enjoy command, don't you?" Roberts asked. "Pity you'll never get another one in armor."

"You seem a good deal more sure of that that I am, Colonel," Lowell said."

"Don't take my word," Roberts said. "But what about Paul Jiggs? Would you take this? Or Bob Bellmon's?"

"You've been talking to them?"

"They've been trying to sell you to me, Major. And you're doing a very good job of unselling yourself, political influence or no political influence."

Lowell just looked at him. Their eyes locked. Finally, Roberts picked up the telephone. "Operator, get me Colonel Paul Jiggs, at the National War College, in Washington, D.C."

Lowell reached over and broke the connection.

"I'm a little surprised that Colonel Jiggs would bring up the political business," he said.

"I shouldn't tell you this, because you're arrogant enough," Roberts said. "But I finally seem to be getting through the layer of smart-ass, and I'll take a chance. Jiggs said that you're a splendid combat commander, a splendid S-3, and a three-star wise-ass. He said that with luck, you may grow out of being a smart-ass, and that I'm going to need both commanders and planners, and that I'm not going to get many to volunteer."

"What you're suggesting is that I could get a command in army aviation," Lowell said. "Of what? A reinforced platoon of Piper Cubs?"

"How about a company of rocket-armed helicopters?"

"You're a dreamer, Colonel," Lowell said. "The air force won't stand still for that."

"I see entire divisions, entirely transported and supported by army aircraft," Roberts said. "That's what I dream."

"A vast armada of L-19s, Beavers, and H13s filling the sky," Lowell said, sarcastically.

"I told you to watch your lip," Phil Parker said.

"That's my brain talking, not the booze," Lowell said.

"OK," Roberts said. "Paragraph Four. Conclusions. Where

you stand now, Major Lowell, is as an officer far too young for the grade you hold, with an efficiency report that will hang around your neck the rest of your career. There is no way, *no way*, that you will *ever* command a tank battalion, and you're smart enough when you're sober to know that. And when your time comes to be considered for lieutenant colonel, if you last that long, and the choice is between you and some officer whose efficiency report does not state he acts impulsively and cannot be recommended for command, you know who will be promoted."

"You've been reading my efficiency reports, too, huh? You get around, don't you, Colonel?"

"Yeah, I do," Roberts said. "I'm generally as unpopular with my peers as you are with yours."

"Who's going to promote an officer who spent ten years flying a Piper Cub?" Lowell asked.

"In ten years, I don't intend that the army will be flying Piper Cubs," Roberts said. "And when they start picking *aviation* battalion commanders, they'll have to pick them from aviators. By your own statements, you consider most army aviators mediocrities and misfits. Against that kind of competition, you just might not have to go from being the youngest major in the army to the oldest, Lowell."

"What's in it for you, Colonel?" Lowell replied.

"I told you. Both Bob Bellmon and Paul Jiggs have been touting you as the best G-3 type I can get. That and the political influence."

"You keep saying 'I,'" Philip Sheridan Parker said. "You sound like you own army aviation."

Roberts gave him a cold look.

"Right now, I'm one of the three officers on active duty who were in the first class, the 'Class Before One,' before they numbered the classes for liaison pilots. The other two are about to retire. To the considerable surprise of my classmates, who to a man felt that I had thrown away my career, I have been promoted with them. Right now, I'm one of the very few people with the vision to see an air-mobile army. Yeah, Captain, I guess you could say I have a certain possessive feeling toward army aviation."

"You really think you can get away with it?" Lowell asked.

"I hope I can," Roberts said. "I work pretty hard at it."

"What do you think, Phil?" Lowell asked.

"He sure do talk it up, don't he?" Captain Philip Sheridan Parker IV said, in a thick Negro accent. "He make a *fine* casket salesman. He make it sound like you *need* the solid bronze."

"I've got to do a lot of things I don't like to do," Roberts burst out, furiously. "But I don't have to take being mocked by assholes like you two."

"Colonel, you have really sprung something on me I didn't expect," Lowell said. "I'd like to think it over. When do you have to know?"

"Right goddamned now," Roberts said, still red in the face and furious.

"I saw my father on the way out here," Phil Sheridan said. "He said that I was making the same mistake a lot of people were making." Confused, both Lowell and Roberts looked at him. "He said that armor wasn't cavalry, and he said that there will always be a place on the battlefield for cavalry."

"What the hell is that supposed to mean?" Roberts asked.

"He said it didn't come down from Mount Sinai engraved on stone that cavalry has to be mounted on a horse," Parker said. "What you said before, Craig. About arming helicopters? What the hell is that, a fast-moving lightly armed force, unrestricted by roads, but cavalry?"

"You think the man has a point?" Lowell asked.

"What happens to me next?" Parker asked. "There aren't many field-grade motor officers around. Count me in, Colonel."

"Don't be impetuous," Lowell said. "This needs some thought. If we fuck this up, Philip my lad, we would really be finished. How soon do you need an answer, Colonel?"

"Right goddamned now," Roberts said. "I need two bodies at the airfield at 0800 tomorrow. Yours or somebody else's."

"Well, in that case," Lowell said. "I think I'd better have another martini."

"What the hell kind of an answer is that?" Colonel Roberts demanded.

"It mean," Captain Philip Sheridan Parker said, again in his thick Negro accent, "look out aviation! Here come duh Duke and King Kong!"

Roberts was still mad. "I hope you two bastards don't think you're doing me a favor," he said. But he got up and put out his hand to both of them.

(Two)

Antoinette didn't seem impressed one way or the other when they came down from their meeting with Colonel Roberts and told her that they were about to soar off into the wild blue yonder, starting at 0800 the next morning. But when they tapered off from the martinis into wine spritzers, she became what Lowell thought of as a royal pain in the ass.

When Harriet finally went home, she got even worse. And then, surprising the both of them, she made a pitcher of martinis, and when asked about the pitcher, said she was in a good mood to drink at least one pitcherful, and possibly two.

"Would you tell me why you're being such a bitch?" Phil Parker asked.

She finished the martini she was drinking before she replied.

"Why am I being such a bitch?" she said. "Right. Good question."

"You're drunk, for Christ's sake!" Phil said to her.

"In vino veritas," Antoinette said.

"Ergo sum," Lowell said.

"E pluribus unum," Parker said. He and Lowell laughed.

"Screw you, Phil!" Antoinette snapped, furiously. And then she started to cry.

"What the hell is the matter?" Phil asked, half angry, half concerned.

"Well, excuse me, kiddies," Lowell said. "Little Craig is going to go tuck it in."

"You stay!" Antoinette ordered.

"What the hell have I done?" he asked, but he sat back down.

"I've had enough of this," she said.

"Of what, honey?"

"Of being a damned camp follower."

"I'm sorry you feel that way," Phil said.

"I'm not like that redheaded tramp of yours, Craig."

"Harriet? Hey, Slim, if Harriet is the problem, it's solved. I've had about all of her I can stand myself," Lowell said. "And now may I go to bed?"

"No," she said. "That's not what I mean. What I mean to say is that I can't go on like I am. I have to make up my mind."

"About what?" Phil asked.

"Every time I come out here, I convince myself that I'll be able to talk you out of the army, and get you home to Boston. And every time, nothing happens."

"Nothing will, Toni," Parker said softly. "I'm a soldier. That's what I do."

"And I'm a doctor," she said. "That's what I do."

"And ne'er the twain shall meet?" Phil said.

She looked at him, and with tears streaming down her cheeks, nodded her head.

"I've had enough of this maudlin bullshit," Lowell said, and got up.

"Watch it, Craig!" Parker said, angrily.

"Either she loves you and wants to marry you and bear your children, or she doesn't. It's as simple as that. You two can fight about it all night for all I care, but for Christ's sake, if she gets hysterical, throw some water on her. I need my sleep."

He stormed out of the room and went upstairs.

Five minutes later there was a knock at his door. Captain Philip S. Parker IV and Miss Antoinette Elaine Ferguson, M.D., wished him to be the first to know that they were to be joined in holy matrimony.

"In a couple of weeks, Craig. Just a little ceremony. My folks and Toni's, and that's about all. You, too, of course."

"But not Harriet?"

"No," Toni said, and leaned over and kissed him. "Not Harriet."

"I suppose this means I'll have to find someplace else to live, doesn't it?" Lowell said.

"This is your home, dummy," Parker said.

"I'll make you a good deal on it," Lowell said, "if you agree to rent me a room. This one."

(Three)
Fort Sill, Oklahoma
14 January 1953

Chaplain (Lt. Col.) James Jackson "Brother Jack" Glover, Fort Sill's senior chaplain, was a Southern Baptist from Daphne, Alabama. He naturally reflected the "mores of his background," as he thought of it, but he prided himself on keeping his feelings about colored people to himself. They were all God's children, after all, and this wasn't Daphne, Alabama, but the U.S. Army. There was no room for prejudice in the armed forces of the United States, and he did whatever he could, whenever he could, to condemn bigotry.

Having said that, there was really no phrase Brother Jack could think of to better describe the colored officer who had come to his office five days before than "an uppity nigger."

His door had been open to him, and his heart, and he had been willing to render unto him precisely the same services that he would render to any of his Protestant military flock, regardless of color.

He had tried to explain to him that marriage was a sacrament and that it should not be entered into lightly and not without a lot of prayer. He had told him that he had regularly scheduled marriage counseling sessions and that he would be happy to schedule the captain and his young lady for the next one.

"Chaplain, all I want from you is to tell me when I can have the chapel in the next five days. I intend to provide my own clergyman, and I'm really not interested in counseling. I've given this marriage a good deal of thought for a long time."

"But has your young woman?"

"My 'young woman,' Chaplain, is a doctor of medicine, and she's given the matter even more thought than I have."

"Captain," Brother Jack had told him, "my marriage counseling sessions have the enthusiastic support of the general. It is official command policy that ɔfficers and enlisted men be encouraged to participate before assuming the responsibilities of marriage."

"With all respect, Chaplain, when can I have the chapel?"

he asked, not even bothering to conceal his impatience.

Brother Jack would not have been surprised if the colored captain's intended had turned out to be a white woman. There was a certain class of white women, mostly Yankee intellectual types, who really chased after big black bucks like this one. But she was a coon, too. She had brought their wedding license to the chaplain's office two days later, after he'd told the colored captain that he would have to see the marriage license before he could turn the chapel over to a civilian clergyman. Good-looking woman, Brother Jack thought. Obviously had a lot of Arab—or white—blood in her. Not one of your flat-faced jungle bunnies. Maybe she really was a doctor. That's the way she signed the marriage license, anyway.

Then things started happening that really began to bother Brother Jack, though the way the liberals were running things and ruining the army, the last thing he wanted was a run-in with the NAACP about picking on the colored.

The first thing that happened was that he walked into the chapel and found the general's aide snooping around. When he asked him what he could do for him, the general's aide said all he knew was that the general had told him to come to the chapel and make sure things were up to snuff.

Brother Jack could hardly call the general and ask him what he was worried about, but just to be sure, he called in all the chaplain's assistants and had them give the chapel a good GI party, top to bottom. It didn't need it, of course, but a chapel could never be too clean.

The next thing that happened was that Mrs. Roberts, the wife of the head aviator, came to the chapel and started nosing around herself. She told him that an old friend of hers was being married there, and she wanted things to be first rate.

He wasn't really surprised when the friend turned out to be the colored captain.

He expected that the civilian minister who was going to perform the ceremony would be in touch with him, but that didn't happen; so Brother Jack called the president of the Lawton Ministerial Association, of which he was a member, and asked him who would be a likely candidate among the colored clergy to marry a colored officer and his fiancée. He got three names, and called all three of them, but they had never heard of a Captain Parker.

On the morning of the wedding, Brother Jack went by the chapel just to make sure things were all right. There was a self-propelled 155 mm cannon, a Long Tom on a tank chassis, parked in front of the chapel. He didn't know what was going on, and he went to the driver and asked him what he was doing, and the driver told him all he knew was that he had been told to bring the vehicle to the chapel, and that the general's aide would meet him there.

And then things really started to happen. Two panel trucks showed up from Lawton loaded with flowers; and then Mrs. Roberts started to arrange them all over the chapel. The obvious thing to do, to show her he had no prejudice, was to help her with that, and that's what he was doing when he saw the front door of the chapel open, and a major wearing a sword came in.

"I got the sabers, Chaplain," the major said. "Where's the condemned man?"

The major's name was Green, and he said that he was president of the local chapter of Norwich graduates, and he just wished to hell they'd given him a little more time; all he could come up with on such short notice was twelve officers, including himself. Brother Jack had never heard of Norwich, and didn't know what he was talking about, and moreover, Major Green had obviously been at the bottle. You could smell it four feet away.

And then what really put the cork in the bottle, the chapel door opened again and a major general came in. Brother Jack saw the stars first, and only afterward the silver crosses on his lapels. There is only one man in the U.S. Army who wears the two stars of a major general and the crosses of Christ: the Chief of Chaplains.

Mrs. Roberts ran and kissed him on the cheek.

"Father Dan," she called him, even though Brother Jack knew for a fact that he was Episcopalian, not Roman Catholic. "I'm glad you could make it."

"Not only that, I came in style," he said. "E. Z.'s here, too."

"Where?"

"The bar at the club is open," he said. "Where else?" Then he saw Brother Jack. "I really hate to just jump in on you like this, Chaplain," he said, "but I went through War II with the colonel, Colonel Parker, that is, and I christened the groom, so I figured that it was my duty to marry him."

"We're honored to have you here, sir," Brother Jack said. "Is there anything I can do?"

"Nothing but clean up the mess afterward," the Chief of Chaplains said, cheerfully. "I know this chapel. I was stationed here. The reason the organ is new is because the old one, when I was here, used to collapse once a month."

Then the guests started to arrive. Including the officer the Chief of Chaplains had identified as "E. Z." E. Z. turned out to be the newly appointed Vice Chief of Staff of the United States Army, General E. Z. Black.

The Vice Chief of Staff of the U.S. Army smelled as heavily of booze as did Major Green.

Fair's fair, Brother Jack decided, admitting that the very brief Episcopalian wedding ceremony had a lot of class, even if it meant the minister didn't have much of an opportunity to exhort the bride and groom on their responsibilities to God and the community as man and wife.

And he really liked the officers lined up outside the chapel afterward, with their sabers forming an arch over the newlyweds. He hadn't been able to find out what this Norwich Association was, but he made a note to look into it. Maybe he could get them to do the saber thing regularly. It added a nice military touch.

The self-propelled 155 mm cannon was a disaster, as Brother Jack knew it would be. First, when they started it up, it made so much noise you couldn't hear the organ music during the recessional. Next, it frightened the bride, when the groom and she got into it. And when she rode it to the officer's club, she got grease all over her white dress.

And, as Brother Jack knew very well it would, it just tore

up the macadam road in front of the chapel and all the way to the officer's club, where there was a party that could only be described as drunken.

But he couldn't say anything to anyone about that. For what happened was that the Vice Chief of Staff of the U.S. Army, a four-star general, obviously in his cups, had called out to the groom's father (whom Brother Jack had learned was a retired colonel). "Come on, Phil," the Vice Chief had said, "it's our last chance, probably," and then ordered the driver and the commander of the self-propelled 155 mm off the vehicle and had driven Captain and Mrs. Philip Sheridan Parker IV to their reception at the officer's open mess.

ABOUT THE AUTHOR

W. E. B. Griffin, who was once a soldier, belongs to the Armor Association; Paris Post #1, The American Legion; and is a life member of The National Rifle Association and Gaston-Lee Post #5660, Veterans of Foreign Wars.